Most Beautiful Princess

A novel based on the life of
Grand Duchess Elizabeth of Russia

Christina Croft

D1228005

Cover Photographs:
Grand Duchess Elizabeth – reproduced by kind permission of Sotheby's.
Peonies and Lilacs – reproduced by kind permission of André Hilliard.

ISBN: 978-0-9559853-0-0

Prologue

In the early hours of the morning 18th July 1918, two carts left the small Siberian town of Alapaevsk and followed the Sinyachikhenskaya road to a disused mine. There, soldiers alighting from the carts ordered eight blindfolded prisoners - six men and two women - to walk forwards and, striking their heads with rifle butts, forced them one after another into the waterlogged shaft. Having hurled hand grenades after them into the pit, the soldiers assumed their task was complete and were about to leave when, to their amazement, the sound of singing echoed from beneath the ground. From a ledge, nineteen metres below, a woman was singing the Russian Orthodox hymn: '*Lord Save Your People.*'

Some weeks later as the First World War drew to its bloody conclusion across Europe, battles still raged for control of revolutionary Russia. With the arrival of the White Army in Alapaevsk, the bodies were recovered from the mine: five grand dukes, a companion and two middle-aged nuns. By the side of the incorrupt body of one of the nuns lay an unexploded grenade, on her breast an icon of Christ.

How did a fairy-tale princess, granddaughter of Queen Victoria, cousin of Kaiser Wilhelm II and King George V, and sister-in-law of two Russian Tsars come to so terrible an end? 'Ravishingly beautiful', 'a thing of dreams', 'saintly', 'enigmatic', revered as a saint by the poor of Moscow, what drove the Lutheran daughter of

Princess Alice to turn her into the Russian Imperial Highness Grand Duchess Elizaveta Feodorovna, then 'Matushka' mother of the poor, and finally Holy Imperial Martyr Saint Elizabeth? Why did the gentle Elizabeth of Hesse-Darmstadt, described by one her admirers as 'the most beautiful creature of God I have ever seen', die of infected wounds and starvation in a mineshaft in Siberia?

This novel is written in tribute to the beauty, courage and inspiration of this remarkable woman.

Who's Who

ALEXANDER II: Tsar of Russia (1818-1881). Serge's father.

ALEXANDRA: Grand Duchess (1870-1891). Daughter of the King of Greece. Pavel's first wife.

ALEXEI: Tsarevich (1904-1918). Ella's nephew. Son of Nicholas II.

ALICE: Princess Alice of Battenberg (1885-1969). Ella's niece and first godchild. Daughter of Victoria.

ALIX: Empress Alexandra Feodorovna (1872-1918). Ella's younger sister.

ANASTASIA: Grand Duchess (1901-1918). Ella's niece. Daughter of Nicholas II.

AUNT ALEXANDRA: Queen of Great Britain (1844-1925). Wife of Edward VII. Sister of Empress Marie Feodorovna.

AUNT BEATRICE: Princess Henry of Battenberg (1857-1944). Youngest child of Queen Victoria.

AUNT LENCHEN: Helena, Princess Christian of Schleswig-Holstein (1846-1923). 3rd daughter of Queen Victoria.

AUNT LOUISE: Duchess of Argyll (1848-1939). 4th daughter of Queen Victoria.

AUNT VICKY: German Empress (1840-1901). Eldest daughter of Queen Victoria. Mother of Kaiser Wilhelm II.

DMITRI: Grand Duke (1891-1942). Serge's nephew and ward. Son of Pavel.

DONA: Augusta, German Empress (1858-1921). Wife of Kaiser Wilhelm II.

DUCKY: Victoria Melita of Edinburgh. (1876-1936). Serge's niece and Ella's cousin. Married Ella's brother, Ernie, and later Grand Duke Kyril Vladimirovich.

EDDY: Prince Albert Victor, Duke of Clarence and Avondale (1864-1892). Eldest son of the Prince of the Wales. Ella's first cousin.

ELENA: Grand Duchess (1882-1957). Serge's niece. Daughter of Vladimir and Miechen.

ERNIE: Grand Duke Ernst Ludwig of Hesse and By Rhine (1868-1937). Ella's brother.

FELIX: Prince Youssoupov (1887-1967). Son of Zinaida.

FRITTIE: Prince Frederick of Hesse and by Rhine (1870-1873). Ella's brother.

GEORGE: King George V of Great Britain (1865-1936). Ella's first cousin.

GRANDMAMA: Queen Victoria of Great Britain (1819-1901).

GRANDPAPA: Prince Albert (1819-1861). Consort of Queen Victoria.

HENRY: Prince of Prussia (1862-1929). Ella's cousin and brother-in-law. Brother of Kaiser Wilhelm II. Married Ella's sister's Irène.

IGOR KONSTANTINOVICH: Prince of Russia (1894-1918). Son of Kostia.

IOANN KONSTANTINOVICH: Prince of Russia (1886-1918). Son of Kostia.

IRÈNE: Princess of Hesse and by Rhine (1866-1953). Ella's younger sister.

IRINA: Princess of Russia (1895-1970). Niece of Tsar Nicholas II. Married Prince Felix Youssoupov.

KONSTANTIN: See *Kostia*

KONSTANTIN KONSTANTINOVICH: Prince of Russia (1890-1918). Son of Kostia.

KOSTIA: Grand Duke Konstantin Konstantinovich (1858-1915). Serge's cousin. A poet who wrote as 'K.R.'.

KYRIL: Grand Duke (1876-1938). Son of Miechen and Vladimir. Cousin of Nicholas II.

LOUIS: Prince of Battenberg (1854-1921). Ella's brother-in-law. Married to Victoria.

MAMA: Princess Alice, Grand Duchess of Hesse and By Rhine (1843-1878). 2nd daughter of Queen Victoria.

MARIA: Grand Duchess (1899-1918). Ella's niece. Daughter of Nicholas II.

MARIE: Grand Duchess (1880-1958). Serge's niece and ward. Daughter of Pavel.

MARIE: Duchess of Edinburgh & Saxe-Coburg (1853-1920). Serge's sister. Married Ella's Uncle Affie.

MAVRA: Elizabeth, Grand Duchess (1865-1927). Wife of Kostia.

MAY: Princess Mary of Hesse and by Rhine (1874-1878). Ella's younger sister.

MIECHEN: Maria Pavlovna, Grand Duchess (1854-1920). Serge's sister-in-law. Wife of Vladimir.

MINNIE: Empress Marie Feodorovna (1847-1928). Wife of Alexander III. Mother of Nicholas II.

MISHA: Grand Duke Michael (1878-1918). Brother of Nicholas II.

NICHOLAS NICHOLAEVICH: Grand Duke (1856-1929). Serge's cousin.

NICKY: Tsar Nicholas II (1867-1918).

OLGA: Grand Duchess (1882-1960). Sister of Nicholas II.

OLGA: Grand Duchess (1895-1918). Ella's niece. Daughter of Nicholas II.

OLGA VON PISTOLKORS: Princess Paley (1865-1929). 2nd wife of Pavel.

PAPA: Grand Duke Louis (Ludwig) IV of Hesse and by Rhine (1837-1892).

PAVEL: Grand Duke (1860-1919). Serge's brother.

SANDRO: Grand Duke Alexander Mikhailovich (1866-1933).Cousin and later brother-in-law of Nicholas II.

SASHA: Tsar Alexander III of Russia (1845-1894). Serge's brother.

SERGE: Grand Duke (1857-1905). Ella's husband.

SERGE MIKHAILOVICH: Grand Duke (1869-1918). Cousin of Nicholas II.

TATIANA: Grand Duchess (1897-1918). Ella's niece. Daughter of Nicholas II.

UNCLE AFFIE: Duke of Edinburgh & Saxe-Coburg (1844-1900). 2nd son of Queen Victoria. Husband of Serge's sister, Marie.

UNCLE BERTIE: King Edward VII (1841-1910). Eldest son of Queen Victoria.

UNCLE FRITZ: German Emperor Frederick III (1831-1888). Husband of Aunt Vicky.

UNCLE LEO: Prince Leopold, Duke of Albany (1853-1884). 4th son of Queen Victoria.

VICTORIA: Princess Louis of Battenberg (1863-1950). Ella's elder sister.

VLADIMIR: Grand Duke (1847-1909). Serge's brother.

VLADIMIR: Prince Paley (1897-1918). Son of Pavel by his 2nd wife.

WILLY: Kaiser Wilhelm II (1859-1941). Ella's first cousin.

XENIA: Grand Duchess (1875-1960). Sister of Nicholas II.

ZINAIDA: Princess Youssoupova (1861-1939). Ella's friend.

Chapter 1 - June 1884

As the train drew into Varshavskiy Station, Konstantin Konstantinovich gazed through the steam in awe. The deafening cheer of the crowd almost drowned out the welcome of the military band as Princess Elizabeth of Hesse and by Rhine stepped from the carriage and, shyly holding her father's arm, floated like an apparition of light across the platform. Whether dazzled by the glare of the sunlight on the swords and medals of the Imperial Guard, or overwhelmed by the radiance of her features, Konstantin could hardly tell but, raising his hand to shield his eyes, he murmured, "My God, Serge! She is…"

"*Now,* you believe me, Kostia," Serge smiled, his grey eyes shining with pride. "The most beautiful princess in Europe."

Smiling timidly, she moved towards the waiting dignitaries and, with the grace of a dancer, curtseyed before the imposing figure of Alexander III, Tsar of all the Russias. Huge, bearded and slightly balding, his firm features softened to a welcoming smile.

"Your Highness, we are honoured to welcome you to Russia!"

The formality complete, he took both her hands in his and laughed loudly, "Ella, we're delighted to see you! My brother's a fortunate man."

"No, Sasha," she said softly, "I am the fortunate one."

He turned and gesticulated, "Come on, Serge, welcome your bride!"

Grand Duke Serge Alexandrovich, tall and erect in the uniform of the Preobrazhensky Regiment, strode across the platform and, though his smile was as nervous as hers, the flicker of his lips revealed his pride in the impression she had made on the crowd. He greeted her with a brief, courteous embrace and, with one hand clutching the hilt of his sword, formally introduced her to the rest of the family.

"Her Imperial Majesty, the Empress Marie Feodorovna."

Konstantin's eyes followed her every step of the way and, as the beautiful and bejewelled Empress embraced her warmly, he couldn't help but think that until now he had never seen any woman whose radiance could compete with Marie Feodorovna's sparkle and vivacity.

"His Imperial Highness, Tsarevich Nicholas Alexandrovich. His Imperial Highness, Grand Duke…"

The nearer she came, the more clearly Konstantin observed the perfect symmetry of her features: her blue, naïve eyes, her soft, tender smile, the faint blush on her fair complexion. It seemed that every line, every curve had been sculptured by some divine hand intent on bringing beauty into creation.

"His Imperial Highness, Grand Duke Konstantin Konstantinovich."

He bowed and his lips brushed her fingers, "Your Highness, we had heard that we were to welcome the most beautiful princess in Europe but, as you can see from the adulation of the crowd, your beauty far exceeds our expectations."

She smiled coyly and Serge, laughing, slapped him heartily on the back, "Ella, you must make allowance for my cousin. He's an aesthete and a poet, constantly overwhelmed in the presence of beauty."

Her eyes widened with interest, "A poet?"

"A very poor one, I'm afraid," Konstantin said. "My words seldom capture what my heart really feels or my eyes truly see."

She smiled pensively, "Sometimes we feel things so deeply and cannot find words to express them. For that we're grateful to the poets who express them for us."

Serge mused for a moment, gazing at her with a wonder that Konstantin had never seen in his eyes before.

"I trust," Konstantin said, "that you will be very happy in Russia."

"I'm sure, I shall."

Serge guided her further along the line and when she had faded into the distance like the amber glow of the fading beams at sunset, Konstantin turned to Grand Duke Alexander Mikhailovich.

"Well, Sandro, I have to admit I am thoroughly ashamed of myself. In spite of all the descriptions, I never believed that a German princess could be so beautiful. Of course, she's half-English but even so I..."

"Damn it, Kostia!" Sandro turned abruptly, stamping like an angry child against the platform, "How can they let this happen?"

Konstantin shook his head, confused as much by the vehemence of his tone, as the question.

"How can they let her marry *him*? Didn't you see the way he looked at her with that haughty expression, showing her off like some prize trophy?"

"Wouldn't you be proud if she were your bride?"

"Yes, I'd be proud but not in the way that he is!"

Konstantin laughed, "There are different forms of pride?"

"I would be proud to serve her, love her, take care of her. But *him*? He's proud like a Philistine with a work of art, proud to possess it as a show of his wealth with no idea of its value or beauty."

"You don't think Serge appreciates her beauty? You don't think he knows what a treasure he has found?"

"Oh yes, he knows but he values her like a miser values his money. You must have seen how his hand rested on her shoulder? That wasn't love or passion, Kostia. That was possession. That's all she is to him - a possession. Something he owns and can show off to the boys in his precious regiment!"

Konstantin looked up at the sky in sham contemplation, "How old are you, Sandro? Sixteen, seventeen?"

"Eighteen."

"Eighteen," he nodded sagely. "That's very young to claim such an insight into men's hearts."

"Hearts?" Sandro's lip curled in disgust, "Serge has a stone in place of a heart. I tell you, Kostia, he'll destroy her. I'd give ten years of my life to stop her walking down the aisle on his arm."

Konstantin frowned, vaguely discomfited by rumours he had tried to ignore, and, as he shrugged to shake away the unwelcome thoughts, he was deeply aware that Sandro was not the only one who would like to prevent this marriage.

The clinking of cups on china saucers and an occasional sigh broke the silence of the tartan-walled drawing room of Balmoral Castle. Queen Victoria tugged at one finger then another, desperately trying to assuage her sense of foreboding.

"It isn't right. It just isn't right," she sighed.

Victoria sat down beside her, "Try not to fret so, Grandmama. I'm sure that she'll be very happy with Serge."

"Happy? How *can* she be happy? He's a Russian! When I think how my poor Aunt Julia suffered in that pernicious country. And Serge's own mother, left to die untended while her husband entertained his mistress and her children upstairs!"

"Every family has its share of good and bad. We surely can't condemn every Romanov for one or two rotten apples. Serge is quiet and gentle and even Aunt Vicky agrees that he is far more refined than his brothers."

"He's still a Russian," the Queen said sharply, refusing to be appeased. Her mind darted from one horrific thought to another, "The climate won't suit her at all. She's never been physically strong and the cold winters there will ruin her health completely."

"Serge has promised that they'll spend much of the year abroad."

"Where? Not here! How can I possibly entertain a Russian Grand Duke? Of course, Ella will always be welcome…but *him!*"

In the rising tension, Victoria reached for her tea cup and clumsily clattered it against the saucer.

"I don't understand her," the Queen thought aloud. "I don't understand her at all. When she came here last summer, she assured me she had no intention of marrying him. In fact she sat where you're sitting now and told me most definitely that she would hate to live in Russia. The next thing I hear, it's all arranged and your father did nothing to stop it. If your mother had lived, this would never have happened."

Victoria smiled gently, "Mama was always fond of Serge when he was a little boy."

"As a little boy, perhaps, but she would never have wanted a Russian husband for any of you. The country's in a constant state of turmoil. Serge's father blown to pieces in the street! Shootings, bombings, murders, to say nothing of the decadence and immorality of the court. And my poor Ella, so innocent and naïve; I can't bear the thought of how that unscrupulous set will spoil her."

"Oh, Grandmama, you know Ella's far too sensible and good to allow herself to be spoiled."

The Queen shook her head despairingly, "I won't even be able to write to her for fear of our letters being intercepted."

When Victoria didn't reply, the Queen stood up and moved to the open window, gazing out across the green landscape and recalling happier visits of her Hessian grandchildren. The memories were so clear. She could see them even now, trotting on their little Shetland ponies or running and laughing in their noisy games. No wonder, she thought, dear Alice wore herself out with so many big children to care for! Victoria, always the dominant one, climbing trees and leaping about like a boy, while dainty Ella cooed over the puppies and ponies, nursing her dolls like babies in her arms. Irène, quiet as though overawed by her sisters; Ernie, enthusiastic and exuberant, and dear little Alix, so shy and nervous in the company of strangers.

She turned back from the window, "You know, since poor, dear Alice's passing, I've always seen you and your sisters as my own children. Haven't I always been supportive to you all?"

"More than supportive!" Victoria swept quickly to her side, "Please, please don't think we don't appreciate everything you've done for us."

"Then *why*? Why did she not listen to my advice? Nineteen years old and throwing herself into that terrible place! Heaven knows she'd be better off not marrying at all. Marriage is such a lottery and if young girls knew what they were letting themselves into, I doubt any of them would go through with it."

"Oh come, Grandmama," Victoria laughed, "you were so happy with Grandpapa."

"Your grandfather was different," she answered brusquely, resenting any comparison to her own idyllic years with beloved Albert. "He was an angel in every way, and very, very few young girls are as blessed as I was." She frowned discontentedly before conceding, "I know your good Louis is an excellent husband...but Serge? If Ella so desperately wanted to marry, there were so many far more appropriate princes. William, for instance, would have given anything if she had only accepted his proposal."

"Cousin Willy?" Victoria laughed.

"Of course, I know how hot-headed he is and how arrogant he can be but, as your Aunt Vicky said, he adored Ella. She would have been such a calming influence on him and one day would have made such a lovely German Empress. *That* would have pleased your dear grandpapa." She paused for a moment with a pang of regret for what might have been, then sighed, "And if not William, there was that nice Fritz of Baden. Your mother would have approved of that match."

"But Ella felt nothing for him."

"And she feels something for Serge?"

"Yes. I am sure she does. I am sure she must."

Queen Victoria shook her head, "She wrote to me, you know? She said she thought she might 'do him some good'. What is that supposed to mean? And, more to the point, what good is he going to do her? They tell me he is very unpopular even among his own people."

"He's shy, that's all. It makes him appear a little aloof sometimes but I am sure when you get to know him, you'll see that he has many fine qualities."

"I have no desire whatsoever to get to know him. The less I see of him, the better."

Victoria sighed and the Queen yielded, "Well, since it's all arranged and there's nothing I can do to stop it, you must promise that you'll inform me at once of any news you have of her. I want to know every detail, you understand?"

"I'll write to you the moment I arrive in Russia, and afterwards will tell you all about the wedding."

"Weddings!" Queen Victoria huffed, "I *hate* weddings!"

"Please, Grandmama," Victoria squeezed her hand gently, "try not to be angry with her. You know she would never deliberately hurt you and perhaps in time you'll see that she has made the right decision."

A chill wind blew threw the open window and a shiver like the passing of a ghost ran down the Queen's spine, "I'm not angry with her. I am afraid; I am truly afraid. I have such a bad feeling about all of this and I honestly believe that your grandfather and your dear mother are trying to warn me of it."

"Try not to think these things," Victoria smiled. "Fear can make our minds play all kinds of tricks on us. Ella will be perfectly alright. I am sure of it."

Unbidden tears burned in the Queen's eyes, "I hope you're right," she whispered, "but it breaks my heart to think that she is lost to me forever. I shudder at the prospect of what will become of her now."

Chapter 2

Cheering masses lined the broad thoroughfares as the gilded state coach moved slowly through St. Petersburg. Looking out across the city, it was clear to Ella why Grandmama had been so fearful that the legendary wealth of the Russian court would turn her head. Already Serge had showered her with so many jewels that she had been unable to stand beneath their weight, and now, as the carriage crossed the ornate bridges of the gleaming River Neva, her eyes were dazzled by the grandeur of the most opulent palaces in the world.

June was the finest time to arrive in St. Petersburg. These were the 'white nights' when the sun barely set and the daylight lasted for twenty-two hours a day. Its glow illuminated the splendours of the Nevsky Prospect, the most fashionable thoroughfare in the city. All along the route, Serge pointed out the sites and landmarks. Here was the Lutheran church in which she would worship; there was the magnificent colonnade of the Orthodox Kazan Cathedral; further along stood the Tsar's city residence, the Anichkov Palace; and on the opposite bank of the Fontanka Canal was the red baroque Beloselsky Belozersky Palace that would soon be her home.

How much more brilliant, she thought, were these magnificent mansions than the damp, gloomy Schloss of her early childhood, where her parents had been driven to beg Queen Victoria for financial assistance! How immense was the power of the Romanov Tsar compared to the limited authority of her father in the little Grand Duchy of Hesse! As the procession moved through the city, she was struck by the sight of people crouching and pressing their lips to the ground.

Her father pressed his face to the window, "What on earth are they doing?"

"Kissing the Tsar's shadow," Serge said.

"Good heavens!" Ella gasped. "I thought the crowds who come to see Grandmama were enthusiastic, but this!"

"Ah yes, but the Tsar is so much more than the Queen of England. He's the anointed one, chosen by God, Head of the Church and the Little Father of his subjects."

"All hundred and thirty million of them?" Ella smiled.

Serge raised his eyebrows, "So you read the books I sent?"

"Yes, I did and I learned a few Russian words, though I doubt I'd have the courage to say them aloud."

Even as he nodded in reply, his eyes darted warily through the crowds and a tingle of fear ran down Ella's spine. Amid all the rejoicing, came the echo of Grandmama's warnings and the English news reports of the extensive security operations in preparation for her arrival. From the comfort of the coach she couldn't see the hundreds of police agents mingling with the crowd nor the armed officers stationed at vantage points, their eyes alert to any sign of disturbance, but she knew they were there. She had heard that the homes of suspected terrorists had been raided; that undercover policemen had hired shops along the route; and that every inch of the station had been inspected daily for bombs. In a country where the possibility of assassination was a daily hazard for ministers and princes, such precautions were deemed a necessity.

Only when the cheering had faded as the carriage left the city, did Serge take his eyes from the window and for the first time he turned to her and smiled.

"You must be tired after your journey but don't worry it's not far now to Peterhof."

"I'm too excited to feel tired!"

"All the same, you'll need to rest. This evening we'll just have a small family dinner so you can prepare for the busy week ahead. There are so many people waiting to meet you. I must introduce you to my regiment and..."

"Serge," her father leaned forward, "you will leave her some time to spend with us before the wedding?"

"Yes, of course."

"It's not easy to part with her, you know? We've always been so close and, since the death of their mother, my children have meant everything to me."

An uneasy feeling churned in Ella's stomach as he reached for her hand.

"Two daughters in two months," he shook his head sadly. "Victoria vanished to England and now..."

"Oh, Papa, we'll visit you often. Isn't that right, Serge?"

"Yes, of course, and you'll always be welcome here."

Her father thanked him and sighed resignedly. Ella looked into his eyes, only too aware of the sorrow that had never left them since the death of her mother six years earlier and, for the first time since leaving Darmstadt, a wave of sadness shrouded her excitement. All that she loved, all she had known would soon be gone forever and, looking out across the vast expanse of foreign soil, she was suddenly overwhelmed by a thousand scattered memories and a longing to return to the safe world of childhood in the little German Grand Duchy of Hesse and by Rhine.

Life had been happy in Darmstadt. Although by royal standards the family was not wealthy as her father waited to come into his inheritance, it had been an idyllic early childhood, loved by doting parents and surrounded by cheerful siblings. She looked out of the coach window and a myriad of images danced before her eyes: the long hours in the schoolroom where Mama, with her wide-ranging interests and deep sense of duty, devised a broad curriculum that placed as much emphasis on practical skills as academic learning. Music lessons, riding lessons, the numerous performers who were invited to the palace to introduce Ella and her sisters to opera and literature; the pets, the ponies, the dogs and the guinea pigs; the imaginative games; parading through the palace dressed up in Mama's old-fashioned clothes; Papa showing her how to grow vegetables and flowers; and Mama teaching her cookery, needlework and housekeeping. Princesses or not, Mama had insisted that the children cleaned their own rooms, laid fires in the grate and made their own beds. Skills, Ella thought, glancing at Serge, that would come in useful now as a wife.

She smiled at him, inwardly whispering a prayer that she would not only make him happy, but also would serve his country well. Beyond the opulent palaces, in Russia no less than in Hesse, there would always be suffering people in need of help. That was the promise she had made to Mama: to follow in her footsteps and do all she could to serve those whose lives were so far removed from her own. It wouldn't be new to her; Mama had never shielded her from the harsher realities of life outside the palace. Ella had often accompanied her on her visits to the hospital and the 'mental asylum' that she had founded, and assisted in her work for wounded soldiers during the Franco-Prussian war.

"Not far now," Serge said and turned to her father who was gazing through the opposite window as though lost in memories of his own. "It will be pleasant for you to have the opportunity to meet up with all the family again. Victoria and Louis are expected mid-week with the others from England, and the Prussians should be arriving any day."

Papa tugged at his beard, "William isn't coming?"

"No. He made some excuse. Military manoeuvres or something of that sort."

Ella smiled with relief, recalling the holidays marred by the arrogance of Cousin Willy, spoiling every game with his irrational mood swings and fondness for boasting of the recent Prussian victory over Hesse.

"I suppose that's for the best," her father said. "If he had come, he'd only have been obnoxious. To be fair, though, who can blame him? I doubt I would take too kindly to being the guest of a rival."

"Rival?" Serge frowned.

"You don't know how desperate he was to marry Ella?"

It was difficult to tell whether Serge's expression was one of shock or annoyance, and, fearful that the news had disturbed him, Ella felt obliged to laugh, "Oh Papa, that was years ago. I was only…what? Fourteen, fifteen at the time."

"Broke his heart though, didn't it?"

"It offended his Prussian pride, nothing more. He couldn't understand how anyone could resist the opportunity of one day becoming German Empress."

"You had a lucky escape," Serge said. "From what I hear he is a most petulant and bombastic character."

Her father smiled, "Only two people have ever been able to reduce him to silence. Ella is one of them. Totally tongue-tied he was in her presence and even now he can hardly string a sentence together when she's in the room."

"Then it's as well I rarely see him," Ella said.

Her father leaned forwards confidentially, "I heard from Aunt Vicky that he still keeps your portrait on his desk alongside his favourite picture of the Princess of Wales."

Serge's lips twitched, "And what does his wife think of that?"

"His wife? In her eyes, Willy can't put a foot wrong! When Ella wouldn't have him, he opted instead for a fawning little creature who would support him in everything and never contradict him."

"Admirable qualities in a wife?" Serge said.

"That depends on whether you want a helpmate and companion who'll speak the truth come what may, or someone who serves only to boost your pride."

Serge's brow furrowed into a pensive frown and, when he looked at Ella, she felt he was weighing the question in his mind and deciding into which category to place her. Seeming to sense her discomfort, he shook away the frown, "So, who was the second person who managed to subdue William?"

"His English grandmother, Queen Victoria."

"Ah! I might have guessed."

"He adores her but she stands for none of his nonsense. I honestly believe she's the only person in the world who really manages to keep him in check. He wouldn't dream of contradicting her. Mind you," he paused and smiled, "nor would I. Amazing, isn't it, that so tiny a woman holds such authority over everyone in the family?"

"It *is*," Serge laughed, "and it would take a stronger man than any of us to go against her wishes."

Ella smiled to herself with an inkling of pride at the stand she had taken in choosing to marry a *Russian!*

The magnificence of friezes and marble garlands and the glorious view across the River Neva did nothing to lighten Sandro's mood as Konstantin led him up the staircase of the Marble Palace. He pushed open the door to the cluttered sitting room where Mavra sat beside a steaming samovar, entertaining Grand Duchess Maria Pavlovna.

"Ah, here's Kostia, at last!" Mavra smiled. "And Sandro, too, you're most welcome!"

Konstantin greeted his wife with an affectionate kiss before turning to Maria Pavlovna, "Miechen, delightful to see you."

"And to see you," she said. "We've been longing to hear all the news and, judging by the look on Sandro's face, the news isn't good. Does the beautiful Ella not live up to her reputation?"

"Absolutely she does, and more!" Sandro said.

"Then why the thunderous expression?"

He shook his head, too furious to respond, and Mavra guided him gently towards a chair, "Come, sit down and take tea and you can tell us all about it."

They settled themselves and, as Mavra served tea, Konstantin took a cigarette from a case and pensively tapped it on the table. "We were blinded," he said at last, "as though by the sun. We haven't seen such beauty in a long time. She was like a dream."

"Dear, dear, dear," Miechen laughed. "Only two months married and already you speak this way of another woman without a thought for your wife!"

He sat forward quickly and was about to apologise but Mavra laughed too, "It's the poet in him, Miechen. He speaks the same way of sunsets and flowers and oceans."

"In that case, we'd do better to hear Sandro's opinion. I'm intrigued to discover what's making him so out of sorts today?"

"Kostia is right," Sandro said. "She's like no one else I have ever seen. It's not only that she's beautiful to look at; there's such a gentleness about her and something that just can't be put into words"

"Oh Sandro, Sandro," there was a hint of scorn in Miechen's voice, "I should have known better than to ask the opinion of a hot-blooded young man. You young fellows are so easily entranced by a pretty face."

"No, no. It's much more than that. There's an atmosphere about her. I don't know how else to describe it. The minute you meet her, you immediately feel so entranced and yet so at ease. It's like being in the presence of...how can I possibly describe it? Pure innocence!"

"Innocence?" Miechen laughed. "How long will that last after marrying Serge?"

Konstantin winced and lit his cigarette.

"I can't bear it," Sandro said. "Serge of all people! It's too awful to even think about. How can we let her throw her life away on someone like him?"

"Serge?" Mavra turned questioningly to Konstantin, "I have always found him affable and good-humoured in a shy sort of way."

"Affable?" Sandro spat. "He'll ruin her, I'm telling you. He'll make her miserable and…"

Miechen leaned across and tapped his hand, "Have no worries on that score. I can guarantee that as soon as the wedding is over he'll be back to the boys of his regiment, leaving the pretty little bird to sing in her gilded cage. She's a trinket to him, nothing more; a mere bagatelle that he can bring out for appearance sake to stem all the rumours and then put back in her case."

"That's *terrible!*" Sandro gasped.

"Not really. If she's as pretty as you say, I'm sure she'll find no end of ardent young men who will be only too willing to make up for Serge's neglect."

Mavra's eyes darted towards Konstantin, compelling him to intervene.

"It's strange," he said quietly, "how everyone seems to have an opinion of Serge, based solely on rumours which, as far as I can see, have no foundation at all."

"What rumours?" Mavra frowned.

"Nothing worth repeating."

Miechen glanced towards the ceiling with a scornful smile, "They say the young officers adore him."

"Which speaks volumes about his capacity and conscientiousness as commander of the regiment," Konstantin said sharply.

"Indeed. And they say he adores them, too, with a schoolboy like devotion."

"Surely, you're not saying..." Mavra began but, before she could finish, Sandro thumped his fist against the chair.

"For God's sake, the man's a disgrace to the family, to the army and to Russia! I've seen him carousing with his boys, his head thrown back and singing at the top of his voice some ridiculous song about peace and love and bliss!"

His outburst led to a moment of stunned silence during which Mavra nervously looked again to her husband, who silently drew on his cigarette.

"I'm sorry, Mavra," Sandro said, "I've no right to speak so boldly in front of you."

But Miechen, it seemed, was not so willing to let the matter drop, "He wears corsets, you know? Vladimir told me of it."

"Perhaps many men wear corsets," Konstantin said feebly.

"Do they? Do you?"

"Well, no but..."

"What about you, Sandro?"

"Of course not."

"Nor does Vladimir, nor..."

"Oh really," Konstantin said, resting his cigarette on the edge of the ashtray, "it's hardly proper for us to sit here discussing his undergarments. The man is about to be married, can't we at least wish him well?"

"I wish Ella well," Sandro said. "I wish her all the good fortune in the world. Heaven knows she's going to need it."

"Don't worry," Miechen smiled, "I'll take her under my wing and help her through. After all, Mavra, she's one of us."

"One of us?"

"German - well, half-German - *and* Lutheran. We're few and far between in the midst of all this Orthodoxy, so we must stick together, wouldn't you say?"

Mavra nodded half-heartedly and Miechen stood up, "And now I must take my leave. I have correspondence to deal with. I promised William in Prussia that I would keep him informed of all the developments."

"I had better go, too," Sandro said. "I am sorry if I have spoken out of turn. I just couldn't help myself when I think of her going like a lamb to the slaughter."

When they had gone, Mavra sat staring towards the samovar, with a troubled expression knitting her brow. Konstantin sat down beside her and took her hand.

"You look anxious, my dear?"

"Serge has always been so pleasant to me."

"And a good friend to me, too."

"You know that Vladimir was opposed to this wedding?"

"So I've been told."

"Why? As Serge's brother you'd think he would want him to be happy with a beautiful bride. Yet, from what Miechen says, they see him as some kind of monster. Am I missing something?"

Konstantin sighed and shook his head, "He's not a monster. He might be a little short-tempered and it's true he can appear stand-offish at times but it's only a mask. He's terrified of appearing weak but, underneath that harshness, he is one of the most sensitive men I have ever known. His servants are devoted to him, his officers respect him and the Tsar trusts him implicitly."

"So why do they speak so badly of him?"

"Sandro is young and impulsive, that's all. And as for Miechen, who knows? Perhaps she's afraid that the legendary Ella is about to steal her thunder."

Mavra leaned her head against his shoulder, "I don't understand."

"Miechen prides herself on running the most fashionable court in the country. The news of the warm welcome Ella received from the crowds in Petersburg will have set alarm bells ringing in her head."

"Jealousy?"

"Perhaps. And then, of course, there's her husband's position to consider."

Mavra frowned questioningly.

"As brothers of the Tsar, both Vladimir and Serge have a lot to gain in terms of power and influence. Miechen is...how shall I put it? She's of the opinion that Vladimir would have made a far better Tsar than Sasha. It colours her judgement of most things. Everything becomes a competition to her. She dislikes Serge because Sasha places such trust in him and she sees that as taking away power from Vladimir."

"Such intrigues," Mavra sighed. "I feel sorry for Ella, and pray that she will be spared all this unpleasantness and jealousy."

"So do I," Konstantin nodded, kissing her tenderly.

"And I pray," she said, "that Serge and Ella will be as blessed and happy together as we are."

He leaned back and, drawing her head to his chest, stared pensively towards the window.

Chapter 3

Serge could not have chosen a more beautiful setting for his bride's introduction to Russia. On the shores of the Gulf of Finland, the Grand Palace of Peterhof overlooked a cascading canal, crowned with bronze statues of classical and biblical figures. Jets spouted water in different directions from the mouths of gilded dragons onto the black and white chessboard cascade, and the surrounding lawns were awash with flowers.

Secluded in the gardens beyond the Grand Palace, stood a smaller pavilion known as The Farm, which, Serge announced, was perfect for an intimate family gathering and would provide a more relaxed atmosphere in which the Hessians might recuperate from their three-day journey. Immediately, the sights and scents of the place transported Ella through so many scenes from her childhood. The Farm's arched windows and verandas were reminiscent of her father's country estate at Wolfsgarten; while the fresh sea air through the heady fragrance of flowers, took her back to her mother's favourite childhood home - Osborne House on the Isle of Wight, overlooking Portsmouth Harbour and the Solent.

But there was little time that first evening to dwell upon the past or appreciate the beauty of the present surroundings. Papa was standing at the door, waiting to escort her to dinner. While Alix and Irène hovered nervously by the window, Ernie marched around the room, examining every detail of the décor, paintings and furniture.

"It's beautiful!" he enthused. "It's all so huge and so exciting. Even more exciting than Osborne or Windsor!"

"I think it's frightening," Alix whispered. "Do I really have to go to this dinner?"

"It's only a small family party and they all speak perfect English."

"It's not the language, it's having to speak to them at all. What will I talk about?"

"Anything!" Ernie said. "You've spoken to them before. Remember when we met Uncle Sasha and Aunt Minnie at Heiligenberg? They were so friendly and we had so much fun."

"It was different there. They were like family. Now, they're the Tsar and Tsarina. It's different."

"They're still the same people!" Ernie laughed. "They're not like you'd think they'd be at all. They have all these beautiful rooms and beautiful palaces and you know what? Their children sleep on camp beds without pillows, and Uncle Sasha wears the same old boots and patched clothes year after year instead of having new ones."

"How do you know?" Irène said.

"Nicky told me. And he told me something else. He said he and Misha jumped out on Uncle Sasha and sprayed him with water until he was drenched. All the soldiers and guards didn't know what to do but Uncle Sasha just stood there laughing."

Neither Irène nor Alix laughed.

"Who's Misha?" Irène frowned.

"Don't you know anything? If you're going to be a guest in another country, and especially if your sister's about to marry into the family, you really ought to find out something about it first. Isn't that right, Ella?"

Ella smiled at his exuberance.

"Nicky, His Imperial Highness, the Tsarevich Nicholas Alexandrovich, is the eldest son of the

Tsar. He's sixteen, same as me. Then there's George, who's just a bit younger than you Alix, but he won't be here tonight because he's ill and they sent him to the Crimea to recover. Then there's Misha and the two little girls, and..."

"Oh stop, stop, please!" Alix said, putting her hands to her ears. "I'll never remember them all!"

"I've not started yet," Ernie laughed, glancing at himself in the gilt-edged mirror and carefully adjusting his collar, "they're only the Tsar's children. On top of them, there are all his brothers and their families. Of course, you know Serge and Pavel but we've not met..."

"Ernie," his father said to silence him, as Alix stood pale and trembling as though she were going to an execution not a dinner. "I'm sure you'll find that they are just like our family and there's nothing frightening about them. And just like our family, they won't want to be kept waiting for dinner."

Her offered Ella his arm and, as they walked down the staircase, laughter echoed from the rooms below. Suddenly, from nowhere, a little girl and two young men in sailor suits came charging along a corridor in a some wild game that came to an abrupt halt as they saw the guests approaching. One of the young men immediately stepped forwards and, with a broad smile, made a slight bow, "Welcome to the family!"

The warmth in his eyes was so striking that it seemed his very soul shone through them.

"Nicky," Ernie said, "may I introduce you to our family?"

"Please do."

"My father, and my sister, Ella."

"We met at the station," Ella said.

Nicky nodded, "I've been wondering whether I should address you now as *Aunt* Ella or should I wait till after the wedding?"

"Aunt?" Ernie laughed. "It sounds so old when there's only three years between you!"

"How about..." Nicky frowned for a moment, *"Tetinka?"*

"Tetinka?" Ella wondered whether it was a compliment or an insult.

"It means 'little aunt'."

There was something so mischievous in those violet blue eyes that provoked a kind of banter in reply. "Then how should I address you? Your Imperial Highness? Or is there a word for 'little nephew'?"

"Nicky," he said firmly. "That will be fine."

He smiled again and in that moment Ella felt that a deep bond of friendship had been forged between them.

"I'm glad that's settled," Ernie said. "This is my sister, Irène, and my youngest sister, Alix."

"Alix," the Tsarevich repeated. She flushed a little but responded to his smile and, when he turned to introduce his companions, her eyes followed him.

"Now it's my turn," he said. "My sister, Xenia, and my brother, Misha."

The pleasantries over, Misha leaped away to continue the game but Nicky called after him, "Dinner will be served soon. We had better go in and join the others. Alix, will you sit beside me?"

He offered her his arm and, when she took it, Papa turned to Ella and smiled, "Such a charming boy. I knew he'd even set Alix at ease."

Soon everyone was gathered at table and, with a total lack of formality or even decorum, the conversation flowed freely. Frequently the huge

Tsar leaned forwards to whisper to Papa and, though what he said was out of Ella's earshot, the laughter that followed suggested he was sharing some kind of bawdy story. In response, the Tsarina - petite, stylish and exquisitely bejewelled - glanced at her husband with exaggerated disapproval before trying, in a soft Danish accent, to distract the guests with talk of her children and the social life of the city. At this, the Tsar laughed even more loudly, "Ah Minnie, what would I do without you to keep me in check?" and he threw her such a look of affection that it seemed, in spite of the glaring contrast in their appearance and manners, no two people could have been better suited.

Ella turned to Serge, wondering if soon they, too, would have such easy familiarity. For now, despite his frequent smiles, conversation with him felt awkward and stilted. Each time she looked directly at him, he fidgeted, nervously twisting the ring on his finger, and seemed grateful when his younger brother, Pavel, intervened to keep the conversation flowing.

"Ella," Pavel said, "will you have any objections if I come along with you to Ilinskoe after the wedding?"

She shook her head, uncertain what answer was expected.

"I promise to keep a discreet distance."

She smiled to conceal her embarrassment and, as Serge fidgeted more wildly than ever with the ring, she caught sight of the Tsar, staring in his direction with an expression of mild concern.

Whether or not Serge had noticed it, he turned quickly to Ella, "You'll love Ilinskoe. It's so peaceful there and so different from the city. It was my mother's country estate and, knowing how much it meant to me, she left it to me when she died. I've taken good care of it, made quite a few improvements and have begun importing all kinds of rare breed animals that I'm sure you will love."

"It sounds beautiful," she said.

"It is," he nodded. Then he looked away, catching sight of Alix and Nicky lost in conversation further along the table.

"Alix has grown so much since I last saw her. How old is she now?"

"She'll be twelve next week."

"Good heavens, twelve already!"

Feeling his eyes upon her, Alix looked up.

"I was just saying to Ella," he laughed, "I can't believe how quickly you've grown. It only seems two minutes since I saw you being bathed as a tiny baby!"

She blinked coyly but when Nicky laughed, she laughed, too, and turned back to Serge with a smile so radiant that Ella marvelled to see her so comfortable in the company of strangers.

When the meal was over and cigars had been brought for the men, Nicky offered to show Ernie, Irène and Alix around the palace while the Tsarina invited Ella to meet her youngest child, who was too small to join them at table.

As soon as the nursery door opened, an excited little girl, all dressed in white, toddled gleefully towards them. The Empress crouched on the floor and hugged her warmly, "Children, I always say, are the heart of a home. A house without children is so sad, don't you think?"

Ella smiled and soon both she and Minnie were crawling on their hands and knees, peeping and playing, while the little girl giggled and laughed and clambered all over them.

"You must have a way with children," Minnie said. "Olga's usually so shy with strangers. I try to encourage all my children to meet many people to give them as much of a normal childhood as possible. I was raised very simply in Denmark, and that is the way I try to raise my family." She paused and her smile became more pensive, "In Russia, though, it is different."

"Aren't children the same everywhere?" Ella smiled.

"Oh, yes, and here at home we are all very simple and like any other family. But outside," she nodded towards the window, "we are different. We have to be different because the people expect it of us. Russia is like no other place. The people here have the warmest hearts and the most passionate souls but they like to be *ruled* and they don't want their Imperial Family to be as they are. They want someone to look up to, to rule them very firmly like a strict but caring father, to be ruled with a…what's the English expression? With a velvet glove on an iron fist."

Ella nodded uncertainly, trying to understand.

"It takes a little time to adjust," Minnie said. "Things are done differently here and at first it might seem strange, even harsh, but it's the way it has to be." She mused for a moment. "The last Tsar wanted to change things. It's hard to believe that not long ago the serfs here were still bound to their masters - something that would have been unheard of in the rest of Europe. My father-in-law liberated the serfs and he would have gone further but you know how the people reacted?"

Ella did know. She had heard in far too much detail the accounts of his horrific death and had seen with her own eyes the effect it had had on Serge.

"It was terribly shocking for everyone," Minnie frowned. "And my poor Nicky, only thirteen years old, seeing his grandfather dying in agony and so mutilated by the blast."

"Serge told me of it."

"But it shows, as Sasha says, that the people don't want that kind of reform. They want to be ruled; they need to be ruled because they are so unused to freedom that they cannot cope with it and it leads only to more violence and suffering."

For a little while there was silence as Minnie took Olga in her arms and gently laid her in her cot, and Ella could think only of how much there was to learn of her new homeland.

"Forgive me," Minnie suddenly smiled, "you've only just arrived. It's too soon to lecture you on politics. Tell me, how is your grandmother?"

"Well, thank you."

"Has she come to terms yet with your marrying a Russian?"

Ella flushed, uncertain how to respond, but Minnie laughed, "Don't worry! My sister in England told me all about her objections to the wedding."

"Grandmama worries so much about all of us."

"And it must have come as a surprise to her, with your having refused Serge's first proposal?"

"I suppose it did."

"What made you change your mind?"

She shrugged evasively, "It's difficult to describe. When he returned to Darmstadt and we were able to spend more time together, we discovered that we have much in common. We both are so fond of nature and animals, and share the same tastes in art, literature and religion."

"Religion? I understood you promised your father to remain Lutheran."

"Oh yes, yes," Ella nodded quickly, "I meant only that Serge and I share the same interest in our faith. We may follow different paths but all roads lead to the same end and I'm sure that as we get to know each other better we will find that our differences will compliment each other."

Minnie smiled thoughtfully and, taking Ella's arm, led her from the nursery. She walked with slow deliberate steps along the corridor and when she eventually spoke, her voice was faltering as though uncertain what she intended to say. "Serge is a good man. Sasha has every faith in him and for that reason entrusts him with a great deal of responsibility."

Ella nodded.

"With responsibility, however, there inevitably comes criticism. Perhaps you have heard that Serge has enemies even here in his own family?"

A pang of fear shot through Ella's heart at the memory of the murder of his father, "Enemies?"

"No, no, that is too strong a word. *Critics*, yes, critics might have been better. Serge is a very private man. He isn't the easiest person to get to know and those who don't understand him as we do, are inclined to misjudge him."

"People are often afraid of what they don't understand."

"That's true and fear can make men vicious."

"They are vicious to Serge?"

"To his reputation. I am only telling you because I think you need to know. You may hear rumours, all kinds of unpleasant rumours about him but that is all they are, *rumours.*"

Ella shrugged, "I have never paid any attention to gossip."

"In that case," Minnie smiled, "you have nothing to worry about. As I said, it is nothing but tittle-tattle from empty minds. Come, let's go back to the others."

As they walked, Minnie commented on the décor and the history of the house but, beneath the small talk, the weight of her warning hung on Ella's heart. *Rumours,* she thought, *what kind of rumours?* Whatever they were, she decided, they would be wrong. She recalled the long conversations with Serge at Darmstadt prior to their engagement. How sensitively he had spoken of music and art, and how deeply he understood when she told him of her deepest, most sacred thoughts! Hadn't his eyes shone with an almost mystical joy when she spoke of her faith in the goodness of God? Hadn't he agreed with her belief that her mother was no less a mother to her after death? And hadn't he also confessed to feelings that his role in Russia compelled him to hide? No, she thought resolutely, whatever people said, they were wrong. They didn't know him. But, even as she drifted back through the over-ornamented rooms, she couldn't help but realize that she herself barely knew him at all.

Chapter 4

Standing gloriously between the Neva and Moika rivers, the thousand windows of the Winter Palace reflected the shimmering light of the summer sun. The white stone gods positioned along the roof had, for almost a century, looked down upon the tsars and princes who dotted the chequered history of the capital. Here, Catherine the Great had entertained her many lovers; Tsar Nicholas I had rallied his troops to crush the Decembrist Rising; across this square came the carriage bearing the bloody Alexander II, hurrying home to die; and now on this glorious Saturday in June, Ella was approaching the door to the chapel.

All morning she had sat in the great malachite halls, in front of the gold mirror of an earlier empress, while the other grand duchesses and ladies-in-waiting attended to her Russian court dress with its long flowing train. Now, moving slowly beneath the weight of the jewels of Catherine the Great, she raised her head and stepped into the chapel.

In the hectic rush of the previous week, greeting Serge's numerous relatives, meeting his regiment and welcoming the royalties who converged on St. Petersburg for the wedding, there had been little time to consider the gravity of the occasion. Here, through the scent of incense and the light of flickering candles, she felt at last the solemnity of the moment. In the simple words of the Lutheran service, she had pronounced her vows with the conviction that the promises she was making before God were binding for life. Now, as the Orthodox priests chanted their rites in a language she couldn't understand, she prayed fervently for the courage to be all that Serge could desire in a wife, and all that the Russian people could wish for in a grand duchess.

Determinedly erect, despite the weight of the jewels that tore into her ear lobes, she stood through the seemingly endless hours of Russian prayers, oblivious of their meaning and mystified by the strange and foreign actions of the priests. She and Serge were crowned with wedding crowns before encircling the altar with lighted candles until at last she emerged from the dimly lit chapel into the sunlight, no longer Princess Elizabeth Alexandra Louise Alice of Hesse and by Rhine but Her Imperial Highness Grand Duchess Elizaveta Feodorovna of Russia.

The rest of the day passed in a haze of greetings, speeches and toasts: line upon line of guests and well-wishers; trying to remember the names and the faces of this huge extended family of which she was now a part. By the time the evening banquet was served, she was too exhausted to eat more than a morsel and, as the celebrations continued late into the night, she longed only to be relieved of the weighty jewels, the noise, the crowds, the polite conversation and the fixed smile that had begun to make her jaw ache.

Eventually, the carriage arrived and, amid a shower of scattered rice, she and Serge were driven through the bright streets of St. Petersburg to the palace that was now her home. It was only then that she realized that not once since her arrival in Russia had she and Serge been alone. Even now, on reaching the Beloselsky Belozersky Palace, rows of servants were waiting to offer the traditional welcome of bread and salt, and, as she entered her dressing room, a whole army of maids and ladies-in-waiting stood in attendance. They set to work removing the jewels and gowns as though she were a Christmas tree being stripped at the end of the season.

At last, they bade her goodnight and, when they had closed the door behind them, she sat for some moments in front of the high triple mirror, uncertain where to go and what was expected of her. Victoria had assured her it would all be alright and there was nothing to fear; but Victoria knew her husband far better than Ella knew Serge. Besides, Victoria and Louis had always been affectionate together, whereas the greatest show of physical devotion she had ever received from Serge was a polite kiss of greeting and his hand enfolding her own. She closed her eyes and tried to pray, wishing more than ever that Mama had lived long enough to see her through this day.

Footsteps creaked the floorboards in the adjoining room and she opened her eyes, breathing deeply for some seconds before tentatively turning the door handle. Beside a vast bed, Serge was sitting in a silk dressing gown, smoke rings issuing from his pursed lips and hovering in the air above him. He turned slowly towards her and, rubbing one eye with a long finger, put out the cigarette.

"You did well today," he said. "I was so proud of you. It can't have been easy with so many people to meet and everything being so unfamiliar."

She smiled and stepped a little closer.

"You must be very tired now?" he said.

"A little."

He stretched, gesticulating towards the bed, and she took off her dressing gown, draping it over a chair before climbing in. He pulled the covers over her, kissed her forehead and extinguished the lamps. She heard his footsteps move around to the other side of the bed and then felt the warmth of his body beside her.

"I'm tired, too," he said, "and there are ten more days of celebrations before we leave the city. For now we'd best rest as much as we can. It will be different when we're in Ilinskoe." He kissed her cheek and rolled away from her and for a while she lay with her eyes wide open, half-expecting something to happen. Soon she could hear the deep flow of his breath in sleep and, with a combination of confusion, disappointment and exhausted relief, she closed her eyes and drifted away into dreams.

Serge was gone when she woke in the morning. A glorious sunlight streamed through the open window and glistened on the golden frames of the pictures and door. From a courtyard below, came the regular clickety-clack of horses' hooves and voices calling in indecipherable tongues. She climbed out of bed and looked down at the courtyard where uniformed footmen and grooms busied themselves with carriages, bridles and plumes. From the centre of a group of young soldiers came the echo of louder voices and, as she leaned further through the window, she caught sight of Serge among them, smiling broadly as the others slapped his back and shook his hand. He looked so at ease and their joyful laughter, reverberating on the walls, suggested a shared affection that was far more genuine than the mere politeness expected of junior officers to their commander-in-chief.

She smiled and pushed open the door to the dressing room where the army of maids was already gathered in attendance. They curtseyed in unison and a lady-in-waiting directed her into an adjoining room where a bath of hot water, scattered with rose petals, steamed. Undergarments and corsets were laid out on wicker chairs beside thick towels embroidered with Cyrillic letters, which, she was told, translated as *E.F.* "Grand Duchess Elizaveta Feodorovna."

She bathed and returned to the dressing room where, to her surprise, the maids were holding out her clothes ready for her to step into.

"Wait," she said, "I haven't yet decided what I shall wear today."

"Forgive me, Your Highness," the lady-in-waiting replied. "The Grand Duke gave orders that you would wear these clothes this morning."

"I see," she said, a little taken aback, but, after a moment's reflection, nodded. Of course, Serge knew far better than she did what a grand duchess was expected to wear for whatever events had been arranged for the day. How thoughtful he was, and how few husbands would even stop to consider what their wives were wearing.

"How very kind of him," she said but the maids' only response was to hurry about their task in silence, turning her this way and that until she was standing in front of the mirror again, viewing herself from every direction and smiling at Serge's good taste. He had certainly made an excellent choice: styles so flattering to her figure, and colours that enhanced her pale complexion and fair hair. The lady-in-waiting led her to a series of cabinets, "The Grand Duke asked me to inform Your Highness that he has added further gifts for you this morning."

When she opened the cabinet doors, Ella gasped with amazement: amethysts, diamonds, rubies, pearls, exquisite jewels of every possible description glimmered and reflected the rays of the morning sun: dazzling brooches, necklaces, bracelets and pins, iridescent as stars against their velvet background. Trying to restrain her awe, she made her selection and, when the maids had finished adjusting the catches, she dismissed them and stood before the mirror, fascinated by the beautiful spectacle reflected in the glass.

In just one day, she thought, *I have been completely transformed from a lowly Hessian princess to this dazzling Imperial Highness!* But no sooner had that thought crossed her mind, than the echo of Grandmama's warning about the wealth of Russian court turning her head, sounded in her ears. She turned sharply from the mirror and, returning to the bedroom, shook at the pillows and began to tuck in the sheets.

"Ella," the door burst open and Serge appeared, "I was..." He stopped abruptly, his face aghast, "What on earth are you doing!"

Before she could reply, he had seized her wrist tightly and was pulling her away towards the door.

"What is it?" she whispered in shock as a hard-steely look replaced all the softness in his eyes.

"What were you thinking? What would the servants think if they saw you doing this?"

The anger in his tone and features was so alarming that she could barely find the words to respond.

"I'm sorry," she stammered, "it's just that at home we always..."

"This is your home now. You're my wife, not a housemaid, for heaven's sake!"

Tears of shock began to well in her eyes and she swallowed, blinking quickly to prevent them from falling. Then, as suddenly as the rage had come upon him, it subsided, and the harshness in his eyes melted. He cleared his throat and, loosing his grip on her wrist, said softly, "Forgive me, you weren't to know. Things are done very differently here than in Darmstadt."

"I'm sorry to have made you angry. I didn't..."

"No," he shook his head to silence her, "*I* am sorry. It's not your fault. I should have told you. It's important that the Imperial Family behave *always* as the Imperial Family. If the servants were to see you carrying out these kind of menial tasks, what would they think? We would lose all respect and the reputation of the whole family would be put at risk."

A series of images flashed before her eyes: Mama on her hands and knees, scrubbing the floor of a squalid slum; carrying the slop buckets at the hospital and bathing the infected wounds of the casualties of the Franco-Prussian War. The message instilled in her since childhood rang through her ears: *never allow the servants to do anything for you that you can do for yourself. Remember how privileged you are and how important it is to set a good example to those who were not born so fortunate.*

Serge rested his hands on her shoulders and held her for a moment as though she were a child.

"I'm sorry, Ella," he said again, "I shouldn't have spoken so harshly. There's so much for you to learn, so much I need to teach you." He looked into her eyes, "So much that I *will* teach you."

"Thank you," she murmured.

He stepped back a little and viewed her as though he were an art critic and she were a statue in a gallery. After a few moments' contemplation, he adjusted the comb in her hair, "That's better," he smiled, taking her hand. "Now, come, breakfast is served." He held open the door and led her towards a staircase, "We'll meet with your family again today. I promised your father that I'd let you spend as much time as possible with them before we go on to Ilinskoe and they return to Darmstadt."

Return to Darmstadt... The words played on her heart like sad cello music but she threw back her head and smiled, "Thank you."

Chapter 5

The engine chugged and a great cloud of steam filled the platform of the Nikolaevsky Station where whole companies of servants bustled to and fro with trunks and cases and a myriad of luxuries to bring comfort to the journey to Ilinskoe. As the regular engine thudded, coupling with the private carriages marked with the Romanov double-headed eagle, Ella smiled.

"Something amusing?" Serge said.

"I was thinking of something Mama told me when I was a child. She had returned home to England and for some reason Grandmama wasn't pleased about her visit so refused to allow her to use the royal train to transport her to Balmoral."

"What did she do?"

"Bought a ticket with all the other passengers and travelled all the way up to Scotland second class."

"Did anyone recognize her?"

"I don't think so."

"Might be an interesting way to travel. It could be useful in gauging the mood of the country and finding out what the people really think, rather than what the ministers would have us believe."

"She often went incognito through some of the poorest parts of London and Darmstadt to see for herself what conditions were like."

He was thoughtful for a second and then sniffed, "An excellent idea. Perhaps one day I'll do that."

Pavel appeared from nowhere, "Do what?"

"Go out incognito to see how the Tsar's subjects live."

"Oh no, dear boy, please!" Pavel slapped his back jovially, "If you go, I'll have to go with you." He winked at Ella, "You know how inseparable we are!"

"I'd go," she said.

"Now that *would* be an impossibility," Serge laughed. "Can you imagine, Pavel, the dangers of letting so beautiful a creature out unprotected?"

Ella smiled, uncertain of the compliment, "But I would like to…"

"Come," Serge said, "the carriage is ready and you're going to love this journey. So far you've only seen Petersburg and now you'll have the chance to see the real Russia."

They settled into their seats and, as the engine pulled out of the station, she looked out across palaces, bridges, canals and shimmering cathedrals.

"Petersburg is beautiful in its way," Serge said, following her eyes, "but when Peter the Great built this city - at the cost of hundreds of workers' lives - he wanted to make the country more European, so the styles here aren't really Russian at all. Moscow is far closer to the true Holy Rus."

"Holy Rus?"

He nodded, eager to explain, "The autocracy was ordained by God, and the Tsar as Head of the Orthodox Church is Christ's representative on earth. Those whom God has chosen to govern this vast empire have a duty to build the Kingdom of Heaven in Russia." His eyes narrowed as though viewing an unpleasant memory. "That's why the murder of the Tsar is so great a crime."

Pavel nodded, "What happened to our father was not only murder, it was sacrilege."

"This is what happens when the people are given too much freedom. It isn't the ordinary

Russians who are to blame. They are like children, you see?"

His eyes were fixed earnestly on Ella, and she nodded.

"They need to be ruled with fairness but also with firm discipline."

"An iron fist in a velvet glove, as Minnie said."

"That's right! You're learning quickly. The ordinary Russians love the Tsar, the autocracy and all that God has ordained. They know where they are and are happy in that security. As soon as we loose the reins and grant more freedom, they're infiltrated by intellectuals who seek to fill their heads with all kinds of nonsense. They make empty promises of a glorious new future where everyone is equal, and what God has ordained is of no consequence whatsoever. It unsettles the people; they become lost and confused and that invariably leads to violence."

Pavel caught her eye and winked, "You must make allowance for Serge's sermons, Ella. He feels very passionately about all of this."

Serge threw him an icy glance and returned his gaze to Ella, "It's important, very important that you understand these things. In Hesse and England the whole culture is so different. Your grandmother is the Queen but she doesn't rule. Her Parliament does that. Here, the Tsar is the only authority and everything depends on his decisions. As members of his family it is our first, our *only* duty to support him. There is no place for gentleness; it's perceived as weakness and, once the people perceive us as weak, chaos and anarchy are sure to follow."

Pavel stretched his legs and lit a cigarette, "Don't worry, Ella," he smiled, "when we reach

Ilinskoe, he'll be in a far less dogmatic frame of mind."

For a moment it seemed that Serge would retaliate but instead he shook his head and flicked open his cigarette case.

"Ilinskoe," he said more softly, "is a haven. There are no anarchists there, only simple peasants with good and sincere hearts."

Ella smiled at him and he returned the smile, "It shows what can be done when people are free of all the trouble-causing stirrers. You see, *there,* my mother was able to do all kinds of things to help the people. She even opened a school for girls as well as boys - something that I'm sure *your* mother would have approved of."

Ella smiled and looked out of the window as the train moved beyond the city to the open countryside where the recently liberated serfs toiled to earn a few meagre kopecks. Beyond them, the golden domes of countless cathedrals glistened on the horizon. Each station revealed some new panorama: Liuban, Likhoslavl, Tver - always a different monastery, displaying the vitality and pride of the Orthodox faith, the very soul of Holy Rus.

While the sights enthralled her, the conversation was scintillating as Serge and Pavel vied with one another to explain countless details of Russian history, of the glory of the three-hundred year rule of the Romanovs, the stories of so many palaces, heroes and tsars. She listened intrigued and laughed with pleasure as Pavel recounted anecdotes from their childhood. She dozed and she woke and they played cards as the carriage filled with cigarette smoke. Then she dozed again only to be woken as the train drew into Moscow.

Breathless in awe, she gazed at the colourful minarets and cupolas crowning the cathedrals and the giant walls of the Kremlin palaces.

"Moscow," Serge murmured, sharing her wonder. "*This* is the heart of Russia."

From Moscow the train continued south for a further thirty-five miles to Odintsovo where a carriage awaited them for the final part of their journey. Here, the roads were narrow and on either side peasants looked up from their labours in the fields to catch sight of their new grand duchess, before abasing themselves, bowing down in the dust with a humility unknown in Darmstadt.

The carriage turned along a winding driveway leading to a simple two-storey house surrounded by balconies, overlooking acres of flat parklands and birch woods leading down to the river.

"Ilinskoe!" Serge beamed.

Pavel slapped his back, "And now, I'll keep my promise and make myself scarce so you can enjoy your honeymoon in peace."

Serge turned to Ella, "I hope you'll come to love this place as I do."

"I love it already," she smiled.

Sunlight shimmered across the Moskva River as the breeze stirred the surface, sending ripples towards the landing stage. The paddles lapped against the water and, from across the woody banks, birds twittered and chirped in the branches of the high birch trees. On either side of the boat, the vibrant hues of the season ran together like a water-colour canvass: bright red strawberries, meshed in light green leaves; amber-gold sunshine in a pale blue sky; dark brown tree trunks in the black mud banks, and cornflowers and lilies lining the woodland paths.

Serge set the oars into their locks and, holding the sketch at arm's length, smiled, "It's perfect!" His eyes moved from the page to the bank, seeking out the details, "You notice everything, don't you? The flowers, the creatures, the landing stage, the plants."

"Perhaps later, I'll paint it to capture the colours, too." Ella said.

"Yes, you must!"

"And if it turns out well, I could send it to Grandmama."

He handed back the sketch, "If you wish, but..."

"You don't think it will be good enough?"

"On the contrary, I know it will be exquisite, so exquisite that I'd like to keep it here as a memento of these beautiful days."

His tone was so affectionate and gentle that she could only gaze at him in wonder. There was such tenderness and sensitivity in those grey eyes and yet something impenetrable; something unknowable or something that perhaps it would take a long time to know.

He reached for her hand, "Ella, there's something I need to say to you." He looked down shyly and thudded his boot against the timbers of the boat. "It's difficult to find the words. I know that I'm not always..." He shook his head and laughed awkwardly, then stopped laughing and inhaled determinedly. "I don't find it easy to express myself. Sometimes I might seem distant or cold but you must know that the days we've spent here have been the happiest, most beautiful days of my life."

She was about to respond but he shook his head quickly, "Please, let me go on. Until we came here, I wasn't sure that I was capable of loving you as you deserve to be loved. In fact, I didn't think I was capable of loving anyone." He smiled briefly before struggling on. "Maybe it's because every time I cared for anyone before, they were taken from me. First my eldest brother, then my mother, my father...I can't stand it, Ella. I can't bear to love someone and then lose them. Perhaps it's a weakness to feel things so deeply."

"No," she shook her head, "it's not weakness."

"It seems that way to other people."

"What does it matter what other people think?"

"In our position, it *does* matter. We can't...*I* can't let them see any chink in this armour or it's as certain as night follows day that they'll use it against me, or worse against Tsardom."

"Who will?" she frowned.

"The people, the aristocracy, even members of the family. There is nothing they despise more than weakness in a man, and in a grand duke it's unforgivable. Any display of emotion appears as weakness, so very early in life I learned to hide all my feelings from other people and I hid them so deeply that at times I thought I had lost them completely. Every time something or someone begins to matter to me very much, a kind of barrier comes up inside. It's as though I've built a wall around my heart so no one will ever see what's really there." He looked across the river and stared earnestly onto the horizon, "I know that people consider me cold and insensitive and it's easier for me that way. It's better to be seen as cold than weak. But the truth is that behind that wall hides a vulnerable and deeply-feeling person who is nothing like the man people think I am."

"Serge," she said softly, "I don't think you're cold and insensitive."

He sighed deeply and twirled the ring around his finger, "Sometimes I might sound harsh or unkind and I hate myself for it but I can't help it. I have hidden my feelings for so long that now, even when I want to express what I really feel, something stops me and instead it comes out in completely the wrong way. Do you understand what I'm trying to say?"

She reached for his hand and clasped his fingers in her own, "You don't have to explain. I know who you are and I love you as you are; I wouldn't have you be otherwise."

"If I don't always tell you what you mean to me, and how fervently I thank God for bringing you to me, it isn't because I don't feel those things. It's just that I..." When he looked at her, his lip trembled and his eyes glistened as though tears were forming. "I do," he whispered, "thank God every day for you."

"And I, for you."

He threw back his head and looked up at the sky, breathing deeply, "Since we're speaking so openly, there's something else I need to tell you if I can find the words."

She sensed what he was about to say and a flurry of embarrassment caused her cheeks to burn.

"I should have spoken of this before we were married but the opportunity never arose. Besides, I hoped that it might be different when we were together. Perhaps it *will* be different when we know each other better."

"Serge, you don't have to say this. It's alright."

"No, it isn't alright. It isn't alright at all." He kicked against the side of the boat, "You must wonder what kind of man I am. Why I can't..." He gasped and a tear fell from his eye and rolled down his cheek.

"I know what kind of man you are," she said, moving to sit beside him and causing the boat to rock frantically. "You're a good man, a kind man."

With delicate fingers she wiped away his tears and drew his head to her till his beard bristled against her cheek.

"We're only beginning to know one another," she said softly. "There's plenty of time for things to change between us."

"And if they don't?"

"There are other ways we can show our love."

His eyes, shining in the sunlight, bored through her, "Don't think that I don't want you, Ella. I do! And yet when I look at you and see such beauty, such *perfection*, I know I'll never be able to hold you, to love you as a man loves a wife. It would spoil you."

She blinked and shook her head.

"You're like a work of art, beyond human, beyond flesh and blood. You're like an angel, other-worldly, ethereal. Don't you see that to reduce you to flesh and blood would be to defile you, to spoil your angelic purity? It would be *sinful* to do that to you."

"Serge," she murmured, "didn't God create flesh and blood? Didn't he make us as we are and sanctify our humanity by becoming a man himself?"

"He also created purer beings and, to me, that is what you are." His lips curled in an expression of disgust, "Bloody flesh and the mess of physical bodies! Ella, you're above that. I could never reduce you to that."

She frowned, perplexed, "I *am* human. I am not a statue or an angel. I am flesh and blood."

The disgust in his expression turned to confusion and frustration, "This isn't the whole truth. There is…I am…There's more I would tell you but I *can't.* I'm sorry to be such a disappointment to you."

"No, you're not!"

"I'm so sorry. I am just so very sorry."

She drew him towards her and he buried his head in her shoulder until his warm tears trickled down her neck as he sobbed like a child in her arms.

"It will be different when we know each other better," she whispered and kissed him and held him until the sobbing subsided and he suddenly drew away from her, breathing deeply and wiping away his tears on a handkerchief.

"You need to learn Russian."

The sudden change in his expression and tone threw her into utter confusion. Whether it sprang from his wounded pride or regret that he had allowed her to see him so vulnerable, his features were suddenly rigid and his voice patronising and cold.

"The people expect it of a grand duchess."

"Yes, of course," she said.

"I'll teach you. We'll begin tomorrow and then…."

A voice from the landing stage distracted him, and Ella turned to see two figures on the bank calling and waving frantically.

"It's my cousin, Kostia," Serge said, reaching for the oars, with a smile that spoke of relief. "We'd better go to him. We can save this conversation for another time."

As he heaved the oars, Ella responded with a wave to the calls from the landing stage, "Is that Mavra with him?"

"No." Serge narrowed his eyes to make out her face, "It's Zinaida."

"Zinaida?"

"Nicholas Youssoupov's wife. Their estate, Archangelskoe, is just a short ride from here."

"Are they part of the family?"

"No, but they're very good friends. They must be one of the richest families in Russia. Youssoupov owns four palaces in Petersburg alone, as well as a mansion in Moscow and estates with oil wells and mills all over the country. Archangelskoe is magnificent; it even has its own theatre and zoo. You'll like Zinaida. I'm sure that as soon as you meet, you'll become great friends."

The boat drew alongside the landing stage and, as Konstantin reached for the rope, Ella looked up at the beautiful woman standing beside him. She made a slight curtsey and, with a radiant smile accentuating her beautiful features, said, "Your Highness."

"Oh, please," Serge laughed as he stepped from the boat, "we're in Ilinskoe. Let's have no formality here. Zinaida, this is Ella, Ella, Zinaida."

Zinaida embraced her, "The beautiful Ella whom everyone in Petersburg is talking about! And you are every bit as beautiful as they say!"

Ella laughed and Zinaida glanced towards Serge and Konstantin already deep in conversation.

"Might we walk a little way together and leave the men to their serious talk?"

They linked arms and strolled through the summer woods, talking of the beauty of the season and surroundings, until they came within view of the house.

"Serge loves this place," Ella said.

"It's not surprising. It's always a relief to be free of the intrigues of the city and, for a man as devout as Serge, the simplicity of the villagers and peasants has great appeal. You've been to the village?"

"We went yesterday. It was so touching to see how the people love him."

"With good cause. He genuinely cares about them and is very modest about the improvements he's made to their lives. It's not every village has a school for girls and boys."

"Serge says that the simple faith of the peasants is far more sincere than anything that is found in Petersburg. I noticed it, too. There's something quite mystical about them; something so deep-rooted that seems to pervade every area of their lives."

Zinaida smiled, "It borders on superstition with their shamans and ancient beliefs, but who can blame them for believing in superstitions? Sometimes I think that we have such an idealised view of our dear Russian peasants as simple, hardworking, devout souls, that we forget quite how difficult their life can be."

Ella raised her eyebrows, eager to know more.

"You've seen them in the summer when everything looks rosy but the winters are very harsh. Few of the babies born at that time of year survive the cold, not to mention the number of mothers who die in childbirth, with no medical assistance at hand."

"There's no doctor in the region?"

She shook her head, "No midwife, no clinic."

Ella turned pensively to look at Serge and Konstantin, striding through the woods behind them, "I could ask Serge..."

"Of course," Zinaida sighed, "there are times when even the best medical assistance is powerless against the will of God. I have lost two children already."

"Oh, I'm so sorry, I had no idea."

"Rich or poor, princess or peasant, it makes no difference. Losing a child is the hardest thing for any woman to bear."

Ella nodded and Zinaida looked at her with a kind of recognition, "You understand that, don't you?" she frowned.

"I had a younger brother, Frittie - a beautiful, beautiful little boy. One morning he was playing in my mother's room when he saw my brother, Ernie, at an opposite window. They waved to each other and suddenly Frittie climbed onto the ledge and fell straight through the window."

"Oh my!" Zinaida gasped, "Was he killed?"

"Not at once. My mother ran out to him and was amazed because he seemed quite unharmed but that night he began bleeding in his brain and he never woke up. He had an illness, you see, the same as my mother's brother, Leopold. Haemophilia."

"Haemophilia?"

"The blood doesn't clot so a slight cut can go on bleeding for days and, if there is internal bleeding, the joints swell and cause crippling pain. Uncle Leo suffered terribly throughout his life so, in a way, my mother thought Frittie's death might have been a blessing to him. All the same, she never recovered from the loss."

Zinaida stared beyond the trees, "She still misses him, even now?"

"She's with him now." Ella smiled.

"Forgive me, I should have known."

Ella shook her head.

"Was it the same illness that killed her?"

"No. Diphtheria. All the family had it, except for me and Mama, and so she sent me away to stay with my paternal grandmother in Bessungen. Mama remained in Darmstadt to care for the family. The doctors warned her that she mustn't touch or kiss any of them for fear of infection, and for weeks she nursed them, covering herself in disinfectant, wearing a mask and gloves so as not to spread the illness but, in spite of all her care, my little sister, May, died."

Zinaida shook her head in sincere sympathy.

"Since Ernie's life was still hanging in the balance, Mama thought it better not to tell him of May's death. She kept up the pretence until he began to recover. When she eventually told him the truth, he was so distressed that she couldn't bear it any longer. She took off the mask, held him and kissed him…" she broke off as the memory played out before her eyes.

"And contracted the illness herself?" Zinaida prompted.

Ella nodded, "After losing May and Frittie, I think she had no will left to fight."

Zinaida sighed, "What a terrible tragedy."

"But, you know what was strange and beautiful?" Ella said. "She had been virtually unconscious for a few days, yet just before her death she opened her eyes and her face was quite radiant as she whispered, "Dear Papa!" It was seventeen years to the day since the death of her father, whom she loved so much. I believe he came back to take her home."

For a while they both stood in silence, listening to the bird song and lost in their own thoughts until the crackling of bracken behind them announced the approach of Konstantin and Serge.

"I'm sorry," Ella said, "I didn't mean to bore you."

"No," Zinaida rested her hand on her arm, "*thank you.* I'm honoured that you told me of it."

"I don't believe Mama has really gone. I don't believe any of them have. Your children, my brother, sister, mother…we simply don't see them now but they see us and their prayers and love are still with us."

Zinaida smiled, "I can see why you're so attracted to the peasants' mysticism. Are you something of a mystic yourself, Ella?"

Serge suddenly stepped forwards, "A mystic?" he smiled. "I thought Orthodoxy had the monopoly of mystics. I never heard of a Lutheran mystic before."

"In that case," Zinaida joked, "if she is like this as a Lutheran, when she converts you'll be amazed! After all, converts are renowned for being far more devout than those born into a faith."

Serge awkwardly dug his boot into the earth, and Ella looked down at the ground.

"Sorry," Zinaida said, "have I said something out of place?"

"Ella isn't going to convert." Serge said abruptly.

She blushed. "Have I put my foot in it?"

"No, not all," Serge said affably. "Ella promised her father she would remain true to the faith of her childhood, and I've agreed to that. It would be different if she were to become Tsarina but I'm so far down the line of succession that's hardly likely. Vladimir is closer to the throne than I am and he was happy to let Miechen remain Lutheran so I could hardly object to Ella's father's decision."

There was something distinctly uncomfortable about hearing him discuss her religion as though she had no say in the matter and it irked her a little to think that Serge saw it as an agreement between himself and her father.

"Serge," she said, deliberately changing the subject, "Zinaida was telling me of the number of infants and mothers who die in childbirth here. I was wondering whether it would be possible to have a clinic built or at least pay for a midwife for them?"

He blinked as though taken aback and his eyes moved from Ella to Zinaida and back again, "I don't see why not," he said and, after a moment's reflection, added, "Yes, my child, that's an excellent idea."

My child? She squirmed inside but his eyes were bright now and he nodded several times to himself as though impressed by her suggestion. "Yes. I'll arrange it straight away."

"Goodness!" Konstantin laughed, "You've only been here a fortnight and already have Serge eating out of your hand. You're good for him, Ella, and with ideas like that, it's no wonder the Russian people adore you!"

Serge laughed, "You're not wrong, Kostia. Honestly, God couldn't have sent me a more perfect wife. She has a lot to learn but she learns quickly and, by the time we return to the city, I'm sure she'll be a perfect Romanov grand duchess."

He put his arm possessively around her shoulder but, when she looked into his eyes, she was certain she saw the unmistakable shimmer of love.

Chapter 6 - St. Petersburg - January 1885

Autumn had passed so quickly in the spree of visits, dinners, theatre performances and receptions planned by Serge to introduce Ella to every aspect of life in the capital. Cousins, second cousins, grand dukes and princes, officers and ministers had filed through the doors of the Beloselsky Belozersky Palace and, at the end of each visit, Ella smiled at her growing confidence and the stunning impression she had made on her guests. Now, as the cold winter winds froze the River Neva and snow drifts covered the carriageways and parks, she felt every inch a grand duchess waltzing into her first St. Petersburg season of magnificent balls.

Stepping from a fur-lined carriage into the glamour of a malachite ballroom, her eyes were dazzled by the resplendence of gilt-edged jambs and mirrors and the glistening jewels and golden threads of ball gowns. Everything was shining, from the flecks of light shimmering in the crystal drops of the chandeliers to the sheen of the polished floor on which dancers floated like ice skaters to the strains of an orchestra, half-concealed by palms and ferns at the farthest end of the room. Candles gleamed through octagons of coloured glass and flickered in glowing candelabra, throwing shafts blue and orange across the brilliant white shirts of the footmen who stood at regular intervals, holding silver trays of champagne to refresh the thirsty dancers.

"Allow me," said Serge, taking her dance card and glancing quickly around the room. He reeled off a list of names of young officers and scribbled them onto the card, "I've only chosen the most handsome partners for you."

"Then I must be first on the list!" laughed Pavel and, taking the card from his brother, crossed out some of the names, replacing them with his own.

Serge laughed and Pavel, offering his hand to Ella, led her onto the floor.

"Can you feel them?" he said.

"Feel what?"

"The eyes of every man in the room fixed on you."

She laughed to dismiss his compliment but it pleased her to know, as she glided in front of the mirror, that her appearance was every bit worthy of such attention. Tightly-laced, her low cut gown revealed a white neck ornamented with tiny emeralds, accentuating her luminous eyes. Matching droplets of emeralds dangled from her ears, catching the light as she floated across the room with her most radiant smile. Pavel's firm hand pressed against her back as he moved her, turned her, guided her across the floor. With no effort, her feet followed his steps and fell naturally into the movements as though they had danced this dance together a thousand times before. It was too much, too easy and too frightening - she dared not look at him, though he was so close she could smell the starch of his stiff white shirt and a faint whiff of champagne on his breath.

"Serge is so proud of you," he said. "You know how much the regiment means to him and can't you see how delighted he is to have all the officers adore you?"

"If they do," she said modestly, "it's only because I am his wife. I know how they admire and love him."

She glanced across the room to where her husband stood laughing with a group of young soldiers. His laughter was so entrancing that she stepped out of rhythm until Pavel pressed her back a little more firmly, helping her readjust. She smiled at him apologetically but he was looking over her shoulder, nodding occasionally to other guests and exchanging a few passing words with other dancers as they floated elegantly by. It occurred to Ella that this moment might have been something she had dreamed of all her life - to be here in emeralds, silk and tulle, dancing with a handsome Russian grand duke. Yet the pleasure she took in the strength of his arms and the touch of his fingers enfolding her own, left her with a strange unease. She wanted to look at him again to see if he was smiling but she dared not raise her eyes to his face for fear of blushing.

Instead, she looked in Serge's direction, hoping his eyes, too, might look on her with the adoration she was receiving from every other corner of the room, but he had turned away, engrossed in conversation with the men of his regiment.

She glanced at Pavel; he was smiling, but not at her. His gaze was directed towards a young princess who returned his smile and fanned her face coyly.

"Who is she?" Ella said.

"Minnie's niece. Alexandra of Greece."

He twirled her more vigorously around the room, and an unbidden sense of disappointment, perhaps even jealousy, gnawed at her stomach.

She forced a smile. "Do I detect a romance?"

"Far too soon to say. She's only fifteen. Besides, I don't know that I'm ready for marriage. I like my life just as it is, though I dare say I can't go on playing gooseberry to you and Serge forever."

"Gooseberry?" she laughed. "Hardly that! We love your company."

"And I yours," he spun her around, "so perhaps I'll continue a little longer before taking on all the responsibilities of wife."

"Good gracious! Responsibilities! You make marriage sound like a burden."

"Not really," he laughed loudly, "but I somehow can't see myself making all the decisions for someone else as Serge makes all your decisions for you."

"Not *all* my decisions," she said, slightly affronted.

"You know what I mean. He appointed your tutors for Russian and music, he decides where you go, what you read, even selecting your dance partners. I can hardly sort out my own life, let alone someone else's."

The lightness in his tone and expression suggested he had no idea that his words had struck her to the core.

"Of course," she said defensively, "Serge makes most of our decisions at the moment but that's because I'm so unfamiliar with the court and manners of Russia, and he is so much more experienced in so many ways than I am. In reality, I'm still a stranger in a foreign country."

Pavel's smile faded into a more pensive expression, "It's part of his character, too. He likes to feel in control and I know he can be a little overbearing at times."

She shook her head, "He's the head of the household and I'm glad that he shows such an interest in how I spend my time and where I go and what I do."

"You're very patient with him," Pavel said.

"Not at all! He's very patient with me."

"Patient? Even when he loses his temper?"

"It must be very trying for him if I make mistakes, and I'm glad that he corrects me."

He looked directly into her eyes and held her closer as they turned through the final diminuendo.

"He's my brother and I love him but I know he can be difficult to live with, and perhaps as a husband he isn't..." he broke off and shook his head. "All I'm saying is that I'm always here for you, Ella, if ever you need a friend."

From an alcove, Sandro Mikhailovich surveyed the guests and gulped his champagne with an ever-increasing dissatisfaction welling in his stomach. A trill from the orchestra prompted a hasty movement towards the dance floor and, for the third time that evening, Pavel took Ella's hand and led her to the farthest end of the room where they paused a moment barely touching each other as they waited for the beat. Suddenly, in perfect unison, they pressed closer and stepped into a polka. Sandro watched transfixed as, smiling, they swayed together, their steps at once graceful and natural as though carried by the music or guided by some shared intuition. Their bodies curved harmoniously through each cadence, and the elegant lightness of their movements brought to mind the graceful beauty of two falling snowflakes floating weightlessly through the sky.

Sandro's heart beat quickly as the tempo increased and he longed to be in Pavel's place; holding her close enough to feel her breath on his skin.

"My dear, what a sorry looking fellow you are!" Miechen's voice intruded on his reverie. "I'd have thought a handsome young man like you would have been the first choice on everyone's dance card but I don't believe you have danced at all this evening."

"I'm not in the mood to dance tonight," he turned towards her, struggling to avert his eyes from Ella.

"Then why on earth did you come?"

"To visit Nicky. It just so happens that my visit coincides with this gathering of mannequins."

"Mannequins!" Miechen laughed, signalling to Konstantin and Mavra to join them, "Sandro is out of sorts tonight, come and help me to raise his spirits."

Mavra smiled gently, "What's the matter, Sandro? Are you not enjoying the ball?"

"What's the point?" he huffed. "Look at them all! Months and months of costumiers, seamstresses, shoemakers, coiffeurs, jewellers and God knows how many other poor wretches toiling away so they can all parade around for a few brief hours like overdressed dummies, talking of nothing but the previous ball and the next."

"You surprise me," Miechen teased. "I would never have thought that you had such concern for the masses or such disdain for your family."

"Oh, the people themselves are alright, or at least they would be if they had the courage to come out from behind their masks. They're all so afraid of what we might discover if we saw what they're really like beneath the silks and uniforms and jewels. Strip away the trappings and I'm sure I would find them a good deal more interesting."

His eyes moved involuntarily towards the dance floor again and Konstantin smiled, "I suspect a case of the pot calling the kettle black."

He frowned irritably.

"Strip away all the masks, you said, and yet there you stand behind a cloak of disdain, concealing nothing but jealousy."

"Jealousy?"

"Oh, come on, confess it," Miechen prodded him. "You haven't been able to take your eyes from Ella all night."

"Nonsense. I just can't stand the falsity of it all. It's so tedious."

Miechen wafted her fan and peered across the room, "Our pretty grand duchess doesn't seem to be finding it tedious. She has been smiling and laughing since she arrived."

Sandro shook his head, "I'm sure Ella hates it as much as I do. She's far too intelligent to want to spend time idling away the hours with Serge's cronies who have nothing more interesting to discuss than their most recent mistress or the latest drinking spree."

"If your conversation is more scintillating," Mavra said, "why not ask her to dance yourself?"

"How can I? Her card is full. Her card is *always* full because he fills it in, in advance. He passes her around among the soldiers of his regiment so he can buy their friendship…or their silence."

"Their silence about what?" Miechen's eyes were wide with interest but, before Sandro could reply, Konstantin stepped between them.

"She looks very happy."

Sandro shrugged, "It's expected of her so she makes the best of it."

"Couldn't it be that she *is* happy?" Mavra said.

Sandro looked directly at her, "Would *you* be happy if your husband spent his evenings in the seediest bath-houses paying for the services of boys?"

The blood drained from Konstantin's cheeks and his heart missed a beat then thudded so fiercely that his hand shook and champagne dripped from his glass to the floor.

"That's a wild and dangerous accusation to make," Miechen said.

"Well, I'm sorry if it shocks you but, if you didn't hear it from me, you'd hear it from someone else sooner or later. It's the talk of Petersburg."

"And who told you?"

"Someone who knows someone who has seen him there."

She leaned closer, "They actually said they saw Serge?"

"Of course they didn't name him. They wouldn't dare but it was obvious: 'a grand duke' - who else could it be but *him*?"

"There are many grand dukes in Petersburg," Konstantin said.

"'A person very close to the Tsar' - which is just a roundabout way of saying one of his brothers."

"Oh heaven forbid!" Miechen laughed. "The very idea would turn my husband's stomach so it's certainly not Vladimir!"

"Nor Pavel. He's transparent and guilt would be written all over his face. And not Alexei - he's seldom here and far too much of a ladies' man. That leaves Serge."

Konstantin shuffled, "This is all supposition and rumour and I'm surprised that you pay any attention to it, let alone repeat it."

"Serge is your friend, so you don't want to hear the truth but…"

"It isn't the truth!" Konstantin responded with such uncharacteristic force that both Miechen and Mavra stared at him in amazement.

Sandro shrugged, "You're good man and only want to see the best in everyone. I respect you for that but it blinds you to what's going on."

Konstantin leaned closer to him, "It's not for you to judge whether or not I am a good man. You have no idea what goes on in my heart any more than you know what goes on in Serge's. Weren't you just saying that we all hide behind masks? What do you think we would see were we to remove them? I will tell you what I think: we would be shocked by many whom we consider to be good men, and we would be amazed by many whom we judge to be wicked."

Sandro was about to respond but Mavra, reaching for her husband's hand, said quietly, "I think if we could truly see into men's hearts, what we would find there would fill us with such pity that we would never judge anyone at all. Everyone has his own private grief and inner battles and it's only the fear of how others might judge us that compels us to wear the mask in the first place." She looked at Konstantin with deep affection and understanding in her eyes, "Come," she said, "I would like to dance."

"Well," said Miechen when they had gone, "what was all that about?"

Sandro shook his head, "He's a poet and a dreamer and Serge's friend. Of course, he feels he has to defend him."

Miechen's eyes moved across the room, "Whether or not your allegations have any foundation, they could lead you into serious trouble. If Sasha were to hear that you have been telling stories, your whole future could be put at risk before you have even begun. May I offer a word of advice?"

"I am sure you are going to, whether I want it or not."

"Be careful to whom you speak. Anything that suggests scandal or division within the family, is a threat to us all. Gossip, by all means, if you must but select your listeners with discretion."

"And join the whole charade along with everyone else?"

"Indeed. That's what we do. It's all a charade; we all play our parts, choose our own roles and, if we don't like the part we are playing, we simply switch masks. Life is much happier once you realize that. It's no longer necessary to take everything so seriously. It's all a game, nothing more."

"And what of those who don't know the rules of the game? The ones who step into it blindly and don't understand what everyone else is playing?"

"We all know the rules. We're none of us quite as naïve as we like to think we are. Some people choose to play the part of the victim or martyr, and that is their choice no less than those who choose to play the blackguard or victor."

He sniffed grouchily.

"You think that Ella is an unwitting victim?"

"I think she is only just beginning to realize what a monster she has married."

Miechen shook her head, "Hardly a monster. That's just an act, too. All that anger and short-temper, it's a cover for his weakness. You needn't worry about Ella. She's intelligent enough to see through it and, if Serge isn't the husband she thought he might be, it seems there is substitute at hand already."

"What?"

"Use your eyes, Sandro! Who has she been dancing with all night?"

"Whatever partners Serge chose for her."

She sighed in sham exasperation, "Whose name has appeared on that card most often? Who accompanied them on their honeymoon, lives in the same house, spends virtually every day in her company and then dances with her most of the evening?"

"Pavel?" he frowned.

"Let's put it this way. Supposing two brothers were inseparable and devoted to one another. One of the brothers," her voice dropped to a whisper, "lacks either the inclination or the wherewithal to be a true husband but doesn't want his pretty little wife to go seeking comfort elsewhere. Wouldn't he naturally turn to his brother to keep the little bird satisfied and silently content in her gilded cage?"

"You think Pavel and Ella are…"

"Ah, ah, ah!" She raised a finger to his lips, "Learn a little discretion. I never mentioned any names, never made any allegations. When you tell a story, you should credit your hearers with intelligence. Drop hints and crumbs and allow them to reach their own conclusions."

"And that way, the story is told and you can walk away blameless?"

"You're learning," she smiled. "And now, run along, Sandro, and tell my husband that I would like to dance."

Chapter 7

With a quaking heart but a firm resolve, Konstantin strode along the corridor of the Beloselsky Belozersky Palace towards Serge's study. Brushing the dust from his sleeve, he tried to breathe deeply to restore his calm but the sound of raised voices echoing from behind an open door only increased his anxiety.

"For pity's sake, have they nothing better to talk about! It makes me so angry to think they can spread these lies and, no matter what we do or say, the minute the story is out the damage is done."

In the pause that followed, Konstantin moved closer and, through the gap in the door, caught sight of Serge standing erect and quite still but for the steady tapping of his boot against the grate of the fire.

"I suppose it can be ignored?" It was Pavel's voice.

The tapping stopped momentarily but there came no reply.

"Yes," Pavel answered his own question. "I suppose it is best to ignore it."

Serge kicked more frantically at the grate, "Damn it! Is there no limit to the depths to which they will sink? No, this is too much."

There was a shuffling then Pavel came into view. He was shorter than Serge, wearing the uniform of the Imperial Horse Guards, and, though his expression was serious, his face lacked the tautness of that of his elder brother.

"Do you think it would be better if I were to move away?"

"No, absolutely not!" Serge's foot hammered the grate. "What's the point? When this story has run its course, they'll only invent another. And besides, to change our arrangements now is as good as admitting that their accusations are true."

Pavel stared at him earnestly, "You know that they're not?"

"Of course I do. I wouldn't even think such a thing."

"In that case, let's ignore them and forget all about it." Pavel moved towards the door where he paused and, resting his hand on the jamb, turned back slowly.

"But if Ella's reputation is at risk..."

Serge stiffened, "Ella's reputation is beyond reproach." With greater vehemence than ever, the toe tapping started again. He fumbled through his pocket, pulled out a cigarette case and flicked open the lid, "It's deplorable that she should be dragged into this. Deplorable that either of you should!"

"Perhaps for her sake, in public, at least, it might be as well to appear a little less friendly."

Serge nodded dejectedly and, as Pavel turned to the door, Konstantin slid back into the shadows until he had disappeared along the corridor in the opposite direction.

For a moment Konstantin stood quite still as a battle raged in his head. A thousand excuses swarmed through his brain but the guilt, which weighed so heavily on his soul, urged him not to yield. It was bad enough to know himself to be a sinner, but that Serge should be slandered for his sin was more than his conscience could bear. He emerged from his hiding place and stepped determinedly towards the study.

Serge was standing in the centre of the room. In one hand he held the cigarette but the other was clenched into a fist that drummed against his thigh as though he had no control over it. When Konstantin tapped at the door, the drumming stopped immediately and the anguish on his face melted into a welcoming smile.

"Kostia, this is an unexpected pleasure!"

His greeting was so sincere and his voice so gentle that it was almost impossible to believe he was the same man who had been cursing only seconds before.

"I was hoping, if it's convenient, that I might speak with you?"

"Of course. Come in, come in," Serge ushered him to a chair. "What can I do for you?"

"It's rather delicate," Konstantin said, praying that his courage wouldn't fail. "It concerns a personal matter."

Serge sighed wearily, "In that case, I think I know what you're going to say."

Konstantin's heart thudded and, when Serge offered a cigarette, his hand shook so violently he could barely take it from the case.

"You've come to warn me of more rumours?"

"Rumours?" he said tentatively.

"Don't look so anxious, Kostia. I know what they're saying this time."

"You do?"

"Pavel and Ella are lovers, isn't that right?"

Konstantin almost laughed with relief and for a moment a puzzled expression creased Serge's brow, "That *was* what you came to tell me?"

Konstantin hesitated but his courage gave way and, cursing his own cowardice, he nodded.

"I've just been speaking of it to Pavel. God knows what evil minds create these stories. To tell the truth I'm so used to being slandered that I'm hardened to it now. For myself, I don't give a damn but to have the reputation of the two people I love most in all the world sullied by vicious tongues is unbearable!" His lips curved into a pained expression, "Why do they do it, Kostia? How can anyone take such pleasure in trying to destroy the reputation of others?"

Konstantin shrugged, "Boredom? A means of diverting attention from their own failings?"

Cigarette ash fell onto Serge's lap and he stood up to brush it into the hearth.

"Or perhaps," Konstantin mused, "they believe that creating misery for others can somehow alleviate their own unhappiness."

"Unhappiness," Serge smiled ironically and threw the cigarette butt into the fire. He moved towards the window and stared out across the Nevsky Prospect. In the ensuing silence, Konstantin struggled to regain his confidence and adhere to his resolution.

"May I..." he began, but at that exact moment Serge turned from the window and, with the plaintive voice of a child, asked,

"Kostia, do you think that Ella is happy here?"

"Happy? Of course, she is! She's won so many hearts already. Even Vladimir, who was so opposed to your wedding, has changed his mind now. She's taken the city by storm and the people adore her."

Serge sighed deeply, "But none of that proves she is happy."

"Why shouldn't she be? She has a good husband who loves her and..."

"A good husband?" Serge glanced sharply towards the door, "Kostia, as a friend, may I confide in you?"

"Of course."

"I realize that what I'm going to say might be distasteful to you but you're the truest friend I have and sometimes I think I will explode if I don't tell someone."

A glimmer of hope flickered in Konstantin's mind. Would this confession ease his own anguish and a shared sense of guilt somehow relieve his conscience?

"Believe me, Serge," he almost whispered, "I have secrets of my own that torment me night and day. Nothing you might say will shock or surprise me."

"Then, perhaps, you'll understand." He cleared his throat and fidgeted wildly with the ring on his little finger, "I love Ella. I love her as I never thought I was capable of loving anyone but I fear I have wronged her, deceived her even." He swallowed audibly as though choking back emotion.

"Deceived her in what way?"

"Kostia, I should never have married her. I am not capable of being the husband she deserves." The foot tapping started again, more frantically now, and Konstantin's mind raced through the rumours circulating round the city. Perhaps now was the time to confess his own secrets; perhaps in doing so he might also ease Serge's pain...but, as he stood up and stepped across the room towards him, the desperation in Serge's eyes, reduced him to silence.

"I love her, I want her and I cannot...I just *cannot*..." He gasped, then inhaled and said firmly, "I am not physically capable of consummating this marriage."

The unexpected announcement threw Konstantin into confusion, "I see," he frowned, barely seeing at all.

"Do you? Do you *really*?" the aggression in Serge's tone and features was clearly aimed more at himself than at Konstantin. "Do you see what I've done to her? *I* am the cause of all these rumours. People know that there is something amiss and it's humiliating for her. And it is all my fault."

"No, no," Konstantin shook his head quickly, "that's nonsense. No one else knows anything about this. How could they?"

"You think servants don't talk? They know these things. And what they don't know they make up. Already I've heard what they say: I'm a pederast, I beat her, I treat her in all kinds of abominable ways, and now the latest story that she takes refuge from my unnatural passions in the arms of my own brother! Don't you see, Kostia, what this must be doing to her?"

"Perhaps," Konstantin floundered, "perhaps in time things will change. There are doctors and..."

"No. Nothing can change. It's how it is. It's how it's always been. God created me with this disability and there is nothing that can be done to change it."

"You knew this before you were married?"

"Why do you think I spent all my time with the regiment and was so much happier in the company of men? I was terrified of women, Kostia. Terrified that if we became close they would discover the truth and how could I stand that humiliation? I'd be the laughing-stock of Petersburg."

Konstantin sat down again, wiping his hand across his brow. His heart brimmed with pity, and the desperate pleading in Serge's eyes seemed to be begging for some miraculous reassurance that he felt utterly powerless to give.

"What does Ella say of it?" he asked feebly.

Serge shook his head and stared down at the carpet, "We don't speak of it. *I* don't speak of it."

"You didn't tell her before…"

"No. I couldn't. I tried to tell her in Ilinskoe and somehow…I don't know. I thought perhaps it wouldn't matter to her. Perhaps she would understand, and all the other things we share would be enough for her."

"And perhaps she does understand and it *is* enough for her."

He shook his head, "She wants children. She loves children. She has never said it in so many words but I know and this is what makes it worse. Every time I look at her, I feel I have deceived her, and feel my own failure and what a disappointment I must be. Sometimes, when I can't stand it, I take out my anger on her. I shout at her, lose my temper with her and it is all because I love her and despise what I have done to her."

He slumped into a chair and stretched his long legs before him.

"Speak with her," Konstantin said eventually. "She loves you, Serge, and no matter how difficult it is, she has a right to an explanation and will only love you more for speaking the truth."

"I can't. I have tried and I can't."

Silence descended between them and, as Serge stared helplessly into space, Konstantin felt his heart like a great weight in his chest.

"Well," Serge sighed at last, "now, you know it all, my friend. Christ! Even the poorest peasant in Siberia can be a husband whereas I, with all these trappings and palaces and titles and the rest of it…" He broke off, shaking his head in frustration. "I would give it all away at once to be in your position, just to be able to be a *real* man and a true husband."

Overwhelmed by his own shame and Serge's anguish, Konstantin leaned forward determined to make his own confession if only to reveal that Serge was not alone in his private torment.

"Serge," he said, "I told you I have secrets of my own, shameful secrets and…"

A faint rustle of silk distracted him. Serge's eyes moved to the door, then swiftly to his feet as Ella appeared in the entrance.

Konstantin stood up and made a slight bow at which she reached for his arms and placed an affectionate kiss on both cheeks.

"Kostia, how lovely to see you!"

Familiarity with her beautiful features had made her no less enchanting. Her hair, crowned with a string of pearls, curled about her ears in natural ringlets and she ran her fingers swiftly over her forehead to brush it from her luminous eyes.

She looked towards Serge, "I am not interrupting you, am I?"

He shook his head and Konstantin felt obliged to speak for him, "I was wanting a second opinion of a play I'm writing and Serge has been kind enough to spare me the time."

"Yes," she said, "he *is* kind."

Serge writhed as though her compliment pained him.

"And," she said, her eyes sparkling with delight, "I'm glad you are here to share the good news."

Serge looked up inquiringly.

"We have a new niece."

"Wonderful!" he responded with genuine enthusiasm. "When?"

"Yesterday afternoon but the news has only just arrived. Grandmama was with her the whole time, and she was born in exactly the same room as Victoria herself was born. Can you imagine?"

Serge turned to Konstantin, "Victoria is Ella's eldest sister."

"Congratulations!" Konstantin smiled. "And does the baby have a name yet? Wait - don't tell me! Another Victoria? Doesn't the Queen insist that all the boys are called Albert and all the girls Victoria?"

"No," Ella laughed, "Alice, after my mother. And better yet, Victoria would like me to be godmother. Isn't that exciting, Serge, my first godchild? I can't wait to see her!"

In the brief silence that followed, Ella's eyes moved towards her husband but he seemed disconcerted by her glance and, turning away, he snatched a document from his desk, "I'm delighted for you and we must send telegrams at once. But now, if you'll excuse me, I ought to give this to Pavel."

"Pavel isn't here," Ella said, "I saw him leaving as I came in."

He hesitated, nervously fingering the papers, then, returning them to his desk, leaned against the mantelpiece, tapping his foot on the grate.

Ella watched him for several seconds before smiling at Konstantin, "Forgive me. I was so excited by my news that I interrupted your conversation. You were speaking of a play. May I ask what it's about?"

"It's too soon to say."

"Will it be one of those deep, brooding Russian masterpieces?"

"Hardly a masterpiece."

"You're too modest, Kostia. Serge has told me what a brilliant writer you are."

"He flatters me."

Ella laughed gently, "I am sure that whatever it is, it will be wonderful and perhaps, when it's finished, you might allow us to perform it? Serge and Pavel are already proficient actors and I am learning slowly."

"Ah ha!" Konstantin said, "I heard of your brilliant performance in *Eugenie Onegin*."

"It was Nicky who made that performance. And of course, the wonderful script."

"You're fond of Pushkin?"

"The more I learn, the more fond I become of all your great Russian writers."

As she spoke, Konstantin was aware that she glanced often towards Serge but he made no response. He stared into the grate and the more frequent her glances, the more frenetic his foot tapping became.

"Serge has been so wonderful in introducing me to whole new worlds of literature that I barely knew existed before."

This time her glance became more persistent and she would not look away until he responded.

"She learns quickly," he murmured, shifting awkwardly from one foot to the other. He pulled out his cigarette case again and fumbled with the catch. "It's always better to read them in the original language rather than in translation."

Ella's eyelids flickered, "I'm afraid I am not sufficiently fluent in Russian to understand all the nuances in the original. Sometimes I read the translations first. At the moment, I have just begun reading Tolstoy."

Konstantin nodded, "Which one?"

"*Anna Karenina.* It's very touching, don't you think? Although what she does is wrong, one can't help but feel for Anna when her husband is so cold and treats her so…"

"For pity's sake!" Serge suddenly snapped, and Ella winced as though stung by a sudden pain. "Why do you fill your head with such nonsense? '*A trifling romance*' Dostoevsky called it and that's all it is - a sordid tale of suicide and infidelity!"

"I'm sorry, I didn't realize that you don't like it."

"I would have thought you'd have seen for yourself how unsuitable it is."

"Yes, I should have done. Forgive me."

Her eyes, sparkling with stifled tears, moved to the window as Serge's brow furrowed and his lips moved slightly as though in some private soliloquy. Konstantin looked down at his feet, afraid that he was intruding, but Ella, seeming to sense his discomfort, suddenly stood up, "I have interrupted your conversation and there are things that need my attention. If you'll excuse me."

"Of course," Serge said. There was a gentleness now about his features and a kindness in his dark eyes, yet he stared so determinedly away from her as though utterly ashamed of his own behaviour.

"Good day, Kostia," she said and he stood up, longing to soothe the pain behind her smile.

Serge watched her leave and when she had gone he thumped his fist against the mantelpiece with an expression of such self-loathing that Konstantin could hardly bear to look at him.

"Damn me!" he grimaced and, pressing his face into his hands, sobbed like a child.

Chapter 8

From her desk in the Beloselsky Belozersky Palace, Ella paused from her letter to listen the Anichkov bell chiming the hour. Outside, crowds came and went through the ornate colonnade of Kazan Cathedral, which housed the miraculous icon reputed to have once brought the Russians victory over the Poles. The reverence of the pilgrims intrigued her. Their devotion seemed so much deeper and more sincere than that of the Protestants with whom she had sat earlier that morning in the church on the Nevsky Prospect. The Orthodox family weddings, funerals and Christenings that she had attended, felt so uplifting compared to the familiar Lutheran rites. Unlike Mavra, she had not refused to kiss the cross held out by the priest but she reassured herself that she had been careful not to go too far nor allow herself to be swept away by mysticism, superstition or the tranquil look in Serge's eyes whenever he returned from a service.

She stepped over to the bookcase and pulled out an ancient volume that she had brought with her from Darmstadt. She turned the well-thumbed pages to the portrait of her ancestor, St. Elizabeth of Hungary, the thirteenth-century queen after whom she was named. She had read this account so often in childhood that she virtually knew each line by heart but it pleased her this morning to read again how the saint was born to wealth and power, *"...and at the age of fourteen, she married King Ludwig of Thuringia...When her husband was killed in the Crusades, Elizabeth disbanded her court and adopted the simple habit of a nun. She spent the rest of her life in the service of the poor, with the simple explanation: 'I want to be able to say to Jesus: 'You*

*were hungry and I gave you food, thirsty and I gave
you drink, naked and I clothed you, sick and I came
to you, a prisoner and I visited you, a stranger and I
welcomed you."*

She looked up from the book and drifted back
to the window. Though her eyes were fixed on the
cathedral, the images dancing through her mind
came from somewhere in a half-forgotten past.
Strange, she thought, how her mother felt so close
to her today. But with the sense of that comforting
presence came a disturbing question that had never
occurred to her before. Had her parents *truly* been
happy together? She had always told herself so and,
perhaps, she mused, that ideal of perfection had
coloured her hopes of all that marriage could be.
Yet now, troublesome memories tainted that image.
Even as child she had been aware that Mama
agonised for hours over matters of faith; and she
remembered now the pained expression on her face
at Papa's careless response to her attempts to
initiate discussion. It seemed, looking back, that
there were so many enigmatic aspects of Mama's
character that Papa could never quite reach.

And what of that mysterious, ancient-faced
visitor, David Strauss, whose presence in the palace
caused such a stir? Though he provoked criticism
from all sides, Mama relished the company of the
old theologian with his unorthodox views that
scandalised the established Church. Perhaps, in him,
she found the soul mate that Papa could never be.
Ella frowned, trying to make sense of it all. Was it
this soul-searching that had led Mama into such
terrible bouts of depression? And was it this that
caused superficial Queen Augusta of Prussia to
brand her an atheist?

"*Atheist!*" she laughed at the absurdity of it. Nothing could have been further from the truth. Mama's concern for the poor and her tireless devotion to the people of Hesse was not simply *noblesse oblige* but the visible expression of a deep-rooted faith.

She looked again at the picture of St. Elizabeth and felt once more her childhood longing to follow Mama's example in helping those who suffer and especially those who suffer the anguish of a tormented mind. How inspired she had been in those days! How much good she had planned to do!

Yet now, as she stood in the glorious palace, looking out across the fashionable Nevsky Prospect, it seemed that the faith that had inspired and sustained her through the sorrows of childhood, through the deaths of her brother, her sister and dear Mama, and even through the confusion of this first year of marriage, had been suffocated in the superficiality of the endless round of social engagements, balls and the thousand trivial details of life in the capital. While devoutly Orthodox Serge gained so much from the practice of his religion, she continued to go through the motions of worship at the Lutheran church though the services had lost much of their meaning, leaving her empty and dissatisfied.

"There must be more I can do than this. There *must...*"

She put down the book, walked out of the room and, calling for the maid, ordered her coat and hat to be brought to the door.

The great Kazan Cathedral was crammed with all the aristocracy of St. Petersburg. Dressed in their finest furs, the scents of their hundred perfumes mingled with the incense rising before the altar and, with every bow and genuflection, it wafted in great waves over the heads of the congregation. For a while, Ella stood transfixed by the beauty of the surroundings until, catching sight of the family, she stepped between the worshippers and made her way towards them.

Konstantin, his head bowed reverentially, seemed oblivious of the actions of the priest, too engrossed in his prayers to notice. His hands were pressed together so tightly that the veins protruded through his white skin like fine blue streams through a soft arctic landscape.

Beside him, Serge stood erect. His face was rigid and taut, his eyes fixed on the iconostasis and his lips so tightly clenched that he might have been engaged in some confrontation with his creator. Across the way, a smiling Tsarina joined in the *Te Deum* and threw occasional approving glances at her children who were as absorbed in their devotions as the adults. The bearded priests chanted the prayers but their meaning was lost on Ella and became little more than a dull hum in the background as she battled to suppress a rising sensual feeling of belonging here; a feeling far more powerful than anything she had experienced in Lutheranism.

Suddenly, Serge turned and, the moment his eyes alighted upon her, his whole face lit up with an expression of joy. He gesticulated to her and she stepped closer.

"You came!" he whispered.

"You don't mind?"

"I was praying that you would."

A mystical feeling ran through her body and she trembled with an unfamiliar emotion of combined elation and fear. For the rest of the service she stood silently bathing in the atmosphere of sanctity, as refreshing to her soul as a crystal spring of clear water in the heat of the midday sun.

When the service was over, the congregation fell into conversation. Pleasantries were exchanged among the family and, as they made their way to the door, Serge greeted an elderly, bearded priest with a deference normally reserved for the Tsar.

"Father Ioann," he said, "you remember my wife."

He bowed, "Your Imperial Highness."

"Father Ioann," she nodded.

"The Grand Duke tells me you have been reading some of the lives of our Orthodox saints. I trust you've found them interesting?"

"Yes, very interesting," she said and felt obliged to add, "I see no harm in reading widely even though I am not of your faith."

His eyes seemed to bore through her as though reading her soul - a sensation at once unnerving and invigorating, "We all find our own way to God. I have never been of the opinion that we can force our beliefs onto others. If it is God's will that we approach him by a particular path, he is sure to reveal it to us in due course."

"But how can we know whether the revelation is from God, or is simply our own whims and imagination?"

"Listen to the silence," he smiled. "The still small voice never shouts, never clamours to make itself heard. Wait in silence and listen for the whisper of the Spirit."

Disappointment sank her heart. She wanted an answer; a clear, unmistakeable sign to direct her, not some vague notion, platitude or philosophy.

Father Ioann stepped closer, sensing perhaps what she was thinking, "Once you hear that voice there is no turning back. It *is* unmistakeable and, though it may lead you along paths you have never imagined and to ways that compel to forget all you once thought was true, it will never leave you. The world around you can fall into chaos but, amid all the storms, that small voice of Truth will remain like a still place within you, sustaining you and strengthening you. Then, just as Christ was able to sleep through the storm at sea, regardless of the panic and tumult around him, you will rest in peace all your days, confident of the power of God within."

His words and his eyes were so hypnotic that she could think of no reply.

"Your Highness," he said, "might I offer you a blessing?"

She hesitated, uncertain as to whether accepting this would be to overstep the bounds of Lutheranism but, even as she deliberated, she heard herself reply, "Yes. I would appreciate that."

He stretched his arm, "May God bless, protect and guide you in this life and reward you in the next."

A tingling sensation ran through her limbs and a warm glow seemed to encompass her body. She closed her eyes and a strange image appeared before her in the darkness: a room filled with children, a nun in a grey woollen habit. Perhaps it was St. Elizabeth or perhaps it was...

"Ella?"

She blinked as though suddenly jolted from sleep. Her eyes darted around the cathedral, desperately seeking out the old priest, but he had disappeared through the crowds.

"Are you alright?" Serge said.

"Yes, yes," she nodded.

He frowned at her and took her arm, "We had better go. I have to leave for manoeuvres with the regiment this evening and there are several things that need sorting before I go."

That afternoon, Serge sat in his study, staring to no obvious purpose at the papers spread across his desk. But for the steady scuffing of his boot over the carpet, the room was silent and yet, in that steady shuffling of his foot, Ella sensed a scream of desperation, so loud and clamorous that it almost compelled her to block her ears. For some seconds she stood in the entrance gazing at him, longing for him to look up but, whether he was unaware of her presence or had no desire to see her, his eyes remained fixed on the papers. She yearned to rush to his side, kneel at his feet and beg him to share whatever burden troubled him so intensely, but twelve months of hoping had taught her that any attempt to penetrate his thoughts only drove him to a deeper silence. She pushed the door until it creaked but even when the floorboards rasped beneath her feet he did not look up.

"Serge?"

He raised his head slightly.

"Are you very busy?"

He shook a wad of papers, "I need to read through these before I leave."

"May I talk with you?"

"Of course." He picked up a pen and struck out a few lines on his documents. She drew closer and waited but his only response was a fleeting glance and a swift, questioning raise of his eyebrows.

"Could you at least..." An unintentional irritation crept into her voice but she restrained it with a shake of her head. "Shall I come back later when you're less busy?"

He sighed, put down his pen and pushed back his chair. She tried to catch his eye but he looked beyond, or rather *through* her, as though she were a ghost hovering invisibly before him. Even an impatient word would have been preferable to his asphyxiating silence. Her eyes wandered desperately around the room, trying to find some common link to start a conversation but there was only the starkness of his study, his papers, his own private world in which she played so small a part.

There was so much she burned to say and her thoughts ran so quickly that she half-expected to hear them tumbling uncontrollably from her tongue, 'Why don't you love me? Why *can't* you love me? What have I done to *repulse* you?'

"Please," she murmured pathetically, "will you sit over here?"

He flinched but stood up and followed her to the sofa where he sat half-turned towards her. He raised one hand to his chin, wiping his index finger to and fro across his lips. Her fingers moved tentatively towards his other hand, resting flat on the cushion between them. When she touched his skin with the lightness of a pianist playing a gentle melody, he neither responded nor moved away.

"I've been thinking about establishing a new charity," she said.

"For anything in particular?"

"Your mother did so much for the education of girls in Ilinskoe. I was thinking of something along those lines."

Serge nodded and Ella, sensing a moment of sympathy, interlocked his fingers in her own.

"I have heard that there are so many abandoned children who receive no education whatsoever and their lives are so wretched. Children are…"

Serge lurched forward and stood up, "Yes."

She frowned at him, perplexed.

"You want to set up a fund to provide schooling? Yes. I'll have someone look into it and we can draw up a…"

"Serge," she caught his hand and drew him back towards the sofa, "there's something else."

"What?" he said gently.

She swallowed, "Perhaps we could adopt one of these children."

He drew back his hand in pretence of searching his pockets for a cigarette, and silence descended between them.

"We have so much room here. We could give them all they need: love, kindness, a real home and family."

He lit the cigarette and with the tip of his finger wiped the smoke from his eyes. "It wouldn't work. Many of these poor children already have families."

"Yes," she nodded, "and I don't want to take them away from their parents. I am speaking of those who have no one. If we were to…"

"No," Serge said firmly. He turned back towards his desk.

"Please," she begged, "at least say you'll think about it and we can discuss it again when you have more time."

"There's nothing to discuss."

She followed him across the room as he sat down at his desk and picked up his papers. "You have no heir, Serge. What will happen to all of this when we're gone? Do you want everything you've ever worked for - your farm, Ilinskoe, your art collections - to pass to strangers?"

"So you want me to take in a stranger?"

"If we adopt someone now, he will be like your own son."

"Do you really think that the family would accept him? One minute he's a waif and stray and the next, the son of the Tsar's brother! Help them, help them by all means. Ella. Give them books, pay for their schooling but that's an end to it."

Her hand clenched so tightly that her nails dug into the skin. She could hear her breath building almost to a scream and, before she had time to stop them, the words flowed from her tongue.

"Serge, have I ever asked you for anything before? You come and you go and sometimes I don't see you for days but have I ever complained?"

He let the papers fall across the desk, "If there was ever anything you wanted, you knew I would always give it to you."

"Anything;" she laughed desperately, "a ball gown, a pony, a necklace, anything except..."

He drew on the cigarette, exhaled the smoke in one long breath and said nothing.

"My sister has a child; all our friends have children. Do you know what people are saying? 'Poor Serge, his wife cannot give him an heir.' Someone actually offered me a cure. They recommend spas, bring me prayer cards...even spells! Do you have any idea how that feels?"

"There's time," Serge murmured. "You're still young."

"If there's something about me or something I have done..." Unwelcome tears of anger and frustration burned at the back of her eyes. She turned to hide her face when suddenly she felt the warmth of his hand on her shoulder.

She turned and looked at him and, for one brief moment as she gazed into his eyes, he seemed almost to see her and perhaps even to like what he saw. His face softened to a vulnerable expression and his lip twitched as though he wished to speak but could not find the words.

"I'm sorry," he whispered, "I don't want you to be unhappy."

Ella gazed at him; the unspoken feelings that had welled for months, the hidden anger, the frustration, the longing for his affection seemed to melt in that one phrase, 'I'm sorry.' She smiled and he responded but his eyes were sad.

She drew him back to the sofa and he let himself be led. Pressing his face to her shoulder, she softly kissed his head, running her fingers through his hair and gently stroking his cheek. The tenseness in his shoulders eased and his breath came more deeply as she moved her lips over his face. She held him closer and his fingers were warm on her neck, her throat, her chest. Her heart beat more quickly as he kissed her, softly at first with a tenderness she had never known, then with more force and a passion that made his breath come in short gasps.

"Serge," she whispered, "*must* you go to the manoeuvres tonight?"

As quickly as he had melted, he froze again. He withdrew from her embrace and backed away from her, "Yes. I must."

"What is it? What have I done?"

"Nothing. I need to prepare to leave, that's all."

"And you'll leave again next week and the week after that and on and on?"

"You know what responsibilities I have."

"Responsibilities to whom? Not to me, not to your wife!"

She hoped he might respond but he stared silently into the fire grate, kicking at the hearth with the flat of his boot.

She turned away to conceal her tears, "I'm sorry," she murmured, "I shouldn't have asked. I will never speak of it again."

In the Vladimir Palace, Miechen signed and sealed another letter to Potsdam in Prussia. Although Ella was her friend, her compatriot and co-Lutheran, there was no harm in passing on the latest news. Besides, Willy was Ella's cousin and he had the right to know the truth about her present circumstances. Miechen looked up and mused: some people might have thought she had good reason to be envious of the younger and more beautiful grand duchess who had taken the city by storm, but poor Ella suffered terribly at the hands of her perverted husband. Even though her friendship with the Tsarina and Serge's closeness to the Tsar were common knowledge, within their own home there was nothing but despair. Serge spent more time with the regiment than with his wife, which probably came as a relief to Ella since, when they were together, he frequently humiliated her even in public.

Naturally, Miechen thought, Ella maintained the façade of contentment and would not hear a word spoken against Serge, but anyone with eyes to see and ears to hear, knew what was really going on. She was nothing more than a pretty bird in a gilded cage and if the Russian aristocracy and peasants adored her, their adoration was inspired by pity and the stark contrast between this gentle, pathetic creature and the unnatural, effeminate man who kept her prisoner.

Miechen handed the letter to the messenger. Willy, the spurned suitor, would surely receive this news with relish. Now that *he* was happily married and the father of five strapping sons, it would please him to know that Ella must realize what a chance she had missed and how wrong she had been to sacrifice her life to Serge. Undoubtedly, Willy would waste no time in ensuring that the stories spread quickly and, as branches of the family spanned virtually the whole of Europe, all the intimate details of Ella's life would soon be providing tittle-tattle for the drawing rooms of countless palaces, and reach the vigilant ears of an inquisitive grandmother in England.

Chapter 9 - Osborne House, February 1887

To the steady clip clop of hooves, the pony-chair rolled along the little pathway, bordered on either side by meadows and woodland. Unperturbed by the freshening wind whistling through the naked branches, Queen Victoria inhaled deeply, delighting in the salty sea air and the faint glimmer of wintry sunlight over the Solent. Here, in this sanctuary, for a few brief moments she could put aside the cares of the day and enjoy the simple beauty of nature that had meant so much to beloved Albert.

Her youngest daughter, Beatrice, sitting beside her, tucked the blanket more tightly around her legs with an exaggerated shiver but the Queen paid no attention. The cold didn't trouble her. Rain, hail, snow or sunshine, there was nothing as efficacious as fresh air to maintain a healthy constitution and calm her nerves.

The rider gently pulled at the reins and steered the pony towards the little Swiss Cottage that had so often echoed with the laughter of happy children. Queen Victoria could see them now: Vicky, conscientiously stooped over a flower, studying the intricate patterns of the leaves; Alice, dreamily gazing at the sky; and Bertie, stomping over the soil, digging his spade into the earth as though he were trying to dig all the way to Australia.

"Mama," Beatrice sighed, "it's very cold. Do you not think we ought to go back to the house?"

"Oh, for heaven's sake!" the Queen snapped. "Am I not entitled to a little respite without your constant fussing and fidgeting?"

Suitably subdued by the reprimand, Beatrice rubbed her arms and silently acquiesced.

"Don't you realize that I *need* this time in the fresh air when there are so many pressing matters weighing on my heart?"

No sooner had she spoken than a whole series of disturbing thoughts clamoured for her attention. Only four months left to prepare for the Golden Jubilee celebrations when the whole royal mob would descend upon her from every corner of Europe and the Empire, invading the palaces and throwing her orderly court into complete disarray. Where were they all to be housed? Buckingham Palace would be bursting at the seams. The Duke of Edinburgh had offered the use of Clarence House, and the Prince of Wales, Marlborough House, but still the guest list was growing and it was vital to ensure that, with so many contrary characters gathered in one place, those with the greatest antipathy to one another were kept as far apart as possible.

"You know," she mused aloud, "Willy wants to come for the jubilee."

Beatrice tugged at the blanket, "Can you not refuse him? After all, his father will be representing the Kaiser so there's really no need for Willy to come, too."

"Vicky seems keen for me to invite him, and I can't help but remember how fond your dear papa was of him. For Papa's sake as much as for Vicky's, I feel I should send the invitation."

"If he *does* come," Beatrice huffed, "I hope I won't be expected to entertain him. You know how unpleasant he has been to me and Liko since our wedding, and he was equally rude to Victoria and Louis. Did I tell you what he said? The Battenbergs are not 'of the blood' and are very unsuitable husbands for daughters or granddaughters of the Queen of England."

"And what of the poor, insignificant princess that *he* married!" The Queen chuckled but Beatrice was in no mood for laughter.

"The less I see of him the better," she frowned. "He's such a frightful snob."

"I'm afraid that's down to the Prussian influence that Papa so disliked. If only Vicky had been able to raise him herself without all that interference from the court, he would have turned out very differently."

She gesticulated to the rider to stop the pony and, holding to Beatrice's arm, stepped down from the chaise and strolled past the nine little gardens planted by her children when they were small. Nine little wheelbarrows, nine little sets of garden tools still neatly stored in front of the wooden cabin that Albert had imported so the children would learn the constructive skills of gardening, cooking and attending their own needs to equip them to live useful and independent lives. She smiled at the memory of their laughter and the shrieks and cries from the neighbouring toy fort; dear Albert taking tea in the cottage and handing out coins for the vegetables that the children had grown.

"Ah," she sighed, "how often I wish your father were still here to advise me. He always knew just what to do and the best solution to every problem."

The scents of winter herbs, damp foliage and wet soil hung in the air and she breathed deeply, trying to conjure the image of Albert beside her, guiding her through the minefield of political and family intrigues.

"Papa," she said, "believed that along with all the trappings and privileges of royalty, comes great responsibility. It's our duty to lead by example and if we're to create a peaceful and settled Europe, it begins by creating peace within our family. Prussian militarism always worried him as one of the biggest threats to peace not only in Germany but right across Europe. When Vicky married dear Fritz, Papa's greatest dream was that they would rid the country of all that aggression and, allied with us, create and sustain peace right across the Continent."

"And that will happen when Fritz becomes Kaiser."

"I hope so," the Queen sighed, "but I am worried about him. All these sore throats and colds that he can't shake off; I can't help thinking there must be something more serious behind it."

"Oh, don't even think such a thing, Mama!"

"I try not to but I can't help it. And worse, I can't help thinking of what will come after."

"When Willy succeeds him?"

She nodded, "Unless he grows out of this Prussian arrogance, all Papa's plans and dreams of peace will come to nothing...and worse than nothing. Can you imagine what would happen if our countries were to find themselves at odds? Brothers, sisters, cousins, parents and children all divided on opposing sides." The sea breeze suddenly felt colder and the afternoon so much darker. "The best thing that could have happened for Willy would have been a good wife who could temper all that arrogance and teach him a little humility."

"And now he has Dona who does nothing but flatter him."

The Queen shook her head, "If only, oh, if only Ella had accepted him."

"You can't possibly blame her for refusing, Mama. How could she bear to be married to such a pompous and bombastic man?"

The Queen raised her eyebrows, "Straight from the frying pan into the fire, then. She hardly did herself any favours in marrying Serge."

"She's happy with him. Her letters are always filled with praise of her husband and telling you how happy they are."

"Exactly. When people are truly happy, they don't require to tell others of it all the time."

"Oh Mama, you don't believe all these rumours coming out of Russia? Half of them come via Germany, and Willy wants us to believe they are true because he never recovered from the fact that Ella chose someone else."

"Of course I don't listen to gossip and I can spot a false rumour when I hear one. Good heavens, she'd barely been married six months when the German newspapers reported that she was about to be divorced! But false rumours usually die down very quickly. In Ella's case, they are *so* persistent and you have to admit that there's no smoke without fire. Even dismissing hearsay, the facts speak for themselves. Almost three years since her wedding and still no sign of a child."

Beatrice blushed, "There could be many reasons for that."

"There could indeed," said the Queen, "and when she comes here for the jubilee, I intend to find out exactly what is going on."

Chapter 10 - England - June 1887

Through the warmth of a midsummer morning, the enthusiastic crowds lining the streets cheered carriage after carriage as the great procession moved slowly towards Westminster Abbey. Never before had Londoners seen such a pageant of so many royalties. Never before had Ella been so proud of Grandmama, or felt what it meant to be part of this unique extended family. Shortly before eleven-thirty, as trumpets sounded the National Anthem to announce the arrival of the procession of princesses, Ella made her way to the left of a raised dais where she took her seat between Aunt Helen, the Duchess of Albany, and Dona, the wife of Cousin Willy. Whispers and waves, hugs and kisses filled the abbey - so many, many cousins to greet and so much news to exchange; so rare were the occasions when what Grandmama loved to call the *royal mob* came together in one place.

The roar of the crowds swelled to a deafening pitch and echoed down the nave, announcing the approach of the Queen's carriage, preceded by a procession of her sons and grandsons on horseback. A clinking of harnesses, swords and medals, the whinnying of horses and clopping of hooves, then the sound of heavy footsteps marching into the entrance. Ella turned to see Serge proudly displaying the medal of the Order of the Bath that the Queen had bestowed on him to mark the occasion. As he took his seat at the opposite side of the aisle, she smiled with pride. How handsome he looked; so tall and so dashing in his smart uniform, his plumed helmet under his arm.

Dona leaned towards her and whispered, "Can you see Willy anywhere?"

Ella smiled, wondering how it was possible for her to miss him now that he was sporting such a ridiculously large handlebar moustache.

"Ah, there he is!" Dona gushed. "Doesn't he look handsome? Every inch a true Prussian prince!"

Ella nodded agreeably and Dona shuffled closer, "It would have been better if Willy, rather than his father, had represented the Kaiser. His father isn't at all well. I am surprised he managed to make the journey. It's cancer, you know, throat cancer."

"Yes," Ella said, "so I've been told. Poor Aunt Vicky must be beside herself with worry."

"It would be far better for everyone if the succession were to go straight to Willy now. As he says, how can a man who can't speak become German Emperor?"

Ella flinched at such heartlessness and turned again to watch the rest of the procession entering the abbey. In strode the Kings of Denmark, Greece and Saxony, followed by the Princes of Portugal, Austria and Sweden. From the farthest reaches of the Empire came the Maharajas of Morvi, Gondal, Holkar, Indore and, as the magnificent Queen Kapiolani of Hawaii stepped towards her place, Dona leaned over again.

"Fancy Her Majesty placing a black woman higher in the order of precedence than the future German Emperor! Willy was most put out."

"She's a queen," Ella said. "Of course, she is higher than a prince."

"But a *European* prince; a Prince of Prussia! I would have thought..."

A second rendering of the National Anthem drowned the end of her sentence. The Queen, for whom this whole spectacle had been arranged, walked slowly to the dais and sat in solitary splendour as the archbishop began the prayers of thanksgiving for her fifty years on the throne.

As she joined in the prayers and hymns, Ella looked up at the blues and reds of the stained-glass windows. How brilliantly the sun shone through the faces of saints and ancient kings, scattering rainbows of light across the stone flags, and reflecting on the shining vessels, the jewels, tiaras and medals. Her eyes drifted to the dais where Grandmama sat, looking so tiny that it was hard to believe that so small a person held together this huge family and the whole of Europe and the British Empire. Who else could hold such sway not only over ministers and kings, but also over such diverse characters as Cousin Willy and Uncle Bertie, Prince of Wales? Who else could keep them all on such a tight rein? Who else but Grandmama knew every detail of all of their lives? That thought suddenly disturbed her. So far, since her arrival in England, there had not been a moment for Grandmama to speak with her alone, but she had hinted already that this was her intention and Ella had little doubt as to what she proposed to discuss. Perhaps the numerous state banquets and dinners and the presence of so many royalties would prevent an opportunity for that conversation.

At the conclusion of the service, the princesses filed towards the dais and curtseyed to the Queen. Tears of emotion burned in Ella's eyes as Grandmama's kind face greeted her with a heart-rending smile and, reaching to embrace her, she murmured, "I have missed you so much."

"And I, you, Grandmama."

"We must speak before you leave. Come to Windsor in a day or two and spend some time with me."

All along the grand approach to the castle, Victoria, without pausing for breath, chattered ceaselessly of everything from the state of the government to Uncle Fritz's failing health.

"And you know," she said, "already Willy is speaking of what he will do when he becomes Kaiser. Aunt Vicky is in utter despair. He is accusing her of employing British doctors just to spite the Prussians! Can you believe it? Goodness knows how Irène will cope with him as a brother-in-law. I couldn't stand it, although Henry *is* very different from his brother and is much more amenable. I must say, though, I was amazed that Willy managed to break his vow of silence in your company. It must be the first time he has spoken to you in years! What did he say?"

Ella shrugged, "We merely exchanged pleasantries. He asked after the health of the Tsar and the Tsarevich."

Alix, who until now had appeared quite oblivious of Victoria's monologue, suddenly looked up, "The Tsarevich?"

"Nicky," Ella smiled.

"How is he?"

"Very well. And he grows more handsome every day."

"Do you see him often?"

"A few times a week when we're at home. He and I often attend the theatre together if Serge is too busy to accompany me."

Alix let out a short gasp of delight which she tried unsuccessfully to smother.

Ella smiled at her, "He's very good company and so unassuming. He's grown up a lot since you saw him. Oh and did I forget to mentioned that he specifically asked me to give you his warmest regards?"

A hue of roses coloured Alix's cheeks, "He remembered me?"

"Of course he did! He is always asking after you. I can't think how many times he has reminded me that you and he carved your names together in the summer house at Peterhof."

Alix's eyes sparkled with delight, "I thought he would have forgotten that by now. There must be so many beautiful princesses in Russia to occupy his thoughts."

"And across the rest of Europe too," Ella teased. "He could take his pick from so many but it seems there is only one who has captured his heart."

Alix's smile faded and Ella laughed,

"She is sitting right next to me now."

"My goodness!" Victoria laughed, "I never saw you blush so much, Alix. Is it love?"

She shook her head coyly, "He was very kind to me, very gentle, and I liked him a lot but that's all there is to it. That's all there could ever be to it."

"Why?" Ella said. "You're beautiful, intelligent and interesting, and he obviously thinks a great deal of you or he wouldn't mention your name every time I see him. In a couple of years when you are older and he has completed his military training…"

"No," Alix said with an air of despondency. "It's foolish to think such things when they can never be."

"They *could* be."

"No, they couldn't. It's impossible. Whoever marries Nicky will be Tsarina one day and the

Tsarina is expected to shine and scintillate. I wouldn't have a clue how to cope with all that."

"You're already as beautiful as Minnie and when you are a little older these things will come naturally to you."

"Can you imagine Alix as Tsarina?" Victoria laughed. "You would have to curtsey to her, Ella."

"I think I could manage that."

Alix turned away, "To even think about this, let alone talk of it, is ridiculous. Of course, it will never happen. It's different for you, Ella. You were able to marry Serge and still remain Lutheran but the Tsarina has to be Orthodox and I could never turn my back on all we believe. It would be so wrong."

Unsettled and remembering Father Ioann's words, Ella said tentatively, "Sometimes what seems wrong to us at one time in our lives, can turn out to be what is right at another. Our spiritual paths often lead us in directions we had never expected."

"But Orthodoxy is so close to Catholicism. They share the same practices with their icons and images. It has such a ring of idolatry about it."

"No," Ella said, "there *is* a mysticism about it that we don't find in Lutheranism but the better you come to understand it, the more deeply you feel that there is something quite unique in Orthodoxy that our Protestant Churches lack. And the people, too, they are so humble and simple in their faith. They make us seem so self-righteous in comparison."

Suddenly aware that Victoria was staring at her, Ella shrugged, "All I am saying is that if someone were required to convert in order to marry the Tsarevich, it need not be such an impassable obstacle."

Alix looked up at the sky, "This is all hypothetical nonsense. There's no possibility that

Nicky and I could ever be married. I'm sure he will find someone far more suitable and I could never live in Russia. Grandmama still hasn't recovered from your going. She would be absolutely devastated if I were to even think of going there, too."

"But when she sees how happy I am, we can put all her fears to rest."

"Ah," Victoria said ominously, "that reminds me. I should warn you, you're about to face one of dear Grandmama's dreadful inquisitions."

Ella's heart sank, "What has she said?"

"She's concerned about you, that's all. You know how she likes to know every little detail of our lives."

"Yes," Ella sighed, "I do."

The Queen was sitting under a tent by the little Tea House not far from Prince Albert's mausoleum. In front of her was a desk stacked with papers which she perused with apparent interest; behind her stood her turbaned Indian servant, arms folded and eyes scanning the horizon, alert to any intruders.

At the sound of the carriage approaching, she looked up and smiled, "At last! Your timing is perfect. I need a break from all this."

As the sisters alighted from the carriage, she picked up one of the papers, "Messages of congratulations from all over the world. People are so kind."

"They love you, Grandmama," Alix smiled as she embraced her. "You must have felt so proud during the procession to see all the enthusiasm and the warmth of the crowds."

"Not proud, my dear, only very humble."

She greeted Victoria and turned to Ella, "You look pale."

"That is because she never allows the sun to touch her face," Victoria laughed. "I swear I think that parasol is attached to her hand."

The Queen, unsmiling, scrutinised her closely, "You've lost weight, too. You are eating properly and taking plenty of exercise?"

Ella laughed gently, "Yes, I am and I am in perfect health."

"In that case, since I have been sitting too long and could do with a little exercise, we should walk for a while."

She nodded to Victoria who took the hint, "Alix and I were thinking of visiting Grandpapa's mausoleum. Would that be alright?"

"Yes, you go, my dears. Ella and I have so much to discuss."

Ella glanced at Victoria who raised her eyebrows sympathetically before leading Alix away into the distance.

Butterflies darted over the daisy-freckled lawns and the heady scents of summer filled the air as the Queen, her arm linked in Ella's, tottered along pathways with neatly-tended borders. Blackbirds and chiffchaffs sang in the branches, vying with one another to produce the sweetest song and drowning the hum of the bees, hovering over marigolds and tulips.

"It's so beautiful and changeless here," Ella sighed contentedly. "I think of it so often when I am away."

"You miss us?"

"Yes, I do, though of course I am very happy in my new home, and Serge is such a good husband.

Mama would be delighted to see how happy we are together."

"Tell me all about your life there," the Queen said, and Ella, determined to prevent her from steering the conversation into areas she would rather avoid, responded with a long-drawn out account of the balls, the season, the people, the rooms, furniture, architecture and scenery.

"We have some friends, the Youssoupovs, who have a zoo on their country estate. I was telling them of the animals that you keep here. Do you still have the ostrich?"

"Yes, we do and he is thriving, which pleases me. I'm never sure about importing animals from other countries. Is the climate suitable for them? Do we have the right food? One often hears of creatures being brought here and the environment is so unfamiliar to them that they simply fade away." She nodded towards the herbaceous borders, "I think of it rather like flowers that look so beautiful growing by the wayside, but take them from their soil and they lose their early bloom."

She looked up with the unmistakable inquisitiveness in her eye that heralded the start of the inquisition.

"And what about you, Ella? Are you flourishing in foreign soil?"

"Russia hardly seems foreign to me anymore. There are such good people there and so much good I can do. I know you were afraid that all the wealth and luxuries would make me forget all I was brought up to believe but you must know, Grandmama, that I will never forget my promise to do all I can to walk in Mama's footsteps and be true to everything she taught me."

"I know, I know," the Queen soothed and squeezed her hand. "I never doubted that you would always be true to your upbringing and dear Alice's example. But," she sighed, "what of your health? You were always so prone to the family complaints - colds, bronchitis. I worry about you in that climate."

"There's no need. Our rooms are well heated and, as soon as the season is over, Serge ensures we're often away for the coldest parts of the year."

"He didn't come with you this afternoon?"

"No. He's with his sister at Clarence House. His visits to England are so rare that it's lovely for them to be able to spend time together."

"I am sure Marie must be glad of Russian company. She never found it easy to settle in England. Our cultures are so different, I suppose, and marrying your Uncle Affie wouldn't have made the transition any easier for her. He's hardly an ideal husband."

Ella tactfully smiled and said nothing.

"There are so few good husbands. A woman's lot is often nothing more than enduring her troubles in silence. And if, like Marie, one marries a sailor, months can pass without even seeing each other. *That* is no use at all in a marriage."

"Victoria misses Louis dreadfully when he is at sea."

"And what of Serge? His work sometimes takes him away from you, I hear."

"Occasionally, but seldom for more than a couple of days."

The Queen mused for a moment, then sighed, "We hear such stories about you...and about Serge."

Ella's heart thudded. "Stories?" she feigned surprise. "What kind of stories?"

The Queen responded with a shake of her head, "If there is anything troubling you, anything at all, you know I am always here for you."

"Grandmama, believe me, nothing is troubling me. I am perfectly happy."

"Serge is good to you?"

"Yes! He's so kind and considerate. If you knew him better you would see what a good man he is. So devoted to the Tsar, so hard working. The soldiers of his regiment adore him and…"

"And you? Is he devoted to you?"

"Yes! Yes, of course, he is. I am so grateful to have found such a caring and generous husband."

The Queen's lips twitched and Ella feared she had protested too strongly.

"I commend your loyalty, Ella. A wife's first duty is always to her husband, and people in our position have the extra responsibility of setting an example to others. That doesn't mean, though, that we cannot unburden ourselves discretely, to those who care about us. If your dear mother were alive, she would be here to advise and support you. I want you to know that, since her passing, you have always been like my own child. If even one fraction of the tales we hear is true, there is nothing, nothing at all, to stop you coming home to me."

It was excruciating to realize that the gossip that had become so familiar in Petersburg, had even reached Grandmama's ears.

"I don't know who invents the stories you have heard but all I can do is assure you that none of them is true. If people say unkind things, I can only think it is because they are jealous and have nothing better to think about."

"You *would* tell me, if anything were troubling you?"

"Of course, I would. Please, think no more of it and, if you hear any such rumours, tell people at once that they have no foundation whatsoever."

The Queen nodded resignedly but her silence said more than any words and it was clear to Ella that she remained unconvinced.

"Have you been able to spend time with Victoria's little girl?" she said eventually and Ella enthused at length.

"I hope Victoria won't leave it too long before providing her with a little brother or sister. I don't go for that baby-worship, which your Aunt Vicky likes to indulge in, but I do think it is better for children to have young companions around them. When I was a child there was no one but my dolls to play with. A brother or a sister would have made such a difference."

"We were fortunate that there were so many of us."

The Queen laughed, "And you were all so boisterous!"

Ella smiled.

"You know that Aunt Beatrice is again in a certain condition?"

"Yes. She seems delighted about it."

"I can never understand women who are delighted by it. I always felt so undignified like a rabbit or a guinea pig at such times."

Ella laughed and the Queen laughed, too, but her laughter seemed forced as though her thoughts were elsewhere.

"The whole process is most unpleasant," she said, "and children are such a trial at times and yet, for all the worry they cause, they can also provide a companionship that can't be found elsewhere."

Ella scanned the horizon, hoping that some unexpected visitor might arrive to prevent Grandmama from continuing.

"Your Aunt Louise has been most unfortunate in that regard. She so wanted a child and sought all kinds of cures but to no avail. Since the doctors here were unable to help, she had to resign herself to the will of God."

Ella nodded and said nothing.

"The doctors here, you see, are the best in the world, and so much more sensitive about these things than some of the foreign doctors."

She paused as though hoping Ella would speak but she could think of nothing to say.

"If there is a difficulty, my dear, if there is a problem with your health, it could be dealt with, with the utmost discretion, while you are here."

Ella felt her cheeks burning, "Grandmama, there *is* no problem. I am perfectly well."

"And Serge?"

"He is perfectly well, too."

"Then why…"

"Please," Ella took hold of her hand and held it tightly, "believe me, Grandmama. I am perfectly well and perfectly happy and that is all I can say."

The Queen's face puckered into a dissatisfied frown and, shaking her head, she sighed, "Then all *I* can say is what I said before. If *ever* there is anything troubling you, you know I am always here for you."

Chapter 11

If Ella floated into a room, Serge's sister, Marie, Duchess of Edinburgh, steamed in like a battleship primed for action. She burst through the dining room doors, greeted Ella and her sisters with customary kisses and, by a dramatic wave of an arm, signalled to the footmen to serve dinner.

"Well," she said with a smile, "this *is* pleasant. It's so refreshing to be able to talk in the absence of our men folk. They always want to dominate the conversation and I am sure that is because if they listened to what we have to say, it would illustrate what nonsense they speak!"

Ella laughed and Marie smiled, "Come on then, tell us all the news. How was your meeting with the Queen? Did she offer her condolences to you for being married to my brother - one of those terrible Russians?"

Ella glanced at Victoria, knowing neither what to reply, nor even whether she really expected an answer.

Marie shook out her napkin, "Let's not be bashful about it. We can all speak openly here. She has never forgiven us for the Crimean War, which, I hasten to add, was *not* our fault, and she considers us all far too ostentatious and decadent for her liking." She leaned back as the footmen served the soup. "At least there is *life* in Russia and a proper court worthy of its name. I mean good heavens! It's so quiet here that, apart from once every fifty years when there's a jubilee, there are palaces full of maids with nothing more constructive to do than dust rooms that nobody's using and make beds that nobody's sleeping in."

Victoria laughed, "Oh surely, you don't think *so* little of England?"

"The food is bland, the men are either cads or bores, and this house is so small that there is barely room to turn around without walking into something." She glanced at a footman, "Thank you. Would you leave us? I'll ring when we're ready."

Alix raised her eyebrows to Ella and stifled a smile.

"What on earth was I thinking, marrying an Englishman?" Her eyes moved between Irène and Victoria, "You two obviously have more sense in choosing to marry Germans. The Germans are far more reliable."

She paused in anticipation of a response and, since the others were engrossed in their soup, that duty fell to Ella.

"It seems to me that people are the same the world over. In every country you find good and bad and all the shades in between."

"I'm not talking about individuals but about nations. The English are so dull and so pompous. They think they have the monopoly on justice, the law, medicine...*everything.* It took a great deal of nerve to stand up to the Queen's insistence that I should have an English midwife and even then she wanted only English nannies for my children. I told her, they stand to inherit the Duchy of Coburg so naturally they should be raised as Germans."

"I can imagine her response to that!" Ella laughed.

"It could have been worse. Had I opted for a Russian nanny, she would probably have never spoken to me again. I hope you told her that we are not the decadent wastrels she seems to think we are."

Ella smiled and Marie asked for details of her impression of the country and its people. She nodded frequently and applauded Ella's expressions of admiration of the Tsar and his family.

"The Russians have more backbone than the English," she said. "We're accustomed to bombings and assassinations and they hold no terror for us. We just carry on doing our duty and, at the same time, manage to sparkle and dazzle - something which cannot be said for the court of Queen Victoria."

"Bombings and assassinations!" Alix gasped.

"We hear of these things," Ella reassured her, "and I know that Serge is aware of the dangers posed by anarchists but, in the three years I have been in Russia, I have seen nothing but loyalty to the Tsar and the Imperial Family."

"That," said Marie, "is because Sasha knows how to rule. He rules with a rod of iron which is exactly what is needed. People here speak of the tyranny of autocracy but they have no idea about the way that Russian society works. My father tried to move things forward and look where that got him! Sasha has adopted a firmer approach and I can only hope that he is training Nicky to be equally forceful when his turn comes." She looked at the empty dishes, "Are we ready?"

From her pocket she withdrew a little bell, which jingled loudly enough to summon the footmen who reappeared with trolleys and trays. In their presence she made light conversation about the Russian railway and only when they had retreated did she return to her original theme.

"It's no good pussy-footing around when it comes to governing Russia. It needs firm hands at the reins and, to tell you the truth, I am anxious about whether Nicky will be capable of keeping so many factions in check. He's too gentle, too kind. I'm not sure he'll be strong enough to hold the country together. "

"He's still very young," Ella said, "and Sasha will rule for many more years. There's plenty of time to train him for the task ahead."

"But that is the problem. We don't know how much time there is. The truth might be unpleasant but we have to be realistic. Tsars are always the targets of assassins and one never knows what tomorrow will bring. After what happened to our father, Sasha should be more aware of that than anyone. That is why Nicky's training should have begun years ago. It amazes me that Sasha hardly involves him in government at all. If it goes on like this, he will wake up one morning with an empire to rule and no idea where to begin."

"I am sure that Sasha is aware of what is needed."

"But is Nicky? That's the crux of it. He is naturally kind and compassionate and he imagines that, because he is gentle, the rest of the world is gentle, too. The sooner he learns what life is really like, the better." She glanced at Ella, "You think I am being harsh on him?"

"I think," Ella said softly, "you can't criticise him for seeing the best in people."

"It's not a question of seeing the best; it's a question of recognising the dangers. In an autocracy, when every decision rests on the shoulders of one man, it is vital that that man is a good judge of character and chooses his advisors with great care. If he is too trustful, he will find himself at the mercy of all kinds of unscrupulous people whose ambition is for their own ends rather than the good of the country. He opens himself to manipulation, which ultimately leads to chaos. The Tsar needs to be his own man and trust his own judgement and, if my experience is anything to go by, men are seldom capable of that kind of discernment, which means that every Tsar needs a strong wife who will be firm and make sure that he is firm, too. Of course, men *think* they make the decisions but in truth, as well we know, it's the women behind them who rule in reality."

Victoria laughed loudly and Marie smiled a little too. "In Nicky's case, because he is so gentle, this is doubly important. I can only pray that Minnie ensures he finds a strong and sensible wife to support him and keep him strong."

Ella's eyes moved towards Alix who was staring pensively into space.

"It's not only true of Russia," Marie said. "The same applies all over the world, wherever a country is ruled by one man. Take your Aunt Vicky, for instance. If, please God, Fritz should live long enough to become Kaiser, we know who will be the real ruler of Germany."

"And what of when Willy's turn comes?" Victoria smiled. "Will it be Dona ruling the country?"

"They should have thought of that when they let him marry her. It would have been better for Germany if he'd married Ella. There he was with his great Prussian pride and vast ambition, reduced to loitering about like a lovelorn schoolboy, drooling over every smile and hanging on every word, and what did she say? She couldn't marry him because she didn't *love* him!"

Ella laughed, "It did seem a necessary requisite for marriage."

"Poof!" Marie brushed away her opinion with a smile, "If that were the case, half the wives in Europe would still be single. I didn't love my husband when we married and I'd be very surprised to hear that he loved me."

"Poor Uncle Affie!" Irène gasped.

"Poor Affie, nothing. He's just the worst kind of husband imaginable. But one learns to adapt. One has to. Love is neither here nor there. The ability to get on well enough and endure each others' foibles is a perfectly sound basis for marriage as far as I can see."

"And if Ella had thought as you do," Victoria said, "you'd have been deprived of such a wonderful sister-in-law."

"Germany's loss is Russia's gain," she smiled, then her brow furrowed to a frown. "But what I never understood was how you could refuse Willy because you didn't love him, and then accept my brother. You *surely* didn't marry Serge for love?"

Too astounded by the question to reply, Ella stared at her aghast.

"It was obvious what Serge stood to gain - the most sought-after princess in Europe - but what on earth did you see in him?"

"I love him."

Marie's eyes were wide with astonishment and it was several seconds before she was able to say, "Don't misunderstand me. I am utterly devoted to Serge but I never thought of him as being the kind of man who would inspire *that* kind of love in a woman."

"He's your brother. You would surely see him differently," Ella said.

"Yes, yes, but brother or not, Serge is..." she shook her head. "Well, each to their own, I suppose. But do you not want a family and children?"

Ella nervously shuffled her fork across the plate, "In time, if God sees fit to bless us with children..."

"If God sees fit to bless you?" Victoria laughed. "The Lord helps those who help themselves. Sea bathing! That's the solution."

"Sea bathing?"

"It's very beneficial. Grandmama strongly recommends it."

"All the sea-bathing in the world won't help if..." Marie, catching Ella's eye, stopped mid-sentence and it seemed in that moment there was something she knew and was uncertain whether Ella was aware of it, too.

"Well," she said, unnecessarily dabbing the corner of her mouth with a napkin, "one thing I will say for Serge, he imports the best horses in Europe. I was asking him earlier if perhaps he could find a suitable animals for my daughters and he was most accommodating."

"He is very kind," Ella said.

"Kind? How odd!" Marie laughed. "It's obviously not a family trait. My husband spends his whole life telling me what an unkind woman he married! But then, he's not deserving of my kindness. All the same, I've learned to put up with the old boot, as I'm sure you've learned to put up with Serge."

Her eyes moved across the table and alighted on Alix, "I hope that when you marry, you do so for all the right reasons. Make sure of a good dynastic alliance and, for heaven's sake, don't marry an Englishman."

"I doubt I shall ever marry," Alix said, "but, if I do, I shall only marry for love."

"Oh dear!" Marie sighed dramatically. "You Hessians are far too sentimental. Dynasties last for centuries but love fades the moment a man puts a ring on your finger."

It was after midnight when Ella, rising from her prayers, climbed into bed and stared up at the ceiling, listening to the faint echo of carriages on the road outside. Marie's words swirled through her mind in a spiral of images. *Dear Nicky,* she whispered, *Marie isn't the only one who worries about you.* Serge had often spoken along similar lines. Was he too good, too gentle and trusting to rule so vast an empire? Even Sasha had occasionally hinted that Nicky's younger brother, Misha, had more of the character of a Tsar. But then, if Marie and Serge were correct, it was Sasha's responsibility to prepare him so that when the day came, he would be well-equipped to take on such responsibility. The thought of Nicky's slight physique and short stature disturbed her. Physically, he hardly seemed strong enough to carry so heavy a burden. How different it was for Grandmama, with her Parliament and ministers making the great decisions, but all of that would be laid squarely on Nicky's shoulders.

A strong wife, she thought, recalling Marie's suggestion. *But more than a strong wife, a wife who loves you and will support you come what may.*

"Alix," she whispered, "is sensible and strong *and* she loves him...and what good is a marriage without love?"

A tap on the door distracted her and, as the handle turned, a thin stream of light rushed into the room.

"Ella, are you asleep?"

She sat up and Victoria came closer.

"I didn't want to wake you but we've had so little time together in all the rush of the past few days and, since you'll be returning to Russia in a day or two, I thought that while the men are still in town we could talk."

"That would be lovely," Ella said, shuffling to make a space for Victoria on the bed beside her.

"It's like when we were children," she smiled, putting her arm around Ella's shoulder.

"Happy days!"

"Happier than now?"

She hesitated, "No, just different. It's so much easier being a child, isn't it? But, in spite of what Grandmama thinks, I *am* very happy now."

"Was her grilling very intense?"

"You know how she is. She likes to know everything."

"She *does* know everything! I don't know how she does it but nothing escapes her about any of us."

Ella smiled, wondering exactly how much she *did* know.

Victoria ran her fingers over her cheek, "She was right. You are pale and you have lost weight."

"It's hardly surprising. The Petersburg season is endless and no sooner is that over than we are travelling. Next year is going to be even more frantic. First Irène's wedding and then we're to go to the Holy Land and on to Athens."

Victoria sat up, "The Holy Land?"

"Serge and his brothers have had a church built in Jerusalem in memory of their mother. It's to be dedicated next autumn."

"How exciting!"

"They say it's in a very beautiful spot on the Mount of Olives. I'm looking forward to it."

"You enjoy those Orthodox services?"

"I do, very much. They're so uplifting, so mystical."

Victoria lay down again and for a few moments there was silence; a beautiful shared silence, mellow and intimate.

"Victoria," Ella said at last, "I can't help but feel drawn to Orthodoxy. It means so much to Serge and he is so good about it. He never tries to coerce me or to press his beliefs upon me but, when I hear him speaking of it and, more, when I see how it moves and inspires him, I can't help thinking there is something in it which I can't find in our faith."

"You are thinking of converting?"

"No...yes...no..." she laughed in frustration. "I don't know. I don't know what to think. I promised Papa that I wouldn't."

"Forget what you said to Papa. That promise isn't binding. You know what Mama would say? We have to follow our own lights and do what we feel we are called to do, otherwise we are untrue to ourselves and living a lie."

"But I don't know. I don't know if I *am* called to convert. I know so little about it and there is so much that remains a mystery to me."

"Then take your time. Find out more. No one needs to know of it and if, in time, you feel it is right for you, you will always have my support."

Ella hugged her, "I'm so glad you're here, Victoria. I don't think anyone in the world understands me as you do."

"Not even Serge?"

"Serge?" Tears suddenly filled her eyes and she was grateful that the darkness concealed them. "I love him but there is so much about him that..." she stifled a sob, unable to finish her sentence.

"Oh Ella," Victoria gushed, instinctively throwing her arms around her. "What is it? What's the matter?"

"Nothing," she choked, "nothing at all."

"You don't cry for nothing. What is it? Something about Serge?"

"No, no. Serge is good to me. He is..." The tears rolled in streams down her cheeks and it was pointless to try to stop them. "It's these incessant rumours. It's bad enough in Petersburg but to know that the whole of the family is discussing every intimate detail of our lives! Why can't they leave us alone? We do our best, we don't bother anyone, so why must they tell these disgusting lies?"

Victoria held her closer, "I don't know, Ella. I don't know why they do it but I do know that Serge loves you and surely that is all that matters."

"Does he?" she sobbed.

"Of course, he does. He adores you!"

"Then why has he never touched me? Sometimes it feels as though he can't even bear to look at me."

Victoria winced, "That can't be true. You're imagining it. You are beautiful, you are kind, you are everything he could ever want."

"One minute he's there, so devoted, so affectionate. Then suddenly his face changes and he stares at me with horror in his eyes as though I am the vilest creature he has ever seen. Three years we've been married and he has never once so much as held me with anything approaching love." She blushed at the confidence she had not intended to share. "Marie was right. What use is sea-bathing or any other cure if he never comes near me?"

Victoria shook her head in amazement, "You mean he has never…"

"No. Never."

"I'm sorry, I had no idea."

She inhaled deeply, calming herself a little, as she wiped the tears from her face, "No, *I'm* sorry. I'm so tired I hardly know what I'm saying."

"Have you spoken with him of it?"

"He won't discuss it."

"But there must be a reason for it. Is he ill? Perhaps he…"

"You know what the gossips say? They say he has no liking for women and is more inclined towards men." She drew her hand over her mouth to conceal her embarrassment. "Maybe they're right. Why else is so he so much happier with the regiment than he is with me?"

"No," Victoria said, "you don't really believe that, do you?"

"No," Ella lay back on the pillow and sighed, "I don't. I know it's not true. And the truth is that I could be quite resigned to it. I could be happy as we are. I *am* happy as we are. If there is some difficulty that he is too proud to share, I can accept it. But what I can't bear is all these lies and stories and people suggesting cures or offering me pity, which is the last thing I need."

Victoria ran her fingers over her cheek, wiping away her tears, "You know that if you wanted to change things, it would be possible. No one would blame you."

"What do you mean?"

"If the marriage is unconsummated and you wanted an annulment..."

"Oh no!" Ella sat upright. "That's not what I want at all. I love him and, in spite of everything I have said, I know he loves me and loves me very deeply."

"I'm sure he does," Victoria soothed.

"And there are other ways for us to be close. We *do* have many shared interests and if we were of the same faith it would bring us even closer."

"Oh Ella," Victoria gasped, "you mustn't think of converting for that reason."

"No, of course not. That isn't what I meant at all. But sometimes, when all of this confuses me, I wonder if this was why God brought me to Serge and to Russia. I feel sometimes as though all of it is leading to something else, something deeper that I can't begin to put into words."

"Only you can discover the answer to that. No one can do your soul-searching for you."

Ella nodded, "It seems at the moment as though my whole life, everything I dreamed and planned, everything that Mama brought us up to believe, has come to nothing. My friends have families and children to care for; other people live useful lives of service; and here I am frittering away the hours in the endless social rounds, one ball after another. But underneath all of that, I feel *something*...Something seems to say just keep going, it's all part of some bigger plan and in time it will all be made clear."

"And the first step is converting to Orthodoxy?"

"Perhaps."

"Well," Victoria kissed her cheek, "I believe in you, Ella. Whatever you decide, wherever your road leads, you know I am always behind you."

"Thank you. That means so much to me."

"And I promise that all you have told me tonight remains strictly between us. I wouldn't divulge any of it to anyone, not even to Louis."

"I know and I'm grateful that you've let me unburden myself. I feel so much better for having had this conversation."

They both lay back in silence and a feeling of peace crept over Ella's limbs, stilling her thoughts and soothing her sadness, like a gentle hand stroking her brow.

"Strange," Victoria whispered, "I could have sworn I felt Mama's presence. Do you feel it, too?"

"Yes," Ella murmured. "I think she is giving us her blessing."

Chapter 12 - The Holy Land - September 1888

Standing beneath the seven spires and golden domes of the Church of St. Mary Magdalene, hearing the unaccompanied chanting, inhaling the incense, and dazzled by the priests' golden vestments, Ella gazed at the icons in awe. Perhaps it was the proximity of Christ's tomb that created so profound an impression that seemed to stir the deepest reaches of her being.

Even when the service of consecration was complete and the family drifted away in chattering groups, their conversation flowed over her, barely heard. Breakfast, dinner in the hotels, the carriage rides, the scents of spices, jasmine and sandalwood, the cries of sellers in the street bazaars, the hours, the days, the whole itinerary from Jerusalem to Bethany and north to Nazareth, floated by like a hazy half-remembered dream while a different reality seemed to be playing out in silence in her soul.

It was early evening as she walked alone on the shores of the Sea of Galilee, scarcely able to compass the overwhelming realization that she was actually treading the hallowed ground that Christ himself had trod. A fishing boat moved silently over the water, and a solitary seagull soared through the pale blue sky. The setting sun spread an amber glow across the horizon like a heavenly vision and, for a moment, breathlessly, she paused. Perhaps it was indeed a heavenly vision: a vision of serenity, simplicity and perfection, so far, far removed from the shallow world of glittering ballrooms and palaces. So deep was the sense of peace that tears filled her eyes and a kind of sadness flooded her soul. She raised her hand to her heart. What a strange pain this was: nostalgia for something she had never known? Or a glimpse into another world of ineffable beauty?

She had known this feeling before but never to such depths. Like the glimmer of a candle caught through the corner of her eye, something so close and yet just out of reach; something so simple yet too profound to grasp; like a whispered word or the echo of a sigh; something, something familiar yet *different.* She recalled one amber evening as a child, running through the meadows of Osborne, suddenly arrested by a sense that she was running through her childhood, running through her life, running through the whole of history; no longer simply an isolated being running on summer lawns, but a part of the great stream of Spirit, timeless and changeless yet endlessly flowing, creating, evolving. Even then, came the paradoxical awareness of the transience of the moment, captured forever in one eternal *now.*

Now, as the silent boat sailed across the Galilean sea, it seemed but a shadow of other boats, sailing the same waters long, long before she was born. She could almost hear the voices of fishermen calling to the other boats to help with the miraculous catch; and see the outline of the Man walking across the waves. Christ, the fishermen, the apostles, all humanity seemed as close to her as her own self, woven into the fabric of her being as they were woven into the fabric of history; woven into *everyone's* being, into Being Itself.

Footsteps crunched the pebbles as Serge came striding along the beach towards her. Reaching her side, he didn't speak but took her hand, intertwining his fingers with hers, and for some time gazed silently across the sea. The waves swished in a steady ebb and flow, and the fading sun cast a crimson beam towards them, enfolding them in a single ray.

"It's so strange," Ella said eventually. "There is nothing I want; nothing I need. Everything is so peaceful, so perfect, so beautiful and yet I feel such *longing*."

He didn't answer but smiled and she knew he felt it, too.

"Where does it come from, this longing?" she frowned, struggling to find the words. "It isn't a longing for the past or for the future but something inexpressible: a yearning for beauty, the infinite, something beyond."

He sat down on the rocky bank and drew her beside him, putting his arm protectively around her shoulders.

"It sometimes feels to me," he said, "as though there is a gap, like a great well, inside us. A sort of wound, an inner loneliness and, no matter how close or intimate our relationships, the wound is so deep that nothing on earth can alleviate it. Do you ever feel that?"

"Yes," she murmured, "I do."

"Perhaps everyone does. Some people run around trying to assuage the pain of it; the pain of being alive. Some try to numb it with vodka or opium or laudanum and all kinds of excesses. Others fill every spare moment with activity or seeking out company, small talk, chatter, noise, *any* noise, being so afraid of silence and solitude because when we're alone and silent we feel it most deeply. But no matter how we try to avoid it, we know it's there and there is nothing we can do to be rid of it."

"Perhaps it's a reminder that we're not simply creatures of the earth. We're pilgrims passing through, longing for heaven."

"Longing for death?" he frowned.

"No, not death but the Infinite. Perhaps it *is* a kind of death, though I cannot think that God would create all this beauty, nature, oceans, skies, dawns, sunsets, flowers and creatures to be so ephemeral. I can only believe that what we see here is the reflection of an even greater beauty beyond this life."

"For here," he said, "we see '*but darkly as through a glass*'. Isn't it strange how desperately and deeply we feel this longing that can only be satisfied when our souls are free of these bodies, and yet, faced with prospect of death, we cling to life how ever mundane, dull, empty and meaningless it seems. Even those who live in the most abject poverty, whose lives are nothing but drudgery and misery, would, if faced with the prospect of death, cling with all their might to this existence how ever painful or sad."

"Perhaps they're afraid of what is beyond."

"Or perhaps they fear there is nothing beyond except total annihilation."

She moved closer to him and rested her head on his shoulder.

"Are you afraid of death, Serge?"

"Not now. Not in this moment when everything is peaceful. Heaven seems so close that I would happily step out of my body and into that life. But," he sighed, "when we're back in the city, amid all the clamour and routine and petty irritations, death will no longer seem like a radiant angel welcoming us home, but rather a dark spectre hovering menacingly over our shoulders. *That* is what I fear, being caught unprepared as my father was. One minute there, walking, talking, breathing...the next minute, blown to pieces." He was thoughtful for a moment. "If it were not for my faith, I don't think I would have been able to live with that. For those who don't believe, such times must be unbearable."

The sun had set and only the moonlight illuminated the waves and the silhouettes of boats and houses on the horizon. In the peaceful night everything was so much clearer.

"Serge," she said quietly, "when we return to Petersburg, I should like to learn more about your faith."

He lifted her head from his shoulder.

"There is so much about Orthodoxy that draws me and so much I don't yet understand. Will you help me?"

"Nothing," he sighed, "*nothing* would give me more pleasure!"

Even through the darkness she could make out his smile and, afraid of raising his expectations, she said, "Of course, there is such a lot to learn and it will probably take years before I even begin to understand it as you do."

"You can take all the time you need."

"And perhaps it would be better not to tell anyone. After all, I..."

He put his finger on her lips, "Don't worry. No one need know. And," he stood up, brushing the dust from his clothes, "we will have more privacy soon and more time to spend alone together when Pavel moves away."

"Pavel?"

"When we reach Athens, he is going to propose to Alexandra of Greece."

Her heart sank and she was relieved that the darkness concealed her expression.

He took her arm and led her towards the hotel, "Of course, we'll miss him but Alexandra is lovely and you and she will surely become the best of friends."

"You think she will accept his proposal?" she said with forced brightness.

"I am certain of it."

Her disappointment was foolish and selfish, she knew, and she battled to suppress it. What had she expected? Pavel was warm, humorous, attractive and he was bound to marry one day and, if her reaction to this news showed how much she cared for him, she should be glad for him and wish him every happiness with his bride.

"Since we came here," Serge said, oblivious of her thoughts, "I have prayed so much for them, that God would bring them together. Somehow it feels that prayers offered in these holy places, are so much more efficacious."

"I have been praying that God will bring two other people together."

"Oh?"

"Alix and Nicky."

He stopped in his tracks, "You think they are suited?"

"He speaks of her all the time and I know that she loves him even though she has so many doubts."

"And would she be able to cope with becoming Tsarina one day?"

"She has many admirable qualities. She's loyal and sensible and has a strong character."

He nodded, "Perhaps that's just what Nicky needs."

"If only they could spend more time together, I am sure being with Nicky would overcome all her doubts."

"Let's invite your family for a visit. That way we can arrange it that Alix and Nicky have plenty of opportunities to get to know each other better."

Chapter 13

It was more than the flush of Alix's cheeks or the light in her eyes that disconcerted Queen Victoria. There was a definite thrill of excitement in her voice and an uncharacteristic eagerness as she told of the holiday in Russia. Barely able to sit still, she rested on the edge of her chair as though about to spring up and dance.

"Ella hasn't changed at all, Grandmama, and the Russian people adore her! When she isn't occupied with all her charities, the house is filled with her friends' children. She makes up treasure hunts, hiding presents all over the place for them to find, and you should see how they cling to her! One little boy, Felix Youssoupov, wouldn't even go to bed until she had been up to kiss him goodnight."

Her enthusiasm was too hot. What better way to cool it than to speak of the weather?

"It must have been bitterly cold in January, and the cold so aggravates rheumatism."

"It *was* cold and, when I first arrived, I caught a chill but it didn't last long. The cold there is different from here. It's not damp, you see, and the air is so fresh. We had wonderful ice skating parties and sledging! Even if we stayed indoors, there was so much to do - badminton, hide and seek. In the evenings there were theatre visits and dances. Serge and Pavel are wonderful dancers, and Nicky dances wonderfully too."

"Nicky," the Queen nodded, disturbed by the blush on Alix's cheeks and the familiarity in using a diminutive name.

"He and Ernie got on ever so well, and Papa thinks he is the kindest, politest young man you could ever meet. He's very different from his father and his uncles, so much gentler. He speaks quietly and listens intently with such obvious interest in what anyone is saying."

The Queen raised her eyebrows, "In what *you* were saying?"

Alix laughed awkwardly, "You would have been proud of us, I am sure, Grandmama. We made such a good impression on the Imperial Family and surely anything which contributes to the friendship between our families and countries is something of which Grandpapa would have approved."

Had anyone else referred to beloved Albert as approving of this visit, the Queen would have flinched and suspected an attempt to manipulate her feelings, and yet Alix was always so transparently honest that there was no doubt at all of her sincerity.

"I have brought something to show you," she said, fidgeting through her pocket. "It's from Ella." She handed the Queen a letter and pointed to a line, "Do you see? She writes here that Nicky recalls our visit with such pleasure. And here she says that, since we only saw the city in wintertime, it would be lovely for us to see the countryside in summer. Their estate, Ilinskoe, is said to be very simple and lovely, and Ella thought that perhaps next year we could stay there."

Unsmiling, the Queen handed back the letter, "Next year is a long way off. Anything can happen between now and then."

"I have spoken of it to Papa and he has no objections and, although the journey is very long, they travel in such comfort that one hardly knows one is moving."

"All the same, I cannot see that traipsing all over so vast a country is good for your health. Being cooped up for days in a train is sure to trigger your sciatica again and that is the last thing you need."

Alix nodded and a fleeting crease of her forehead suggested that the mention of her health had succeeded in dampening some of her enthusiasm. It seemed an appropriate point to end the conversation before she had a chance to rekindle it.

"My dear, some important business demands my attention. Do you think we might continue this later?"

"Yes, of course," Alix stood up and placed an affectionate kiss on her cheek. "I will go now and write to Ella."

"On the way out, would you ask your Aunt Alexandra to come and see me?"

"Of course."

She closed the door behind her, and the Queen sat down at her desk, frowning pensively.

Ella, closing the hefty tome, sat back and rubbed her eyes. She had pored over the same pages for so long that the words were running together in her head and each inspiring sentence she had read, was met by an opposing thought of her own. For every idea that captured her imagination, a whole host of fears sprang from nowhere, desperately warning her to put aside such notions. But then, as soon as she tried to oust them from her mind, the memory of the emotions she had experienced in the Holy Land came back to haunt her. Logical reasoning was useless against such powerful feelings and, besides, whatever complex argument she invented to contradict these Orthodox theologies, Serge was able to refute with a single line.

She smiled. He had been so patient with her; never tiring of her questions, responding with the utmost gentleness to her illogical reasoning, correcting her mistakes without trying to rush her into any decision. The truth was, she knew already that how ever many objections she raised, how ever many discussions she initiated, he would win hands down every time because he was speaking from the depths of conviction, and she was merely playing with words, looking for excuses to postpone the inevitable and take the final step towards conversion.

A tap at the door distracted her and, glad of an opportunity to put the soul-searching aside, she smiled and called, "Come in."

Her smile was even brighter when Nicky stepped into the room. She sprang from her chair, reached into a drawer and pulled out a photograph set into a border, "This is for you."

His smile was radiant, "You, Ernie and Alix!"

"I painted the border. These are all scenes from their visit last winter."

"It's beautiful! Thank you! I'll treasure it."

"I'm so glad you like it. I wanted it to be a reminder of how much we all enjoyed being together. Alix writes of it often. She speaks constantly of your kindness to her and what a pleasure it was to be in your company."

His smile faded, "It's about Alix that I came to see you. Well, partly about Alix…"

She smiled and led him to a chair where she sat down beside him.

"I hope I'm not disturbing you," he said. "I really needed someone to talk to."

"You never disturb me, Nicky. You know I am always here for you."

He smiled and relaxed, "I don't think there was ever a time in my life when I was so happy. I love being with the Hussars and the fun of military life. It's so much better than all those hours in the schoolroom."

"You take after your father. Sasha loves the outdoors, too."

He nodded, "I'm never happier than when I am out chopping wood, camping, tramping through the forests - all the things that life in the regiment allows me to do. And the other officers are great company. When I'm with them, I no longer feel like the Tsarevich, always having to behave in a particular way. I'm just myself, Nicky, among friends."

"Serge feels exactly the same. Being with the soldiers is very different from all the polite conversations and small talk of drawing rooms."

"It's more *real*. It allows you to meet so many different people with whom we'd never normally come into contact; interesting people, beautiful people like…" he hesitated and she detected a slight blush on his cheek, "Matilda."

"Matilda?"

"Matilda Kshessinska. She's a ballet dancer, very beautiful and very discreet. I have been seeing her for some time."

"I see," Ella nodded, trying not to sound disapproving.

"She means a lot to me but, as Papa pointed out, there can be no future in it."

"No."

"So Mama has decided that it's time I found a wife. Someone more suitable."

Hope glimmered in Ella's heart, "Someone who will one day make an excellent Tsarina."

"I don't want to think about that. Papa will rule for many more years yet."

"Yes, of course," Ella said, standing up and moving to the window, "but it's important to be prepared. We always believed that Uncle Fritz would rule Germany for many years and yet, after only a couple of months on the throne, he is dead and suddenly Willy is Kaiser."

Nicky's face fell.

"I'm not suggesting that anything like that will happen here but it shows the importance of being prepared. The power of the Tsar is so immense that it's vital that he chooses his wife carefully as someone who will love and support him."

He nodded and she could see that she had caught his attention.

"Whomever you marry will need time, too. Time to acclimatize herself to life in Russia and learn how things are done here, just as your mother did. And you will want time to spend together so you can come to know each other and share carefree days before you're burdened with all the affairs of state. Perhaps that is why Minnie is urging you to think of marriage now."

He sighed deeply, "She's been making lists of princesses from all over Europe."

"And?"

"None of them means anything to me. In fact one of them is so hideous that I'd rather become a monk than marry her!"

Ella laughed and sat down beside him again, "You had better not tell me who that is. She's is probably one of my cousins."

"She *is,*" he smiled.

"So no one on your mother's list appeals to you?"

He shook his head.

"In that case, we should start from a different perspective. Let's think about what qualities you'd like in a wife and whose company you already enjoy."

"I enjoy *your* company."

She laughed, "And I, yours, but I am afraid I am spoken for."

"I enjoy the company of all your family. I like Victoria and Irène and Alix."

She tried to suppress her smile, "Victoria and Irène are spoken for, too. But Alix…"

"She is lovely, isn't she?"

She nodded with forced nonchalance, "You're exchanging letters with her, I think?"

"Yes. We always seem to have so much to talk about. She is different from other girls I have known."

Ella raised her eyebrows, "Is she?"

"Yes she's just…"

"Different?"

"I can talk to her." He looked at Ella and, smiling, nodded, "Yes, alright, I love her. I have loved her since I first met her at your wedding but there's no point in allowing myself to even hope she'll ever marry me."

"Why not?"

"She has told me already she would never change her religion, and whoever I marry must be Orthodox."

"She says that now but that is only because she knows nothing about Orthodoxy. If I were to explain a little about it, she might see everything quite differently. And if she had an example to follow…"

She glanced at him but Nicky seemed too preoccupied with his own thoughts to understand her implication.

"Mama doesn't believe Alix is the right person either."

"She said that?"

"Alix is shy and also so honest, isn't she? It's one of the things I love most about her. She doesn't like all the show and the falseness that dominates so much of our lives in Petersburg. Mama thinks that, while that might be admirable for most people, it would be impossible for the Tsarina who has to lead the social whirl and flatter and dazzle everyone."

"There are hundreds of women in the city who can flatter and dazzle and I am sure there are many princesses who would be overjoyed at the prospect of becoming Tsarina. But how many of them would make you happy and truly love you, be devoted to you and offer you unflinching support every single moment?"

He shrugged.

"Ultimately, it's your decision, Nicky. Do you want a wife whom you love and who loves you, not for your title or position but for the person you are? Or will you settle for someone simply because she can spend hours in idle chatter and look pretty in a ballroom?"

"If I could choose, if I could choose anyone at all, I would marry Alix but…"

She leaned forward and seized his hand, "That's *it* then. That's your choice. Never mind the apparent obstacles. Believe me, with prayer and faith any obstacle can be overcome. Serge and I will support you in any way we can and I have no doubt at all that this will come to a very happy outcome."

150

His youthful eyes shone with hope, "What do you suggest I do?"

"Write to her, that's all. Tell her how you feel about her and, for my part, I promise I will do everything possible to bring you together."

The Princess of Wales, late as usual, stepped through the door and curtseyed to the Queen, who looked up from her desk and said urgently, "Alexandra, my dear, what on earth is going on in Russia?"

The Princess shook her head, "Going on?"

"As sister of the Tsarina, I'm sure you'd be one of the first to know if something of a *romantic* nature is afoot with the Tsarevich."

Still she frowned, uncomprehending.

"Alix's recent visit to St. Petersburg?"

"Ah," said the Princess, straightening her dress as she sat down, "I have heard mention of this. I believe they became very fond of one another during the visit."

"Fond?" she frowned. "It's a preposterous idea and I want it nipped in the bud. Before this goes any further, I would like you to tell your sister that Alix will *never* be allowed to marry a Russian."

The Princess of Wales smiled, "Minnie will be pleased to hear that. She is as opposed to such a match as you are and has already been seeking out other possible brides for Nicky."

"Has she indeed?"

"I think there is a feeling that a Hessian princess isn't quite grand enough to become the wife of the future Tsar."

The Queen bristled, "A granddaughter of the Queen of England is grand enough for *anyone.*"

"Oh yes, yes, of course. I was speaking only of how the Russians view these things."

"The Russians have some very strange notions and too great an idea of their own importance."

The Princess smiled indulgently, which rather irked the Queen.

"That aside," she said brusquely, "at least we agree that this must not be allowed to develop. Would you see that my views are conveyed to the Tsar and Tsarina as soon as possible?"

"I will, of course, but, with respect, *they* are not the ones who need to be told. It is Ella who is behind all of this."

"Ella?"

"According to Minnie, Ella is prepared to move heaven and earth to bring them together."

The Queen huffed indignantly, "Then we must move heaven and earth to keep them apart. It's one thing to marry a grand duke, quite another to even consider marrying the Tsarevich."

The Princess lowered her eyes.

"Yes, I know that Minnie did exactly that but Alix is a different person altogether. She doesn't have the constitution for that climate and she is far too sensible and reserved to squander her time in all that socializing. Whatever is Ella thinking?"

"Maybe she thinks it would be pleasant to have her sister's company in Russia. From all accounts, her marriage to Serge isn't the happiest."

"Ella is perfectly happy with Serge. She has told me so herself and I will not hear otherwise, but that is no excuse for her to meddle in someone else's affairs."

"To be fair, she might have noticed a certain romantic attachment between them. Even Minnie had to concede that Nicky never seemed happier than when in Alix's company."

The Queen frowned thoughtfully, too aware that she had never seen Alix so happy as when she spoke of him.

"If that *is* the case," she said eventually, "there is only one way of dealing with it. I'm not so old as to forget how sensitive young hearts can be, but sensitive hearts are also malleable and fickle. Firstly, we must prevent them from meeting and, while they are apart, we must find someone else, someone closer to home who will soon shake all these silly notions of a Russian marriage from her head."

The Princess of Wales smiled, "Am I correct in thinking you already have someone in mind?"

"I do, indeed," said the Queen, "and it is the perfect solution."

Chapter 14

The dinner party was an intimate affair of the kind Konstantin most enjoyed and, after the days of celebrations for Pavel's wedding, it was refreshing to relax among a small group of friends. Only six at table: Mavra and himself, Minnie and Sasha, Serge and Ella. This evening, Ella appeared more stunning than ever. Beyond her natural beauty there was a glow about her; an aura verging on the divine. As she entered the room and took her place at the table, his eyes couldn't help but follow her, and returned to her frequently throughout the first course, as Mavra and Minnie chattered of Pavel's lovely bride, Alexandra.

Minnie said, "I do hope she will settle quickly here. She is such a delicate creature and I am sure she must bring out all of Pavel's protective instincts."

Konstantin was uncertain as to whether he detected a shade of sadness in Ella's eyes when she replied, "He loves her dearly. How could she fail to settle with such a caring husband?"

"Of course," Mavra said, "being Orthodox, it will be easier for her than it was for either Ella or me."

"Speaking of which," Minnie said, as the footmen collected the soup dishes and replaced them with plates and fish knives, "Serge was telling us that you visited St. Isaac's Cathedral this afternoon, Ella. What did you make of it?"

"Wonderful! The mosaics are so impressive and the Resurrected Christ in the stained-glass window almost took my breath away."

"Did you see Father Ioann?" Serge asked.

"I did. We spoke for a little while."

"He's in Petersburg?" Sasha said.

"Yes, but only for the day. He told me a little about his work in Kronstadt. I was quite amazed."

Sasha reached for the wine and refilled his glass, "The man is a saint."

When Ella looked up inquiringly, her eyes were shining with interest and it was Konstantin's pleasure to explain, "Father Ioann has done so much for the people of Kronstadt that he can hardly step into the street without a great crowd gathering around him, venerating him and asking for his blessing."

"The place is very poor, I believe?"

"It's an old naval base."

"And like many old naval bases," Sasha frowned, "it has attracted the worst possible sorts of people. All the dregs and criminals of Petersburg have settled there."

Serge nodded, "Before Father Ioann, even the priests were too afraid to go out in some parts of the town."

"That's not surprising," Sasha said. "The whole place stinks of depravity: prostitution, neglect, vice of every kind."

Minnie coughed disapprovingly and dabbed her lips with a napkin but Ella had no such qualms, "What did Father Ioann do about it?"

"He went out among them as Christ would have done. When he came across sick people, he tended their wounds, nursed them, prayed with them and even healed them. Some of his healings are truly miraculous."

"Yes," Ella's voice was so soft it was barely audible, "I felt that air of sanctity about him."

"He also works with the children. He teaches them, provides for their needs and through them he reaches to their parents. The difference he has made is quite amazing."

Ella turned to Serge, "Could we visit Kronstadt some time?"

"Good gracious!" Minnie laughed. "That is the *last* place I would want to visit. It is an ugly place, filled with ugliness."

"All the more reason to see it and to discover ways of bringing beauty into it. If people live in squalid conditions, surrounded only by ugliness, and their lives are filled with nothing but drudgery, how can they find beauty in their souls?"

"My child," Serge said with a patronising smile, "your life is so different from theirs. You're too innocent to know how their minds work. Beauty means nothing to them."

"But surely, that is only because they have never known beauty."

"They wouldn't appreciate it if they did."

There was a mounting tension in Serge's voice and, as Ella deftly sliced the skin from her fish, Konstantin felt the unease he had so often felt when Serge and Ella were together.

"If we were to go there and learn of..."

"Ella," Serge said with the restrained impatience of a father addressing a demanding child, "I know where this is leading and the answer is no."

She rested her knife on the edge of the plate and leaned earnestly towards him. "If people never experience beauty, how can they learn to appreciate it? By changing the external conditions, we give them an opportunity to lift themselves out of all that depravity and show them their true dignity."

"Dear God!" Sasha laughed loudly in an attempt to dispel the tension. "Changing their conditions? You sound like an anarchist!"

"No, no, not at all," she insisted. "I just feel that because we are always surrounded by beautiful paintings, statues, architecture, music, it's so much easier for us to understand what is meant when the priests speak of the love of God. People who have never known these things must sometimes ask themselves what evidence there is of God's love. My thought is that if we..."

Serge cut her short, "Your sentiments are admirable but completely impractical. Father Ioann has his role and we have ours, both ordained by God, and our sole duty on earth is to apply ourselves to the tasks that God has given us."

"But, Serge, it is the duty of every Christian to learn all we can about the lives of our brothers and sisters and to bring beauty into..."

"Don't contradict me!" Serge slammed his hand down on the table with such ferocity that even Sasha seemed shaken. "I have lived here far longer than you have. You have no idea what these people are like. You *cannot* step in and start trying to change everything without any understanding whatsoever."

Konstantin stared at his plate, hardly daring to raise his head. For a few moments there was silence until Ella said very quietly, "Forgive me, I have said too much. I was thinking only of what could be done to improve the lives of some of the loyal subjects of the Tsar."

"You think we're unaware of these things?" Serge reached for the wine and it glugged into his glass. "We think of them no less than you do."

Ella didn't answer but when Konstantin glanced towards her, he saw that her brow was knitted with a wounded frown.

"Besides," Serge said, "the place is rife with typhoid and every other kind of illness. It would be very unwise for someone as delicate as you are, to wander about there."

Ella winced and, by reflex, Mavra's hand moved across the table towards her but her pity seemed only to increase Ella's humiliation.

"I'm sorry. I seem to have spoiled a pleasant evening," she said. Her face was so pale and her eyes so sad that Konstantin longed to offer her some comfort but all he could do was look away. For a long time no one spoke and the only sound was the clattering of cutlery and the occasional scuffing of Serge's boot on the floor beneath the table.

It eventually fell to Minnie to lighten the mood. She embarked on a cheerful family anecdote that soon revived the conversation and, though Ella succeeded in making appropriate comments and smiling at the right moments, her eyes were distant as though she were no longer there but lost somewhere amid the squalor of Kronstadt. Only another outburst from Serge startled her back to the present. He suddenly dropped his knife onto the plate with a loud clatter, "I almost forgot. A letter arrived for you from Darmstadt."

"Darmstadt!" The joy returned to her face.

Serge fumbled in an inside pocket and pulled out an envelope which he placed on the table in front of her.

"It's my sister, Victoria's writing," she said, running her fingers over the envelope.

Minnie smiled, "Please don't wait on our account. We can see how you're longing to read it."

"I couldn't, not at the table."

"Nonsense!" Sasha boomed. "There's no formality here. If you want to read it, read it."

She hesitated until Minnie insisted, "Please read it. There might be some news we could share."

Everyone's eyes were fixed on her as her fingers moved over the words and her expression displayed so many various reactions provoked by the contents. First a smile, then a blink, a slight frown, a deeper frown, another smile and then a gasp, "Eddy!"

Minnie leaned forwards, her eyes wide with interest, "What is it?"

Ella held the letter at arm's length and shook her head, "I can't believe it! It's quite ridiculous."

"Oh tell us," Minnie urged, smiling broadly, "we can't stand the suspense."

"Grandmama is quite set on a marriage between Alix and Eddy. She says Eddy is very happy about it and plans to propose to her."

Minnie smiled with delight, "How wonderful! Eddy is such a sweet boy and what a high position Alix will one day occupy!"

"No," Ella put the letter down on the table, "it's absurd. Eddy is…forgive me, but he is quite stupid."

"Oh really," Minnie said, the smile never leaving her face, "that's not so. He is utterly charming and it was only his hearing difficulties that prevented him from doing well in his lessons."

Konstantin looked from one to another, baffled as to whom they were discussing and, when he eventually caught Minnie's eye, she was eager to explain.

"Eddy is my nephew, eldest son of the Prince and Princess of Wales, and a future King of England."

"Eddy," Konstantin said, his mind struggling to recall all the complicated relationships of Queen Victoria's huge family.

"Eddy's his family name. Officially he is Prince Albert Victor, Duke of Clarence and Avondale."

"He is pleasant enough," Ella conceded, "but he and Alix are so unalike. They would have absolutely nothing in common."

"Your grandmother is a very astute woman," Minnie said. "She obviously sees that Alix has all the qualities required of a Queen Consort. After all, she chose my sister to marry the Prince of Wales for that reason and that was a wise choice. Now she is applying the same wisdom to the next generation."

"But Eddy?" Ella sighed and picked up the letter again.

"Does Victoria say anything else?" Serge asked.

"One or two reprimands for me from Grandmama," she smiled ironically, then turned the page and her eyes grew wider, "Oh this is better news! Alix *is* coming to stay with us in Ilinskoe next summer."

As Ella's smiled widened, Minnie's shrank, "The travelling isn't too much for her?"

"No, not at all. She will be fine and we've been so looking forward to showing her the beauty of the countryside, haven't we, Serge?"

He nodded agreeably, "Why don't you come and join us there, too? We could have a wonderful holiday with both families together again. The young people enjoyed it so much last winter."

Minnie's smile had vanished completely, "I'm afraid that won't be possible. Sasha and I have already made other arrangements."

"In that case, perhaps Nicky and Misha could come and..."

"No," she said firmly, "Nicky will be away on military manoeuvres."

Serge frowned and even Sasha looked at her with disbelief, "They have planned manoeuvres so far ahead?"

She threw him a clandestine glance, "Nicky will *definitely* be away on military manoeuvres. Still, I am sure Alix will enjoy the visit and perhaps Eddy will come with her if they are married by then."

When the meal was over and the ladies had retired to another room, Sasha put his feet up on a chair and sent for more wine.

"Well, gentlemen," he said, holding out a cigarette box to Konstantin and Serge, "even the Tsar of all the Russias is powerless to understand the intrigues of women."

Konstantin smiled and took a cigarette.

"We think we're in command but, when it comes to the decisions that affect us most, it's the women who rule the roost. So many things go on between them that only they understand. What's all that about Nicky and manoeuvres? They've never arranged them already but I can guarantee that if Minnie says that's where he'll be, that is exactly where he will be. Do you know what they are playing at, Serge?"

He shook his head evasively.

"Leave them to it, eh?" Sasha laughed, topping up their glasses. "Women think differently from us and the best way to deal with them is to agree with them. No point in arguing. Don't you think so, Kostia?"

"Mavra is far more competent than I am when it comes to making decisions, particular about the children."

Sasha smiled, "What about you, Serge? Do you agree, too?"

He silently inhaled his cigarette and pressed his hand to his forehead.

"Was there any need to react like that to Ella? She was only expressing an opinion."

Serge sighed, "She's too trusting. Even after all these years, she doesn't understand that life here is so different from life in Darmstadt. She saw her mother going into ordinary people's houses and doing all kinds of things for them and thinks she can do the same. She doesn't understand that it isn't safe here."

"Hmm," Sasha grunted and Konstantin looked into his glass hardly daring to speak.

"I encourage her in all her charities but she is an idealist and she would take things to extremes. She is so *good* and so Christian that at times I feel totally inadequate in her company but, at the same time, it's necessary to protect her, for her own good."

Sasha raised an eyebrow.

"You think I am heartless?" Serge said.

"I think you hurt her."

He shook his head, "You don't understand."

"No, Serge, *you* don't understand. She's an intelligent woman. If you listened to her instead of always telling her what to do, you might begin to really understand. Women need to be treated gently not yelled at and humiliated. They need to be told they are loved."

"I do love her, Sasha, and she knows that." He closed his eyes again and sighed, "But I am *so* unworthy of her."

Sasha swung his feet from the chair and slapped him on the back, "Enough of the self-pity! We've more important things to discuss. I have a proposition for you that you will need to think over and I want you to discuss it with Ella before coming to a decision."

Konstantin, afraid of intruding, pushed back his chair, "Perhaps it would be better if I..."

"No, no, sit down, finish your drink. I trust you to keep this in confidence." He turned back to Serge, "In a year or so, I'm planning to appoint a new Governor General of Moscow."

Serge looked up with interest.

"I'd like you to offer the position to you."

"Me?"

"It know it would be a huge upheaval for you. You'd have to leave your post in the regiment and it would mean moving away from your friends here."

"My God," Serge gasped, "it's beyond an honour. I don't know what to say. What about Vladimir? He is the obvious choice, being older than I am."

"I need someone there in whom I have absolute trust. I think you're the best man for the job and, with all the entertaining that's required of the Governor's wife, Ella is the perfect choice, too. If you're willing, I would really like you to take it. Think it over, talk to Ella about it and we'll speak of it again another time."

Chapter 15

Whether it was Pavel's absence or the tedium of routine, the St. Petersburg season with its endless rounds of balls, had seemed interminable to Ella that year. So often, engrossed in the writings of the Bishops Feofan and Anthony, she would have preferred to stay alone with her books but always the maids were waiting to attend to her dress, or Serge was standing at the door, ready to escort her to yet another evening of idle chatter. It had come as a relief when the long Lenten fast brought respite from the social whirl and, as the ice sheets melted on the Neva, she had been counting the days until, at last, they could escape from the city to the simple haven of Ilinskoe.

The first morning after their arrival, she woke early and, with an unfamiliar alertness, climbed out of bed, threw open the windows and gazed across the gardens. The rising sun shimmering over the pond beckoned her like a lover. Without waking Serge or calling for the maids, she tiptoed from the room, dressed quickly and crept down the back stairs into the gardens. As soon as she stepped outside, the freshness of the countryside wafted over her like a wave of pure light, and she hurried with a rising anticipation through the birch groves and maze of bushes, across the woodland leading down to the river.

A musky scent rose from the water plants and mingled with the fragrance of the late summer foliage, oozing its sweetness into the air. As the sun streamed over the wet grass, dew began to evaporate into a fine mist that settled on her face like tiny beads of perspiration. Suddenly, filled with longing, she yearned to hurl herself into the water or to fly through the sky, to be no longer the person she had been for the past five years, but only a drop in the river or the song of the birds; the flapping of their wings; the scent of the flowers; the rays of the sun; to be nothing, to be everything, to blend with the sheer, overwhelming beauty that saturated every sense with bliss.

She glanced around. No one was there. No one would see and, in that moment, even if they did, she didn't think she would care. She slipped off her shoes and, raising her skirts above her ankles, stepped into the water. Rippling in the fresh morning breeze, the waves teased the stones on the bank and sprinkled over her legs, so icily cold yet so invigorating that the sensation travelled the length of her spine. Deeper and deeper she stepped until the waters covered her knees and, letting the hems of her skirts drop, she stretched out her arms and raised her head to the sky, *"Now,"* she thought, *"now I can be..."*

Across the shimmering surface of the river, danced the reflection of the half-risen sun. A single yellow shaft of light pierced through the gossamer wisps of a cirrus cloud until the shaft, gaining more intensity as the sun climbed higher through the sky, cleaved through the mists hovering over the water and in one sudden, dazzling moment, swept over her face with such force that it seemed to penetrate even to her soul. She gasped and a soft breeze sifted over the surface of the river, sending ripples spiralling outward and outward in wider and wider ever increasing circles to the very edge of the bank. *"Now,"* she whispered, "now I am *free."*

Slowly, slowly the ripples came to rest. Ella's breath deepened and her arms dropped to her side. She stepped back onto the bank and, crouching to the ground, nestled her feet into the earth. She had no desire to move. She half-hoped, in that ecstatic moment, that her soul had escaped from her body and all that was left on the earth was an empty shell to which she might never return. She wished that the sun might hold this position steady forever, never rising beyond this first light of dawn, so the busy day wouldn't come and she could remain in this blissful freedom of eternity.

But the sun continued to climb and to spread its glory across the sky. Still she sat there unmoving, as the breeze, sifting over the dew, brought goose pimples to her skin. Perhaps a minute or perhaps an hour had passed; she had no idea what time it was, for that moment was timeless, the eternal *now* and she would have been happy to remain in it always.

Laughter echoed through the woods behind her and, gathering her shoes, she hurried back in the direction of the house but had walked only a few yards when she met a merry party. Serge and Ernie led the way, followed closely by Victoria, Alix, Pavel and Alexandra, carrying baskets and blankets.

"Ah, there you are," Serge smiled. "I said you would be down here so we decided to bring you breakfast. This way!"

He led them to a clearing where they spread the blankets over the grass and set out the picnic. Soon everyone was laughing as Pavel and Serge drifted effortlessly into an impromptu scene from a play, alternating between English and Russian.

From somewhere in the branches of the over-laden trees, came the song of a solitary bird: melodic, heartfelt, passionately singing of love. Ella held her breath to listen and, within seconds, a response came from far across the horizon. Soon other avian voices joined the theme until it seemed a

166

whole orchestra had gathered in the branches to
perform a magical symphony - the swansong of the
trees before they shed their leaves for the winter.
From the clear flute-like sweetness of the
blackbird's threnody, to the deep oboe tones of the
doves; the piccolo trills of the crickets in the
undergrowth, and the deep percussion of the
chattering magpies, the music rose to a great and
harmonious crescendo that set Ella's heart dancing
with a lightness that she, so accustomed to the
sounds of the city, had almost forgotten.

"Well," Serge said, "what would everyone like
to do today?"

"There is a fair in the village," Ella said,
glancing towards Alix. "It would be an ideal
opportunity to meet some of our tenants in a less
formal setting."

Everyone agreed that it was an excellent idea
and, when breakfast was over, they set off in
troikas, laughing like children.

"It's a pity that Nicky couldn't be here," Ella
said, watching Alix's face for any response. "He
would so love to have seen you."

Alix's cheeks flushed but she said nothing and,
as the village came into view, a slight nervousness
was visible in her manner. It occurred to Ella that
the devotion of the peasants might be overwhelming
for someone who preferred to shy away from public
gaze.

"Let's walk from here," she suggested. "That
way we can enter the village unnoticed."

Alix smiled and, as they strolled, she trailed her
hands over the leaves along the pathway, pausing
now and again to finger them like a merchant
examining fine silks. The fresh morning air tingled
on Ella's tongue and, with every step, the light

seemed to seep more deeply through her skin, her bones, her muscles, strengthening her limbs and filling her heart with deep contentment.

On either side of the dusty road, labourers toiled through the harvest, hewing and shearing and clicking their tongues to the dappled horses that snorted and shook their knotted mains. Copper-coloured crops ripe for reaping, late golden roses and reddening ivy around the doors of cottages; green grass, green leaves tinged already with the hint of autumnal amber; yellow haystacks and the dark brown earth! Oh this was music in crystallised form - the sheer transcendent beauty of a paradise on earth.

Voices echoed from the village where peasants in their bright Russian costumes haggled over market stalls of dolls and scarves in deep colours, musical boxes and musical instruments, wooden toys, hand-crafted tools and painted icons and eggs. Jugglers and gymnasts vied for attention, spinning and leaping to the twanging of balalaikas. The smells of the food stalls hung in the air as the vendors offered blinies covered with cream and honey, tvorogs with jam and cheese, cold soups, hot soups, pickled fish and pumpkins.

Alix's wide eyes travelled over the stalls and a smile of sheer wonder illuminated her face. Serge put his hand on her shoulder, "Forget what you've seen in St. Petersburg. These are the real Russian people."

It was too much to expect that so well-dressed a party could pass unrecognised and, in no time at all, the villagers were abasing themselves, face down to the earth, uttering praises in their own dialect.

"I will introduce you," Ella said as a small crowd gathered around them.

The peasants responded to her introductions with gracious smiles, kissing her sisters' hands and bowing to her brother. A wrinkled face, weather-beaten and worn, grinned toothlessly towards Alix and mumbled in Russian.

"She says that you are beautiful," Ella translated and, to her delight, Alix responded by taking the old woman's hands in her own and squeezing them gently.

The old woman gesticulated that she should follow her towards a stall where she ladled a liquid into a wooden cup and handed it to her, indicating that she should drink.

"What is it?" Alix whispered.

"Okroshka - a cold vegetable soup. Try it."

Alix took a sip, and the gathering crowd waited expectantly for her verdict. Whether or not she had actually liked it, Ella couldn't discern, but her response to the onlookers was more than Ella could possibly have hoped for from one so shy, and her smile drew a cheer and applause from everyone around.

The day passed quickly and by the time they returned, laden with the purchases they had made, the sun was already setting.

"There is another fair in another village tomorrow," Serge said as they reached the house. "Perhaps you would like to see that, too?"

When Alix enthused, Serge wasted no time in telling her of all the other delights of the region before embarking on the same gentle lecture about Holy Rus that he had given Ella when she first arrived in Russia.

The days sped by in boating trips, tours of village churches, and visits to the Youssoupovs at

Archangelskoe, and each day it seemed to Ella that Alix was more and more at home.

On the last evening of their visit, they walked down to watch the sunset over the river and, as the others strode ahead, Victoria and Ella dawdled behind.

"This has been such a wonderful holiday," Victoria said. "It's so pleasant for us all to have been together. If only Papa and Irène could have been here, it would have been just like the old days."

Ella smiled, "Perhaps next time they'll come, too."

"It would do Papa good to see you so happy."

"Then you must tell him."

"You *are* happy now, aren't you?"

"Very, very happy."

"In spite of all that you told me in London?"

"Oh, the rumours continue but we close our ears to them."

Victoria walked more slowly, "Something about you has changed. I can't quite tell what it is but I'm not the only one to notice it. At Archangelskoe, Zinaida commented on it, too. There's a kind of glow about you. It's impossible to describe." She frowned for a moment then laughed, "The only thing I can compare it to, is that atmosphere that people have when they first fall in love."

Ella smiled. *Yes,* she thought, *that's how I feel...like someone in love...or like someone who has found what she has been seeking all her life.*

"Victoria," she said quietly, "do you remember what else we discussed in London?"

"About Orthodoxy?"

"If I were to convert, how do you think the family would react?"

"Whatever you decide, you know will always have my support."

"But will I have Papa's?"

Victoria's lips twitched hesitantly and Ella shrugged the conversation away.

"It doesn't matter. I haven't made a decision so there's no point in upsetting him about something which might come to nothing."

"No."

Ella said brightly, "I think Alix enjoyed this holiday. I have never seen her so at ease among strangers. I really wanted her to meet the Russian people because I knew she would love them and they would love her."

Victoria raised her eyebrows, "And one Russian person in particular?"

"Oh Victoria, they're so suited! They love each other!"

"Grandmama isn't at all pleased."

"I know. Your letters made that clear but she has never seen them together. If she did, she would know that they were destined for one another."

"It's not going to happen, Ella. Alix will never change her religion. She's adamant about that."

"Five years ago, I was adamant about that, too, and now…"

Pavel's voice echoed through the trees, "Ella! Victoria! Come on, we're waiting for you!"

They glanced at one another and quickened their pace.

"We have some news," Pavel said proudly, putting his arm around his wife's shoulders. "Shall I tell them, Alexandra, or will you?"

Her coy expression was an announcement in itself, and Serge leaped to his feet, kissing Alexandra's cheek and slapping his brother on the back.

"So I'm to be an uncle again! Congratulations, both of you. I am delighted for you!"

His delight was obvious. He could not have been more elated had it been his own child, and the pang Ella felt witnessing his joy in their happiness, while he denied that same happiness to her, was deep and painful but she blinked it away and joined the others in their felicitations.

As the celebrations continued, she drew Alix to her side and gently steered the conversation to Nicky.

"He loves you, Alix. You know that, don't you?"

She sighed, "If we were different people it would be like a dream but that's all it is - a dream and it can never be in reality."

"But dreams can come true. There's nothing in your way except yourself."

"And my faith, my beliefs, everything I know to be true. It would be selfish of me to sacrifice that for my own happiness."

"And for *his* happiness."

She shook her head despondently.

"You will keep writing to him?"

"Grandmama thinks that Eddy and I are well suited."

"Eddy!" Ella laughed, "You're not really even considering such a thing, are you?"

"I like him and he says he is very fond of me."

"Fond? What's that compared to what Nicky feels for you, and what you feel for Nicky?"

"It's Grandmama's dearest wish and I think Papa would be pleased."

"But what about Eddy? Do you honestly believe you could ever make him happy when your heart already belongs to someone else?"

Alix shook her head and lay back on the grass.

"Then it's wrong to even consider marrying him, and you must tell him so. The longer you leave it the more difficult it will be."

"I will write to him."

"And you'll continue to write to Nicky, too?"

She nodded, "I can't help but write to Nicky. I think of him constantly and there isn't a moment when I don't wish that things could be different for us. If only it wasn't all so hopeless."

"No," Ella reached for her hand, "it isn't hopeless. Never say that. There is *always* hope."

Chapter 16

Snow, gathering on the ledges, muffled the sounds of the city, creating the atmosphere of a safe cocoon far from the outside world. Wood smoke hung in the air and there was silence but for the crackling of logs on the fire and the rustling of paper as Ella turned the pages of Victoria's letter.

"Any news?" Serge said, lying across the sofa and gazing contentedly into the flames.

"Mainly stories about the children and messages from Papa. *'How quickly time passes. It's hard to believe it is eighteen months since we were all together in Ilinskoe...'*" She looked up. It *was* hard to believe and the more so to realize that, apart from the birth of Pavel's baby, little had changed in those eighteen months. Alix and Nicky were as far apart as ever; and she herself still lacked the courage to take the final step into Orthodoxy.

Her eyes moved over the page when suddenly a startling line caught her attention, "Oh good gracious! You wouldn't believe it. You remember my cousin, Sophie - Willy's sister?"

"The one who married the Crown Prince of Greece?"

She nodded, "A couple of months ago she converted to Orthodoxy."

Serge swung his feet from the sofa and sat upright, beckoning her to his side.

"Apparently," she said, turning a page of the letter, "Willy absolutely forbade her to abandon Lutheranism."

"What business is it of his? From what I've heard he has no religion at all."

"Wait, there's worse to come. Willy's wife said that, since the Kaiser is Head of the Church in

Germany, if Sophie disobeyed him, she would suffer eternal damnation! Can you imagine?"

"Since when was Dona appointed God's judge?"

"When Sophie ignored him, Willy wrote to Grandmama saying that the shock had caused Dona's baby to be born prematurely and if the child died, he would hold Sophie responsible for murder!"

"Good grief!" Serge laughed. "What did Queen Victoria say to that?"

"She didn't even bother to reply."

"Good for her!"

Ella laughed, too, but there was fear beneath her laughter, "Willy is so affronted that he's banished Sophie from Germany."

"Much good will that do. I can't see that she would *want* to be in a country that is ruled by such a bigoted mad man."

"She wants to visit her mother and he says that if she so much as sets foot on German soil, he will arrest her."

Serge leaned closer to see the letter.

"*So,*" she read aloud, turning the page, "*Uncle Bertie has suggested that Sophie goes to Germany with her husband because even Willy wouldn't dare to arrest the Crown Prince of Greece!*"

Serge sat back laughing, "To think a man like that should be on so powerful a throne. If he can respond so irrationally to his sister, there's no telling what he is capable of."

She smiled pensively and put down the letter. "It must have taken a great deal of courage for Sophie to have risked the disapproval of her family."

He ran his hand over her cheek, "If she believes that Orthodoxy is the true religion, she had no choice."

"How do you think my family would react if I were to convert?"

"I think they would understand."

"Even Papa?"

"He brought you up to be true to yourself and your conscience. What more could he ask?"

"My conscience?" She leaned her head on his shoulder, "Serge, I am not being true to my conscience. I'm living a lie."

He lifted her head and gazed at her face.

"These past months I have known in my heart that I am already Orthodox in everything but name. Fear has led to me make so many excuses."

She hoped he would speak but his eyes were fixed on her in silence.

"It's a great sin, isn't it, to lie before God?" She looked down humbly, "That's what I've been doing and I repent of it. And there is no repentance without making amends." She looked up again and saw that his eyes were filled with tears that immediately caused tears to spring from her own eyes, too, "Serge, I want to convert."

The tears overflowed and as they rolled down her cheeks, he took her face in his hands.

"I have prayed and prayed for this," he whispered.

"I know. I have *felt* your prayers."

"Oh Ella, I can't tell you what this means to me. It is…" He shook his head unable to finish and, when he pressed her face to his own, their tears mingled on her cheek.

For some time they remained still and silent until at last she drew back from him, "What should I do?"

"We'll speak to Father Ioann together and we can arrange everything. He might ask you to take a couple of months to be sure you understand exactly what everything means but," he paused thoughtfully, "it would be wonderful if we could arrange it before Easter so you can take part in all the ceremonies with us."

"I would like that very much."

"You will need a sponsor."

"I was thinking of asking Minnie."

"That's a perfect idea. I am sure she'll be honoured and, being a convert herself, she will know what this decision means to you. And what of other guests? Would you like to invite your family?"

"No," she shook her head quickly, "let's keep it a small private ceremony. It's too sacred to have it turned into some kind of show. Perhaps just Minnie and Sasha, Pavel and Alexandra and one or two other friends."

He smiled, "I think you're right. Though, of course, other people will know about it."

She sighed, "I will have to tell them but I am dreading telling Miechen. She has always been so pleased to have another Lutheran ally. Goodness knows what she will think of me now."

"It doesn't matter what *anyone* thinks. It's none of their business. Don't be anxious. We'll do it together and I'll help you in any way I can."

He kissed her again, then stood up and took a cigarette from his pocket, "It seems it's a day for revelations. I have some news, too." He lit the cigarette, "You remember some months ago I told you that Sasha mentioned the position of Governor General of Moscow?"

She nodded.

"He has asked me again and this time it is a definite offer. He is only waiting for my reply."

"That's wonderful!" she said, trying to conceal her sudden panic.

"It's such a great honour. I would be acting with Sasha's full authority so my decisions for the region would be as binding as if the Tsar himself decreed them."

"It shows what faith he has in you and if anyone deserves that, Serge, you do!"

He lowered his eyes modestly, "I *am* deeply touched by his faith in me. I know that he wants me to accept it but I will only do that if it's what you want, too. After all, if I am to be his Viceroy, you would be the Vicereine. It would mean a great deal more responsibility and a huge amount of work for both of us and, of course, it will mean leaving the regiment and all our friends here."

"But you *want* to accept it?"

He moved his head from side to side as though weighing his answer, "It's my duty. When I took my oath of allegiance to the Tsar, I swore I would do everything in my power to support his decisions."

"And he has decided that you are the best man to govern Moscow."

He opened his hands in a gesture of sincerity, "So it would appear."

She took his hand, "I agree with him. There is no one in the country more loyal to him than you are, and no one better equipped for such responsibility."

"You think I am capable of it?"

178

"I *know* that you are."

He smiled gratefully, "So we say yes?"

"Yes."

"In that case, your decision to convert couldn't have come at a better time. If Petersburg is the brain of Russia, Moscow is her heart and Orthodoxy is the very soul of that city. It's the ideal place to nurture your new religion."

"We must have been guided there by Providence," she smiled.

Miechen's soirées were always thrilling events, featuring the finest musicians and actors in the country, and this evening, for Konstantin, came the added delight of reading his poetry to music composed for him by Peter Tchaikovsky. The response was genuinely enthusiastic and his heart swelled with pride as he bowed to his audience and raised a toast to the composer.

"And while I have your attention," he said, "will you join me in a toast to congratulate my dear friend, Serge, on his new appointment? To Serge!"

Glasses were raised and the applause continued for several minutes until everyone fell into small groups, chattering livelily and making gracious comments about his work. He drifted towards an alcove where Sandro stood laughing beside Miechen, whose face was anything but cheerful.

Sandro shook his hand heartily, "Wonderful, Kostia, wonderful! Your poetry was so touching it even put me in a good enough humour to drink Serge's health!"

"I am sure you would wish him health and success whether or not you had heard my poems."

"This evening," Miechen said, "Sandro is in such a state of intoxication that he would probably drink the health of the devil incarnate if he were asked."

"Intoxicated?" Sandro stared aghast into his glass.

"Intoxicated by love; and few people are more irritating or nauseous than those besotted by love."

He laughed too loudly, "I have no idea what you mean."

"No?" She raised her eyebrows, "So it was merely my imagination that had you paying such attention to a certain young lady?"

"What's this?" Konstantin smiled, "Is Sandro in love?"

"I'm afraid so."

"And is the young lady equally enamoured?"

"Judging by the flush of her cheeks whenever he is with her, I should say so."

"May I ask who she is?"

"No lesser person than the daughter of the Tsar."

"Xenia?"

Miechen nodded, "He spends an inordinate amount of time in her company. "

"Nonsense!" Sandro laughed, "Nicky is my friend and so it's natural that I should often see his sister but…"

"But nothing," Miechen said. "I would stake a fortune that in a year or two we'll be hearing wedding bells."

"Well, well, well," Sandro shook his head, "I never knew you were psychic, Miechen!"

"One doesn't have to be psychic to read the signs of the times, and there are some things I can see now that are sure to end in heartbreak."

Konstantin pulled up a chair and sat down beside her.

"You see the glow in Sandro's eyes when we speak of Xenia?" she said. "I have seen that same look in my own son's eyes, though I doubt he is even aware of it."

"Kyril's in love, too?" Konstantin smiled. "There must be something in the air giving rise to all this romance!"

"Alas, the romance in Kyril's case can only end in disaster."

"Why so?"

"Because the object of his affection is Victoria Melita, who, for some bizarre reason no doubt invented by the English, goes by the name of Ducky."

Konstantin frowned, confused, "The name is an impediment to their romance?"

"No, no, no," she shook her head irritably. "Ducky is the daughter of Duke of Edinburgh and Coburg, and my husband's sister, Marie."

"Ah ha!" Konstantin nodded as the problem began to make sense. "She's Kyril's first cousin."

"*Exactly.* Anywhere else, that wouldn't matter one bit. Good heavens! The Queen of England married her first cousin; Ella's sister married a first cousin, and a good many of my relations married first cousins but oh no! Not in Russia! Orthodoxy forbids such a match."

"Well," Konstantin said tentatively, "there *is* a scriptural foundation to the rule. It says in Leviticus that…"

"Oh, don't quote the Bible at me Kostia. If you followed every word in Leviticus, you would never trim your beard or cut your hair; and what you would do to women doesn't bear thinking about. It's all open to interpretation, and Orthodoxy chooses to create a sin out of something that every other religion considers perfectly acceptable."

Sandro rested his foot on the rung of a chair, "Is it really Kyril's romance that's behind this sudden attack on Orthodoxy, or is there another reason why our religion is so out of favour with you today?" He nodded across the room to where Ella stood, laughing with Pavel.

Miechen sniffed, "I make no secret of my opinion regarding Ella's conversion. I think it is diabolical. And I am not the only one. I heard from Willy in Prussia that her sister, Irène, is shocked to the core and her father is so outraged about it that Irène fears it will damage his health. Who can blame him when she is deliberately turning her back on all she was brought up to believe?"

"Really!" Konstantin huffed with indignation, "This is none of our business. How can you possibly criticise someone who is following her conscience - and at great cost to herself regarding the relationship with her family?"

"Her conscience? Must you be so naïve, Kostia? This has nothing to do with conscience and everything to do with Serge's ambition. Ella hasn't made this decision on her own. He has forced her into it."

"Oh, come now! If that were the case, she would have converted seven years ago when she first came to Russia."

"It wasn't necessary then. *Now,* of course, it's blatantly obvious. His appointment as Governor General of Moscow would be untenable unless he had an Orthodox wife."

"Not necessarily."

"He's setting himself up as a tsar in Moscow, and tsarinas are always Orthodox. This has nothing to do with religion or faith; it has everything to do with his ambition."

"Nonsense! Utter nonsense! Serge is far too devout to abuse his religion like that and he has far too much respect for Ella to even consider forcing her into something like this."

Sandro shook his head, "He rules every other aspect of her life, why should he make an exception for her religion?"

Konstantin stood up, "Because when it comes to religion, Ella knows her own mind, and what happens between her and God is no one's business but her own."

"According to stories I have heard," Sandro said, "this appointment to Moscow isn't the honour it appears to be at all."

Miechen looked at him inquiringly.

"There's been some scandal in his regiment - a scandal of the very worst kind - involving Serge himself. As a result, it's impossible for him to continue as commander-in-chief there. To avoid it becoming public knowledge, Sasha thought it best to have him moved as far away as possible from Petersburg."

Konstantin shook his head in disgust and started to walk away but not before he overheard Sandro laughing, "A joke is going around Moscow, which is far too base to repeat in polite company, but the gist of it is that the Muscovites are about to be governed by the biggest bugger in the country."

Miechen said, "God help Ella! She's going to need all the help she can get, far away from all her friends and stuck with only Serge for company while he lords it over the city like a self-proclaimed tsar."

Chapter 17 - Moscow 1891

All morning the rumbling of carriage wheels echoed on the walls and resounded through the windows of Nieskcushnoe Palace as the dignitaries gathered for Serge's formal inauguration as Governor General. Line after line of officials to greet, so many lips pressed to Ella's hand, and still they arrived in such vast numbers that their carriages blocked all the routes to the Kremlin. At each introduction, the immensity of the task ahead became increasingly clear. So many departments, so many bureaucrats, and Serge was responsible for them all.

The smile never left Ella's lips as the line continued: Alexeyev, Mayor of Moscow; Vlasovski, Chief of Police; Count Vorontsov, Minister of the Court; and suddenly the cadaverous countenance of an aged and bespectacled man appeared before her eyes.

Serge greeted him with a firm handshake, and said to Ella, "I don't think you have met Konstantin Pobedonostev, one of the wisest gentlemen in all of Russia."

As he kissed Ella's hand, his gaunt features twisted into the briefest of smiles, "Your Imperial Highness, as Procurator of the Holy Synod, may I congratulate you on your conversation to the true faith."

She thanked him and he turned to Serge, "Your appointment will be of great benefit to the city and the country. Your predecessor was far too lenient, particularly in regard to the Jews."

"The Tsar has given me the clearest instructions and I will carry them out to the letter."

184

"I know you will. That's why I advised him on your appointment."

Ella flinched at the notion that this corpse-like creature could have offered advice to the Tsar.

Serge said, "I have a report from Alexeyev stating that there are over one hundred and twenty thousand Jews in Moscow. Is that so?"

Pobedonostev nodded, "A menace to the stability of the city. They control most of the businesses and flour mills in the region. They offend Christianity and are at the heart of every disturbance. They need to be dealt with quickly."

"Steps have already been taken?"

"Yes, indeed. The programme began in March with the expulsion of Jews from the government of the city, followed by the removal of various artisans and brewers. Of course, it's a gradual process and will continue with further expulsions on the fourteenth of each month until Moscow is free of this scourge."

Serge nodded in a manner that left Ella feeling deeply uneasy and, as Pobedonostev passed on and other dignitaries came forward, the sense of discomfort heightened. Repeatedly came the call for firmness and, each time it was voiced, Serge's expression became more taut. Even when the introductions were complete and the atmosphere was less formal, he strode among the guests with such tenseness on his face that it seemed to Ella that he was deliberately demonstrating his intention to stamp his authority on Moscow from the start, with a determination that would tolerate no contradiction or dissent.

"Your Imperial Highness," a gentle voice said.

Ella turned around, delighted, "Zinaida, how wonderful to see you! I hadn't realized you were here."

"We were passing through the city and I thought a familiar face among so many strangers might be welcome."

"It is!"

"So, what do you think of Moscow?"

"I am *fascinated* by it! We visited a couple of times on the way to Ilinskoe but, living here, I am beginning to realize how much I missed before."

"It has a completely different feel to Petersburg, doesn't it?"

Ella nodded, "Serge says that Petersburg is far too Western, and Sasha has even been considering restoring Moscow as the capital."

"That would make sense. After all, tsars have been crowned here for centuries," Zinaida smiled. "And, with all the enthusiasm of the newly-converted, you have surely noticed that there are thousands of churches here, each with their own icons and relics and history."

"I have a visited a few of the Kremlin cathedrals - the Dormition, St. Basil's, the Annunciation and Chudov monastery."

"I always think," Zinaida said, "that the Kremlin is like a city within a city, with its own palaces, monasteries, cathedrals. You need never go beyond the walls and still you will know what it is to be truly Russian."

Ella's eyes were drawn to the windows overlooking Red Square, "I want to know what's beyond. If I'm to help Serge in his work, I need to see it all, not just the beautiful parts but *everything*."

"I wouldn't recommend it. There are places where things go on that would literally turn your stomach. Moscow has more than its share of filthy back streets and hovels where every kind of vice is to be found."

Memories of Father Ioann's work in Kronstadt floated through her mind with a powerful sense that fate had brought her to this place. She stepped closer to Zinaida and lowered her voice to a whisper, "I would like to visit the whole city incognito so I can see exactly how the people live."

Zinaida's eyes opened widely in horror, "Serge will let you do that?"

She shook her head sadly, "He says it's not safe."

"Quite right, too! There are streets that even the police fear to walk down. For a beautiful young woman to go there would be utter madness and it's hardly fitting for a grand duchess to be seen in such places."

"Maybe so," Ella murmured, "but some people have no choice but to live there and, if their lives are so wretched, the least we can do is discover why they turn to vice and violence. Only then can we help them."

She looked around the room and caught sight of the gaunt man engaged once more in conversation with Serge.

"Zinaida, what do you know about Pobedonostev?"

"He's Procurator of the Holy Synod so he's responsible for the administration of Church affairs. He's probably one of the most powerful people in the country, being advisor to the Tsar and tutor to the Tsarevich…as he was to Serge, of course."

"Is that so?"

"They call him the Grand Inquisitor because he's such an arch-conservative and has no time whatsoever for any form of democracy or representative government."

"He's right, of course," Ella said more in an attempt to convince herself than Zinaida. "In Russia no form of government other than an autocracy would work. After all, as Serge said, the Tsar is God's anointed."

"And what Serge says," Zinaida smiled, "comes straight from the mouth of Pobedonostev."

Ella frowned, "He said he had advised the Tsar on Serge's appointment as Governor General."

"Well," Zinaida said slowly, "my husband says that Prince Golitsyn, one of your neighbours at Ilinskoe, happens to be a friend of Pobedonostev, and he sounded Serge out for the position during your visit last summer."

"Sounded him out?"

"Perhaps that's rather flippant but they were looking for someone to replace Prince Dolgorukov because they felt he was too lenient with the Jews."

"And they thought Serge would be less lenient?"

"Apparently."

"But why? What have the Jews done?"

"Apart from crucifying Christ?"

Ella shook her head, "Christ himself was a Jew."

"A truth that people find it convenient to forget. The Jews are a useful scapegoat. If there is disorder or the poor complain that they are hungry and cannot afford bread, it's easiest to put the blame onto the Jews who own most of the flour mills, and then expel them from the city."

"But that is only creating a new problem. Who will be left to run the flour mills? Who else has the experience or the skill?"

Zinaida shrugged.

"And they surely can't expel all of them. Serge says there are a hundred and twenty thousand Jews in Moscow."

"A hundred and twenty thousand!" Zinaida laughed. "More like twenty or thirty thousand. They use these figures to scare people."

Her eyes moved beyond Ella to Serge who was striding purposefully towards them.

"Zinaida," he greeted her with a nod, "you seem engrossed in your conversation."

"We were discussing my children," she smiled tactfully. "I was telling Ella how much Felix adores her and how we're looking forward to seeing you in Ilinskoe in the summer."

"Summer is a long way off when we have so many immediate duties here." He looked pointedly at Ella, "If you will excuse us, Zinaida, there are many people waiting to meet my wife."

He took her arm and led her away through the crowds.

Spring passed quickly in endless receptions, entertaining and the organization of a new household and, as Serge worked from dawn till dusk, even when there was a spare hour to spend together, he was too exhausted for conversation. On many occasions, if his meetings continued into the night, he stayed at the Governor General's House on the main Tverskaya thoroughfare, and Ella saw him only at meal times when he was too preoccupied with the tasks ahead to pay her any attention. At first it had seemed a lonely existence far from her friends in St. Petersburg but, as the evenings lengthened and the lingering sunset glistened on the ornate domes of the cathedrals, the silence became more of a friend than a foe. Now, undisturbed, she could kneel for hours before the sacred icons given to her as gifts at her conversion, or study more deeply the Gospels and the writings of the great Russian saints. Even adhering to Serge's insistence that she remain, for her own safety, within the walls of the Kremlin, there were ancient churches steeped in so many centuries of prayer that the air of sanctity was almost tangible. Then there was the Ascension Convent, housing the enclosed order of nuns whose wisdom and holiness was etched into their faces. There, though treated with the utmost deference, she knew she was no longer Her Imperial Highness, but simply another pilgrim soul searching for guidance. There, too, she could speak freely of her thoughts and the inspirations that came to her in prayer.

"Put your hand into the hand of Christ and let yourself be led," said a wizened face with shining eyes, looking at her through the bars of the convent enclosure.

"I cannot help feeling," she whispered, "that when Jesus said, '*I was hungry and you gave me to eat, thirsty and you gave me to drink, naked and you clothed me,*' he was speaking directly to me, giving me a command."

"His message is meant for each of us," smiled the nun.

"But then he said, '*I was hungry and you didn't feed me, I was thirsty and you didn't give me to drink...If you failed to do this for the least of my brothers, you failed to do it for me.*' As long as there is one hungry or thirsty person whom we fail to help, we have neglected our duty."

"We all do what we can in the circumstances in which God has placed us. Here, in the convent, it is our role to pray and, free of earthly distractions, we unite our lives with the sacrifice of Christ. Out in the world, you have different duties. Neither way of life is more blessed than the other. It is all part of God's great design."

"In Catholicism," Ella said, "there are two kinds of religious orders: the contemplatives who remain in their enclosure, and the active orders who run schools and hospitals. I have not heard of any such orders in Russia."

"No. All the Orthodox orders for women are enclosed."

Ella would have liked to say that there was such a demand for active orders in Russia that it would be of great benefit to the people but, looking into the saintly eyes of a woman who had dedicated her entire life to her faith, to even consider making a suggestion seemed arrogant.

Sensing, perhaps, what she was thinking, the nun smiled, "You, Your Highness, have a position of great importance. That is a very great gift because you have the opportunity to do so much good for people."

"Yes," Ella nodded but inwardly sighed. *What good can I do if I am forbidden to even go into the streets and find out how people really live?*

She returned to the palace to find Serge pacing the sitting room, drawing frequently on his cigarette. Without a greeting, he launched immediately into an account of his evening.

"I followed your mother's example and went out incognito. You wouldn't believe the squalor! There's an area, south of the river, called Zamoskvoreche, and I can hardly get the stench of it from my nostrils. It's a filthy, squalid hole like a painting of hell itself! Drunks, whores, beggars and I even saw children offering their bodies for sale."

"I would like to see it, too," she said quietly.

"Absolutely not! I was fortunate to come out of there alive. Some of the scum that I saw there would kill you as soon as look at you and, if I had been recognised, there's no telling what might have happened. Something has to be done about it. Something *will* be done about it."

"Yes, something must be done. No one should have to live like that. If we could…" she began, but he was too engrossed in his own thoughts to hear her.

"Anarchists and nihilists prey on these vulnerable people. They turn them against us, fill their heads with ridiculous dreams of a new world without leaders or governors and where everyone is equal."

"Before God we *are* all equal," she murmured.

"Before God, yes," he nodded impatiently, "but God has ordained that some should be rulers and some should be ruled. Entrusted with that authority, it's my responsibility to see that those who strive to wreck the whole balance are rooted out before they can do any more damage. I know who's at the heart of this: Jews and intellectuals. The universities are hot beds of sedition and the Jews are behind every plot against Tsardom. I won't rest until I have cleared the whole of Moscow of their influence."

Ella gasped in horror and Serge looked at her as though she were an ignorant child incapable of comprehending.

"Russia," he said, "is founded on Orthodoxy. We are here to build Christ's kingdom on earth. Of course, the Jews who killed Christ will do everything to prevent that."

She reached for his hand, "It is hardly Christ-like to drive them from their homes, confiscate their land and close their synagogues. Jesus himself prayed in the synagogue."

He shook her from him, "You have no idea. Their influence is pernicious and underhand and, if I had my way, I'd string every one of them up." He walked to and fro, frowning and rubbing his hand across his forehead, "I need to tighten the restrictions on the university appointments. It's necessary to stop these hot-heads from gathering support. And then I'll increase the restrictions on the Jews. Many of them claim the right to be here because they are descended from soldiers in my grandfather's army but that doesn't mean anything now."

Ella stood up, "I know you might think my ideas are naïve but it seems to me that as long as people live in such appalling conditions it is impossible to build Christ's kingdom on Russian soil. I have been speaking with the nuns at the Ascension and…"

He turned quickly, "Again?"

Taken aback by the disapproval in his tone, she nodded, "I have prayed so much about this, as well as speaking with those wise nuns and some of the priests, and I feel that there is much more I could do to help you to help all those people. I honestly believe that God is calling me to do more for them and…"

"Ella," he shook his head and sat down beside her, taking her hand in his. "I'm anxious about you. There's something I should have warned you about; something that I believe is a great pitfall for many new converts. Perhaps one of the priests might have spoken to you of it?"

She blinked, uncomprehending.

"As soon as we commit ourselves to a different, better way of life, the devil strains every nerve to lead us from the true path. All kinds of charmed spirits speak to us, telling us we should go this way or that way or that our immediate duties aren't enough to please God. It's a clever trick on the devil's part. It distracts us with whims that prevent us from carrying out our real task, by making us believe we should be doing something completely different - something quite impractical for us - and so we are left paralysed and doing nothing."

She looked down humbly, trying to accept his superior knowledge of Orthodoxy, yet she couldn't help replying, "But this isn't a whim, Serge. Ever since I was a child I have wanted to help those who suffer."

"And you *do*," he said patting her hand. "You help them with your charities and you help them by serving in your role as wife of the Governor General. I need your support and I know I have it. If you want to do more, you could visit the hospitals now and again or maybe call in at an orphanage. It would be good for people to see you doing that - they would know that we care about them and it would reflect well on the family."

She sighed, "I will do that, of course, but…"

"And I'm establishing a new charity to help assist pilgrims to visit the Holy Land. I'm thinking of calling it the Palestine Society. You could help with the paper work, if you like." He stood up and moved away, "I haven't time now to discuss these things in detail. When we go to Ilinskoe I will find an opportunity to explain it better. For now, concentrate on your duties as a hostess instead of allowing yourself to become carried away by all these excessive devotions."

Her heart sank and she could barely restrain her tears. Could it be that their spirituality - the one thing she truly believed would bring them closer together - was now the greatest wedge between them?

She stood up to leave. "I read in the newspapers today that the farmers are predicting another poor harvest due to the all the bad weather last year and the excessively long winter."

He grunted, "They predict poor harvests every year. It's a means of avoiding paying taxes."

"But if they're correct and the grain supplies will be limited, won't it be necessary to have experienced people running the flour mills and ensuring nothing is wasted?"

He looked up and frowned.

"If the Jews have that skill, why send them away?"

He laughed condescendingly "Dear child, you're so trusting. It's probably the Jews who predicted a bad harvest for that very reason! You'll see when we go to Ilinskoe, the fields will be ripe for a bumper crop."

She turned away and moved towards the door when, with the remorse in his voice that so often came after a patronising comment, he said, "It will be lovely to go to Ilinskoe this year. We can spend more time together, and Pavel and Alexandra will be there with their little girl. You always enjoy their company."

"Yes," she continued towards the door.

"You heard that Alexandra is expecting another child? I think it's due in late autumn or early winter."

"Yes, I know."

She opened the door, walked up the stairs and knelt in prayer before her icons.

Chapter 18 - Ilinskoe - Summer 1891

"Good grief!" said Pavel, whipping the newspaper from beneath Serge's boots as he lay sprawled across the sofa reading through pages of documents. "You're supposed to be on holiday. Can't you take a break from all that?"

Serge didn't reply.

"He's become such a dreadful bore since he moved to Moscow. How do you stand it, Ella?"

She smiled and her eyes alighted on the newspaper headline, "May I see that?"

Pavel wrinkled his nose and handed it to her, "I hope you're not becoming as dull as he is."

"Look," she said, "there are more warnings of another poor harvest. Nizhni-Novgorod, Tula, Kazan and many more places. Don't you think that this is becoming serious?"

"They always predict bad harvests," Pavel said carelessly as Alexandra leaned over Ella's shoulder to read the report.

"They recommend that we stop exporting the grain or there won't be enough to feed our own people."

"We can't stop the exports," Serge said without taking his eyes from his documents. "It would damage the whole economy of the country."

"The economy of the country is surely less important than preventing starvation. According to this, the ground is so dry that seeding will be late and thousands of peasants could be left with nothing for the winter."

"Ella, you know nothing about economics or farming. Don't meddle in things you don't understand."

She bit her lip to restrain a reply and, seeing Pavel's sympathetic smile, masked her humiliation with a shrug.

"Shall we visit the Youssoupovs this evening?" she said but, before anyone could answer, a knock at the door heralded the entrance of a homely-faced woman carrying a little girl.

"Ah, thank you, Nanny Fry," Alexandra's eyes opened wide with pleasure. "Marie, come to Mama!"

Nanny Fry put down the little girl and, as she toddled across the room, Serge dropped his papers, swung his feet from the sofa and opened his arms, "Come to Uncle Serge!"

But the child continued towards her mother who greeted her with an affectionate hug. Pavel beamed proudly, "A boat trip is in order! What do you say, Marie, would you like to come sailing?"

Nanny Fry coughed pointedly, "With respect, Your Highness, the little grand duchess came to bid farewell to her mother before her afternoon nap."

Like a reprimanded schoolboy, Pavel murmured an apology and, when Marie had been suitably hugged, coddled and praised, he returned her to her nurse with promises to see her later.

"Good heavens!" Pavel huffed when they had gone, "What is it with these English nannies? They put the fear of God into me!"

Ella laughed, "It was the same when we were children. Nanny Orchard ruled the nursery and Mama wouldn't dream of contradicting her."

"No wonder my sister prefers German nurses! And before Nanny Fry decides to pack us all off for a nap I say we go for a boat trip."

Serge looked at his papers but, before he could protest, Pavel snatched them from him, "You're on holiday. Come on, let's make the most of the sunshine!"

It was an exceptionally warm afternoon and the sight of the Moskva River glistening in the sunlight, brought to Ella's mind the deep-seated peace she had felt the first time she came to Ilinskoe.

"Seven years," she murmured, and Alexandra, strolling slowly beside her, moved closer.

"Seven years?"

"Since first I came here."

Alexandra smiled pensively, "Did it take you a long time to settle in Russia?"

Ella shook her head sadly. It had taken no time at all to settle into the dream of what Russia might be, but now it seemed that each day reality shone more clearly through that dream, and it was with more than hint of nostalgia that she said, "Serge was so wonderfully kind."

"Pavel, too." Alexandra nodded and, as though to reassure herself, added, "He is *still* kind, of course, and yet..."

Ella looked into her eyes and recognised the loneliness. "And yet?" she whispered.

"Pavel told me many times what a stunning impression you made on everyone when you first came to Russia. I'm afraid I lacked your confidence. I found it all rather overwhelming."

"It *is* overwhelming," Ella said reassuringly. "Life here is very different from anywhere else. Even after seven years, I feel I am only just beginning to understand it. Converting to Orthodoxy has opened my eyes to so many things that I wasn't aware of before."

Alexandra reached for her arm and linked it in her own, "I am sorry your father took it so badly."

"So am I. I had hoped he would understand but he sees it as a betrayal, bringing shame on him and the family."

"Do you miss your family and home very much?"

"At first I did but not now. Not really."

Alexandra's lip trembled as though she were about to cry.

"You miss yours?" Ella said softly.

She nodded, "I can't help it. I try not to think of them but when Pavel took me home last year, I was dreading coming back here."

She looked so lost, so frail and so worn with the weight of her pregnancy that Ella, by reflex, reached to put her arm around her shoulders.

"No, please," Alexandra stopped her. "If you are kind to me, I will cry and Pavel mustn't see me crying. It would break his heart if knew how I feel."

"I'm so sorry," Ella whispered, "I had no idea you were so unhappy."

She forced a smile, "It's probably my condition making me feel this way. When I was expecting Marie, I wanted to cry all the time. It's just that sometimes I feel so…" she shook her head unable to find the right word.

"Lonely?"

Alexandra nodded, "You feel it, too, don't you?"

"Sometimes."

"It's difficult, isn't it? When Pavel is with me, it's different. He's so attentive and loving and he makes me laugh so I forget how much I miss my family and home, but, since his promotion to Commander of the Horse Guards, whole days pass sometimes without my seeing him and I miss him dreadfully."

"I understand," Ella said honestly.

"Of course, you do. Serge is so busy with his work, you must feel his absence dreadfully."

Ella nodded trying not to admit even to herself that it was Pavel's absence she felt most deeply.

"That's why it's beautiful coming here," Alexandra said, looking up at the sky. "Pavel and Serge enjoy each other's company so much and when they are happy, we are happy, too. It's lovely the four of us being together."

"Yes," Ella said, "it *is*. And you know what we must do? We must see to it that even when we're apart and you return to Krasnoe Selo and I to Moscow, we keep in close contact. I shall write to you regularly and we'll visit each other as often as we can so, if ever you feel lonely or sad, you know there is someone here who understands."

"Thank you. That would make such a difference to me."

Ella smiled, "Do you not think…" she began but Alexandra's face suddenly brightened, "Look, they have the boat ready!"

Bright rays of sunlight streamed between the wooden slats of the landing stage, making the surface of the river glisten as though sprinkled by a thousand stars. Ducks gathered by the dozen, quacking like old women sharing a secret joke: greenheads, brown heads and fluffy little ducklings and among them floated two proud swans, arrogantly surveying their shabby offspring in their dowdy brown feathers.

The tethered boat creaked on its moorings as Pavel gripped Ella's hand when she jumped from the jetty.

"Can you swim?" he laughed as the boat rocked frantically.

"I hope I won't have to!" She leaned back on the cushions and trailed her hand through the water to let the ripples trickle between her fingers. Such serenity, such stillness and...

Suddenly there was a splash and the boat began to shake so violently it seemed it might overturn. In an instant she saw Alexandra lying across the timbers, her limbs trembling uncontrollably and her unfocussed eyes rolling wildly.

Pavel, calling her name, lurched forwards to take her head in his hands, and the oars fell into the water.

Serge, standing on the landing stage, holding a rope to keep the boat steady, looked down in horror, "Is she alright?"

But Pavel was listening to no one. His eyes were wide open in dread and, as Ella struggled to steady Alexandra's limbs, the tremors increased.

"It's a fit," she said urgently. "Serge, fetch a doctor. Fetch someone, quickly!"

Six days had passed; six days, during which Alexandra lay quite still, oblivious of the hands that mopped her face, turned her, bathed her and gently soothed her forehead. No doctor could be found in the region, only the midwife who hovered as helplessly as the others, waiting, praying, waiting, praying for any sign of improvement. Night and day Pavel barely left her side, whispering to her until exhaustion overcame him and he dozed fitfully in a chair, without letting go of her hand.

"Your Highness," said the midwife gravely to Serge, "Grand Duchess Alexandra is in a very serious condition. I fear you must prepare your brother for the worst."

Serge stared through the bedroom door, his cheeks almost as pale as the ashen face on the pillow.

"She's going to lose the baby?"

"How can the child survive when the mother is so weak?"

He sighed and pressed his hand to his forehead, "Then we must resign ourselves to the will of God and concentrate now on Her Highness' recovery."

The midwife's voice dropped to little more than a whisper, "Sir, she is utterly exhausted and, in her present condition, I doubt she has the strength to withstand the birth of the child. "

"So what can be done?"

The midwife shook her head helplessly.

Pavel turned from the bed, "No," he whispered. "No! She *will* recover. She's so young. Of course, she'll recover!"

His eyes darted from the midwife to Ella and Serge, desperately seeking a reassurance that none was able to offer.

"No!" he said, lunging towards his wife. "She isn't...she cannot..."

"Pavel," Serge rushed to restrain him, "more than anything she needs absolute quiet and peace. Any noise or disturbance will only aggravate her condition."

Pavel dropped to his knees by the bed, took her hand in his own and kissed it softly. The tenderness in his eyes and the heartrending anxiety on his features seemed to Ella the most tragic scene imaginable. She leaned against the jamb, longing for Alexandra to open her eyes and see how fondly her gazed at her.

She turned to the midwife, "There is *some* hope, isn't there?"

"I honestly don't know."

Serge put his arm around her shoulders, "We must try to be strong for Pavel's sake. Come."

He led her further into the bedroom where Pavel remained kneeling and stroking Alexandra's hand. Her face was clammy, and damp strands of hair clung to her forehead.

"You will feel better soon, I promise," Pavel whispered, leaning so close that his lips were almost touching her cheek. He slipped his arm beneath her shoulder and raised her gently, beckoning Ella closer.

"Ella, tell her she will be alright."

Tears stung her eyes at the sight of his desperation, and she inhaled deeply before murmuring the words that he wanted to hear but that she couldn't believe.

"I know," he said, "Marie will waken her. She'd love to see Marie!"

Serge glanced hopelessly at Ella who nodded and backed towards the door, "I'll bring her."

Pavel smiled at her gratefully but there were tears in his eyes.

Marie was sitting on a nursery maid's lap while Nanny Fry busied herself with linen and blankets. They curtseyed when Ella entered, and inquired as to whether there was any improvement in the patient. Shaking her head slightly, Ella smiled with forced brightness and took Marie in her arms,

"Mama would like to see you. She's very poorly but seeing you will make her feel so much better."

"A child in a sick room?" Nanny Fry sniffed.

Ella hesitated before replying, "I was not there when my mother was dy.." She stopped abruptly, seeing the little girl's eyes fixed upon her. "One of my greatest regrets is that I didn't see my mother at the end. Come, Marie, Mama would like to see you."

But, before she had reached the door, the sound of heavy footsteps running along the landing brought her to a halt.

"Ella," Serge burst in, "Marie must stay here. The baby is being born."

"Oh Lord!" said Nanny Fry, bustling past both of them.

Ella handed Marie to the nursery maid, and she and Serge followed the nanny to the sickroom.

There was little anyone could do and the flurry of activity around the bed seemed only to heighten the sense of utter desperation.

After what seemed an eternity, the midwife looked up sadly, "You had a son, Your Highness."

"He's alive?" Pavel said.

She shook her head and placed the scrawny little bundle on a linen pile.

"Then concentrate on his mother," Pavel said urgently.

Alexandra's breathing, at first laboured, gradually slowed to an occasionally gasp.

Serge, tears rolling down his cheeks, murmured, "Shall we send for the priest?"

"No," Pavel said, "she needs to rest. She can see him when she's better."

"Pavel," Serge put his hand on his brother's shoulder.

"No," he said, frowning to restrain his tears, "not yet. She'll recover. She *will* recover."

But the gasps became more infrequent until there was silence.

Pavel stood up and, wiping his shirt sleeve over his eyes, crossed the room to the door where he stood resting his elbow on the jamb and pressing his fist to his head.

Silence seeped like a fog through every corner of the room, broken only by occasional agonised cries as Pavel crouched to the floor and, burying his head in his hands, sobbed uncontrollably. Numbness paralysed Ella's limbs. She could neither reach to comfort him, nor wipe the tears from her own face. Everyone stood unmoving as though the shock had turned them all to stone, when suddenly Nanny Fry began fussing and jabbering in the corner of the room.

"For Christ's sake!" Serge stared angrily in her direction but, undeterred, she continued until eventually there came the sound of a baby's cry. Nanny Fry turned and stepped towards Pavel, holding a bundle of linen in her arms.

"Your Highness," she whispered, stooping down to him, "your son is alive."

Ella sat at the piano, her eyes closed, her fingers gliding effortlessly through the strains of Chopin's dirge. Absorbed in the music, she had been unaware of anyone entering the room until the sense of a gentle presence beside her brought such an unfamiliar warmth to her heart that for a while she was convinced it must be an angel or a ghost. She played on, bathing in the serenity of the music and only when the final diminuendo faded away did she open her eyes.

Pavel was sitting by the window, staring out across the gardens.

"Go on," he said gently, "it was beautiful."

She closed the piano lid, "Is there anything I can do for you?"

He shook his head. "The funeral will be in Petersburg. Serge is making the arrangements. He's sent word to her family. God knows how they'll cope."

The sorrow in his voice gripped her heart like a vice, "She knew how deeply you loved her."

"Love wasn't enough, was it?" He stared out of the window. "I failed her."

She wanted not to hear him. She wanted to feel nothing, but his grief was tangible and the vice around her heart was slowly tightening.

"She loved you, Pavel. She was talking of you only moments before it happened. She spoke of the happiness you brought her."

He trembled and Ella could stand it no longer. She slid from the piano and, standing behind him, rested her hands on his shoulders. He turned and his dark eyes moved over her face. She wished that she did not love him. She wished that she could be strong but the sight of tears welling in his eyes was more than she could stand. She moved to face him, "I know it's unbearable but, for your children's sake, you have to be strong."

He gulped to stifle a sob and covered his eyes with his hand.

"I'm so sorry," she said.

"No," he blinked back the tears, "*I'm* sorry."

Slowly, tentatively she moved his hand from his face. She kissed his cheek gently and his skin tasted of tears. When she moved back, his eyes were closed and his words came out in a whisper, "I can't even think of the children. I need to get away, far away. I can't…"

His pain was so intense. His eyes were red, his jaw unshaven and his lips curled in fatigue and despair.

"You're exhausted. Why don't you try to sleep for a while?"

"I couldn't sleep even if I wanted to."

"You could at least lie down and try to rest."

He looked up and stared intently at the crucifix around her neck.

"A just God? Isn't that what they say? How is it then that he could see her lying there suffering and yet he didn't lift a finger to help her?"

"I don't know. We can only go on believing that everything happens for our good, no matter how hard it seems."

"I'm sorry but I don't have your faith," his face crumpled. "Why? Why did this happen to her?" Tears rolled down his cheeks, and Ella held him to her heart. His shoulders shook in convulsions of grief and the few words he tried to speak came out as nothing but incomprehensible gasps. She stroked his hair until, in one terrible moment, the awful realization dawned on her that she would gladly have prolonged his grief if it meant prolonging his proximity and warmth of his body in her arms.

An image of Alexandra flashed through her mind and an intensity of guilt flowed over her like a wave. Releasing him from her arms, she stepped back and was grateful that he barely seemed to notice her or that she was blushing in shame.

Chapter 19

Autumn faded into a dreary winter with little to lighten the gloom. Even the miraculous survival of his son, Dmitri, could not rouse Pavel from his grief. In a desperate attempt at distraction, he had thrown himself with greater fervour into his military duties, leaving his children in Serge's care. Serge seemed hardly less grief-stricken than his brother. Clinging to the key of the now-locked room where Alexandra had died, he withdrew into silence and the lines on his brow deepened, rarely relieved by smiles. Only in the presence of Pavel's children did he seem to find relief and if, at first, it had delighted Ella to see him tenderly holding Dmitri or speaking softly to Marie, the affection he lavished upon them contrasted starkly with the sternness in his eyes when they alighted upon her. Nor could she prevent the pangs of resentment on seeing him play the role of a father to them, when he had denied her the opportunity of ever becoming a mother.

In the long, dark evenings she knelt before her icons, remorseful of her resentment, and seeking guidance as to how she might put her gifts to greater use. The winter days after New Year brought little respite. In January, a telegram, followed by a heartbreaking letter from Grandmama in England, told of the unexpected death of Cousin Eddy only days after his twenty-eighth birthday. The death of the British heir presumptive temporarily displaced the famine from the newspaper headlines but, as the days passed, that reality could no longer be ignored. The truth of the situation - the deaths of thousands of people, too malnourished to withstand infections or the cold - had finally reached St. Petersburg. Sasha had ordered a ban on exports and donated more than half of his income to the relief committee, which he had appointed Nicky to supervise. Since the Tsar and Tsarevich were actively involved in the aid programme, Serge couldn't refuse Ella's request to establish a series of bazaars to raise money for the victims.

Her carriage crunched over the ice and the driver jumped from his seat to open the door.

"There's no need to wait, Rudinkin. We'll walk back."

With her ladies-in-waiting, Princess Troubetzkoy and Countess Olsuvieva, scurrying behind, Ella crossed the snowy yard where a long queue of would-be purchasers bowed and curtseyed in unison. The countess pushed open the door and immediately a huge woman stomped around a table, "Ah, Your Imperial Highness! We thought perhaps you were unable to come today."

"Princess Vassilshikova," Ella nodded. "We were delayed at the hospital but we're here now and have brought more items for sale."

The princess took a parcel from the countess' hand and spread the embroidered handkerchiefs and cushion covers over the table, "I hope you've not been too close to the patients. They say tuberculosis is rife."

"Well," Ella smiled, placing the samplers at regular intervals across the table, "perhaps our visit raised their spirits."

"And His Imperial Highness, are his spirits raised too?"

Ella frowned, uncomprehending.

"When we didn't see you at the ball last week, we thought perhaps he was unwell."

"My husband was away in Petersburg last week."

"I suppose there must be a lot of coming and going between Petersburg and Moscow when one is representing the Tsar," the Princess said and, for some obscure reason, laughed loudly. "I hear His Highness has completely redecorated the Governor General's House. Such an artistic man, isn't he? Some years ago, I don't suppose you recall, I visited your palace in Petersburg and I remember being so impressed by the Grand Duke's art collection."

"My husband is quite a connoisseur," Ella smiled.

The huge princess mused, "It's such a shame to think of all the time and labour that's gone into amassing the collection, building everything up and for what? If he has no heir..."

Ella winced, "The collection isn't solely for my husband's pleasure. It is a means of preserving the artistic heritage of the country."

"Yes, of course, but a man must have an heir," the princess persisted. She leaned closer and in a booming whisper said, "Apparently the Roman Catholics believe that St. Rita is very good for this sort of thing. I heard of a woman who lived in Madrid, married for fourteen years but not blessed with children. She'd tried cures and spas to no avail until her husband took her on a pilgrimage to Cascia. For three solid days she did nothing but pray and what do you know? Within a year she'd had twins!"

Ella, bristling with humiliation, turned away.

"Someone brought me a prayer card from Cascia, with a tiny relic of St. Rita sewn into it - a bit of her dress or something. It's no use to me but, if you like, I could let you have it."

When Ella didn't reply, Countess Olsuvieva fidgeted frantically and spread more items across the table.

"Then again," said the unruffled princess, "from what I hear, Grand Duke Serge is as good as a father to his brother's children now. Perhaps he will make them his heirs since he has none of his own."

Ella restrained a retort and was relieved to catch sight of a priest, clad from head to toe in black, moving purposefully towards them.

"Ah," said the princess, "if I am not mistaken, this is Metropolitan Leontius."

"Your Imperial Highness," he bowed low, "forgive me for approaching you like this but I would be so grateful for a moment of your time."

"By all means," Ella said, glad to escape from Princess Vassilshikova.

She led him away from the table and he stood nervously fingering his beard, "I appreciate that Your Highness has so many commitments so I hesitate to ask this of you, but I did not know who else to turn to."

He hesitated, prompting her to offer a word of encouragement, "Please, speak freely. If I am in a position to help, I will."

"You have seen, I think, the Foundling Hospital?"

She nodded.

"Until a short time ago, it was open to the children of poor families and orphans as well as those whose parents are deemed unfit to care for them."

"It does great work, I believe."

"Unfortunately, the number of illegitimate children and foundlings now being admitted means that it is no longer possible to take in other needy children. Consequently, hundreds of them remain living in squalor and depravity."

"Is there a reason why the number of foundlings has suddenly increased?"

"It's difficult to pinpoint one specific reason, but the rise of industry has brought many more people into Moscow in search of work. The city was not prepared for such vast numbers and so the shortage of suitable housing has led to overcrowding and hastily built slum dwellings."

"I suppose the famine in the countryside will be increasing the numbers arriving, too?"

He nodded, "Living in such foul conditions gives rise to all kinds of vices. Quite often the only escape these people have from their miserable existence is to numb their minds with vodka, which in turn leads to promiscuity. The outcome is literally hundreds of abandoned babies. And then there is the plight of the women workers."

He paused as though afraid he had said too much but she nodded to encourage him to continue.

"It has to be said that many of the factory foremen abuse these women terribly, compelling them into all kinds of acts against their will."

"Surely, there are regulations to protect them?"

"Regulations are very difficult to enforce. The women are too frightened of losing their jobs to complain when the only alternatives available to them are starvation or…forgive me, prostitution."

Ella frowned, "What can be done about it?"

"There is only so much we *can* do, and that we *must* do. While the Foundling Hospital does great work for all these abandoned children, others are left in appalling conditions. Some as young as nine or ten years old become addicted to alcohol or are forced by their own parents to sell their bodies. We would like to establish another institution to help these poor little ones but that requires permission from His Majesty."

"You would like me to speak of it to the Tsar? Yes, of course, and perhaps..." The idea dawned as she spoke, "Perhaps I might be involved in this new venture which, I am sure, will be a complex task requiring a great deal of organization."

"It will, it will."

"Do you not think it is better, as far as possible, that children remain with their parents rather than being removed into institutions?"

He nodded and shook his head in one movement.

"Obviously, there will be some cases where that's impossible but I am firmly convinced that many children suffer neglect not because their parents are uncaring but rather because they are uneducated. People who have been raised badly, have never learned how to care for their own children and so it goes on generation after generation. If it were possible to educate the parents, it would have very far reaching and beneficial consequences."

As though stunned by her understanding and cooperation, he stood wide-eyed and silent.

"It would be necessary to involve people who know these families well. The priests, perhaps, in local parishes would be in the best position to do that since they have direct contact and are aware of who is most in need. That way, too, the venture would be under the auspices of both the Church and the secular authorities." Her mind raced ahead through a thousand possibilities, "Do you not think that, rather than creating one institution like the

Foundling Hospital, the people would be better served by a society in which institutions and other programmes could be established."

"Yes, yes indeed!"

"It will be necessary to draw up a statute and present it to His Majesty. Once we have his approval, I will do everything in my power to support it financially and, if you wish for my patronage, I would be delighted to do anything I can in the way of its organization and promotion."

"Your Highness," the Metropolitan shook his head in amazement, "I had heard that those whom you visit in the hospitals and orphanages esteem you so highly but I never expected such…"

Reluctant to hear his praise, she interrupted him, "You would need a name for the society. A name that is instantly recognizable so we can seek donations and support from many quarters."

He mused for a moment, "With your permission, Highness, *The Elizabethan Charitable Society* sounds most appropriate."

She smiled, "We shall see what His Majesty says. I will write to him as soon as I finish here."

"Your Highness, what can I say? I…"

"I will contact you the moment I hear from the Tsar. And now, if you will excuse me, I have a bazaar to open."

It was a delight to read Sasha's response to the request. Not only had he given the Elizabethan Society his full approval, but he had clearly paid attention to every detail of the statutes that Ella had devised, and added various suggestions and provisos of his own. Once sanctioned by the Tsar, Serge was quick to offer support, and throughout February and early March there was so much to do that the days flew by in a haze of ceaseless activity that not only distracted from the grief of the previous months but inspired Ella with a new sense of purpose.

With so many meetings to attend, letters to write and documents to read, she barely noticed the growing distance between herself and Serge; and the loneliness that for so long had been a constant companion returned now only when he raised the subject of her devotions.

"Did you see Count Olsuviev in church this morning?" he said as they sat down for dinner one evening in early March.

She looked at him quizzically.

"If you didn't see him, you must at least have heard him. All that noise he was making! The man's a disgrace."

"I didn't notice."

"How could you have failed to hear him?" He frowned and added sarcastically, "I suppose you were too engrossed in your prayers."

If he hoped to provoke a response, he was to be disappointed and, when Ella simply shrugged, he drummed his fingers on the table.

"I understand the importance of reverence but I am sure that it isn't right for you to be so enraptured in your devotions as to be quite oblivious of what is going on around you. You must try to temper your faith with a little more reality."

As always when he spoke of these things, there came a sense of deflation and the feeling of being a child reprimanded by a stern father.

"You remember I warned you of the dangers of being carried away by charmed spirits? You must be careful."

"I *am* careful," she sought to reassure him. "I judge everything by its fruits. If what I feel when I pray leads to good works, to helping people, to inspiring me with ideas for the Elizabethan Society or..."

"No, no," he shook his head, "don't trust any of your own ideas. We can all imagine we hear the voice of God inspiring us. You must refer everything to the priests and do only as your confessor tells you. You know that..."

The approach of a footman, bearing a silver tray, distracted him, "What is it?"

"There is a telegram for Her Imperial Highness."

Ella stared at it anxiously; telegrams almost always brought bad news.

"You'd better open it," Serge said.

"It's from Alix in Darmstadt," her heart sank. "Papa has had a stroke and is dangerously ill."

Serge pushed back his chair, strode around the table and, in an uncharacteristic display of affection, put his arm around her shoulders, "We must go to him. We'll leave at once."

Queen Victoria pressed her lace handkerchief to her eyes and dabbed away the tears.

"Utterly broken. That's how I feel. Not ill, but utterly broken."

Beatrice nodded sympathetically.

"Poor, poor Louis, such a good man and so kind and so attentive to me and to his dear children!"

"It is a blessing that they were all with him at the end and that Ella was able to reach him in time."

Grief weighed like a stone in the Queen's stomach as she forced herself to reply, "I can only hope that he found it in his heart to forgive her before he died or she will feel his death even more acutely."

"He was such a good and forgiving man, I am sure that he will have done."

The Queen pushed herself up from the chair and stared out of the window, "Dear Ella. What a difficult time she has had! And Pavel! That poor young man, widowed and left all alone with two children. Life really is nothing but sorrow."

Beatrice sighed unhelpfully.

"I think I will invite Ella and Serge to join me at Balmoral next year and they might bring Pavel with them. After all this sadness they would all benefit from the good Scottish air."

"Ella always loved Balmoral," Beatrice said.

But the Queen was too distracted to respond. Her thoughts were of Darmstadt: the lovely carriage rides, Louis' attentiveness, those beautiful girls and Ernie, always so bright and so gentle.

"Dear, dear Louis," she sighed again. "You know, after Alice's death I doubted he would be able to cope with raising his family alone. At one time I entertained the idea that perhaps you might have married him so that you could have been a mother to those dear children."

"Yes, I know," Beatrice said indignantly.

"If the Church hadn't interfered with the ridiculous rule forbidding a man to marry his late wife's sister, it would have been a happy arrangement."

The expression on Beatrice's face implied disagreement but the Queen chose to ignore it.

"No matter, Louis did a very good job on his own. Dear Ernie and Alix will miss him terribly. Alix must be with me more than ever now. With no father or mother to protect her, I will have to be both to her and, since poor Eddy's passing, there is nothing here to make her feel uncomfortable."

"But what about Ernie?" Beatrice said. "So young and unprepared to rule the Grand Duchy. He will surely need Alix there with him, to help him."

The Queen frowned pensively, "It isn't Alix's place to play the Grand Duchess. What Ernie needs is a wife, as soon as possible." She pondered for a moment and her thoughts suddenly brightened, "I know exactly the right person for him. Yes," she nodded as the pieces began to fall into place, "and if Ella and Serge come next year, they will be in perfect position to bring this to a happy resolution."

Chapter 20 - Balmoral 1893

Autumnal sunlight streamed through the purple heather, over the orange bracken and shimmered on the mountain streams. Only the distant crack of gunshots and the occasional calls from the hunters shattered the silence and, as the pony carriage returned to the castle, it seemed to Ella that Balmoral was the most secluded haven on earth.

On these afternoon outings with Grandmama, or pony trekking through the hills, it was possible to ride for hours without meeting another soul. Here, more than anywhere, they were all able to forget the high demands of their station; no one distinguished between Queen, Grand Duchess, lady-in-waiting, or maid - the same warm greeting was extended to all. Rough speech wasn't tempered by deference; outspoken honesty was the order of the day, and these country folk thought nothing of offering the Queen advice or a nip of whiskey to keep out the cold, in a manner that would have been unheard of in London. The staff in Mr. Simon's shop, the worshippers leaving Crathie Kirk, the crofters in their cottages might doff their caps or make a slight bow but Ella was certain that this courtesy extended to all, not only to royalty. Had she had any desire to stand on ceremony, it would have been impossible here. Shopkeepers, servants, staff and locals remembered her from childhood and, if her lady-in-waiting, Princess Troubetzkoy, was initially a little surprised by their familiarity, it did not take long to relax into the way of things in Highlands.

Disembarking from the pony-carriage, she took Grandmama's arm and together they walked into the castle. The smell of the place was identical to that of Osborne and Windsor: the lingering scent of

Grandmama's orange blossom perfume and the smokiness of log fires - at least, Ella smiled to herself, that was what they told the Queen with her aversion to cigarettes.

"Since the men have not yet returned from the hunt," Grandmama said, "you and I might sit and talk for a while."

"Of course," Ella smiled and, as servants scurried to take their coats, she followed the Queen into the tartan-walled sitting room where they settled themselves and she prepared herself for a further interrogation.

"Pavel seems to be bearing up well after his terrible loss."

"Yes," Ella said, "I think he is slowly coming to terms with it. His children are with him more often now, although I believe his duties prevent him from spending a great deal of time with them throughout the day."

"Serge must miss them. I understand he is very attached to them and, according to his sister, has been quite a second father to them."

Ella nodded.

"And you? You miss them, too?"

"I think it is better for them to be with their father. Pavel loves them dearly even if he doesn't always demonstrate it in an outward show of affection. That is the way with Russian men."

"With most men," the Queen said. "Your father and your grandfather were exceptions."

"Yes." Ella said sadly.

"What a great loss he is to me. First your Uncle Fritz and then dear Louis: two of the dearest sons-in-law any mother could hope for." She sniffed away her grief, "And what of Ernie? How is he managing?"

"He is determined to live up to Papa's high standards and he has made a good start. He is very popular with the people, and Alix is a great help to him as hostess."

"Indeed," nodded the Queen, "but good as Alix is, Hesse requires a grand duchess. You know yourself what a difference your mama made as a helpmate and guide to your dear papa. Ernie needs a reliable wife who will fill that role."

Ah, thought Ella, *so this is where the conversation is leading.*

"The truth is," she said cautiously, "I don't believe Ernie is ready for marriage. He is very young in his ways and enjoys his freedom so much."

"I'm afraid his freedom vanished with the death of your father. People in our position forfeit our freedom the moment we accept our responsibilities. We no longer live for ourselves but for our countries. There are times I look at the crofters and farmers in their tiny cottages and how I envy them! Their lives might be a struggle but their responsibilities are few and their decisions do not have far-reaching consequences on hundreds of thousands of people as ours do. For that reason we need to be sure of a strong and supportive helpmate. That was true for me when I became Queen, and the same is true now of Ernie as Grand Duke of Hesse."

"Victoria mentioned that you were encouraging him to pursue a match with Ducky."

"It's the best thing all round. Now that Ducky's father has become Duke of Coburg, I can think of nothing better than a union of Coburg and Hesse and, since their mother insisted on raising those girls as Germans, Ducky will immediately endear herself to the Hessians. On a more personal level,

Ernie and Ducky have always been such good friends. They have always seemed very happy in each other's company and I have often seen them laughing and dancing together."

"Yes," Ella agreed, "they are good friends."

"And yet," the Queen peered at her closely, "you seem less than enthusiastic about this match? Since Ducky is Serge's niece and also your cousin, is there something that you have heard that makes you so cautious?"

Ella clasped her hands together to prevent herself from fidgeting. Had Grandmama heard the rumours of Ernie's preference for the company of young men? Had Alix hinted to the Queen, as she had hinted to Ella, that Ernie might be happier to remain single?

Fortunately, the Queen spoke again before she had time to reply, "Is it true that Ducky has a fondness for a Russian who is equally fond of her?"

"Ah," smiled Ella with relief, "Miechen's son, Kyril. Yes, I believe they were attached to one another at one time but nothing can come of it. The Orthodox Church forbids marriage between first cousins, and Kyril cannot marry without the Tsar's permission. Sasha would never consent to a match that contradicts the Church laws."

The Queen smiled, "Thank goodness those laws don't apply here."

"And yet," Ella said hesitantly, "the close ties of kinship between Ducky and Ernie might still be a hindrance."

"Oh, this is your Orthodoxy speaking. If the Church of England had forbidden first cousin marriages, England would have been deprived of the wonderful services of your grandfather."

"No, no," Ella said quickly, shaking her head, "it isn't for that reason. Mama always told us that Grandpapa believed the family needed strong blood from other royal houses. Considering the possibility that..." Reluctant to continue, she sighed, "Forgive me."

"You are thinking of the illness of Uncle Leopold and your dear Frittie?"

Ella nodded, "There is a suggestion that it might be carried in the blood and passed through generations."

"That thought has crossed my mind. We *do* seem to be cursed by this family illness and, for that very reason, I have consulted with Dr. Jenner. He has assured me that the children of two healthy people of strong blood will be even stronger than the previous generation. I have passed this information on to Ernie."

"Did Dr. Jenner speak of the possibility of the illness being carried through any of us?"

"There's no reason to believe that. Of all my nine children, only dear Leopold suffered from it. Your mother had six healthy children and only poor little Frittie was struck by it. Victoria's children are perfectly healthy so perhaps it has run its course and we are all free of it now."

"I pray that that's so."

The Queen sat forwards. "So," she said, "the doctor has set our minds at rest on that account. Ducky is quite ready to marry and, after some initial misgivings, her mother is eager to see her settled with Ernie. The only thing that's preventing this from reaching a happy conclusion is Ernie's reluctance to make a commitment. I have no idea why he is being so dilatory about it." She raised her eyebrows in expectation of an explanation but when

Ella had none, she continued, "Since you will be visiting Darmstadt on your way back to Russia, you might speak with him of it and let me know of his response?"

"Yes, I will."

"Good! And while you are there, I hope you will remember that this is the *only* match in the family that we need to pursue at this time."

Ella looked at her questioningly.

"Don't be filling Alix's head with tales of the young Tsarevich. As I told your father and have told Ernie, too, Alix will not be *allowed* to go to Russia."

Ella smiled and said nothing.

When Ella had left to dress for dinner, Queen Victoria sat for some time by the open door, with one eye on the corridor outside. It would have been useless, she knew, to press Ella for more details of her life with Serge, but there were always ways and means to find details from the most unsuspecting sources, and what lady-in-waiting would fail to answer any questions posed by the Queen of England?

At the tread of dainty footsteps, she stood up and the carefully contrived chance encounter fell perfectly into place.

"Ah, Princess Troubetzkoy!"

The young woman curtseyed politely.

"We have a few minutes before I need to dress for dinner. Perhaps you would care to join me in the sitting room?"

The princess glanced back along the corridor as though about to make an excuse but clearly thought better of refusing such a command and nodded in acquiescence.

"Most people who visit us here complain of the cold. I never feel it myself so I hope you are quite warm enough."

"Yes, quite warm enough, thank you, ma'am," nodded the overawed princess.

"I suppose you are used to a far colder climate in Russia. It has been a great trial to my nerves to think of my dear granddaughter enduring such bitter winters."

"Her Imperial Highness' rooms are always kept warm."

"It's important that she takes great care of her health. She was never strong."

The princess said nothing, compelling the Queen to adopt a more direct approach, "She is in good health generally?"

"Yes, very good health. Sometimes she suffers from colds and perhaps a little rheumatism but that, she says, is something that afflicts all of her family."

"Mm," the Queen nodded. "She is very popular in Russia, I understand?"

"Oh yes, ma'am, the people in Moscow adore her! She was loved in St. Petersburg but everyone has noticed such a change in her since her conversion. There's such a glow about her that the Muscovites call her a saint!"

"A saint?" said the Queen doubtfully.

"Her charities are so well-organized and she delegates very little as she wishes to be totally involved in all that is happening."

"I hope she doesn't overtire herself?"

The princess' lips twitched, "I couldn't say, ma'am. She works very hard but, as you see, she is in perfect health."

"And the Grand Duke? I suppose he must have many responsibilities now that he is Governor General."

"Many, many responsibilities. Even when he is supposed to be resting at their country estate, he takes his work with him so he hardly has a moment to himself. Sometimes they are both so busy that they barely see each other at all."

"I see," said the Queen, at which the princess blushed as though fearing she had said too much.

"Tell me honestly, in complete confidence, my dear, would you say they are happy together?"

An involuntary sigh issued from the princess' lips, "I really couldn't say, ma'am. Her Imperial Highness always seems very happy."

"*Seems,*" nodded the Queen, "which is quite a different matter to *is.* We hear so many stories that it isn't always possible to discern the truth. Perhaps you could enlighten me?"

"I will try, ma'am."

"During this terrible famine that ravaged your country, the Grand Duke was involved in the relief effort?"

"All of the Imperial Family were involved, ma'am. They donated large sums of money from their own accounts as well as raising funds in all kinds of ways."

"And the Grand Duke's efforts were appreciated?"

The princess' hesitation was revealing.

"I am sure this is all nonsense but we were led to believe there was strong feeling against him. Rumours of his acquiring some of the relief fund for his own personal use."

Princess Troubetzkoy opened her mouth but no words came out.

"And again, we were told that during these terrible purges against the Jews, he was accepting bribes to allow some of them to stay."

"Ma'am," she looked one way then another, "I couldn't really comment on these things except to say that His Imperial Highness has no need whatsoever to accept bribes or anything of the sort. He has such a fortune of his own that he wouldn't even think of doing these things."

The Queen nodded and changed tack, "Of course, I wasn't suggesting that the Grand Duke would stoop so low but the fact that these rumours are rife and even reach us here in Britain, suggest he is very unpopular in the city. Is that so?"

"Perhaps."

"And why is that?"

"I couldn't say, ma'am. Her Imperial Highness is greatly loved; everyone admires her."

"In contrast to her husband?"

The princess nodded, "Aware of what his father suffered, the Grand Duke takes a very hard line. He believes the people need to be ruled with firmness. I think that sometimes Her Imperial Highness finds his measures rather severe."

"I see," nodded the Queen sadly. "It must be extremely difficult to be married to so unpopular a man, and all the more difficult to try to support him when their views are so disparate."

"But she *is* happy, ma'am," said the princess unconvincingly.

"I hope she is," the Queen sighed, "but if her husband is so disliked I dread to think what might happen in so violent a country."

Chapter 21 - 1894

Ella couldn't sit still as she waited for the Tsarevich to arrive. Striding from one side of the room to the other, a mounting excitement welled in her chest and a whole scenario played through her imagination. This was surely the answer to her prayers, and all these years of waiting had not been in vain. One chance, and he must be sure to take it; one golden opportunity that must not be missed.

The door opened and there he stood, smiling despite the shade of sorrow in his eyes.

"Nicky," she rushed to greet him, "there's some wonderful news!"

"You've already heard?" he said with surprise. "I thought I was to be the one to tell you. How on earth did you hear it so soon when Papa has only just given his consent?"

A moment of confusion, then she laughed, "I think we have different news. Mine came by telegram from England this morning."

"It doesn't concern Xenia and Sandro?"

She shook her head and he slumped into a chair, "They're to be married."

"That's wonderful! I'm so happy for them."

"So am I," he said, though his expression belied his words, "but I do wish they could restrain themselves a little. They're all over each other, kissing and cuddling and…"

"Young and in love!" Ella laughed. "Romance must be in the air."

"Not for me. Look at me: twenty-six years old and still no nearer to finding the happiness that blesses everyone else."

"Ah," she smiled, holding up the telegram, "that's where you're wrong. My news is going to change that for you."

He lurched forwards, his eyes open wide with anticipation, "Alix has changed her mind?"

"No, but…"

He sat back, deflated, "It's impossible, isn't it? Nothing is ever going to change for me. Is it any wonder that I was born on the feast of Job the long-suffering?"

"Come on," she chivvied, *Faint heart never won fair lady!* You're not going to give up so easily."

"Six years I've waited and it hasn't made the least bit of difference."

"If you give up now, that's six years wasted. Didn't Alix write to you and send you her photograph?"

"Only because you persuaded her to do it when you were in Darmstadt."

"She wanted to be persuaded."

He raised his eyebrows.

"She loves you, Nicky. Everyone can see that. Even your mother has come round to the idea that you're made for one another. You have to keep trying."

"How can I, when there is never an opportunity to see her?"

She shook the telegram and smiled, "Coburg in April! Can you think of anywhere more romantic and beautiful?"

"Coburg?"

"Ernie and Ducky are to be married."

He forced a smile, "More romance."

"Exactly! And in such a romantic atmosphere, how could Alix possibly refuse you? You must attend your cousin's wedding; Alix must, of course, attend her brother's. Hey presto! Both of you in the same place at the same time. This is your chance, Nicky!"

Some of the sadness shifted from his eyes, "You really believe there is hope?"

"No," she shook her head, smiling, "it's far more than hope. It is certainty."

The questions revolved and revolved in Alix's head as she crept into the chapel on Sunday morning, hoping she wouldn't be noticed. Why had she written to him; why had she sent him her photograph; why had she given him any encouragement at all? The thoughts that had burned through her mind all night had swelled to such proportions that she was convinced that if anyone should catch sight of her face, her confusion would be apparent. She tiptoed past the household and crept into the bench where Ernie, greeting her with a smile, shuffled along to make her a space, then closed his eyes.

As he slumbered or prayed, Alix stared at the altar, begging every angel in heaven to calm and guide her, but the recurring image of Nicky's face only increased her apprehension. That handsome profile; his innocent smile; those deep, pensive eyes, so expressive and so kind...*Why*, she cursed herself, why had she kept in contact with him? And why would he not listen to her refusal and understand that it was cruel to keep pressing her when nothing could ever come of it?

She must tell herself that she didn't love him. Yes, that was the only solution. She must be strong, unemotional, rational and yet...why had she spent the whole night tossing and turning and beating her pillows, trying to drive his face from her mind? Through all of Ernie's wedding plans, it was Nicky and herself whom she imagined standing at the altar; it was Nicky's eyes she saw whenever Russia was mentioned; it was Nicky's lips that she felt gently brushing her cheek in the breeze.

She pressed her hands together and stared more fervently at the altar, "Take this feeling away."

But beneath the supplications, her prayers were insincere. This clutter of emotion was something that no one else had ever inspired: the excitement when his letters arrived; the racing heart when someone spoke his name; the longing even to breathe the air he had exhaled. Did she really want to let this feeling go?

Feeling? This was so much more than a feeling. This was *love*. It was love that no one else had ever known. She wanted him to know how she suffered in his absence, just as he suffered without her. She imagined herself, a latter day Joan of Arc, riding beside him into battle, shaken by canon fire, pierced by swords, brought to the point of death before the last minute rescue, when he would take her in his arms..."I love you...I love you...I love you..." she whispered and he, holding her close, pressed her head to his pounding heart.

The congregation rose, and Alix absent-mindedly chanted the rote-learned prayers, *"To you, o Lord, I lift up my soul..."*

She didn't want to let the feeling go; but it bothered her this strange, irrational, irresponsible love. Was true love really so passionate, so powerful and inflammatory? Or ought love to be gentle, steady and true, like Ella and Serge's, or Ernie and Ducky's? She recalled her aunts and uncles dragging themselves wearily through their routine lives; wives disappointed in their husbands, husbands complaining of their wives; occasional glimmers of affection on birthdays or at Christmas, and months of stagnant endurance in between.

This wasn't Alix's dream of love; a dream which bore no resemblance to Ella's love for Serge. Their love that was steady and stifled and devoid of all passion. Alix's dream was a love that blazed; where lovers rolled through poppy fields, soared like birds, swam in oceans. But it bothered her deeply this strange, impassioned, impossible love.

The minister droned through the scriptures, "*If your virtue goes no deeper than that of the Pharisees...*"

And suddenly the sight of the pious congregation overwhelmed her with guilt. How could she stand here before the altar of God, dreaming of Nicky, when she was already bound to the faith of her childhood?

"*If your eye causes you to sin, pluck it out. If your hand causes you to sin, cut if off.*"

She would put him from her mind. She wouldn't think of him again. She would replace his image with thoughts of duty and service and abide by the answer she had given him. She must write to him and tell him that there would never, *could* never be any future together. Then, perhaps, he would not come for the wedding and she would harden her heart and never have to face him again.

She joined her hands and prayed, "Please, God, please take these thoughts away. Teach me to forget him."

When the service was over and the congregation had dispersed, Ernie wandered with her through the gardens and into the glasshouse where the strong scent of hyacinths hung in the clammy air. Ernie named the plants and fingered their leaves with a feminine concern.

"I've been thinking," he said eventually, "you're probably anxious about what will happen when I am married."

"Why should I be anxious?"

"About your place here. I know it won't be easy for you to give way to Ducky. After all, since Irène married, you have more or less been the mistress of the house. Now, with a new Grand Duchess of Hesse…"

"Oh, Ernie, you know me better than that! I've never enjoyed the limelight. Ducky will be far more suited to that kind of thing and I'll be happy to hand it over to her."

"Well," he said, "I just wanted you to know that you will always have a place here. Nothing will change between you and me, and this is your home for as long as you want it to be."

She thanked him and opened the door to let the breeze dispel the asphyxiating scents of the flowers.

"Of course," he said, "you won't want to stay here forever. You'll want to be married and…"

"No," she said quickly, "I'll never marry. But don't worry, I won't stay here and be in your way. I will go to England and keep Grandmama company. She would like that and so would I."

"Grandmama won't be here forever," he said, reaching for her hand and leading her to a wrought iron bench.. "Since we were children, with Frittie and May and then Mama, we have always known how fragile life can be. Sometimes it seems to me that our lives can end so abruptly and unexpectedly that we should seize every moment of joy with both hands and never miss an opportunity of happiness."

"At any cost?"

He shrugged, "I know how Papa reacted to Ella's conversion but we are a different generation. As head of the family now, I would have no objections if you were to convert."

She pulled away from him, "I *cannot*. It goes against everything I believe. At my confirmation I promised to adhere to our faith and I can't go back on my promise. I know that when Ella comes for your wedding, she will begin again but there is nothing I can do."

"Do you honestly believe that the God of love would want you to sacrifice your happiness and Nicky's, too, because you feel bound by some man made doctrine?"

"You mustn't say that. These rules aren't man made. They are the results of hours of study. There are very clever men in the Church who have examined all these things and they understand it all far better than we do."

"They know what's best for us, better than we do?"

"Yes, yes they do and it behoves us to listen to them."

"When they lay burdens on our shoulders that are too heavy to bear? Didn't Christ teach love and kindness, forgiveness and mercy? Didn't he heal the sick and raise the dead to make people's lives happier? Did he want people to suffer? No, he didn't and he never condemned anyone for love."

Flustered, Alix stood up, "Ernie this kind of talk is dangerous."

"More dangerous than wasting our lives in some misplaced idea of martyrdom or sacrifice? Think about it, Alix. Isn't love the very heart of God? How then could he inspire love in us and, at the same time, condemn us for following our hearts?"

The more he spoke the greater became her confusion.

"Listen," he said gently, "I'm not telling you to do anything against your conscience. All I am saying is that, if you love Nicky, there is no obstacle between you except your own scruples."

A sudden pang thudded in her chest and she raised her hand to her heart, "My conscience..." she murmured as tears stung her eyes. "I *cannot* go against my conscience. I am going to write to him now, and to Xenia, too, and make it clear once and for all that he must forget me."

The April evening was particularly warm as the imperial party boarded the train for Coburg. In spite of the crowding, the atmosphere was jovial and, as Serge, Michen, Vladimir and Nicky settled into the luxurious compartments, Ella reached for her cross and uttered a silent prayer.

"Cheer up, Nicky," Serge slapped him on the back. "A long face won't win her heart!"

"I already have her heart. It's her conscience that keeps us apart."

Miechen said, "It would be quite wrong to try to tempt her away from all she was raised to believe." And, despite Ella's efforts to be charitable, she was certain that there was a double-edged attack in that remark. Perhaps it was difficult enough for her to accept that Ella had converted, but the prospect of a Hessian bride for the Tsarevich seemed to rouse even greater antipathy.

"I'm sure her refusal is for the best," Miechen said. "No offence to your sister, Ella, but Alix is such a shy girl that the responsibilities of a tsarina would have been too much for her."

"Nonsense!" Serge said gallantly. "Alix's shyness is a mask for real strength of character. It took a great deal of strength to refuse Eddy's offer of marriage, and it has taken a great deal more strength to hold out for so long in spite of Nicky's constant pleading."

Nicky frowned thoughtfully, "I hope my presence doesn't distress her. I wouldn't have come but Mama said it was too late to withdraw my acceptance of the invitation."

"Of course, you had to come," Serge said. "This is the best chance you'll ever have of winning her."

"But she has told me already that it's hopeless. She even wrote to Xenia asking her to impress upon me that she will never change her religion."

"Yes, yes, yes, dear boy," Serge laughed, "but now you hold the trump card."

Nicky raised his eyebrows.

"Queen Victoria will be at the wedding. Never mind pursuing Alix, just win her grandmother over to your way of thinking. Alix is devoted to her so, if you have the Queen's approval, you have your bride."

Ella looked out of the window. The possibility of gaining Grandmama's approval was even more remote than persuading Alix to convert. Nevertheless, unwilling to add to Nicky's troubles, she nodded and smiled, "Grandmama's support would make so much difference."

"I have to say," Miechen sniffed in an obviously intentional change of subject, "I was rather surprised when I first heard that Ernie and Ducky were to be married. I never thought they were suited to one another. Ducky is such a strange girl, high-spirited and strong-willed but prone to moodiness, I believe."

"And *I* believe," said Serge, "that you are only consoling yourself for the fact that she couldn't marry Kyril."

"Poof! That brief infatuation between them was over a long time ago."

"Over before it started," said Vladimir. "It was nothing more than a young girl's fancy."

Miechen smiled without sincerity, and Ella turned back to Nicky, "I think I shall retire now for the night so I can pray for the best possible result tomorrow."

"What time do we arrive?"

"We break for lunch in Bavaria and then a few more hours to Coburg so we should be there by about five in the evening."

"So by five you must look your best," Serge laughed. "Put on your smartest uniform. Women can't resist a man in uniform!"

Chapter 22

Not since Queen Victoria's jubilee had there been such a gathering of royalties and, as the carriages rolled through the streets of Coburg, the crowds turned out in force to cheer and wave and welcome their guests. With each kiss of greeting and each happy reunion, Ella's excitement intensified. Spring was in the air; so much laughter and merriment! Moment by moment the exhilaration swelled - how could Alix fail to be swayed at the sight of Nicky, so handsome and dashing in his debonair uniform? Even the presence of Cousin Willy couldn't dampen her spirits. He was in a particularly jovial mood the evening before the wedding, as the family mingled in the dining room of the old Schloss. With his left hand tucked into the specially designed pocket to conceal the deformity of his arm, he stood fingering the tip of his handlebar moustache until, catching sight of Ella, he strode over and in a booming voice said,

"I hear that Nicky intends to propose to Alix. It's to be hoped she accepts him this time."

Mildly surprised by his support, she raised her eyebrows.

"She would make an excellent tsarina. And a German princess behind the throne of Russia, would be the perfect way to cement the bond of friendship between our two countries."

She couldn't resist, "Even if it means she must convert to Orthodoxy?"

He waved his right hand dismissively, "It's the same God whatever one's religion."

Overcoming the temptation to ask why then he had threatened to banish his sister from Germany, she said, "Nicky proposed to her yesterday morning.

I invited them both to my rooms in the hope that seeing him alone and face to face might change her mind but it only made things worse and left Alix in tears. Grandmama's arrival last night didn't help. You know that she insists that Alix won't be allowed to go to Russia."

"Alix is a German princess. She is *my* subject, not Grandmama's."

She tried to conceal her amusement at the thought that he would not dare voice such an opinion in the Queen's presence.

"You forget, too," he continued with an air of authority, "that Grandmama can never resist a romance. When Cousin Eddy took a ridiculous notion to marry the daughter of the deposed king of France, didn't he find a willing supporter in Grandmama, even though such a marriage would have done irreparable damage to Anglo-French relations? You see, before being a Queen, she is a woman and, like all women, her heart is so easily moved by a love story that logic goes out of the window."

She looked across the room to where Nicky stood gazing like a lovelorn schoolboy in Alix's direction.

She sighed, "I don't think there could be a truer love story than this one."

He looked into her eyes and, for a moment, his features softened and she detected an air of sadness about him like the fading embers of the candle he had once held for her.

He said, "Even if Grandmama doesn't approve of this match, it won't be the first time that she has been disappointed in a granddaughter's choice of husband."

Uncomfortable at his insinuation, she nodded towards her brother, "She is certainly pleased about Ernie and Ducky."

"I heard she engineered the whole thing from start to finish and virtually forced Ernie to propose."

His laughter caught Serge's attention and he strode quickly towards them, possessively linking his arm into Ella's.

Willy said, "I was telling Ella that I hope Alix will see sense and accept Nicky's proposal."

"That was our hope too," Serge said, "but, since she refused him yesterday, the poor boy thinks it's hopeless and has given up trying."

"Given up?" Willy laughed. "Doesn't he realize that the Hessian sisters have a habit of refusing proposals and then changing their minds? How many times did you have to ask Ella before she agreed to marry you?"

Serge, rankled, gripped her arm more tightly.

"Leave Nicky to me," Willy said. "I know how to deal with him and I can guarantee that he will pursue this until we have the desired outcome."

He clicked his heels Prussian-fashion and strutted away. Serge stared after him with an expression of astonished irritation, "*He* can guarantee? What an arrogant, puffed-up..."

"I feel rather sorry for him," Ella smiled. "I don't think he realizes that being so bombastic makes him sound quite ridiculous."

"He's not worthy of your pity."

She mused and said quietly, "I think he behaves in this way because of his arm. He blames his mother for it, you know?"

"I thought he was born with the deformity."

"It was an accident at birth. Somehow his shoulder was dislocated and the nerves must have been damaged, because his arm never developed properly. He went through torture with it as a child as doctors tried all kinds of strange contraptions to make it grow. He couldn't use a knife and fork until he was ten years old, and his balance was affected so he had a terrible time learning to ride. It was only through sheer force of will that he eventually succeeded."

"That's no excuse for his arrogance."

"No," she said, "but I think it has left him with a horror of any sign of weakness so he goes out of his way to appear strong and in control." She looked directly at Serge, "Sometimes people who are deeply insecure about something, try to hide it behind a mask of strength and a desire to dominate others."

His lip curled in annoyance and he fidgeted with the ring on his finger, "So you've become a mind-reader now, have you? Willy is simply the product of the militaristic Prussian Court and, judging by his erratic behaviour, it wouldn't surprise me in the least to discover that his brain was affected, too, by this accident at birth."

Two days later, Alix stood looking out of the window, watching a gentle rain fall over the pretty gardens of the Schloss. The wedding had passed cheerfully as weddings do and, after the months of preparations and the past few days of family gatherings and outings, there came a predicable sense of anticlimax. Nicky had been so kind and understanding about it all. It surprised her that, in spite of her refusal, he still wanted to be in her company and there had been no lessening of the warmth in his manner or the feeling of ease in his presence. Now he was standing at the entrance to the room, his tentative smile accentuating the beauty of his expressive eyes.

"May I speak with you?"

Her heart thudded. This was it; it was now or never. If she refused him this time, it would all be over. He would go back to Russia and she might never see him again.

He closed the door and invited her to sit down beside him.

"Where is everyone?" she said with a brightness that disguised her inner turmoil.

He gesticulated towards the wall, "In the next room. They're all waiting to hear what..." He shrugged without finishing the sentence.

"I suppose they're all discussing weddings?"

"Oh yes," he smiled, "and everyone has an opinion about marriage."

"What are they saying?"

"Aunt Marie thinks that love doesn't come into it. It's more a question of convenience and toleration."

Alix smiled, recalling the careless way that the Duchess had dismissed any notion of loving her husband.

"Aunt Miechen agrees with her. She told me that it's the duty of the Tsarevich to marry and produce heirs to the throne. It makes little difference whom he marries, as long as she is of a suitably distinguished family of royal blood. It's possible to live amicably with anyone, she says, and there's little point in chasing after some elusive dream that, one way or another, will only bring disappointment in the end."

"Do you think," Alix whispered, "that you could live happily with someone else?"

He raised his eyes to the ceiling, "It would be wrong to marry anyone but you. In time, I suppose, my affection for whoever it was would deepen but I know that every day I would ask myself what would have happened if I'd waited for you. My heart could never belong to anyone else. I never dreamed of anyone else; was never so excited when I heard someone else's name; I have seldom missed anyone else in their absence. With you, everything is different. The days I don't see you seem wasted. When you're not with me, my life seems to stop as though I'm no longer real but merely a shadow. It's as though my soul leaves my body, to be with yours. Do you understand?"

She nodded silently and he leaned a little closer. "You feel that, too?"

Her eyes moved over his face, "Yes," she said, "I do."

"Then you'll understand why I could never give my heart to anyone else."

Tears welled in her eyes, "Neither could I."

"Alix, believe me," he took her hand, "nothing would induce me to ask you to go against your conscience, but Willy said something the other day that might change things for you. Converting to Orthodoxy doesn't require a denial of the faith you have followed until now. You could become Orthodox without rejecting Lutheranism."

Suddenly, like the unexpected brightness of the sun piercing through the rain clouds after a storm, light seemed to fill the room.

"I will ask you once more and, if your answer is still the same, I promise that I will never raise this subject again. Will you marry me, Alix?"

"Well," said Willy strutting to and fro and twitching the edges of his moustache, "they're taking a long time so she can't have rejected him outright."

"She's in love with him," Ella murmured. "How can she possibly continue to refuse him?"

"In love?" Serge's sister said flippantly. "What does that have to do with anything?"

"Oh Marie," Ella smiled, "is there no romance at all in your soul?"

"In our circles, romance is of no consequence. Falling in love is a luxury reserved for the lower orders. Tsars and tsarinas, princes and princesses marry each other because they must, to keep the blood line going."

"The blood line," Miechen said thoughtfully. "I suppose one must be very careful of the blood line. It would never do to introduce a strain that could be damaging to an entire family or even an entire nation."

When no one responded, Marie babbled on, "If anyone in my family said they were in love, people would have looked at them as though they had two heads! It's not a thing anyone would have discussed. It…"

"Even if they didn't discuss it," Ella interrupted, "it doesn't mean they didn't feel it."

"Not everyone feels as deeply as you do, Ella," Serge said.

She heard herself swallow. "Perhaps not everyone does but I believe that Alix and Nicky do."

"So do I," said Willy loudly, approaching Serge with an air of confrontation. "Not allowing one's heart to rule one's head is important but there is nothing worse than a cold fish devoid of all feeling."

Serge turned away and fumbled with his ring.

"I agree with Marie," Miechen said. "In this case, the question of feelings doesn't enter into it. What matters is whether or not Alix will make a suitable tsarina. I think everyone is aware of my opinion about that. Considering the blood line..."

Suddenly the door flew open and Alix and Nicky appeared. Their faces were grave and Ella's heart sank. Then Nicky, gazing at Alix, began to speak, "I have asked Alix if she would do me the honour of becoming my wife and, to my amazement, she has accepted."

A moment of stunned silence, then a shriek of delight and Ella flew from her chair, threw her arms around each of them in turn, kissing and hugging them and gushing with congratulatory excitement.

"Oh, thank God! I am so very, very happy for you both! Truly I am! Oh thank God! Thank God!"

With a hundred good wishes, she chattered excitedly and soon everyone, even Miechen, joined in the embraces and kisses while the Kaiser's laughter boomed and everyone fussed and pressed them with questions about when the wedding would be.

"The sooner the better," Nicky said. "We have waited long enough already."

"Spring would be best, don't you think?" Ella said and, while she and the others gushed about arrangements, chapels, cathedrals and relatives, Alix smiled silently, with a rising apprehension in her stomach. Everyone had an opinion: where and when she should convert, whom she should speak with, where they would be married, and she felt herself increasingly caught up in an eddy that was swirling her uncontrollably into places she would rather not go. If only, she thought, she and Nicky could run away together and be alone; a secluded church and a quiet ceremony...But, even as that dream crossed her mind, there came the awareness that in consenting to be Nicky's wife, she was also consenting to the public role of consort of one of the most powerful rulers in the world.

"Your parents will be ecstatic," Ella smiled at Nicky.

"Yes, I will send word at once."

"Well," said Marie, "with so much to be grateful for, perhaps you would all like to join me for a service of thanksgiving in the chapel?"

"Yes, yes," Ella said, already almost falling to her knees with gratitude, "but first we must go and break the news to Grandmama."

The cold wet weather and the solemn religious services of Holy Week could not dampen Ella's elation. Though the rain poured all week, there was nothing but laughter and merriment as she and her sisters visited Darmstadt, shopped for gifts, had their photographs taken, visited a toy factory in Coburg and gathered flowers in the countryside. Even through the sad pilgrimage to her parents' grave, she smiled, convinced that through their prayers her dream had been realized.

It was with a lighter heart than when she arrived, that she bade goodbye to Alix when she and Victoria set off for England. It was touching to see how, despite her fears, Grandmama had graciously given Nicky her blessing.

"You will take great care of her, won't you?" she said to Ella.

"Of course, I will. I will do everything I can to ease her into her new role. Try not to worry. She will flourish in Russia. There is so much good she can do for Nicky and the country, and I just know that the good Russian people are going to love her!"

Chapter 23 - October 1894

Konstantin stood at entrance to the library, watching Ella busy herself among the shelves. So engrossed was she in her task that he had little inclination to distract her, preferring instead to relish the sheer aesthetic pleasure of being in the presence of beauty. Time and familiarity had not lessened her loveliness. If anything, he thought, she was even more beautiful now than when he first saw her a decade ago on the platform in Petersburg. She ran her fingers over the spines of the books with the same delicate touch with which she played the piano, and the tranquil expression of her features was that of a musician enraptured by some gentle air.

At length, pulling two hefty tomes from the shelf, she turned and caught sight of him, "Kostia, what a pleasant surprise!"

"I came to see Serge but he's in a meeting and they said I would find you here."

She set the heavy tomes down on the desk beside several other volumes, "I was just selecting more books to send to Alix."

He tilted his head to read the spines: theological discourses and lives of the saints.

"She's studying Orthodoxy avidly in preparation for her conversion," Ella smiled, "and she devours everything so eagerly that I can hardly find enough books to satisfy her." She paused for a moment, "I'm glad you're here. Maybe you could give me your opinion on something I've been wondering about."

"For what my opinion is worth."

She smiled, "I know that Alix would like her conversion to be a quiet, private service but do you think it would be better if she could be persuaded to make it a more public event?"

"What difference does it make?"

"It will be her first official ceremony and it will give people the opportunity to see her. People have some odd ideas and, if it's done in private, they might think she has something to hide. First impressions are so important, aren't they?"

He nodded and picked up one of the books, "She understands Russian?"

"Not fluently yet, but I sent my reader, Ekaterina Schneider, to give her lessons. I hear she's making good progress."

"Quite a daunting prospect, isn't it, for one so young?"

"Learning Russian?"

He laughed and shook his head, "I meant marrying the future Tsar."

"I'm sure she's equal to the task and we are doing everything we can to prepare her for it. I was rather hoping that Nicky would be able to take these to her in Darmstadt as planned but, since Sasha's unwell, he thought it better to postpone the visit."

"Ah," Konstantin said, "that was why I wanted to speak with Serge. Before Sasha left Petersburg, he was complaining of a weakness in his legs but he didn't make much of it so I was surprised to hear that illness had prevented him from travelling abroad as he intended. He's alright, isn't he?"

"It's overwork," Ella sighed. "His doctors advised him to rest but he wouldn't. While he was at the hunting lodge in Spala, some kind of kidney complaint was diagnosed but now that they've moved on to the Crimea, the sea air is doing him a world of good."

Konstantin smiled with relief, "I'm pleased to hear it. Rumour had it that he was at death's door."

"Oh good heavens, no!" Ella smiled. "He just needs a rest. If it were anything more serious, Serge would have gone to him at once. As it is, he and Vladimir are trying to keep everything running smoothly until he recovers."

Konstantin sat down and rested his elbow on the library table, "What about Nicky?"

"He's with his parents, of course, keeping their spirits up."

"But isn't he taking on some of the Tsar's responsibilities? I mean, as heir, wouldn't this be an ideal opportunity for him to learn the ropes, as it were?"

She appeared startled for a moment, then said brightly, "You know, Kostia, you're right. Perhaps you would mention it to Serge and he could start to involve Nicky more."

"Hmm," Konstantin thought aloud, "it might be better if *you* were to speak of it to Serge. I don't think he would take too kindly to my interference."

She laughed, "I am only a foolish woman. What do I know about government?"

There was such a mischievous light in her eyes, and such depths of understanding that warmth seemed to emanate from her like a radiant glow of pure light. He carelessly flicked through the religious tome on the table in front of him and, before he had even realized what he was thinking, he found himself saying, "Ella, if a man has a weakness, a vice, a sin that he struggles to overcome and yet he cannot overcome it, do you think that God takes into account his efforts to amend his ways even when he fails?"

She sat down at the other side of the table and looked at him curiously.

"I mean," he struggled to explain, "if a man feels driven to do something and he knows it's wrong and he prays that the desire for this sin will go away but it doesn't go away, what does it say of him? What does it say of God?"

"I suppose that as long as we're alive, we are subject to all kinds of temptations. It's the nature of our humanity, and God doesn't condemn us for that. Christ himself was tempted in the desert."

"But he didn't yield to temptation."

"No, he set us an example that we, too, can overcome whatever the devil throws at us. We can only try to act on our higher impulses and, little by little, overcome our weaknesses and learn to resist temptations."

"And if we fail?"

"We try again and keep on trying."

He sat back, stretched out his legs and sighed. For so long he had wanted to unburden himself, and here, with her, in the serenity of her atmosphere, the words that had eluded him, flowed freely.

"Supposing that we are tempted but do not act on our temptations, then no sin is committed?"

"No."

"But if the desire for sin remains?"

"Then we must pray for strength and try to replace that desire with a better one. It seems to me that all our unlawful passions are simply misplaced desires for what is good and true. We can't crush them but we can redirect them and transform them. There's great liberation in that."

He leaned forwards, "Sometimes I don't *want* to lose the desire for sin. Part of me despises myself for it and I make firm resolutions to change but then

I find myself thinking of the sin and it becomes so attractive and irresistible to me that, even when I avoid acting on my lower impulses, in my mind I am still sinning."

Suddenly he felt a warmth on his hand as her fingers clasped his own, "Kostia," she whispered, "you look so troubled. What is it that's disturbing you so much?"

"People think well of me, don't they?"

"Yes," she squeezed his hand and smiled, "everyone loves you! You're a kind man, understanding and perceptive and…"

"They don't know me. I have something on my conscience that weighs me down and, if people knew of it, they would despise me."

"No," she said, "we're all sinners. There are faults in all of us that cause us shame but, whatever it is, you can overcome it."

He withdrew his hand, "I can't! I try and try and I can't. I'm sorry, I had no right to burden you with this."

He stood up and moved towards the door but she flew around the table and caught his arm, "Kostia, don't leave like this. I'm your friend. Let me help you, if I can."

Her eyes were so transparent that her very soul seemed to be shining through them - a soul so luminous and so pure that even to look at her heightened his sense of his own vileness.

"My sin," he said, "is a vice so…"

"Ella," Serge suddenly burst through the door, "we need to…" Catching sight of Konstantin he broke off. "Kostia, I'm sorry I haven't time to be more hospitable but news has just arrived from the Crimea."

"Sasha?"

"His condition has deteriorated. Minnie has sent for Father Ioann. We must leave for Livadia at once."

It was hard to believe that the invalid lying in the Livadia Palace was the same gentle giant whom Ella had grown to love. The Tsar, who had once supported the roof of a train on his shoulders, could now barely raise his own head. Determinedly bright in his presence, Minnie assured him that soon he would feel better but later, out of his hearing, she tearfully confessed her deepest fears.

"Father Ioann has the gift of healing," Ella said desperately.

"This time his prayers are of no avail. I think Sasha is beyond healing."

"No," Nicky said, determinedly, "he *will* recover."

Ella reached for his hand and he gripped hers tightly, choking back his tears, "I need Alix. I need her with me now more than ever."

"Yes," Minnie sniffed, "we should send for her."

A telegram was dispatched and the reply came promptly, followed by further messages for Ella.

"Victoria will travel with her as far as Poland, if someone could meet her at Warsaw?"

Blank faces stared back at her gloomily. Nicky dared not leaves his father's side.

"I'll go," Ella whispered.

The two-day journey to Warsaw seemed to last an eternity and, with each passing mile, she prayed that they would make it back to Livadia in time. The façade of optimism had collapsed and her hope for Sasha's recovery was replaced by prayers that the family would cope with his loss.

It was an anxious Alix who greeted her on the platform in Warsaw, and there was little time for exchanging pleasantries with Victoria before changing trains for the return journey.

"How serious is it?" Alix eventually found the courage to ask.

She could only shake her head in reply.

"Oh, dear Nicky!" Alix gasped. "What a responsibility lies on him! Imagine having to carry on and run the country in his father's place and, at the same time, bearing all the anxiety and sorrow of seeing him so ill."

"Vladimir and Serge have taken on most of Sasha's responsibilities," Ella said reassuringly.

"But they refer everything to Nicky?"

"He is so distressed at the moment. He has enough to endure without the added burden of government."

Alix nodded and Ella reached for her hand, "I know what a difficult time this will be for you. It's not going to be easy meeting all of the family in such circumstances but you need not be nervous. I am there for you and will help you in any way I can."

"And I will be there for Nicky," she said.

They spoke very little for the rest of the journey but, as train crossed the Polish border, a terrible thought struck Ella. In all the haste and panic, no one had given due thought to the importance of Alix's arrival. With no guard of honour to receive her, the future Empress of all the Russias was making her unceremonious entry into the country unnoticed. Something seemed dreadfully wrong. The whole atmosphere of death and mourning seemed to portend a future far darker than anyone could imagine. She tried to shake the thoughts from her head and told herself it was only fatigue that brought such ominous feelings of imminent disaster.

At last, the train reached the station in Alushta where Serge and Nicky were waiting to accompany them for the three and a half-hour carriage ride to Livadia. Nicky, beside himself with worry, embraced a tearful Alix, while Ella whispered to Serge,

"Is there any improvement?"

He shook his head. His face was pale and his eyes narrow from lack of sleep, "I fear the worst."

"Poor Nicky," Ella murmured.

"Poor Russia!" said Serge.

The bedroom door was ajar and, on the corridor outside, everyone spoke in hushed voices, turning their faces away from the weeping Tsarina who paced to and fro, trying to stem her tears. At the sight of his mother's distress, Nicky stifled a sob and, when she opened her arms to greet him, he flew to her and they stood for several minutes unmoving in their shared grief. At length, he stepped back and Minnie turned to Alix, "Thank you for coming," she said.

Too choked to reply, Alix could only nod.

"Sasha is so pleased that you've come. He insisted on getting up and dressing for the occasion. Would you like to come through?"

After wiping her tears and preparing a smile, Minnie pushed open the door.

"Sasha," she whispered, "Alix has arrived."

His cheeks hollow and his eyes sunken, he was sitting in a military uniform that hung loosely over his wasted limbs and, were it not for his medals and stars of office, Alix might not have recognized him. On seeing her, he smiled and tried to stand, causing

Minnie to rush to his side, "No, no, don't tire yourself!"

He yielded and, sitting down again, opened his arms in greeting. In a voice so weak it was scarcely heard, he said, "Alix, it is so good of you to have come."

She knelt before him, "You need not have dressed. You should be resting in bed."

"It would never do for the Tsar of all the Russias to greet Russia's future Empress in his pyjamas!"

More as a release of tension than amusement, everyone laughed but the laughter was short lived.

"Nicky needs you," Sasha said, "now more than ever. He is going to need so much help, so much support. What a legacy I am leaving him!"

"I *will* support him, always," she said, barely able to restrain her tears.

"I know," he nodded, then leaned back exhausted.

Minnie tapped Alix's shoulder, "Come, let's leave him to rest now."

The days dragged slowly by in bedside vigils, prayers and streams of tears. Daily, more members of the extended family arrived and, as each one came and went from the sickroom, it seemed to Alix that there wasn't a moment when someone wasn't weeping, and the weight of Nicky's grief lay so heavily on her heart. Only the beautiful views from the windows, and the presence of the saintly Father Ioann eased the oppressive gloom. Servants carried bags of oxygen into the sickroom, and the doctors stood in conference with Minnie, while Vladimir and Serge strutted along the corridors, armed with documents and issuing orders. Nicky, paler by the day, stood helplessly on the balcony, gazing over the Black Sea, his hands clasped as though in prayer, his eyes dimmed by fear.

Alix moved to his side and gently took his arm, "What do the doctors say?"

"Ask Mama. She has all the dealings with them."

"But you're the heir, Nicky. They should come to you first."

"Mama prefers it this way. It's the only comfort she has."

She looked down at the courtyard below, where Serge was handing documents to messengers bound for Petersburg.

"Nicky, you have to take charge. Your papa's authority belongs to you now. Don't let them push you aside, like this."

He seemed startled, "They know what they're doing, far better than I do."

"No," she said firmly, "you have to be strong. You have to tell them, demand it of them. Tell the doctors they must come to you first each day, and tell Serge and Vladimir that they are not to issue orders without informing you. If you let them take charge now, what will happen when…"

His blue eyes were fixed on her with such sorrow.

"Please," she said, "I know it's a terrible time but you must try to be strong."

He nodded and bit his lip, "I will. I will."

They stood in silence clasping each other's hands and letting the sea breeze blow the sadness from their eyes.

"If Papa…" Nicky stopped, swallowed and began again, "If anything happens to Papa, Alix, I don't think I can continue on my own. If you go back to Germany, I don't know how I will cope."

"I won't leave you," she promised, "I won't *ever* leave you. You're not alone now. I'm with you and I'll help you to be strong."

He kissed her and they turned back to the bedroom where a great crowd of relatives had gathered, some standing erect, others cowering in corners, dabbing their tears with handkerchiefs.

Nicky's eyes travelled around the room, "Poor Ella," he said, "what a way to spend her thirtieth birthday."

"I think she has quite forgotten it. Neither she nor anyone else is in the mood for celebration."

Sasha's breathing was laboured and he gasped as he tried to raise his arm from the bed to summon the priest. Father Ioann leaned over him, and everyone dropped to their knees, blessing themselves as he spoke the prayer.

"Minnie," Sasha whispered. She pressed her face to his and he kissed her.

One lingering breath. Everyone waited. Silence.

The Tsarina pierced the silence with a loud sob, and the priest chanted his prayers for the dead.

"Sandro," Nicky choked, as his cousin took him in his arms and led him to the balcony, "what am I going to do? What are we all going to do? I'm not fit to be Tsar; I never wanted to be Tsar! I'm not ready for this! Oh, poor Papa, poor Mama, poor Russia!"

Chapter 24

"Man proposes but God disposes," sighed Queen Victoria, moving slowly from the window to her desk.

Beatrice nodded, "And what a ghastly ordeal that funeral must have been. Two whole weeks the coffin lay open as they moved him from place to place and at every stop the whole family kissed the corpse. Can you imagine?"

"A very gloomy race, the Russians," said the Queen, choosing to forget her own excessive mourning for beloved Albert.

She glanced at the sketch of Alix and Nicky's wedding in the newspaper, "All the plans in disarray. Everything rushed: her conversion, the wedding...Good heavens! There can't have been such a gloomy wedding since Alice's just after your dear papa's passing." She closed her eyes, recalling the dreary scene in Osborne House over thirty years before.

Beatrice picked up the newspaper, "The reports say that Nicky looked pale and both Alix and his mother wept throughout the ceremony."

"It's hardly surprising, is it? They say he's totally unprepared for all that responsibility, and his dear mother is heartbroken. They all are."

"At least the crowds were enthusiastic," Beatrice's eyes moved over the article and her expression became more serious, "or rather *some* of the crowds were enthusiastic."

"What does it say?"

She folded the paper and shoved it across the desk, "It's probably something invented by the journalists. You know how these newspaper people like to create melodramas."

260

"What does it say?" the Queen asked more forcefully.

With obvious reluctance, Beatrice picked up the paper, "*There were whispers in the crowd that 'she has come to us behind a coffin'. Is this an ill-omen for Tsarina Alexandra Feodorovna?*"

The Queen shook her head in despair, "This is the worst kind of start for her. A private conversion, the joyless wedding, plunged totally unprepared into all that responsibility, and such an unsafe throne, where her husband's life is constantly threatened. My blood runs cold when I think of them."

"I'm tired of this game," Miechen placed her cards on the green baize table and looked from Vladimir to Konstantin and Mavra. "Card games are so tedious and this one seems to have been going on for hours. After all this gloom we could do with a ball or something lively to cheer everyone up."

"A ball," Vladimir said, "is hardly appropriate in a time of mourning."

"And we have a great deal to mourn," she replied. "We've not only lost Sasha but also the prospect of any more great St. Petersburg seasons."

She pushed back her chair and, to Konstantin's astonishment, put music on the phonographic cylinder and invited him to dance.

"I don't think..." he began, but she took his hand, dragged him from the chair and waltzed him around the room. He moved stiffly, unwillingly and, when she realized he would not participate in her frivolity, she sat down again with a sigh.

"Minnie was so *good* at arranging these things. She knew how to organize the best balls in Europe. Alas! They're all over now."

"Once the year of mourning is over," Mavra said, "things will be back to normal."

"You honestly believe they can *ever* be back to normal with the little mouse of a Tsar and his little mousy Tsarina?"

"Miechen!" Konstantin looked to Vladimir for support, "That's outrageous, treasonous even!"

She laughed, "Oh, don't be so stuffy! He might be the Tsar to the rest of the country, but within the family he is just a boy and very foolish and lost little boy, I should say."

Vladimir cleared his throat and it seemed to Konstantin he was stifling laughter.

"He is God's chosen Tsar," Konstantin said, with rising anger. "He is anything but foolish and, if he is lost, it's our duty to support him until he finds his way through the intricate web of government."

Miechen's laughter faded, "He has all the guidance he needs. Serge is going out of his way to see to that. Interesting, isn't it, that he's not yet returned to Moscow? Obviously, he's not satisfied with ruling that little domain; he wants to dominate Petersburg as well."

"He postponed his return to Moscow so he and Ella could be of help to the young Tsar and Tsarina."

"He was certainly quick to get his snout in the trough, and it's all worked out wonderfully for him." She picked up the playing cards and built them into a pyramid. "Everything perfectly balanced," she smiled cynically. "Serge dominates Ella. Ella dominates her little sister. Her little sister dominates the little Tsar. So Serge dominates all of them and, since he hasn't a thought in his head other than his own ambition..." She flicked the cards over, "Poof! The whole lot comes crashing down."

Konstantin pushed back his chair, "I refuse to hear any more of this. It surprises and shocks me, Vladimir, that you allow this kind of treasonous talk. Come, Mavra, we're leaving."

Vladimir jumped to his feet, "Oh please, please, Kostia! Don't you see Miechen is just goading you? It's a release, that's all, after the sadness of recent weeks."

Konstantin looked at her dubiously and she lowered her head in sham repentance.

"Nicky's a good boy," she said eventually. "He's kind and loving and if he simply adopts the views of the last person he spoke to and has no ideas of his own, it is only because he's so trusting and caring and takes time to listen to people."

Her thinly disguised insult was more than Konstantin could stand and he would have walked out at that moment had Mavra not reached for his hand and gently pulled him back to his chair.

"It must be very difficult for the young Tsarina," she said. "Everything is still so foreign to her, and the way she rose to the occasion and agreed to bring the wedding forward, with no fuss or anything, is truly admirable."

"Yes," Konstantin nodded firmly, "it *is* admirable. And it's admirable that she loves him and he loves her. They will set a fine example of domestic harmony and morality to the whole of the country."

"Yes they will," Miechen smiled, "and domestic harmony and morality is just what the bourgeoisie love! They'd make a perfect English squire and his lady, or the grand duke and duchess of some little backwater in Germany. The question is, are they able to play their part on the glittering stage of the finest court in the world? I can't for the life of me imagine Alix shining in a ballroom as Minnie did. Her French accent is atrocious and she barely speaks a word of Russian. In fact she barely speaks a word in public at all. She stands there tongue-tied and blushing with little red blotches all over her neck. The people want sparkle, verve, gusto! Not a meek little hausfrau!"

"I don't think," said Vladimir quietly, "she is quite as meek as she appears. She certainly knows her own mind and, even at Livadia when she'd just arrived, she wasn't backwards in telling Nicky to exert more authority. I think she might surprise us all."

Arm in arm, Alix and Ella strolled through the snow-covered gardens of the Anichkov Palace, sharing memories of Darmstadt and enjoying the afternoon sun.

"It's so lovely to be outdoors," Alix smiled, breathing the fresh winter air. "I think I must take after Grandmama with her dislike of stuffy rooms."

"I know it can't be easy living here with Minnie. When you're first married you need to arrange your own household and have things done your way. It would have been like that if the wedding hadn't been brought forward."

Alix nodded, "I'm not complaining. It's just how things have worked out and our rooms here are so cramped."

"It won't be for much longer. Your rooms in the Winter Palace will be ready soon after New Year."

"It's not only for our sake," Alix said, kicking at the snow. "I can't help feeling that Minnie doesn't really like us being here. Or rather, doesn't like *me* being here. I feel she resents me."

Ella stopped, "In what way?"

"It's hard to put my finger on it. I just feel it. It's as though she wants Nicky all to herself. She is always telling him what to do and discussing all kinds of governmental things with him but she excludes me completely."

Ella nodded. Though reluctant to confess it, she had noticed it, too.

"It's difficult for her," she said tactfully. "She's still heartbroken about Sasha and misses him so much and she's so used to being the Tsarina that handing over that role, on top of all the other changes, is probably too much for her all at once. Little by little, she'll let go of the strings and leave you to get on with it."

"I *do* appreciate what she's going through," Alix said, "and I am trying to be understanding but I wish she would show the same deference to Nicky as she showed to his father. He is perfectly capable of making decisions without all her interference."

"She is only trying to help. Nicky's responsibilities are so vast and, as his mother, she wants to support him."

"But people seem to forget that he is the Tsar now. They still treat him like a son, a nephew, a cousin, a child...and Nicky is so kind-hearted that he won't demand anything for himself because he doesn't want to upset them."

"All that will change in time. It's such early days, that's all."

"And *because* it's early days, it's vital that we show them who is in charge. If they get away with these little infringements now, there'll be no stopping them. It's much easier to let out the reins slowly than it is to draw them back in. He has to show them, all of them, that he is the Tsar and he doesn't need them to tell him what to do. And I mean *all* of them, Ella, *all* his uncles."

Taken aback by the intensity in her tone, Ella frowned, "Serge is only trying to help him."

"I know that and Nicky knows that, too, and we appreciate it, but he doesn't need that kind of help. Nicky is the autocrat. Nicky makes the rules and if he wants help and advice he will ask for it."

Too stunned to reply, Ella nodded and walked on.

"I've noticed," Alix said, after a while, "that Grandmama was right about the aristocracy here. The decadence is quite appalling. They seem to find all the flirtations and affairs amusing and they fritter away their lives and their fortunes, going from one distraction to the next without doing the least bit of good."

"Some of them, perhaps," Ella smiled, "but…"

"I saw a woman with her dress cut so low that she was almost falling out of it. What kind of example is that setting? These things wouldn't go on in Grandmama's court."

"But this isn't Grandmama's court. This is Russia."

"And Russia is *my* court now."

Is this really Alix? Ella thought. She was so adamant and certain of everything; not at all the malleable little girl she remembered from Darmstadt.

"I intend to give them something better to do than waste their time in a useless round of entertainment. Aunt Lenchen established a wonderful nurse training school in England. I'm going to do that here. If I set an example as Mama did, visiting the sick in their own homes as well as in the hospitals, I might be able to engage some of the aristocracy to participate in similar ventures. That way they will win the hearts of the people and use their positions and their wealth for good, rather than just squandering everything."

"They're wonderful ideas," Ella agreed, "but it might take a little time to implement them. It would be better not to rush into anything too quickly. It's quite a different place from Hesse or England. The people are happy for us to patronise charities but they don't expect us to become too actively involved as they think it spoils the mystique of the Imperial Family. The aristocracy are so set in their ways that any attempt to rush them into change would be only give rise to resentment. I know when I first came here I wanted to go out and do all the things Mama used to do but Serge wouldn't allow it. He said it was demeaning to the family."

"Yes," said Alix, "but you were only a grand duchess bound by the mores of the court. *I* am the Empress and, whether the aristocracy like it or not, I set the standards now."

Chapter 25 - Moscow - May 1896

From dawn till dusk the hammering of builders, joiners, masons and decorators echoed across Red Square and pounded through the Kremlin windows. From the streets, crowded with workmen making the final preparations for the coronation, the fresh spring winds blew thick clouds of dust into the Nieskcushnoe Palace where Ella worked her way through countless letters and requests.

There was so little time to rest. As Governor General, Serge was responsible for the whole operation and, with characteristic diligence, he was wearing himself out, ensuring that everything would go perfectly. New buildings had been erected, old buildings cleaned, painted or whitewashed. Every detail required minute organisation, from the order of precedence in the procession to the role of each individual guest. Princes, dukes and ambassadors had to be accommodated, and arrangements made for the masses of ordinary Russians lining the route. Not forgetting the fate of his father, Serge had to guarantee the safety of the Imperial Family without alienating the crowds by preventing them from drawing close enough to see their new Emperor.

All day, amid the noise and turmoil, Ella had worked through the letters - a countess requesting a role for her son, a princess asking for a place at the ceremony - and, besides all the foreign dignitaries, there were numerous members of the family to house. She sat back and stretched. Her joints ached from the hours at the desk but she smiled in exhausted satisfaction. Everything would be perfect. Everything had to be perfect. This was the one chance for Alix and Nicky to reveal themselves as the true Tsar and Tsarina: the Little Father and Little Mother of the people, the leaders of society, and the stars of the glittering show that was the Russian court.

Now, more than ever, Alix would step into the limelight and shine sufficiently to impress not only Nicky's subjects but also the aristocracy and the whole Imperial Family. Now they would see that she was an empress worthy of respect and love. It was impossible to deny that the eighteen months since her arrival in Russia had been difficult for Alix and, despite her best intentions, she had not endeared herself to the court. Her shyness was mistaken for arrogance, her morals mocked as prudishness, and her efforts to engage the aristocracy in useful work had met with nothing but contempt. Ella sighed. Compared to her own spectacular entry into Russia, Alix appeared to be failing in every respect but Ella cheered herself with the thought that, in one area at least, Alix had the advantage. A year after the wedding, she had given birth to a daughter, Olga. True, her pregnancy had brought a recurrence of the illnesses she had suffered since childhood. Constant headaches, sciatica and fatigue had kept her confined to bed for long periods and her seclusion increased the public perception of her haughtiness. True, too, that since the Salic law precluded females from the throne, the country was still awaiting an heir, but Olga was healthy and strong and it was only a matter of time before a boy-child would be born.

Ella folded the last of her letters, handed them to Countess Olsuvieva and sauntered towards Serge's study. As she neared the door, familiar laughter echoed along the corridor and she quickened her pace, eager to greet the visitor.

"Pavel!" she smiled brightly and he turned to greet her with a kiss.

"Your last evening of freedom before the onslaught!" he laughed. "Serge tells me all the family is arriving tomorrow. Are they all staying here?"

"Nicky and Alix are staying at the Petrovskoe Palace," Serge said, distractedly shuffling papers across his desk. "They can't stay within the city as they have to make their symbolic entrance on the day of the coronation."

Pavel turned to Ella, "All your family are coming, too?"

"Yes, *all* of them."

"Wonderful!"

She looked at him for several seconds, trying to work out what had changed. There was something different about him: a brightness, a gleam in his eye that had been absent since the death of Alexandra, and he laughed readily as though brimming with an inexplicable joy.

"What is it?" she said, smiling. "There's something different about you. You look so…"

"Happy?" he skipped from one foot to another.

"Yes."

"I *am* happy. I haven't been so happy since…I can't remember."

"Do coronations always have this effect on you?"

"Coronation, what coronation?" He laughed again, "Coronations are ten a penny but the love of a beautiful woman is priceless."

Ella's heart sank but she forced herself to smile, "Who is she?"

He tapped his finger on the side of his nose, "That would be telling."

"I think this is complete," Serge said, suddenly standing up, with his eyes fixed on a paper. "The ceremony, the singers, the lighting…" He broke off and looked up, "The Khodinka meadow! I must check with Vorontsov that it's all arranged."

"Khodinka?" Pavel frowned, "The old army training ground?"

He nodded, "It's the best place for the free food and souvenirs to be distributed to the people after the coronation. There's plenty of room there and it shouldn't be too difficult to police. Will you excuse me?"

Clutching his papers, he strode out of the room. Pavel, shaking his head, turned to Ella, "He never stops, does he? All work and no play…"

"He wants to make sure everything is perfect," she smiled. "He's exhausted but he won't rest until he's covered every eventuality to make sure nothing can go wrong."

Pavel sat down at Serge's desk, took a cigarette from a box and, lighting it, smiled up at the ceiling.

"Come on," Ella said, moving closer, "I can see you're longing to tell me. Who is she?"

He smiled.

"Is there to be a new grand duchess?"

His lips flickered and his smile faded slightly, "I don't think that will be possible."

Intrigued, she leaned across the desk, searching his eyes for clues.

"She's called Olga. Olga von Pistolkors."

The name was unfamiliar.

"She's beautiful, Ella. After Alexandra, I never thought I would find happiness again until I met her. And now, suddenly everything is brighter and the future holds so much promise."

Torn with the conflicting emotions of joy in his happiness and the powerful longing she always felt in his presence, she asked, "She's not royal?"

"No."

"So marriage is impossible?"

He nodded, "And there's another impediment. She's already married. Her husband is a captain in my regiment and Vladimir's aide-de-camp."

She stepped back in shock, "You're having an affair with a married woman?"

"Her husband means nothing to her. She wants a divorce and if it wasn't for her children..."

"Oh Pavel! Can't you see what you're doing? This is wrong on every level. For one thing, you're responsible for the men in your regiment - you can't take their wives! It's a serious abuse of your position. And for another thing, it's...adultery!"

"Don't be like that," he said, pushing back the chair and coming around to her side of the desk. "Just see the effect she has on me. I found it so difficult after Alexandra died. I could hardly bear to spend time with the children because of all the reminders of her. Yet, since I met Olga, I enjoy their company so much more and I..."

She stepped back from him, "What of *her* children? What of her husband?"

"I hoped you'd understand," he said disappointedly. "I hoped you'd be happy for me."

"I'm sorry but I don't understand, and how can I be happy to watch you making such a terrible mistake? Nothing can come of it, you know that. Why put yourself and her family through something that can only lead to unhappiness?"

He silently put out his cigarette.

"Does Serge know?" she said.

"Yes."

"What did he say?"

"Same as you."

All the excitement had gone from his eyes and in its place was a wounded expression.

"Oh, Pavel," she said gently, reaching for his arm, "you know that we only want what's best for you."

"No," he shook his head, "you're not interested at all in what's best for me. You're only interested in what's best for the family - what *looks* best for the family. It's all sham and appearances."

"In our position, we have a duty to..."

"Don't preach to me, Ella. I don't need it. I love Olga, and no sermon is going to alter that."

Whether it was the knowledge that he loved another woman or the fear of how this would end, the optimism she had felt all day evaporated into a cloud of foreboding.

"You've changed, Ella," he said bitterly. "I didn't expect Serge to understand but I thought your heart was big enough to share in my joy."

"I'm sorry," she said, "but I can't."

The next morning, the arrival of Ernie, Ducky, Victoria and her husband, Louis Battenberg, distracted Ella from her thoughts of Pavel; and the arrival, in the evening, of Irène and her husband, Henry of Prussia, revived her high spirits. When Nicky and Alix reached the Petrovskoe Palace, the family reunion was complete and the celebrations began in earnest. Serge led the family onto the balcony to hear a choir of a thousand singers performing a serenade. The voices of the crowds, already gathering to display their fidelity to the Tsar, echoed from the city. Through the warm summer night a new moon appeared in the sky like a portent foretelling a great and glorious reign, and when the sun rose the next morning it spoke of the dawn of a new era.

Through the peal of bells and the resounding cheers of his people, Nicky, mounted a white horse and, surrounded by Cossacks, rode into Moscow. Behind him, in a golden coach, came the Dowager Empress and, after her, the young Tsarina Alexandra. As each coach was greeted with the same fervent acclamations, there was every reason to believe that the people truly loved their Emperor.

At nine-thirty in the morning, Ella took her place with the other grand duchesses to the right of the throne in the Uspensky Cathedral. While choirs chanted and bishops prayed, Nicky, as Head of the Orthodox Church, crowned himself before crowning Alix. One after another, the grand dukes and grand duchesses stepped forward and knelt to take their oath of allegiance to the twenty-eight-year-old Autocrat of all the Russias.

Emerging from the dark cathedral into the sunshine, Ella breathed a sigh of relief. The months of preparation had proved worthwhile: the impressive processions, the splendid ceremony and above all the enthusiasm of the crowds were reward in themselves, but the festivities were only just beginning and Serge still had a special surprise for them all. That evening from a balcony of the Kremlin, the Imperial Family stood in awe as, at the flick of a switch, the beautiful red walls were illuminated by thousands of electric light bulbs.

Day after day, the celebrations continued with balls and receptions and, as Ella and Serge returned one evening from a gala performance at the Bolshoi Theatre, she was too exhausted to pay much attention to the crowds gathering on the Khodinka meadow. Serge commented, "They are coming in their thousands and there's plenty to go round. This will do Nicky's reputation so much good."

Almost sleepwalking, she drifted through the palace and, as she climbed sleepily into bed, Serge said, "Wonderful as all this has been, won't you be relieved when the celebrations are over and we can go back to a quieter life? Tomorrow I have a photograph session with the regiment, and then it's the French ambassador's ball; the next night our ball and after that things will begin to wind down and we can take a welcome break in Ilinskoe."

"I can hardly wait," she smiled and, closing her eyes, dreamed of the peaceful river and birdsong in the birch woods.

Bright morning sunlight streamed through the windows of the Kremlin where Ernie and Ducky sat at opposite sides of the room, staring in different directions: Ernie absorbed in the intricate details of a statue, and Ducky, it seemed to Ella, absorbed in a figure of a quite different kind. Standing lugubriously in an alcove, Miechen's son, Kyril, puffed at a cigarette and threw her occasional glances. Sandro was flirting outrageously with Xenia, while Pavel crouched on the floor, playing a game with his children. Speckles of dust danced on the light-beams and glistened like diamonds through the scents of coffee, cigarettes and cigars. There was a stillness about the morning. Serge sprawled lazily in an armchair, basking in the compliments offered him for having everything planned to perfection.

Suddenly there was a hammering at the door and an ashen-faced officer stepped in and bowed before Serge, "Your Imperial Highness," there was such urgency in his voice that the entire room fell silent. "I have news for you. May I speak with you in private?"

Clearly alarmed, Serge jumped to his feet and, ushering the officer from the room, closed the door behind him.

"What was that all about?" said Ernie, and all eyes turned to Ella.

No wiser than they were but eager to quell any unease, she smiled, "Serge has a photograph session this morning. There's probably some confusion about it. I'll go and see what's happening."

She had convinced no one, least of all herself, but she continued to smile until she had left the room and was almost running to Serge's study. He was standing as he had stood so many times before, drawing frantically on his cigarette, his foot tapping uncontrollably against the hearth. The officer, visibly trembling, mumbled the conclusion of his message, "Count Vorontsov has organized firemen to collect the bodies."

The bodies? Ella felt a tremor through her own, "What's happened?"

Serge turned and his face was as white as the officer's.

"Khodinka," he said, "the stupidity of it. The bloody stupidity of it all!"

He dismissed the officer and kicked viciously at the hearth, "All those crowds gathering on the meadow last night…"

A bomb, she thought, *it must be a bomb.*

"Some ridiculous rumour began in the early hours that there weren't enough souvenirs to go round, so they all started to push closer to the tables where the gifts were. In the darkness no one could see what was happening and, when the people at the back surged forward, a stampede began. The ones at the front were pushed into the trenches and…It's so bloody stupid!"

"Were many people hurt?" she asked, already reading the answer in his eyes.

"Thousands of them," his voice came out in a whisper. "Bodies strewn like litter across the meadow. At first estimate, over a thousand dead."

"Dear God!" she gasped. "We must go at once. We must…" In the horror of the moment her mind leaped from one thought to another, "Nicky needs to know. We must tell the others and then…Shall I go and tell them? No, we'll go. I'll call a carriage…"

Suddenly he was gripping her wrists, "Calm yourself!" he said in an aggressive whisper. "Pull yourself together! We must act as though nothing has happened."

Wide-eyed in horror, she stared at him, "As though nothing has happened? You can't ignore something like this! Nicky needs to be told at once. He'll have to cancel all the celebrations and…"

He shook her violently, "For Christ's sake, shut up! How can I think when you're blabbering like this?"

He let her go and he paced the room, sucking at his cigarette as though gasping for life. "This isn't my responsibility," he said, more to himself than to her. "It's Vorontsov who's to blame. He should have policed it better. We must distance ourselves from it."

"Serge, a thousand people dead! What does it matter who's to blame? What matters now is…"

He glanced at her sternly, "Don't tell me my duty. I *know* my duty. The priority is to protect the family and the Tsar. I will go to the Petrovskoe at lunchtime to tell Nicky what has happened and advise him to continue with all the plans. If people see that we go on as normal, they will know we have a clear conscience."

She shook her head, appalled and astonished. Over a thousand dead and hundreds of others injured and yet he could stand there thinking only of reputations. She turned away from him in disgust, "We must at least go to the meadow and offer what help we can."

"To do that now would be as good as admitting responsibility. It has nothing to do with us. I will go there with Nicky this afternoon for the distribution of the gifts. Right now I have a photographic session to attend."

He walked past her to the door where he turned back, "There was plenty to go round. I organized it to perfection. None of this has anything to do with me."

"May *I* go to the meadow?"

"No."

"Serge, please, I..."

"If people see you there, they will think I sent you." He gripped the door handle, "You are my wife, remember, and you vowed before God to obey me."

Chapter 26

Wagons piled with corpses passed along the road, and Serge turned his face to the opposite window, his lips twitching in some internal conversation. The taut expression of his gaunt features gave him the appearance of a skeleton and the stifled intensity of his emotion was so immense that it filled the closed carriage like a volatile gas in the air. Konstantin dared not speak for fear that a word would ignite his temper and his bottled anger would burst out in an explosion as terrifying as a bomb.

Sandro had no such qualms. Sitting with his back to the horses, he fixed his eyes on Serge with such determination that they might have been pinning him to the seat, "I saw the soldiers of your regiment dispersing before you arrived. They assumed that under such circumstances any decent man would cancel something so trivial as a photograph session."

Without acknowledging him, Serge turned to Konstantin, "Vorontsov is to blame for this."

"Ha!" Sandro shook his head in disgust before muttering, "He's happy to receive the accolades when things go well but as soon as they go wrong he passes the buck."

Again Serge ignored him and this time Konstantin felt obliged to speak.

"Has the French ambassador been informed?"

"Yes."

"So he'll understand why his ball has to be cancelled."

"The ball isn't cancelled. It goes ahead as planned."

Konstantin stared at him in astonishment and even Sandro seemed too stunned to speak.

"It seems," Serge said, looking out of the window as the carriage drew up at the pavilion in the meadow, "that last night's events haven't deterred people from coming to honour the Tsar."

As soon as the carriage stopped, Sandro leaped out as though he could no longer bear to breathe the same air as Serge. Konstantin followed him onto the platform where Alix and Nicky stood surveying the thousands of subjects gathered before them. Nicky's face was pale and, as the crowds joined in the rousing anthem, *God Bless the Tsar,* Alix's eyes filled with tears that she struggled to restrain.

Konstantin stepped closer, "The people love you, Your Majesty."

"Kostia," she whispered, "we have been to the hospital and seen the wounded. So many of them! So many families affected by this tragedy, and still they stand here singing."

"It's a sign of their devotion to the Tsar and to you."

"We will repay their kindness."

The anthems over, Nicky made an address and the distribution of gifts began but even the enthusiastic response of the crowds could not distract from the thick clouds of dust filling the meadow or the sight of the last wagons in the distance, bearing away the dead.

Nicky stepped back into the pavilion and turned to Serge, "Have you informed Montebello that we cannot attend the ball?"

Serge fidgeted with the ring on his finger, "You *must* attend the ball. It's vital. I have told him we continue as planned."

Nicky shook his head, "How can we? Over a thousand of my people dead, so many families in mourning. How can we possibly attend a ball? All further celebrations must be cancelled."

Vladimir stepped forwards and, physically towering over the Tsar, said, "Nicky, this is no time for sentimentality. Franco-Russian relations are vital for the country. After all the expense and effort Montebello has gone to, it would be madness to insult him - to insult his country - by declining his invitation."

"Montebello will understand," Nicky said, "and will report back to his government the reason why it was necessary to cancel."

"And what sort of impression will that make on the French?"

Alix moved closer to Nicky's side, "The impression of a man who has a noble heart and cares deeply about his people."

Vladimir guffawed and Serge shook his head, "They will think the Russian Emperor is weak. A man who cannot control his emotions, will be seen as unfit to control so vast an empire."

A flame of anger shot through Alix's eyes causing Serge to explain, "It makes no difference how things *are,* it's how they appear that matters. We all know why you might want to cancel but we cannot afford to insult the French. What's more, the people here need a strong leader who can show them how to bear their sufferings and continue unaffected by tragedy."

Vladimir, standing close to the Tsar, stretched himself to full height, "Absolutely! The Tsar can't afford to be sentimental."

Nicky looked at Alix, who shook her head helplessly.

"We will attend the ball," he said at last, "but only to show our faces. We are neither of us in the mood for dancing."

Vladimir and Serge smiled at one another triumphantly, and Nicky turned to his aide-de-camp, "See to it that the treasury provides funds so that all my poor subjects who have died today can be given a decent Christian burial. And I want their families and all the injured to be compensated. Use my personal income if necessary."

The heat in the Embassy was stifling with the overpowering scents of the millions of roses imported from the south of France and, though the spectacle was magnificent, to Konstantin's view there was an ominous air about it, reminiscent of Versailles prior to the revolution. The longer he looked around the ballroom, the greater was the sense of impending doom. Sandro and his brothers, in a conspiratorial huddle, threw glances like darts across the room to where Serge and Vladimir laughed and joked before the eyes of the bemused French diplomats. Other guests seemed uncertain whether to celebrate or commiserate with the Tsar and Tsarina who sat in a stupefied haze as though the terrible images of the meadow were too deeply imprinted on their eyes.

A kafuffle and a clicking of heels. Nicky and Alix rose from the supper table, preparing to leave. The next moment, Vladimir and Serge were towering over them with expressions that seemed threatening. Konstantin stepped closer.

"They will be so insulted!" Vladimir was almost bellowing and it struck Konstantin to the core to think he should dare to speak in that way to the Tsar to whom he had so recently taken an oath of allegiance.

Sandro, breaking away from his brothers, took his wife's arm and led her towards Konstantin.

"Serge has to resign. There's nothing else for it."

Xenia agreed, "It's bad enough that he refuses to take responsibility for it, but that he couldn't even be bothered to go at once to the meadow and hasn't shown the slightest remorse is unspeakable!"

Much as it pained him to do so, Konstantin silently concurred.

"You're his friend, Kostia. Has he spoken of it to you?"

"He says it's nothing to do with him."

"He primed Ella to say the same thing to me," Xenia said. "When I tried to discuss it with her, all she would say is, 'Thank God, Serge has nothing to do with all that.'"

"Does Nicky propose to dismiss him?" Konstantin asked.

"He's going to set up an inquiry. He's thinking of appointing Count Pahlen to deal with it."

"And if Count Pahlen does his job properly," Sandro said, "Serge is certain to be found wanting. Nicky will have no alternative but to dismiss him."

"It would be better if he resigned," Konstantin sighed.

The music began and, as Nicky led Alix to the dance floor, Sandro gasped, "I don't believe it! They said they were leaving straight after supper. They're surely not going to dance?"

But they were already dancing and, as they moved in perfect harmony with graceful steps, they seemed to Konstantin no longer two separate beings but one soul in two bodies. The obvious love in their eyes, however, was dimmed this evening by a sadness they could not conceal. The assembled royalties and aristocrats applauded and Sandro's anger seethed.

"Vladimir and Serge have bullied him into this. This isn't what Nicky wanted at all."

"How is this going to look?" Xenia said. "You know what people will say? The callous Tsar danced on the graves of hundreds of his dead subjects."

As soon as the dance was over, the Tsar and Tsarina bade their farewells. Konstantin followed them to the door and, as their carriage disappeared into the night, he wandered on foot into the darkness of the city. At the side of the road, a small group had gathered and were passing a bottle of vodka between them.

"He's worse than the last one," a voice growled. "Even *he* wouldn't have danced on the dead."

"What can you expect with a German bitch of a wife?"

Konstantin stepped back into the shadows.

"Look at us, working like slaves while they strut around in their gilded palaces. We toil and they reap, we die and they dance."

"I'll tell you who's the worst of the lot," a drunken voice slurred, "Grand Duke bloody Serge Alexandrovich."

Someone laughed, "The greatest bugger in Moscow!"

"He beats his wife you know?"

"Aye, and that's not all he does to her!"

More laughter. Cruel, desperate laughter like the laughter of taunting demons - the demons in Konstantin's head.

"If I could get hold of him, do you know what I'd do to him?"

"Blow him to bits like his father?"

"Nah, that's too quick. I'd string him up from the Kremlin and leave him there to rot till the crows pecked out those evil eyes."

A bottle was hurled towards the gates and smashed into a thousand smithereens, "Death to the whole bloody lot of them! Death to the Romanovs! Death to the Tsar!"

Suddenly the glare of a flash lamp dazzled Konstantin and, as he raised his hand to shield his eyes from the light, the silhouettes of several policemen with raised batons appeared. In a moment, amid oaths and cries, the little group was bundled away and only two policemen remained. One shone the flash lamp towards Konstantin.

"Another anarchist, eh? Skulking there in the shadows won't save you." He drew his finger across his throat in a murderous gesture, "Either that or freeze to death in Siberia."

He lunged forwards and suddenly stopped and, shining the lamp more closely, examined Konstantin's features.

"Oh," he bowed, "forgive me, Your Imperial Highness. I didn't recognize you. Forgive me."

Konstantin nodded.

"We can't be too careful, you see. Scum like that need clearing out."

"You make many arrests like this?"

"We keep our eyes and ears open and nip any dissent in the bud. There'll always be anarchists and trouble-causers but we're under strict instructions from the Governor General to stamp them out. We have our spies all over the place so there's nothing for you to worry about, sir."

They bowed again and went on their way, leaving only the echo in Konstantin's ears, "Death to the Romanovs! Death to the Tsar!"

Chapter 27 - Ilinskoe

Sunlight through the lattice of leaves cast a shadow, like a mosaic, across children giggling and rolling like puppies across the lawn. Nicky, relaxed and smiling, gazed fondly at his little daughter, Olga, in the centre of the group. Serge, sitting upright on the garden chair, his legs crossed, his eyes narrow, fingered his beard and stared pointedly at Zinaida's son, Felix.

"Strange little fellow, isn't he?" he said.

Though Ella smiled at him fondly, she had to agree. Twirling his long curls, he skipped daintily to and fro, curtseying like a princess to the daughter of the Tsar.

Zinaida laughed, "I wanted daughters and only have sons so, if Felix likes to play girlish games, I don't complain."

Hearing his name, Felix stepped closer and curtseyed to Serge before putting out a finger and running it over his side.

"You wear corsets like Mama," he said, "I can feel them."

Serge irritably slapped his hand away, "You should teach him some manners, Zinaida."

"He speaks his mind. What can I do?"

"You spoil your sons. It's not good for children to be spoiled."

Felix ran to Ella and she put her arm around his shoulders and smiled affectionately. How could she help but love this strange little boy? His openness was so endearing and, if at times his behaviour lacked decorum, he had a character that never failed to keep her amused. Pavel's son, Dmitri, toddled towards them and, with one hand still clinging to

Ella, Felix slipped the other into Dmitri's hand, drawing him closer.

"You're my very best friend, Dmitri," he said, placing a kiss on his cheek. Then an anxious expression clouded his smile and he looked ruefully at Ella, "My joint best friend with you," and he kissed her cheek, too.

All the while, Dmitri's sister, Marie, sat sulkily on the grass, viewing the whole proceedings with a surly expression that suggested she was about to cry.

"Oh dear," said Alix. "That is not a happy face."

The surly expression became more of a pout, "Where is Papa? I want to be with Papa."

"Dmitri, go and play with your sister," Serge said sharply, and Felix cheekily stuck out his tongue.

Ella concealed a smile and pretended not to notice as Felix, laughing now, went galloping away into the trees, pursued by Dmitri and Marie and a fluster of nursery maids and nannies.

Alix pushed back her chair and took Olga in her arms, cooing over her and smothering her face with kisses.

"I thought Pavel always used to come here with you," she said. "Why didn't he want to join you this year?"

"Pavel," said Ella bitterly, "has found better company."

Alix frowned and Nicky sat forward, "I can't approve of it but I love Uncle Pavel and the last thing I want is to drive him away from us. If I were to condemn all the grand dukes who keep mistresses, the palaces would be empty."

"He should be *here* with his children," Ella said. "They are not our responsibility and he has a duty to them."

"I have no objection to caring for them," Serge said, which irked Ella still more. He pushed back his chair, stood up and stretched, "Actually, Nicky, I have some worse news. She's expecting his child."

Ella swallowed.

"Does her husband know it's Pavel's?" Nicky said.

Serge nodded, "He's divorcing her, and Pavel is speaking of marrying her now."

"No," Nicky said adamantly, "absolutely not. There's no way I can sanction that."

"I know. I have told him so and he has given me his word that he won't do anything without your permission."

"I can never grant him that permission. If he married her, I would have no alternative but to impose the strictest penalties on him and banish him from the country as my father did when Uncle Mitia married without permission."

"And in Mitia's case," Ella said, "the woman he married wasn't the wife of a captain in his regiment."

Not wanting to prolong the conversation, she reached for her parasol and stood up, "It's very warm here; shall we walk in the shade for a while?"

They strolled along the pathways and gathered wild strawberries as they had done on her first visit to Ilinskoe. Nicky's easy manner and Zinaida's laughter were refreshing after the stress of recent months and the customary stiltedness of Serge's conversation. There was something so restful in their company that she began to dread the day of their departure and the thought of being alone again with Serge.

She glanced at him: how thin he had become and how tired he looked after devoting himself so diligently to the coronation preparations. It seemed unjust that, after all his painstaking planning, the tragedy had marred the entire event and led to even greater antipathy towards him within the family and right across Moscow. She pitied him and her heart softened towards him but almost immediately came the memory of his response to the news: his utter disregard for the wounded and dead; his denial of all responsibility and his unyielding insistence that he knew what was best for everyone, even the Tsar. All these things had created such a rift between them and any attempt she had made to bridge that gulf had been met with rebuttals or a refusal even to discuss it.

She recalled the earliest days of their marriage when he sat in the boat, here at Ilinskoe, confessing his difficulty in expressing emotion. *"I learned to hide all my feelings from other people and I hid them so deeply that at times I have thought I had lost them completely...It's as though I built a wall around my heart..."* he had said. For a few brief months she had hoped that she might help him dismantle that wall and regain the gentleness that fear had hidden away. But now? She sighed inwardly. Since the move to Moscow, he had strengthened that wall and turned it into an impenetrable fortress that, for all her prayers, she could never breach.

"It's so beautiful here," Nicky said, craning his neck to view to the tops of the trees. "If only we could stay here forever and forget all the business in the city."

"Wouldn't that be wonderful?" Alix smiled.

"Alas! Even here they bring me so many reports, so many papers to sign, so many departments demanding my attention."

He walked more slowly as though something preyed on his mind and he were trying to find the most tactful way to speak of it.

"Even here," he said eventually, "we need to keep abreast of all that's happening in the rest of the country, to prevent any simmering unrest."

"Moscow is firmly under control," Serge said, "and when we return, I intend to impose further restrictions on the universities. They are the breeding ground of revolutionary ideas and I mean to crush any hint of unrest before it has chance to take hold." He walked on a little before adding, "With your permission, of course."

Nicky looked at him thoughtfully, "There's something else that we need to settle. In view of the tragedy at Khodinka, and out of respect for the dead and their families, I've appointed Count Pahlen to set up a commission to look into the cause of the disaster. He's the best man for the job. Very discreet but also very just."

Serge stopped in his tracks and fumbled with his ring.

"Hopefully, once he discovers who is responsible and you are exonerated, the people will be satisfied that justice has been done."

"Exonerated!" Serge's voice echoed through the trees like a gun shot. "You're saying *I* am to be investigated?"

"Not you alone. I've given him authority to interview everyone who played any part in the preparations so we can get at the truth. I trust you'll cooperate with him."

"No, I will not." Serge stood his ground and for a moment there was silence as Ella looked from him to Nicky and back again. Was he saying 'no' to his nephew, or was he saying 'no' to his Tsar - the Tsar to whom he had sworn an oath of allegiance; the Tsar in whose name and in whose best interests he claimed always to act?

Perhaps the same question crossed Serge's mind as he stood scraping his boot across the earth. Several times he opened his mouth to speak but no words came out until he said, "Nicky, it's unthinkable that a member of your family should be subject to an investigation by a mere minister. What message does that send to the people?"

"The message that everyone, from the lowest peasant to the highest grand duke, is subject to the Tsar's authority," Alix said.

Serge shook his head, "No."

Alix lips narrowed with indignation bordering on anger, "Would you have spoken like this to Sasha?"

Serge stuttered to reply, "My allegiance to the Tsar is beyond doubt but the message such an investigation sends out is that we are a family divided. Supposing that Pahlen should find me wanting in some way? What then?"

"You've already told me," Nicky said in a conciliatory tone, "that it wasn't your responsibility and Vorontsov was to blame. Why not allow Pahlen to question you? That way, you will be vindicated and the Muscovites will be content?"

"No, no. I'm sorry, Nicky, but it's too great an indignity. I will not be questioned by a commoner. Rather than bring shame on the family, I offer my resignation and, with your permission, will leave Moscow and return to my regiment in Petersburg."

Though Nicky seemed taken aback by the humility in his tone, it appeared to Ella that Serge's offer was more was more of a threat than a suggestion.

"I can't afford to lose you," Nicky said wearily, "and besides, I've already received letters from Uncle Alexei and Uncle Vladimir stating that if you resign, they will resign their positions, too. It would be too great a risk to lose all three of you at the same time when you all hold such crucial positions."

To Ella, Serge's recent meetings with his brothers and the new camaraderie among men who were normally rivals, began to fall into place. If this had been planned in advance, it couldn't have worked out better. Between them they were holding Nicky over a barrel. He knew he needed their support; they knew he would have to back down. Alix was right. Serge would never have treated Sasha in this way. And, for his part, Sasha would have ridden roughshod over anyone who dared to pressurise him like this, but Nicky's kind heart and respect for his uncles could lead only to one conclusion.

"I don't accept your resignation," he said.

Serge smiled, "You'll disband this ridiculous commission?"

Nicky nodded.

"You understand why I have had to do this, don't you? I would hate there to be any bad feeling between us."

"Yes," Nicky said, "so would I. And after all your hard work and the good you have done in Moscow, it would be a great tragedy for you to leave the city."

"In that case," Serge said with a tone of pompous triumph, "may I make another suggestion? In order to prevent any future confusion about roles and responsibilities, wouldn't it be better to put all aspects of the city under one command? If I were given charge of the troops in Moscow and the Moscow district, I could oversee all the departments instead of clashing with other authorities."

"Yes," Nicky said, "that's for the best. Before I leave, I will draw up a charter to appoint you Commander of the Troops for the entire district."

Chapter 28 - St. Petersburg

Had he not been born a grand duke, Konstantin thought as he and Mavra took their seats in the box of the Mariinsky Theatre, he would have spent his life on the stage. The very scent of the place filled him with such a sense of belonging, and an actor's life, though precariously dependent on whims and fashions, would have suited him to the core. And of all the theatres in the world, there was none so stunning as the Mariinsky. With a profound sense of satisfaction, his eyes travelled over the blue and gold décor and ornately sculptured details of the cornices and balustrades. On evenings like this he was proud to be Russian, proud of the great musical and theatrical heritage and proud that he had done so much to promote and patronise the arts. Art, literature and music, he thought, are the life blood of humanity; it is the aesthetic which raises man from his animal state to that of an angel; and in the act of composing, writing, painting or performing, he finds his true nature and co-creates with God.

"Soon," he said to Mavra, "we must bring the children here. It's important to introduce them to the arts while they are still young."

She smiled, "They would appreciate it and they will take after their father and become great poets and playwrights."

"Better ones than their father, I hope," he laughed.

A sudden ripple through the waiting audience distracted him and he sat forwards to discover its cause. All heads were turned towards the shadows moving into the imperial box.

"I didn't know Nicky was coming this evening," he said, shuffling to the edge of his seat in anticipation of the National Anthem that always greeted the Tsar. For some reason, though, the music wasn't forthcoming and, as the murmuring through the audience grew louder, Mavra peered across the theatre, "Is that Alix? No, it's…"

"Miechen," Konstantin frowned.

"Are Alix and Nicky with her?"

He shook his head, "Only her sons, I think. They must have been given permission to use the box tonight."

"Who's the young woman?"

"I'm not sure. She's vaguely familiar but…"

Miechen stepped forwards and, raising her hand above the golden eagles that decorated the box, acknowledged the stares.

"Good Lord!" Konstantin gasped. "Does she think she's the Tsarina now?"

The curtain rose and Tchaikovsky's chaotic passion boomed from the orchestra pit. Rousing, ardent, fervent then softly falling, tender, sorrowful; each cadence and trill played through Konstantin so powerfully as though the composer had read his soul and somehow transformed the darkness of his inner turmoil into beauty through music. *Prince Seigfried* leaped onto the stage: his form so perfect, like Michelangelo's *David,* animated for the dance. With every pirouette, fouetté and plié, his slender body curved and stretched, his sinewy limbs extending and reaching, and Konstantin's heart raced. His eyes transfixed by the loveliness of so perfect a creature, he sat back and the music carried him like a ship bearing its cargo across the ocean; great breakers rising, exhilarating, powerful as a storm, then slowly, slowly easing and calm. The gentler notes, the softer sounds flowing into the alcoves and niches, washing over the enraptured audience, over the tiaras and diamonds, over tulle and chiffon and lace and silk, over the tiers, the balconies, the boxes...

Suddenly shaken from his reverie, he looked towards the imperial box. Miechen's eyes were fixed on the stage, as were those of the young woman sitting beside her, but her sons were laughing and chattering like Philistines, signalling to an attendant who disappeared then returned with champagne.

At the interval, the theatre manager appeared in Konstantin's box.

"Excuse me, sir. Her Imperial Highness Grand Duchess Maria Pavlovna asks if you would care to join her."

Looking across the theatre, Konstantin saw Miechen smiling in his direction. The whole situation seemed wrong and, though he doubted the tact of his question, he couldn't help but ask, "Has His Majesty given permission for the imperial box to be used tonight?"

The manager shuffled uncomfortably, "We did not receive any word from His Majesty."

"Surely you know that the box can only be used with express permission from the Tsar?"

"Yes, sir," his discomfort was obvious, "but Her Imperial Highness said that it would be alright and we did not feel it our place to..."

Konstantin stood up, "It's alright. Of course, His Majesty will have granted her permission to use it. He probably forgot to inform you."

The manager smiled with relief and, bowing, backed out of the box and disappeared.

"You don't really believe that Nicky gave her permission, do you?" Mavra said.

"No, I don't and I must ask her about it. Will you wait here?"

Laughter echoed from the box as he approached and, pulling open the door, he was greeted by Miechen.

"Kostia," she beamed, "come, come in, take a seat."

Her three sons, Kyril, Boris and Andrei, greeted him with smiles, "Is Mavra not joining us?"

"No," he remained standing by the door, "and I am not…"

"Have you met my son's friend, Matilda?" Miechen said.

The young woman, leaning on Andrei's arm, turned and smiled. In spite of his irritation, politeness demanded a response so Konstantin made a slight bow, "I don't think we have been introduced but I am sure we've met before."

"You will have seen her on stage," Andrei smiled, "the star of the Petersburg ballet."

"Ah, yes, of course," Konstantin nodded, eager to leave.

"But tonight," Andrei winked at her, "she dances only with me."

Boris laughed coarsely, "Then she must have come down in the world. There was a time when she *danced* only with the Tsar."

Matilda shook her head urgently, "That was before his marriage."

"And you might say," Andrei said, stretching himself to full height, "that she has come up in the world. I'm sure I'm a far better dancer than the Tsar. Much stronger, much more passionate, am I not?"

Boris laughed at the innuendo, "Come on, Matilda, confess, was the Tsar a good dancer?"

She didn't reply.

"Surely not," Boris said. "The way he allows his wife to dominate him is indicative of a man who always needs to be told what to do."

Matilda blushed, "His Majesty was always very good to me. I esteem him highly and it would be most inappropriate and demeaning to speak of what once passed between us."

Though they continued to smirk, her comment silenced them for a moment and Konstantin seized his chance.

"Miechen, may I speak with you in private?"

She fluttered her fan, "There's nothing that needs to be kept from my sons. Speak openly."

"Has the Tsar given you permission to use this box?"

"If I'd asked, he would have said yes. After all, he seems incapable of saying no to anyone."

Konstantin's indignation was all the greater that she dared to speak this way in front of a commoner.

"You're aware that no one should be here without his express permission."

"Oh dear, Kostia," she sighed and shook her head, "why make mountains out of molehills? I'm a member of the Imperial Family, why should I not use the imperial box?"

"You know why not. Undermining the Tsar's authority like this causes irreparable damage to the whole autocracy. You would never have done this when Sasha was Tsar."

"Perhaps not, but Sasha commanded respect. The same cannot be said for his successor."

"Both as God's anointed Tsar and as a man who diligently and selflessly carries out his duties,

His Majesty deserves as much respect as was given to his father."

"Indeed," she said, "in theory that is probably true but somehow that little man…"

"He may be smaller in stature but he is equally great in his devotion to Russia and his determination to serve his people."

She smiled insincerely and looked at Kyril, smoking a cigarette and staring into space.

"His stature is irrelevant. The old Queen of England is a tiny woman - no more than five feet tall, I believe - and yet she keeps an entire family and an empire in line. You see poor Kyril, sitting there so sadly because the love of his life is unhappily married to a man who, from all accounts, prefers the company of footmen to his wife's."

Konstantin shook his head, "I don't know what you're talking about."

"The Tsarina's brother, Ernie of Hesse. His wife despises him. If it weren't for Queen Victoria refusing to allow it, she would have divorced him by now, but that little Queen has real authority and no one dare contradict her. I'm afraid the same can't be said for the Tsar. Anyone can marry whomsoever they choose here now. It's only a matter of time before Pavel marries his mistress, with or without Nicky's permission."

"Pavel would never do that. He is devoted to the Tsar and he knows his duty."

"Does he? He's virtually abandoned his legitimate children into the care of Serge and Ella, while he spends all his time with his new family."

Konstantin sighed pleadingly, "Miechen, don't you see that this isn't Nicky's doing? We are here to support him and uphold the autocracy. We're not children who need a strict father to control us and who go off the rails at the first whiff of freedom. Nicky doesn't treat us in that high-handed way because he is trustworthy and upright, so he trusts us to be the same and to do our duty without having to be bullied into it."

That reply seemed to floor her temporarily and she shook her head and waved her fan across her face.

"Please," Konstantin said, moving his eyes from Miechen to her sons, "come and join Mavra and me in our box. We have plenty of room and it really would be more respectful."

Miechen raised her eyes to the ceiling, "It would be such a shame to let this beautiful place go to waste. Since Nicky and Alix spend all their time out of the city in Tsarskoe Selo, playing happy families, the whole fabric of society would collapse if I were not here to keep it going. Consider it this way: people need to have a flamboyant Tsar and Tsarina to capture their imagination and keep them fascinated. Nicky and Alix fail to do that and I am simply stepping into the breach and carrying out that duty for them."

Konstantin turned to the door, "How very altruistic of you."

As the curtain rose for the second act, he sat down beside Mavra, "She refuses to move."

"There's no point in her moving now. Everyone has seen her so the damage is already done."

He sighed pessimistically, "Don't they understand that whatever they do to Nicky, they ultimately do to themselves? If the Tsar falls, we will all fall with him."

Chapter 29 - 1901

A chill sea wind blew through the windows of Osborne House where Queen Victoria peered through clouded eyes at the shadowy figures surrounding her bed. Their voices were muffled. Were they talking in whispers or was her hearing fading with her sight? The touch of their hands was comforting but why, she wondered, were they weeping when her own eyes were dry? There had been so much grief in recent years that her tears had frozen in this bitterly cold winter. So much death; so much sorrow; so much suffering. It's a terrible thing, she thought, for a mother to outlive her children. Three times she had endured that agony: dear Alice, Leopold and Affie, and now the dreadful news from Prussia that Vicky's cancer had spread to her spine.

To outlive one's children was tragic but to outlive one's grandchildren was agony beyond expression.

"I have lived too long," she murmured.

Eddy, and Marie's son, young Affie, had gone before; then came the appalling news from South Africa that yet another grandson - brave, young Christian Victor - had perished while fighting the Boers. All those poor, heroic young men, she thought, for as mother of her country the loss of every soldier pierced her heart. *War is so dreadful.* And this war was dividing the family. Half the Germans, like the Greeks, understood and offered support, but Willy and the Russians spoke only of the antagonistic feelings towards England and the supposed atrocities her soldiers committed against the Boers.

She dozed for a while, escaping through dreams of the past. Dear Albert and those happy, happy days that seemed an eternity ago. Half-forgotten names and faces drifted through her mind. Prime Ministers and princes - so many of them had come and gone that she might have lived since time began. Children, grandchildren and great-grandchildren…How many of them were there? So many that she had lost count. How many did Victoria have? Was it four or five? Ernie's beautiful little daughter; Irène's little boys; and Alix in Russia with her three little girls and the hope that the child she was carrying now would be a son.

How quickly everything had passed. It seemed only a moment since they woke her in the middle of the night to tell her that Uncle William was dead and she was now Queen. How long ago was that? Twenty…thirty…sixty-four years ago. It wouldn't have surprised her if it were sixty-four minutes or sixty-four thousand years ago. Time had lost all meaning as images, past and present, melted into one.

"I will be good," she had said at the moment of her accession, and now, as she lay in the dimming light, feeling gentle hands soothe her, she wondered if she had lived up to her promise. *Yes,* she thought, *I have done my best to fulfil Albert's dream and pave the way for a more peaceful world. Germany, Russia, Greece, Roumania, Denmark, the Empire*…All were safe in the hands of her children and grandchildren. The family would stand united. Peace would reign over Europe.

An arm slid beneath her shoulders and held her tenderly. Was it Bertie? Was it Albert? Her eyes flickered…Willy. How lovingly he embraced her.

Yes, I am leaving the world in safe hands. I have done my duty. I have been good.

Ella dried her eyes and knelt to pray. Perhaps, she thought, she should go to Alix and offer what comfort she could. Alix more than anyone would feel Grandmama's absence so deeply and the exultant newspaper headlines could only cause her more grief. Gloating in the death of the Queen, they shouted only of the hope that her successor would bring an end to the Boer War. Didn't they understand what a momentous event had occurred? The 'Grandmama of Europe' had been the lynchpin holding the family and all their subjects together. What would happen now? Would Uncle Bertie be strong enough to take over that role? Would he be able to keep Willy in check? It seemed unlikely. After all, Willy deeply loved Grandmama but despised Uncle Bertie as he despised his own mother. According to letters from Prussia, he was even refusing to allow her to see English doctors or be prescribed sufficient morphine to ease the pain of her cancer.

Prayer was particularly difficult that lonely afternoon as Ella's mind raced from one thought to another but, with unapproachable Serge absorbed in his work, and Alix and Nicky so far away in Petersburg, to whom else could she turn but to God? And there was so much to pray for. From all sides, from ministers, princes and people, came endless warnings about a rising tide of unrest sweeping the country, while Alix, clinging to her belief in Nicky's divinely appointed role, refused to believe it. These advisers, she claimed, were scare-mongering in an attempt to manipulate the Tsar. St. Petersburg was full of intriguers; the real Russians, like the peasants she had met at Ilinskoe, were totally loyal and devoted to the Emperor.

But how could she know, Ella wondered, clasping her hands together desperately in prayer. Secluded in Tsarskoe Selo, Alix was deluding herself. In Moscow, life was very different. Serge might attempt to shield her from it but she had sufficient contacts through her charities and staff to know that students were making revolutionary speeches calling for the overthrow of the autocracy. Good heavens! They had even shot at Trepov, one of Nicky's most trusted ministers. If only Nicky's response had been more decisive!

"The only way of preventing further violence," Serge had said, "is the swift execution of the rebels."

But what had Nicky done? First he said he would exile them to Siberia, then, swayed by his more liberal ministers, changed his mind. And while he prevaricated, the family mocked him, took advantage of his good nature and bandied about the idea that he was weak. Now even Serge, coping with student riots, was exasperated by him and it was too painful to hear him criticised.

She gazed at the icon of Christ and prayed fervently for Russia, for the family, for Nicky and for Alix. *Alix* - what a difference it would make if the child she was carrying were a boy. The three daughters she had borne were beautiful and loved beyond measure but the country was awaiting an heir. The birth of a son would be greeted with so much rejoicing and restore the people's enthusiasm and love for the Tsar.

"Oh Lord," she prayed, "this time, grant them a son."

Chapter 30

Ella smiled with satisfaction at the latest reports from the Elizabethan Society. Two hundred and twenty-four parish committees in the city and a further fourteen throughout the Moscow district; donations were pouring in from all sides and the work was extending to include private orphanages and nurseries. She added her signature to the latest request before turning to her other charities. The widows and orphans of soldiers of her Kiev regiment; the hospitals asking for her patronage; the nurse training schemes...

A cough distracted her and she looked up to see a radiant figure hovering in the doorway.

"Zinaida!" She pushed back her chair and rushed to greet her, "What a delightful surprise! I didn't know you were in Moscow."

Zinaida kissed her cheek, "Forgive me for calling unannounced but I couldn't pass through the city without seeing you." She nodded towards the desk, "I can see you're very busy. I am not disturbing you?"

"No, not at all. I could do with fresh air. Shall we walk outside for a while?"

Parasols raised against the midday sun, they strolled through the cast iron gate of the Alexandrovsky Gardens and along the northern wall of the Kremlin, talking of Zinaida's children, the warmth of the season and how quickly the time had passed since their last meeting.

"What news from Petersburg?" Ella said.

Zinaida bit her lip.

"Don't spare me. Tell me everything."

"Of course, you know what a disappointment it was that the Tsarina had another daughter."

Ella nodded, "But little Anastasia is thriving and Alix is still young enough to have other children."

"And she's *enceinte* again already, I believe."

Ella stopped and stared at her, "Is she? I haven't been told."

"Ah," Zinaida said hesitantly, "then perhaps the rumours aren't true."

"There's something you're not telling me, isn't there?"

"Gossip, that's all. Though, I must say it's rather strange gossip and there seems to be some substance to it."

Ella looked around the park. The police guards were far enough away to be out of earshot, "What is it this time?"

"Have you heard of Philippe Vachot?"

She shook her head.

"The Tsarina has become very attached to him, apparently. He's a Frenchman, a mystic, they say, who has the gift of miracles."

There was nothing surprising in that. Mystics and holy men crowded the streets of St. Petersburg. Many were sincere, some were insane and others were simply charlatans preying on the desperate and vulnerable. The Orthodox Church accepted the staretzy who devoted themselves to prayer and meditation; and then there were the holy fools, dressed in rags and jabbering incomprehensibly to demonstrate to the worldly the ephemeral nature of human existence.

"A staretz?" she asked.

Zinaida shook her head.

"A holy fool?"

"No. This man is quite different. At one time he was part of Miechen's circle but I don't think she entertains him now. He claims to be a healer and hypnotist and they say he can determine the sex of an unborn child."

"I can see why that would appeal to Alix."

"It's all far-fetched but some of the stories that are circulating are too bizarre for words. They say that he sleeps at the foot of the imperial bed so that Alix might conceive a son."

"Oh my!" Ella laughed in disbelief, "I have heard some rumours in my time but that is the most outlandish yet!"

Zinaida laughed, too, but her laughter quickly faded, "It's nonsense, of course, but the truth is the Tsar and Tsarina *do* spend an awful lot of time with him and it all goes on in such secrecy. They meet in Grand Duchess Militsa's Palace. No one knows exactly what happens but they say that, after their meetings, the Tsar is elated and quite vacant as though under the influence of some drug."

The peculiarity of the story was becoming disturbing and though, having been so often the victim of gossip herself, Ella knew better than to give credence to rumour, the mention of Militsa suggested something was awry. Militsa was known to have studied all kinds of strange Eastern rites, to mix with fortune-tellers, table-rappers and mediums and to involve herself with séances and the like.

"How long has this been going on?"

"Since shortly after Anastasia was born."

"And no one knows anything about him?"

"Apparently, the Minister of the Interior dispatched an officer to France to examine his background and the report that came back was quite clear. This Philippe is a swindler and charlatan with previous convictions for practising medicine without a licence."

"Surely, when Nicky heard that, he dismissed him?"

"On the contrary. The Tsarina persuaded him to grant Philippe an honorary medical qualification and now, rumour has it, she is pregnant again and has dispensed with the medics who saw her through previous pregnancies because this so-called doctor has assured her that the child she is carrying is male."

Ella stared at her askance, "*Is* she pregnant?"

"Who knows?"

Ella sighed and Zinaida looked at her apologetically, "I'm sorry if it's worrying for you. I just thought you might be able to help."

"Yes," Ella nodded, "I will. We'll be in Petersburg next month for Miechen's daughter's wedding. I'll speak to Alix then and find out what is happening.

The journey from Moscow to St. Petersburg had been exhausting and it would have been pleasant to spend a restful evening alone but the arrival of Minnie and Pavel at the Beloselsky Belozersky Palace put paid to any such hope. It was clear from the moment he stepped into the drawing room that Pavel was in no mood for conviviality and, for the greater part of the evening, his sole contribution to the conversation was an occasion disgruntled sigh. There was no doubt in Ella's mind that he was dreading the forthcoming wedding - after all, he was spending so much time with his mistress that he had all but cut himself off from the family and, to make matters worse, Miechen's daughter was about to be married to his late wife's brother.

It was Minnie who eventually triggered his anger.

"Elena's wedding will be delightful," she said. "There are so few opportunities nowadays for us all to meet together and I do so love a big family party, don't you?"

Pavel huffed, "These things bore me to tears. The same trivial conversations with the same trivial people who have nothing better to talk about than the latest scandals."

"Particularly," Serge said with a smile, "if you are at the centre of the scandal."

"There is no scandal in wanting to be with the woman I love. The greatest scandal is that I am expected to attend this wedding without the mother of my child."

Ella let out an involuntary gasp and Pavel turned sharply towards her, "How you can be so judgemental? You're half-English and in England these things are permitted. Why, your own grandmother provided a home for that princess of Hanover whose father threw her our when she married a commoner."

"This isn't about marrying a commoner," Ella said quietly. "That woman is already married."

"Was. She's divorced and, before you dare to pass judgement on that, think closer to home. Isn't your own brother divorced now?"

"That isn't his fault. Ducky abandoned him."

"With good reason from what I've been told."

Ella, shaking her head in disgust at the implication, didn't bother to reply.

"The truth is, Pavel," Serge said, "though I am sure you're loath to admit it, the real reason for your ill humour is that you're afraid of meeting your in-laws again."

"Afraid?"

Serge stood up and strolled around the room with an arrogant air that heightened Pavel's anger.

"Afraid to face Alexandra's parents because of how they feel about your liaison."

"My *liaison,* as you so carelessly call it, is none of their business. Alexandra is dead and they can't expect me to spend the rest of my life as a monk. You might choose to live like that but I..."

Such an intimate attack was more than Ella could stand and her anger flared, "It *is* their business. They care about their grandchildren, which is more than can be said for their father."

"What would you know about how I care for my children?"

"I know that they can't understand why you have abandoned them and prefer to spend all your time with your mistress instead."

"I love Marie and Dmitri. They know that."

"Do they? Then why are they always with us and never with you?"

"It is *because* I love them that I leave them with you. They need a proper home with a mother as well as a father."

"And you think," Ella laughed in amazement, "that *I* should play mother to your children while you carry on with your new family!"

"Having no children of your own, I thought that...well, as Serge said..."

Ella's eyes darted across the room, "What did Serge say?"

"That, since my military duties often kept me away from home, it was better, especially for Marie, that they stayed with you."

She could not tell which wounded her more: that Serge, who had denied her children of her own, had used her as an excuse for creating the family he wanted, or that Pavel considered her so pathetic that, like some ancient maiden aunt, she needed someone else's children to love.

"What a convenient excuse," she said bitterly. "Do your military duties extend to stealing the wife of one of your officers?"

Pavel stood up, "There's no point in continuing this conversation. I will leave you to your self-righteousness and bid you good night."

Without waiting for a reply, he strutted from the room, slamming the door behind him.

Serge raised his eyebrows, "I had better go after him and try to calm him down."

Good, Ella thought, feeling so used and abused that she could hardly bear to look at him.

Her anger simmered and it took some time to realize that Minnie, who had been no more than a silent observer throughout the whole tirade, was looking at her with an expression of affection and understanding.

"Hot-headed obstinacy seems to be a trait among those Romanov brothers," she smiled.

Ella forced a smile as her anger gradually abated.

"I trust for Nicky's sake that Pavel won't do anything rash."

"He has given his word to Serge and Vladimir that he will never marry without Nicky's permission."

Minnie nodded, relieved, then sighed, "I don't know what's the matter with everyone nowadays. Men have always kept mistresses but now they all seem to be demanding rights, regardless of their responsibilities or the effect it has on the rest of the family. It puts Nicky under terrible pressure."

"I know."

"I suppose you have heard that Ducky and Kyril have more or less settled together in France? It's only a matter of time before they start pressing Nicky to allow them to marry. Poor boy, he has so many demands made of him from every side." She was thoughtful for a minute, "Has Alix written to you about this Philippe fellow?"

She shook her head, "Zinaida told me of him and I am hoping to find out more about him when I see Alix tomorrow."

"I hope you have more luck than I've had. Nicky usually tells me everything but he's very cagey about all of this. And so little has been said about Alix's pregnancy. I thought perhaps she wished it to remain a secret so as not to disappoint everyone again if it's another daughter, but even the doctors seem to be in the dark about it."

"She still won't let them examine her?"

"She says this so-called Doctor Philippe has assured her she will have a son so she refuses to listen to anyone else. To be honest, I'm not even convinced that she's pregnant. Xenia thinks it's all in her mind. You hear about these things, don't you? When someone so desperately wants a child, they can actually go through all the symptoms but in the end there is nothing there."

Ella sighed, "Let's pray that in this case, there *is* a son, for her sake and for Nicky's and for Russia's."

There was so little warmth in Alix's greeting when Ella arrived at Tsarskoe Selo that it seemed her visit was more of an inconvenience than a pleasure. Though she grudgingly agreed to a carriage ride through the palace grounds, she was no more forthcoming in conversation than Pavel had been the previous evening, confining herself for the most part to monosyllabic replies to Ella's questions. Yes, she was in perfect health. Yes, the baby was due in August. Yes, this time it would be a son.

"And this new doctor," Ella said as the carriage rolled through the shade of the dark green trees, "who is he?"

"A man of God."

"Was he recommended to you by your confessor or one of the bishops?"

"No."

"But you've spoken with them of him?"

"What passes between my confessor and me is none of your business."

Suitably reprimanded, Ella nodded humbly, "I'm sorry. It's just that I have been so anxious. Perhaps you could put my mind at rest. I've been hearing such strange things about him."

"I didn't know you paid attention to gossip."

"I don't as a rule, but when stories reach Moscow..."

"Of course, there are calumnies. It's an occupational hazard for a holy man. One only need read the Bible to see how many prophets were rejected by their own people."

"And this Philippe is a prophet?"

"He is a gifted man of God."

"Then why has he not been brought to the attention of the priests? And why is there such secrecy around your meetings with him?"

"Secrecy? Do you honestly believe there can be anything secret about our lives? We're constantly surrounded by guards and policemen who report everything. We can't even sneeze without someone writing it down."

Ella smiled but Alix turned her head in the opposite direction.

"Do you see him often?"

"We have seen him several times."

"With Militsa?"

"Sometimes."

Ella reached for her hand, "Alix, I know how it feels to long for a child and I know how important it is for you and Nicky to have a son, but surely you don't need to turn to these superstitions."

Alix sharply withdrew her hand, "Superstitions? You know nothing about it!"

"I know that if you need guidance, you can turn to the priests or your confessor. And there are so many Orthodox saints whose prayers are so powerful."

"I don't need *you* to tell me how to pray."

"That's not my intention. It's just that these stories are so disturbing and I only want to help."

"The best way you can help is to pay no attention to these lies and remind anyone else whom you hear repeating them, that to slander the Empress of Russia is tantamount to treason."

Chapter 31

The wedding celebrations had done nothing to improve Pavel's humour. Determinedly avoiding Alexandra's family, he made no effort to appear cheerful, reacting to Serge's attempts to chivvy him with grunts and glowers. Ella's eyes were repeatedly drawn to him throughout the service, as she prayed for some means of healing the rift between them, but later, when the guests fell into chattering groups, he was no more inclined to respond to her words or smiles than he had been to Serge's.

After the banquet, he sat silently at the table where five or six cousins were heatedly debating the future of the Empire.

"What we need," someone was saying, "is greater access to the Pacific. If we're to compete with the rest of the world in exporting Russian goods, it's vital that we have more ice-free ports. Vladivostock is useless in the winter."

Pavel sucked at a cigarette and pulled his fob watch from his pocket, tapping it as though he could barely believe time was moving so slowly.

How he misses that woman, Ella thought sadly, *every moment away from her, is tedious to him.*

"Acquiring Port Arthur has made a big difference and with the expansion of the Trans-Siberian railway…"

"Pavel," Ella said quietly, "I'm sorry for what passed between us the other day."

He exhaled a cloud of smoke and stared beyond her towards the door, "What's done is done."

Someone reached for a dish of salt, tipped it over the table and traced the outline of a map with his finger, "The best thing would be to occupy Korea, here, and take over the whole of Manchuria so the Empire expands across Asia."

"The Japanese would object."

"They can object all they like. They're hardly in a position to stand up to the might of Russia."

"And if they did?"

"We'd defeat them in no time."

"Perhaps," said a prince, "that might not be such a bad thing. A small war and a great victory would work wonders in bringing the people together with a strong sense of patriotism and loyalty to the Tsar."

Ella tried again, "I *do* hope you understand that I wasn't meaning to be critical of you. Heaven knows I have enough faults of my own..."

"It doesn't matter now." He sounded exasperated and the longer she looked at him, the greater his exasperation seemed to grow.

"War isn't necessary," Serge said. "All this is already underway. Our soldiers have already moved into Korea."

"Surely not? We would have heard about it."

"No one knows they are there." Serge said. The men huddled closer as he stuck his finger in the salt. "There's a private timber company just here, and our soldiers have moved in, disguised as workers. Gradually, more and more of them will be stationed there until there's a large enough presence to establish it as a Russian colony."

A prince leaned over Pavel's shoulder, trying to follow the plan.

"By the time the Japanese..."

Pavel sat back suddenly, throwing the prince off balance, then, swishing his hand across the table to wipe out the map, huffed, "This is supposed to be a wedding and you're treating it like a council of war."

"Dear boy," Serge said, "I haven't seen you making any effort at merriment. You're simply in a very bad mood again."

The provocation was clearly too much for Pavel. With a curl of his lip he stood up, knocking over his chair as he stormed from the room.

"Dear me," Serge said, scooping the salt together to re-draw the map, "he becomes more like an adolescent schoolboy every day."

Ella longed to go after him to find some means to placate him but following him now would only give rise to more gossip and would undoubtedly be met by another rebuttal.

"Assuming that we *do* take Korea," said the prince, "and the Japanese are in no position to prevent it, how will the rest of the world respond?"

"Our allies will be content. As long as we expand eastwards rather than into Europe, they have nothing to fear from us."

"Can we be sure that the Japanese are as weak as we think they are?"

The evening dragged slowly by as Ella longed for Pavel's return and, when she slipped from the group of princes to circulate among the other guests, her eyes were scanning every alcove and every chair in the hope that he had come back. At length, she could stand it no longer. She wandered onto the adjoining corridor where footmen scurried to and fro with trays of champagne. No sign whatsoever of Pavel - only Miechen strolling purposefully in her direction.

Ella forced a smile, "Elena looked so beautiful. I'm sure she will be very happy in Greece."

"She could have done better for herself," Miechen said, "but who am I to stand in the way of true love?"

Ella smiled again, knowing full well that Miechen had searched far and wide for a crown for her daughter, and this marriage was more the result of desperation than true love.

"It is a great pity," Miechen said, "that Kyril is being denied the same happiness. He and Ducky could be so happy together if only they were given permission to marry."

Ella, determinedly non-committal, nodded.

"It could be so easily resolved if Alix weren't so obstinate about everything."

Loath as she was to enter into a dispute with Miechen, Ella knew she had no option but to respond, "It isn't Alix's decision. It's not possible for Nicky to contravene Church law."

"I don't see why not. As Head of the Church, he can make the rules."

"It's not as simple as that. The laws are there for a purpose and it's the duty of the Tsar to uphold them."

"Particularly when it suits his wife to uphold them," Miechen said acerbically. "There must be many sour grapes since Ducky abandoned your brother, and I have to say that is colouring your judgement of the whole situation. Alix despises Ducky for what happened with Ernie, and now she is positively gloating in Ducky's unhappiness."

"No, that's not true at all!" Ella said vehemently. "Alix is never vindictive. She may be obstinate at times but she would never deliberately cause unhappiness to anyone. She sets very high moral standards for herself..."

"And what gives her the right to expect everyone else to live up to them?"

"The right as our Empress," Ella said firmly.

"Of course, blood is thicker than water so you're bound to defend her even when she is in the wrong."

Miechen smiled sarcastically and made to walk on but had barely taken two steps when Serge came rushing along the corridor.

"Miechen, have you seen Pavel?"

She shrugged carelessly and, as she continued on her way, Serge turned urgently to Ella, "I've looked everywhere for him. He must have left."

"Let him go. If we go after him now, it will only lead to more arguments. Tomorrow, perhaps, we can speak with him and try to settle our differences."

Serge wasn't satisfied and his eyes darted along the corridor towards the door, "But *where* has he gone? Something isn't right about this. All day his whole demeanour was so strange. I'm afraid of what he's planning to do."

"What *can* he do? He's given you his word that..."

Before she could finish, he was gripping her hand and leading her at a rapid pace towards the entrance, pausing only to inquire of footmen and guests alike, if they had seen him. Only when they had reached the door did a liveried servant step forward with a low bow, "Forgive me, sir, I was told you were seeking His Imperial Highness Grand Duke Pavel Alexandrovich?"

"You've seen him?"

"He left about two hours ago. His steward was waiting for him and…forgive me, I wasn't deliberately listening in to their conversation…"

"Just tell me what was said," Serge demanded.

"His Highness asked the steward if he had brought the money he requested and the steward handed him a case."

Serge looked desperately at Ella, then back at the servant, "Did he say where he was going?"

"I overheard mention of Italy, sir."

"Oh dear God," Serge slapped his hand against his forehead, "he's done it! The other night he threatened to do this but I thought it was all bluff. I never believed he'd actually do it!"

"What?" Ella said, already fearing the reply.

"He's eloped."

On the landing outside the imperial suite of the Alexander Palace, Nicky paused and turned to Ella and Serge, "Anaemia, according to Dr. Ott. That explains the symptoms."

"So she wasn't pregnant at all?"

He shook his head and looked towards the bedroom door. His face was drawn and weariness had settled in his eyes.

"How has she taken it?" Ella said softly.

He shrugged helplessly, "We'll let it be known that it was a miscarriage. The humiliation will be too great otherwise."

Serge nodded and Ella reached for Nicky's hand, "I'm so sorry, so very sorry."

He tried to smile, "Would you like to go in and see her? Perhaps you can cheer her up."

"I will try."

"She would probably rather see you alone," Serge said. "I'll wait here. Nicky, if you wouldn't mind, I would like to speak with you."

The shutters of the bedroom were half-closed, allowing only a shimmer of light to illuminate the incongruous furnishings that said so much about Alix's complex character. In any other room, the simple chairs and chintzes, imported from *Maples* in London, would have appeared quite incompatible with the Russian icons and photographs of her children that cluttered the walls and ledges, but here was a perfect blend of Alix's innate Englishness and the deep mysticism of her Orthodox beliefs. It was small wonder, Ella thought, that this place was Alix's haven. Far enough from the city to provide some seclusion, here she could create her own private world filled all that most mattered to her: her husband, her family, her faith and the high moral standards instilled in her by Grandmama in England.

Alix was lying on the bed, her eyes closed and her hands clasped as though in prayer but, as the floorboards creaked beneath Ella's feet, she stirred and blinked.

"How are you feeling?" Ella whispered.

"A little tired."

"Anaemia can be very exhausting. It's important that you eat well and regain your strength."

"Anaemia?" Alix frowned.

"I understand that the doctors…"

"The doctors don't know what they are talking about. Monsieur Philippe assured me that I would have a son."

The sorrow in her eyes was so profound that it tore at Ella's heart and she wanted to hold her as she had done when she was a child. She moved closer but Alix folded her arms defensively to preclude any intimacy.

"It's very painful," Ella said in all sincerity, thinking back to the events of recent days, "to have absolute faith in someone only to find they have deceived you."

"*Deceived?*"

"I suppose there will always be people who take advantage of us when we are at our most vulnerable and, when we want something very much, we can make ourselves prey to the unscrupulous. I understand that you trusted that man and, of course, anyone would have done in your position."

Alix stared at her icily, "You understand *nothing* about it. Philippe is the truest friend Nicky and I have ever had. People can think what they like but they have no idea of what he has done for us."

"You really believe that? Even now, after all his false promises?"

"It was *my* lack of faith that failed to bring his prophecy to fruition. I let him down and now he must leave us. His work is taking him elsewhere but, even though I have disappointed him, he won't completely desert us. He has promised that another guide will come after him and the next one will have even greater power to help us."

Ella stared at her askance, "Alix, you don't need guides, like this. You have the Church! There are so many holy priests who can pray with you and for you. Why turn to these…"

"Do I interfere in what you believe?" Alix snapped. "Do I tell you whom to speak with, whom to trust? Do I presume to read your soul and what passes between you and God?"

Utterly confused, Ella shook her head.

"Then how dare you come in here and start preaching to me of things that are way beyond your understanding and are certainly none of your business?"

"No," Ella whispered, "that wasn't my intention at all."

"But that is exactly what you are doing. It's what you have *always* done. You think that somehow you have the monopoly of faith? That you can tell me what to believe and how to believe it? Is your own soul not enough for you, that you have to come here and claim responsibility for mine, too?"

"No," Ella said, "I came here only to offer you my support."

"If you truly wanted to support me, you'd accept that I'm capable of making my own decisions without all this interference and criticism."

Ella shook her head sadly, "No criticism was intended. Believe me, I only wanted to help."

"If ever I need your help, I will ask for it. And now, I'm tired and would like to rest."

She closed her eyes and, whether her sleep was genuine or feigned, it was obvious that there would be no further conversation with her that day. Ella stood up, "I will keep you in my prayers," she whispered and kissed the top of her head.

Alix didn't respond and, as Ella left the room, consoling herself that, for now at least, the spectre of Philippe had vanished from Petersburg, she couldn't help but wonder how long it would be before another wolf dressed in sheep's clothing came to prowl around the palace.

She found Nicky and Serge in the Maple Room. A map was spread out across the table and, though both of them were looking at it, their conversation had taken a different turn.

"...and, much as it pains me, I have no alternative," Nicky was saying. "Unless I act as my father did with Uncle Mitia, the floodgates will open to all kinds of abuses. How long before Kyril and Boris do the same?"

"He won't be permitted to return to Russia?"

"No. I will write to him and tell him so."

"And the children? You will grant me full legal guardianship?"

"That's in their best interest. They can't possibly go to him now and they have been with you and Ella so much that they are already like your own family."

Serge threw back his head with what Ella believed was a triumphant smile. She stepped into the room, expecting a full explanation but none was forthcoming. Instead, once Nicky had asked how she had found Alix, Serge pointed to the map.

"The Japanese wouldn't dare to oppose us and, even if they did, our army is far superior and we would crush them in no time."

"De Witte isn't convinced," Nicky said. "He thinks it could prove very costly to us."

"Finance ministers are always cautious. Plehve is in favour of it and you have the backing of the German Kaiser."

Nicky nodded, "If it is truly in Russia's best interest, it's the only course to take."

Serge put his hand on Nicky's shoulder and said condescendingly, "It's good to see you taking such a decisive step."

No longer able to restrain herself, Ella moved closer, "What has been decided about Pavel?"

"Don't worry about it," Serge said. "Nicky and I have made all the arrangements. The children are mine now."

Mine, she thought. Not *ours* - not our children. Pavel had gone. Serge had what he wanted and her opinions counted for nothing.

Chapter 32 - 1904

Waves of tulle and satin flowed across the dressing room floor where the dressmaker stood like an artist surveying a masterpiece.

"Or this one, Your Highness?" she raised a pale green silk to Ella's shoulders. "Or this? Yes, blue suits you better, if I may say so."

"I'm not sure," Ella said, reaching for the design she had drawn. "Would you hold it against me."

The dressmaker loosened another roll and pulled the material tightly around her waist. Ella twisted and turned before the mirror to view herself from every angle and caught sight of the reflection of a surly child, staring at her from the corner of the room.

"What do you think, Marie? Blue or green?"

The child's only response was an awkward shrug.

Ella stepped to one side to block the reflection from view but, even as she continued her conversation with the dressmaker, she felt Marie's irksome presence like a hovering nimbus cloud. If only she could *like* her or at least feel some inkling of affection - after all, she told herself, it was it was hardly the child's fault that she had been forced into this household – but, try as she might, there was always a barrier between them. It might have been easier, she thought, if there were something about the girl to inspire affection but there was not a spark in her. Rarely speaking, she mooched around miserably, lurking in doorways or complaining of her father's absence; and even when she did speak, her comments were most inappropriate.

The dressmaker gathered her materials and Ella's designs and departed. Now there was silence and still the child stood there staring. Ella wanted to smile at her but couldn't and the antipathy she felt, preyed on her conscience. Was she transferring to this innocent the anger and disappointment that was due to Pavel? If so, why did she not feel the same antagonism towards Dmitri? Moreover, how could she be expected to engender any affection for Marie, when Serge totally excluded her from any decision-making on her behalf? It was Serge who decided everything for the children, from the appointment of their tutors and nannies to how often they should be allowed to write to their father and, if Dmitri accepted that, Marie made it clear she resented it…just as Ella resented the fact that Serge could always make time for these children but was always far too busy to discuss her plans and dreams.

"Marie," she said, "go and find Nanny Fry and tell her that…"

A hammering and the door burst open. Serge stood in the entrance, smiling triumphantly and holding a telegram aloft, "The Japanese have attacked our fleet at Port Arthur!"

Ella, confused by the incongruity of the news and his joyful expression, shook her head.

"Don't you see what this means?" He came closer, "Ella, it's a declaration of war."

"How dreadful!"

"On the contrary," he was almost leaping for joy, "it's exactly what we need. The whole country will unite behind Nicky, and the anarchists and nihilists will see that their cause is hopeless. Before you know it, you'll be calling back your dressmaker to create something wonderful for the victory ball."

He spotted Marie, cowering in the corner, and his enthusiasm waned a little, "What a pity Pavel has forfeited his opportunity to play his part in this." He put out his hand to the child, "Come, Marie, you must write to your father and tell him that every true patriot stands proudly behind the Tsar."

He led her from the room.

Ella waited until the echo of their footsteps faded along the landing, then she walked to the library where she unrolled a map of the region. Using her fingers as guides, she measured the distance from Moscow to Korea and Manchuria.

"It will take weeks," she whispered to herself, thinking of the long trek the soldiers would face on their way to battle. An even more disturbing thought dawned on her: how much longer would it take to bring the casualties home?

Throughout early spring, the whole of Moscow echoed with the tramp of marching boots and the rousing strains of *God Bless the Tsar*. As the soldiers boarded the trains, flags waved and crowds cheered. For a few brief weeks it seemed that Serge's optimism was well-founded. The country was united in its eagerness to serve the Tsar, and for once everyone, from the lowliest peasant to the Tsarina herself, was working together for the sake of Mother Russia. Caught up in the patriotism, Ella found a sense of liberation. Opening workrooms in the Kremlin to make up packages of clothes, medicines and prayer books to send to the Front; organizing the Red Cross trains to transport the wounded, it seemed that at last there was an opportunity to put her skills to good use. Better yet, as Serge encouraged her to visit the wounded and widows and orphans, she was finally able to venture among people she had been longing to meet. From Petersburg came frequent reports of Alix's new popularity as she, too, worked tirelessly for the war effort, and by February her doctors had confirmed that she was pregnant. For those few months, there was lightness in the air. The country might be at war but there was a sense of euphoria and wouldn't it be wonderful, Ella thought, to crown a military victory with the birth of a Tsarevich?

But, as soon as the Red Cross ambulance trains returned to the city, and the newspapers reported the number of Russian losses, euphoria turned to resentment. There was no cheering now, only silence. Then came a muttering of discontent and, within a few months, outright hostility. Even within the family, discordant voices were heard. When Miechen's son, Kyril, almost drowned when his ship was sunk by a mine, the hero's welcome on his return could barely gloss over the dissatisfaction that Nicky had permitted the country to engage in so disastrous a war. In the heat of mid-summer, as Ella was about to make her way to the hospital to visit the wounded, news came from Petersburg that Plehve, Nicky's reactionary Minister of the Interior, had been assassinated.

"Treason!" Serge growled. "How unpatriotic can they be? In war time, too! The anarchists use anything to turn the people against us. I'll make certain this kind of unrest doesn't spread to Moscow."

"What more can you do?" Ella said.

"Have more police infiltrate their groups. Send spies into the city. They won't *dare* to so much as speak one word against the Tsar or his ministers when I have finished."

She slipped from the room and called for Rudinkin to drive her to the hospital. A stench filled the air as she entered the ward, amid agonized cries from behind screens and groans from the beds where men lay tossing and turning.

"Perhaps Your Highness would care to visit the day room where some of our patients are almost ready for discharge?" said a doctor in an apologetic tone as though he were responsible for their pain.

"No," she said, "show me the worst cases."

"Your Highness, it's really not very..."

"Please," she said quietly. "I won't disturb them. I will just offer what comfort I can."

Many lay unconscious, their faces as ashen as if they were already dead. She rested an ungloved hand on their foreheads and whispered a prayer for each one, for their souls, for their wives and their children who would soon be widows and orphans. At length she came to a bed where a man lay murmuring - praying perhaps. His eyes were open but he seemed not to see her approach.

"Gangrene," the doctor whispered, "I doubt he will last the night."

Ella, determinedly ignoring the thick stench of decaying flesh, sat down beside him and took his hand in her own. He turned his head towards her, blinked several times and slowly, as recognition dawned on him, struggled to sit up.

"Your Highness, forgive me," he gasped, struggling frantically.

"No, no, please," she soothed, "just rest."

He smiled like a child, "I never dreamed I would touch the hand of a grand duchess."

"I never dreamed I would touch the hand of a hero," she replied.

"Why have you come to *me,* of all people?"

"To thank you for all you have done for Russia and the Tsar."

"The Tsar," he nodded. "Will you give him a message from me?"

"Of course."

"Will you tell him that I am proud to die in his service?"

She nodded and choked back her tears.

"Tell him we hoped to bring him victory but the enemy outnumbered us and was well-prepared. We were too far away and the supplies couldn't reach us, four thousand miles from home. Tell him we did our best."

"He knows that and he is grateful."

His eyes glazed and for a moment she thought his soul had already left his body but he stirred and turned to her again.

"Will you tell His Majesty, too, how we live? If he knew, if he only knew, he would help us but they keep it all from him."

"I will tell him everything."

"I joined the army to fight for him but who will fight for my family now? Two of my sons died at birth and the third is still a child. What will happen to him and to my wife, with no one to support them? Will you ask the Tsar…will you…"

"I will take care of your wife and your child, I promise you. I will see that they are well cared for and have all they need. Where do they live?"

"Zamoskvoreche, south of the river. They share a room with three other families and all the men have gone to the war. It's very cold in the winter and unless I can find work…"

She gripped his hand and the light caught the dazzling diamonds on her fingers. *Just one of these,* she thought, *is probably worth more than this man could earn in a lifetime.*

"I promise," she said resolutely, "I will do everything in my power to help them."

"I know you will," he said. "And I know that…" His eyes moved beyond her as though someone had suddenly appeared above her shoulder. "God bless you, Your Highness." He exhaled one long, slow breath and his eyes glazed over.

She summoned the doctor and, closing her eyes, prayed for his soul.

When the doctor had finished his ministrations and covered the man's face with a sheet, Ella said, "I would like you to send me the details of this man's family."

He nodded and she turned to leave, then turned back to him, "Would you send me the details of all of your patients whose families are in need?"

A wry smile crossed his lips, "Your Highness, there are so many."

She looked at the diamonds on her fingers, "It doesn't matter how many there are. I would like all the details."

Suddenly a great cheer echoed through the ward, drowning the groans and cries and, before she had time to discover the cause, a spontaneous chorus of *God Bless The Tsar* broke out.

A nurse with a beaming smile, curtseyed, "Congratulations, Your Highness! Please convey our good wishes to Her Majesty!"

Ella looked at her quizzically.

"You haven't heard? The birth of the Tsarevich!"

Had she been in any other place, Ella thought she would have dropped to her knees in thanksgiving. Ten years, she thought, ten years they had waited for this!

She hurried from the hospital and found Rudinkin sitting atop the carriage, throwing his cap through the air and smiling as brightly as if the new baby were his own. He leaped down to open the door, almost falling over himself in his enthusiasm.

"As quickly as you can!" Ella told him, barely able to contain her eagerness to hear all the details. On every corner, cheers greeted her carriage as it rattled apace through the streets; bells chimed from churches and cathedrals, and all along the route people were gathering in groups to celebrate the birth of the heir.

As soon as she entered the palace, Serge flew down the staircase to greet her. With an unexpected display of affection, he took her in his arms, swung her around and laughed loudly.

"Is Alix well?"

"Very well. It was much quicker than the previous times."

"And the baby?"

"Alexei, after the great Russian saint."

"He's well?"

"Perfect!"

"I'm longing to see him."

"Then you won't have to wait long. He's to be Christened at Peterhof and every soldier in the army is being named as his godfather." He danced her around the hallway, "Isn't this just what the country needs? In the middle of all these disasters and losses, at last we have something to celebrate!"

334

Chapter 33

Never, since her arrival in Russia, never in the whole of her life had Alix known such joy. All the disappointments, the suffering and humiliation had been worthwhile if they were leading to the birth of this cherubic child. She gazed at him and, beholding his chubby pink cheeks, his golden curls and bright eyes, so healthy and so alert, she felt she was holding the most precious treasure on earth. It was difficult to know what brought the greater pleasure: the sight of this beautiful angel incarnate, or the joy and pride in Nicky's eyes whenever he held him. She laughed at the thought of the ministers whose meeting were interrupted so that Nicky might introduce them to his son and their future Tsar; and she smiled fondly at her little girls, crowding round, eager to nurse their little brother. They doted on him, as she and Nicky did, and the happiness of each contributed to the greater happiness of all.

These were the loveliest times: free from outside interference, a cosy evening in her daughters' nursery. She couldn't deny that the Christening had been a far more joyful event than the coronation or even her wedding. Nor could she deny the pride she felt that all those who had whispered and mocked her for so long were silenced now that she had done her duty and given the country an heir. At times like this, cut off from the world, she was no longer the Tsarina of All the Russias, but a mother alone with her children in an atmosphere of love.

Nicky came in smiling and gathered the girls in his arms. They kissed and hugged him and swung on his hands.

"Has your brother been good today?"

"Oh yes, Papa. He's always good," Maria said.

"But not as good as I've been," Anastasia insisted. "I've drawn some pictures of Alexei to send to our brave soldiers."

She pushed the papers under his nose and he eyed them critically, "Anastasia, I fear we shall have to remove the Rembrandts and Vermeers from the gallery and replace them with these masterpieces."

Anastasia giggled and Nicky kissed the top of her head before sprawling in a chair and reaching to take his son in his arms.

"I saw Misha earlier," he said. "He's so delighted that he is no longer next in line to the throne. He says he's in retirement now."

"What a great weight off his mind that must be," Alix laughed and, leaning over Nicky, stroked Alexei's cheek. "Oh but you, little sunbeam, what a great weight will one day be laid on your shoulders."

"Don't worry, we will see that he is well prepared for it," Nicky said.

He handed him back to Alix and, standing up, moved towards the door.

"You're going already?" Alix said.

"I must. There is so much work to do. I only called in to say goodnight to my beautiful girls. Uncle Serge has sent dozens of documents from Moscow that I need to look over. Apparently, there is a lot of unrest in the city. Even the birth of this little fellow," he tousled Alexei's curls, "hasn't quelled all the hostility towards us."

Alix shook her head, "Serge has always been over-cautious and pessimistic. To tell you the truth, I think the death of your grandfather has made him expect trouble and hostility where there is none.

Didn't he see the crowds at the Christening? The people love you, Nicky, and these scaremongers only invent these stories in an attempt to make you do things their way."

"Perhaps so," he nodded. "All the same, I must read what he sent."

"You work so hard, Papa," Olga said.

He smiled, "It's nothing to what my brave soldiers are enduring. It seems almost wrong that I can even spend these few minutes with you when they are so far from their families and home." He stepped towards the door and hesitated, "Shall I take Alexei to the nursery on the way? With so much to do, I want to spend every possible moment with him."

Alix handed him the child, "I'll go along and see him in a few minutes."

When Nicky had gone, she tucked the girls into their beds, lay down on the sofa and, at Tatiana's request, began a story.

"Close your eyes," she whispered, "and let me paint a beautiful scene for you. It's a landscape of a season long, long ago. The stars are shining and the trees shimmer with rime in the moonlight, as Petersburg lies under a veil of snow. Cathedral bells are chiming and all over the land thousands of voices are singing *God Bless the Tsar.*"

The images in her mind shone with such clarity as the story unfolded: a beautiful tale of a mythical tsar who ruled his people with justice and brought glory to Mother Russia, making her the envy of the world. How the people adored this wonderful emperor, whose dynasty lasted for centuries and whose reign brought a Golden Age of art, literature, music and prosperity for all of his subjects. And, at the back of her mind, the emperor bore the face of beautiful Alexei, grown to manhood - so tall and noble, so brave and so strong.

When the story was complete and the girls were murmuring softly in sleep, she tiptoed from the room and along the corridor to Alexei's nursery. Standing by his cot, with a mildly concerned expression, stood the nursery maid holding a wad of lint. Perhaps, thought Alix, it was only the dim light that gave the lint its deep red colour but, as she drew closer, her heart thudded.

The nursery maid curtseyed, "It's coming from his navel, Your Majesty. It started just a few minutes ago. Would you like me to send for the doctor?"

"Yes, yes, do so at once," she tried not panic and, as the girl scurried from the room, she leaned over and peered closely at Alexei's healthy cheeks and plump little body. It was nothing, nothing at all, she told herself. There was no cause for alarm but it seemed an eternity before the doctor arrived and offered the reassurance she needed.

"It's quite natural," he said. "I will bandage his stomach and that should solve it."

All night she lay awake, praying to drive the vague memories of Frittie and Uncle Leopold from her mind. Irène's little boy had inherited the family illness but Victoria's children were perfectly healthy, and how could God possibly grant her this miraculous child, only to blight him? No. God wouldn't do that. It would be too cruel, too harsh, too great a burden to bear.

"Nicky, are you awake?" she whispered.

"Yes. I couldn't sleep."

"Supposing it *is*..."

"No, don't think that. It's probably just a small cut or something. You know how tender babies' skin can be."

She propped herself up on her elbow and leaned over him, "But if it is?"

"Then we will find the best medical treatment and the cleverest doctors in the country."

"No amount of medical treatment will help. There is no cure."

He was silent.

"Nicky, if it *is* haemophilia, it's all my fault."

"No, no," he sat upright, "don't *ever* say that. It's God's will and we must accept it."

"The people won't accept it. They will say I have tainted the dynasty."

"The people won't know. No one needs to know, not even the family, except your sisters because they will understand."

"But the poor child, how he will suffer! I can't bear that thought, Nicky, I really can't."

"We might be worrying over nothing," he said but his voice lacked conviction, "and if the worst is to come, you will bear it because I will bear it with you."

He drew her towards him and held her close.

As soon as dawn broke, they returned to the nursery and ordered the covers to be removed. Trembling, Alix hardly dared open her eyes for fear of what she might see. *"Please, please God,"* she prayed silently, *"let it have stopped bleeding."*

The maid pulled back the covers. The bandage was soaked in fresh blood.

Serge pushed his chair back from the desk and looked up at Ella, "How did it affect your brother and uncle?"

She breathed deeply; it was almost too painful to remember, "Frittie was so young that we didn't really have time to see it develop, though I do recall his bruising and bleeding. For Uncle Leo it was worse. He was such a lively, sociable man but the illness was so debilitating that it crushed all his enjoyment of life. There were spells when he was well but then the tiniest knock or cut could have such a dreadful effect, leaving him crippled and virtually paralysed with pain. It was worse when the bleeding was internal because then his joints swelled and he could hardly move. Even on his wedding day he had to walk down the aisle with a stick."

Serge's lip curled and he stood up, striding to the window before voicing the fear that she had not dared mention, "Do you think he will survive?"

"He will have the best care, and Alix and Nicky will do everything to protect him but..."

"The best care in the world can't prevent an occasional knock that could prove fatal?"

She nodded.

"Alix must be frantic," he said.

"I can only begin to imagine how she must be feeling. I don't know how she will cope and I pray that she finds the strength."

He turned from the window and took both her hands in his, "Alix is a strong person. She *will* cope and she has Nicky's full support, which is a blessing."

"I can't help thinking that this decision to keep it a secret will only make things more difficult for them."

"No," he said vehemently, "it *must* be kept secret. Can you imagine how the people would react if they thought their future Tsar was an invalid?

They want to see strength in the Emperor not weakness."

"But you know that they speak so cruelly of Alix, already. They call her haughty and proud and make no effort to understand her at all. Now, it will be even more difficult for her, having to appear in public, smiling as though everything is wonderful, when all of this anxiety will be weighing so heavily on her mind."

"That is exactly what she must do - act as though nothing is wrong. It's our duty to appear strong and in control, no matter what we are going through."

She withdrew her hands from his and turned away. *Role, duty, control, strength...*

"If they knew what Alix is going through, the people would be sympathetic and appreciate how difficult it is for her and for Nicky."

"No, they wouldn't. It would make her even more unpopular. They would blame her for the sin that's carried in her blood."

Ella winced, "Is that what you believe? A *sin*?"

"No, no, of course not," he shook his head and fumbled through his pocket for his cigarette case. "But it's how they will see it. They'll accuse her of infecting the dynasty and, when you think about it, the dynasty *is* affected. It's not only little Alexei whose future is in jeopardy." He clicked open the cigarette case and, finding it empty, pulled open a drawer and rummaged through piles of papers.

"What do you mean?" she said.

"If it's carried in the blood, what royal family is going to want to risk introducing the strain into their lineage? Nicky's daughters might have made great dynastic marriages to strengthen our alliances abroad. Now, who knows what will happen?"

He found another cigarette case and, as he pulled it from the drawer, papers fluttered to the floor. "Perhaps now you see it's a blessing that you didn't have children."

She was certain he did not intend to be callous but the heartlessness of his comment struck her to the core. To distract from the blow, she stooped to pick up the fallen papers.

"No, don't!" He leaped to snatch them from her but her eyes had already alighted on the words and she stared aghast: vile accusations, death threats and warnings. Frantically, before Serge could stop her, she reached into the drawer and pulled out other sheets until the table was covered in paper.

"Where did they come from?" she whispered.

"They pay street urchins to deliver them so there's no way we can trace the fiends who write them."

"Why didn't you tell me?"

"I didn't want to frighten you."

Her eyes moved over the disgusting words - *pederast, sadist, bugger, death, death, death...*and scrappy sketches of Serge with his head blasted from his body.

All her animosity melted and, when she stepped closer, he opened his arms and let her hold him.

"Tell me," she whispered, "that they're meaningless and just idle threats. Tell me you don't believe they mean what they say."

He couldn't answer but reached into an inside pocket, "Another came today, addressed to you. Forgive me, I opened it and was going to tell you of it later."

He unfolded a note and handed it to her: "*Grand Duchess, we respect your concern for the people of Moscow and we have no desire to harm you. For your own safety, we urge you not to appear in public with your husband."*

She tore it into shreds and threw it into the fireplace, "I'm your wife. I will always be by your side."

"Thank you," he whispered and kissed her, then stepped back, lit his cigarette and shook his head. "I *do* believe these threats and think we must take them seriously. I truly appreciate your love and loyalty but I can't bear the thought of them harming you. It would be better if we don't appear together in public and avoid as many social engagements as possible. And there's something else. It's me they want to kill, not you. As long as we're together, I put you at risk. It would be better if I alter all our routines so they can't predict my movements. Some nights I'll stay here, some nights at the Governor's House or one of the other palaces."

She nodded sadly, "But there are some things I *must* do. I have already promised to patronise events for the Red Cross fund. If I back out now, what message will that send to the people?"

"Alright," he conceded, drawing on his cigarette, "we must decide which are the most important engagements and cancel all the lesser ones."

"The concert next February is vital. Months of planning has gone into it and, besides, if we don't attend, people will think we are hiding and you are afraid."

"Ella, I *am* afraid." His response was so totally unexpected that she could only put her arms around his shoulders and hold him as though he were a child.

"I have done my best," he said, without self-pity. "From when we first came here, I have done my utmost to keep the city loyal to the Tsar. Have I failed?"

"No, of course not. Events have been against you, that's all. Who could have predicted that this war would be so disastrous or the terrible events at the coronation?"

He stared beyond her, "I have made mistakes. I see it now and I didn't see it before. I could have acted differently after the Khodinka meadow tragedy. I could have done so many things differently."

"And when this war is over and all this hostility dies down, you will have a chance to rectify any mistakes and the people will see that you have always wanted the best for them."

He shook his head sadly, "I have failed. The people hate me and, since I am the Tsar's representative here, it reflects badly on Nicky. For his sake, I need to leave and let someone else take over Moscow."

Though deeply moved by his humility and the sorrow in his voice, Ella sensed a glimmer of light through the gloom.

"You have worn yourself out here," she said. "You have become so thin and so exhausted by it all. You deserve a break, Serge. It would do you good to be away from here, if that is what you really want."

"What I want is irrelevant. What matters is what is best for the Tsar. I'll wait till New Year to ask him to relieve me of my duties here. We can go back to Petersburg. I'll return to the regiment and you'll be closer to Alix. After all, she is going to need all the love and support we can give her."

He looked at her with a tenderness she had seldom seen in recent months and, in one moment, the love in his eyes transported her back to Ilinskoe in late June twenty years before.

"I love you, Serge," she whispered and kissed him softly, "I love you more than you will ever know."

Chapter 34 - 1905

An icy wind blew through the streets of St. Petersburg, and the morning sun glistened on the icicles hanging from the door as Konstantin emerged from the bath-house. The crisp, bright freshness of the morning only added to the sense of his own darkness and he cursed himself as he stumbled into the street. *"How many times,"* he wondered, *"must I beg God's forgiveness? And how many of my penances are meaningless when I know I will sin again?"*

The frost glistened like diamonds beneath his feet; like the diamonds that studded his cuffs; like the diamonds that ornamented his fob watch; like the diamonds that bedecked his wife's neck and wrists and the radiant combs in her beautiful hair.

"And now I return home, sullied and foul, kiss her trusting lips, tell her lies and spend all Sunday morning standing in prayer like the Pharisee in the Temple."

He furtively crossed the street, cut through an alley and turned the corner so that the coachman might believe he had come from a meeting at the palace.

"I can lie to them and they believe me but God knows the truth and sees all."

The all-too-familiar conflicting emotions raged in his head: disgust and shame, followed by remorse that turned into anger, *"Didn't I pray to be released from my sin? Yet still I sin. I can't help but sin so you never hear me and never answer my prayers!"*

But it was useless to rage against heaven for his own foul failure, and the anger sank deeper into self-loathing. He stepped out onto the open street, half-hoping he might be caught and exposed for then hypocrisy wouldn't be added to his crimes.

A galloping of hooves startled him and the sudden approach of a patrol of Cossacks threw him into a panic. His indulgence was not only a sin, it was also a crime - had these soldiers been sent to arrest him? No sooner had the thought entered his head than he laughed at his own self-absorption. Half the city was on strike, the factories picketed by anarchists and socialists. Would the army waste resources on so despicable a creature as him? The Cossack patrol passed but he had barely taken a few more steps when a group of Hussars appeared and among them was the familiar figure of Prince Mirsky, the assassinated Plehve's successor as Minister of the Interior. Konstantin stepped back into the shadow of a building but the prince had already seen him and, dismounting, saluted.

"Your Highness, it's not safe in the city today. May I suggest you return home as soon as possible?"

"What's happening?"

"Some damn socialist priest by the name of Gapon is planning to march to the Winter Palace to petition the Tsar."

Konstantin, regaining his composure, frowned, "His Majesty isn't at the Winter Palace. He is still in Tsarskoe Selo."

"I know," Mirsky nodded. "I visited him last night and advised him to remain there for his own safety."

"You think this priest intends to cause trouble?"

"He claims to have over a hundred thousand followers marching with him. Even if he means no harm, there's no telling what could happen if the crowds were let loose on the city. But have no fear, sir, we're taking strong measures to prevent any disorder."

"Strong measures?"

"We've stationed soldiers at each of the Neva bridges. If the crowds attempt to cross, we'll open fire."

"Shoot our own people?" Konstantin gasped.

"It won't come to that. A few warning shots will be enough to disperse them. And now, if you will excuse me, Your Highness, I must press on."

"Yes, yes, of course."

"And may I suggest you return home and remain there until all this is over?"

Further posses of troops passed along the road as Konstantin hurried towards the waiting carriage.

"Go quickly as you can," he told the coachman but they had barely turned the corner when the amassing crowds blocked the route, bringing the carriage to a halt. It was not, Konstantin observed, a deliberate ploy by the masses, for there was no aggression on their faces, simply that there were so many of them that there was not room for the carriage to pass. With some difficulty, the coachman succeeded in turning around and attempted a different course but every street he tried was equally crowded. For over an hour, Konstantin sat as the carriage moved at a snail's pace until, at length, he could stand the claustrophobia no longer. He pushed open the door and called to the driver, "Wait for me here. I'll walk ahead and see if I can find someone to direct us to a clearer route."

"Are you sure that's safe, sir?" asked the coachman. Only then did Konstantin realize that he felt safer among these people than he did walking alone through the streets at night. The atmosphere was peaceful - even joyful - as men, women, elderly people and children, greeted one another in an air more reminiscent of a church procession than a protest. Many carried icons, while others held aloft portraits of the Tsar and Tsarina, and banners asserting their allegiance to the Little Father and Little Mother of Russia. As Konstantin elbowed his way among them, there came the echo of the opening line of a hymn. Soon, all around him, the same refrain rang through the streets: songs of peace, songs of faith and songs of loyalty to the Tsar.

An old woman appeared beside him and, with a toothless smile, reached for his sleeve, "You're a gentleman, sir. I can tell by the cut of your clothes."

He smiled at her.

"I saw you step from the carriage. You might even be a prince?"

He glanced around and, despite the lack of hostility, hoped that he wouldn't be recognized.

"Tell me, sir, have you ever met His Majesty?"

"Yes," he said quietly, "I have."

The old woman gasped, clasped her gnarled hands to her face in awe, then seized his hand and kissed it reverently.

"Today is a great day! We're going to show him how we love him and we know he will show us he loves us, too, because does love us, doesn't he?"

"Yes," Konstantin said, "of course he does. He has dedicated his whole life to his people."

"I know," she gushed, "and if he knew how we suffer, he would help us. That is why we must see him. When we tell him how conditions are, he will change it for us, won't he?"

Konstantin, both humbled and disturbed by her faith, stuttered to reply, "If he *can* change things for you, he will, but it's not always so easy."

She laughed, "Of course, he can. He's the Tsar! God's anointed one. With God's help, he can do anything."

He wanted to reply; he wanted to tell her that Nicky was no more nor less a miracle worker than she was, but simply a man burdened with the weight of so many aspirations laid on his shoulders. She had fixed him in so hopeful a stare that he shrank from the task of disillusioning her.

"Yes," he said, "he loves you and is God's anointed Tsar."

She kissed his hand a second time and, still smiling, croaked the refrain of the hymn. Konstantin jostled his way into a side street and watched the remnant of the procession pass.

It was almost midday by the time he returned to the carriage. Leaping inside, he called to the driver, "They've gone towards the Winter Palace. We can take any other route now."

The driver shook the reins and, as the carriage moved off, it seemed at first that the crackling sound was nothing more than the clacking of the wheels on the cobbled side street. Soon, though, the cracks resounded into a thunderous rumble followed by screams and cries.

"Christ!" Konstantin gasped, "They're shooting them!"

Ella dropped the newspaper onto the table and turned to Marie's governess, "It was a massacre, Hélène. There's no other word to describe it."

"They say that the soldiers panicked. They asked the people to go back but when they kept walking, the soldiers took fright and opened fire."

"There were women and children there. Surely they could see that?"

"I don't know, Your Highness."

"Hundreds of His Majesty's loyal subjects murdered! They were not rebels, they were not anarchists. They were…"

The door creaked open and Serge gloomily drifted into the room.

"Is there news from Petersburg?" Ella said.

He nodded and looked pointedly at the governess who curtseyed and tactfully slipped from the room.

"Nicky and Alix are distraught. They had no idea what was happening in the city. If Nicky had received the correct information, he would have gone to the Winter Palace but he was completely misinformed about the whole situation." He picked up the newspaper, "Bloody Nicholas the butcher, isn't that what they're calling him now?"

"This can never be rectified," Ella said, "but somehow we have to try. The people need to know that we care."

"It's too late," Serge slumped into a chair. "The damage is already done."

She wouldn't, *couldn't* allow herself to believe that. There had to be hope; there had to be some means of healing the rift between the Tsar and his people; a means of showing that he cared and loved them.

"I must go to the hospital," she said. "They brought in more wounded from Korea today and I ought to see them."

"No," he sat forward and reached for her hand. "The streets aren't safe anymore. Moscow is even more volatile than Petersburg, and the hatred they feel for the Tsar right now is at fever pitch. I'm not even sure you would get through the street. The rebels are building barricades all over the place and the troops are stretched to the limit trying to keep control."

"All the more reason for me to go among them and show the people that we haven't abandoned them."

"Don't you see? If they can't get to him in Tsarskoe Selo, any member of his family is a target. It's too risky, Ella. Wait till it all calms down."

She loosed his grip on her hand, "The soldiers face death every day in Korea, fighting for Russia. The least that the Imperial Family can do is show the same fearlessness and devotion to duty. I must go to the hospital."

He sighed deeply and rubbed his eyes, "I know you're right."

"Then I have your permission to go?"

He nodded wearily and she wished she could find some good news to cheer him but with the Russian losses mounting daily, the hatred aroused by the events in Petersburg, and the constant anxiety for the health of the baby Tsarevich, there was nothing she could say. She turned towards the door when an idea occurred to her.

"The charity concert at the Opera House has all been arranged. They've even managed to book Chaliapin."

"Chaliapin?"

"Feodor Chaliapin, the bass singer."

"Ah, yes." He nodded and frowned, "Do you think that I should attend on my own? In view of the warning you received…"

"No." she said. "It's for my charity so I must be there. Besides, I *want* to be with you."

"Perhaps we should take the children, too."

She hesitated before agreeing, "Why not? It would be good for them to be seen more in public and I am sure they'll enjoy the concert."

He smiled, "Just another couple of weeks and we'll be free of all this and can go back to Petersburg and have concerts of our own again."

"Will you miss Moscow?" she said.

"I don't think so. Will you?"

She raised her eyes thoughtfully, "You told me once that Moscow is the soul of Holy Rus. Somehow I think that no matter where we go now, my heart will always be here."

Chapter 35 - Moscow - February 1905

The staff of the Moscow Opera House bowed and curtseyed as Ella and Serge emerged into the street. Rudinkin jumped down from the carriage and, brushing the snow from his sleeves, held open the door. Marie and Dmitri were chattering excitedly of Chaliapin, and the cold winter wind seemed hardly to touch them as, draped in their furs, they stepped into the silk-lined carriage.

"It was a great success," Serge said, leaning back in his seat, "and the reception we received was tremendous."

Ella smiled at him. He appeared so much more at ease than in recent months. Perhaps the death threats would cease now; after all, he had only two days left in office and already his successor was prepared to take over his duties.

Lanterns aglow, the carriage pulled away from the theatre, and Ella turned to the window to take in the last glimpses of Moscow by night. She *would* miss this place; already a kind of nostalgia for it hung on her heart. It was here she had discovered the depths of Orthodox mysticism; here, she had found her heart's true home. Memories of Petersburg were crowded with the superficial balls and receptions, the gossip and hours and hours of idle chatter. Moscow had depth, substance, a sense of purpose.

Little groups of bystanders shivered on the pavements and huddled into doorways, seemingly oblivious of the carriage as it turned into Voskresensky Square. Suddenly, from the corner of the street, a man in a peasant's coat ran forwards. His arm was raised as though he were about to hurl something but in that second in which Ella's heart thudded, he met her eyes. His arm dropped and he lowered his head, pulled up his collar and was gone.

"Did you see that man?" she said.

Serge leaned over to look through the window, "Where?"

"He's gone. It was very strange. He ran towards us, then he just seemed to vanish."

Serge laughed, "We're all so jumpy nowadays. He was probably just running to keep out the cold."

"Yes," she smiled, "I'm sure you're right."

But even as he squeezed her hand affectionately, the face hovered like a ghost before her eyes.

Two days later, the early evening sunlight, glistening on the window ledges of snow, reflected Serge's mood as he strode into the Kremlin rooms where Ella, Marie and her governess were working on their Red Cross projects.

"Look," he beamed, "this just arrived from Tsarskoe Selo!"

He placed in Ella's hand a miniature portrait of Sasha, "It's a gift from Nicky; a token of his gratitude for all we've done here. He's so thoughtful. Even amid all his own worries and difficulties, he still thinks of us."

"It shows the high regard he has for you." Ella smiled.

Serge looked down modestly, "Once we are back in Petersburg, I'll be of greater use to him. In fact," he looked up suddenly as though struck by a new idea, "I could go to him this evening. In these troubled times, he needs all the support I can give him and there's so little left to do here. What do you think?"

A vaguely disturbing atmosphere filled the room, and the suggestion only increased Ella's sense of foreboding.

"I think it would be better to wait. It's dangerous to travel at the moment. Why not wait until everything is finally completed here and then we can go together?"

He moved his head from side to side, weighing up her suggestion before yielding, "Yes, you're right. Besides, I need to go to the Tverskaya and clear my office." He smiled to himself, "My last duty as Governor General and once that is done we're free to go wherever we choose."

"And for the first time in months you'll be able to relax," she smiled.

"Yes. I'll go and clear the office and when I come back we can have a lovely restful evening together for a change."

He was laughing as he left and Ella smiled, too, but, even as she returned to the Red Cross packages, her apprehension had not abated and she was in no mood to chatter with Hélène and Marie. An eerie silence, like the muffling of dark clouds before a lightning storm, drenched the room when suddenly an explosion shook every window in the palace. Stunned, nobody moved for a second. Then cries and racing footsteps echoed from the square below. Ella sprang from her chair in horror.

"It's Serge!"

Hélène followed her from the room, down the stairs, through the entrance where she urgently summoned a sleigh to speed them to the scene. As they neared Senate Square, she was hardly aware of the soldiers from the neighbouring barracks trying to hold her back. Her limbs empowered by panic and desperation, she forced her way through the soldiers and beyond the gathering crowd.

"No, please, Your Highness," someone was saying, "don't look…"

But already her eyes had alighted on the appalling sight: two dead horses, splintered planks; the shattered fragments of a carriage; Rudinkin bleeding and moaning in agony; and a tangled mass of flesh and bone: all that remained of Serge.

It was too much to take in. Too vast, too vile, too unreal. His head had been blown off. One arm and part of his leg were severed from his torso, and pieces of bone, tissue and cartilage lay scattered across the snow.

"He hates blood and mess…he hates blood…" she heard herself thinking as she dropped to her knees.

"Bring a stretcher from one of the ambulances!"

There was nothing to hold - no hand, no head. She scrambled through the snow and the gore for the treasured icons and medals that Serge always wore around his neck, and she clung to them in desperation. When the soldiers returned, she gathered the bloody remains in her hands and carefully placed them on the stretcher.

"We must take him to the church," she thought aloud and, as the soldiers placed their coats over his tangled flesh, she felt a strong arm around her, helping her to her feet. A small crowd had gathered and she could feel their eyes fixed on her with compassion and horror.

"Place him on the steps of the altar," she whispered.

The crowd followed her into the chapel of the Chudov Monastery where she knelt, too numb to pray. Blood seeped through the soldiers' coats and trickled down the steps of the altar in a dark stream.

"Serge...Serge..." It wasn't real. It *couldn't* be real but it was too horrific even for a nightmare. Sobs came from the gathered crowd - soldiers and workmen alike - and yet her own eyes were dry. If only the tears would fall, if only, if only...

"Your Highness," a voice whispered and she turned to see Marie and Dmitri, their faces white with shock, staring towards the bloody stretcher. They mustn't see it. They mustn't see him like this. She opened her arms and, when they ran to her, she held them close, trying to find words of comfort. Serge loved these children, "He loved you, he loved you," she told them.

"Aunt Ella," it was Dmitri's voice, "let's take you home."

She let herself be led back to the palace where she sat rigid in a chair, unable to erase the horrific images from her head. Again and again, her mind re-ran the terrible scene until it gradually became clear that Serge wasn't the only one who had suffered that afternoon.

"Rudinkin," she murmured and turned to Countess Olsuvieva, "Rudinkin? Did he survive?"

"His condition is critical, Your Highness. The doctors don't think he will last the night."

She stood up and, though her legs felt barely able to support her weight, with a determination that seemed to come from beyond her, she said, "I must go to him at once."

"But Your Highness, you have suffered such a terrible..."

"Serge would want me to go to him. Have a carriage brought."

She was barely aware of the journey to the hospital but suddenly found herself gazing at the astonished face of a doctor.

"Your Highness, we're so sorry for your loss. Your husband was greatly respected. We..." Even in the midst of her shock, she was so aware that bereavement, like some terrible disfigurement, causes discomfiture that drives people to turn their faces away and, as the doctor stuttered through his condolences, she pitied his embarrassment.

"Our driver, Andrei Rudinkin..."

"Forgive me," his embarrassment only seemed to increase. "His wounds are fatal and there is nothing we can do. His one concern is for his master so, to avoid causing him furthering suffering, we told him that His Highness survived."

With all the self-possession she could muster, Ella neared his bed and the coachman's eyes turned towards her.

"The Grand Duke," he grimaced in pain, "he is uninjured?"

She smiled gently, choking back her tears, "It was he who sent me to you."

"Thank you, Your Highness." He drew her hand to his lips and kissed her fingers, "Now, I can die in peace."

The dark, Gothic interior of the small dining room heightened the sense of eeriness that pervaded the Vladimir Palace that evening. Miechen and Vladimir were sitting at the table in silence and, judging by the untouched food spread before them, it was obvious to Konstantin that their horror was as great as his own. As he and Mavra entered the room, Vladimir stood up and opened his arms to clasp him in greeting.

"What can I say?" Konstantin murmured. "What can *anyone* say?"

Vladimir shook his head, unable to reply.

"The whole country," Miechen said, "is in such a state of turmoil. Where is it all going to end?" She looked at Mavra, eight months pregnant and her eyes red with weeping, "Come, come and sit down."

"Poor, poor Ella," Mavra said. "She actually *saw* him after it happened. What a terrible, terrible sight it must have been! I wanted to go to her at once but Kostia is concerned for my condition."

"You couldn't have gone anyway," Miechen said. "Nicky has forbidden any of us to go to Moscow. It's too dangerous at the moment."

"Kostia is going," Mavra said, looking towards him for confirmation.

He nodded, "I sent a telegram to Nicky and he's granted me permission."

Miechen, with an expression of alarm, immediately turned to her husband, "Vladimir can't go."

"No, I can't. I'm responsible for the security of Petersburg and that is more vital now than ever."

Whether his response was inspired by genuine devotion to duty or fear that what had happened to his brother could happen to him, Konstantin couldn't tell, but it irked him and there was a bitterness in his tone when he said, "Ella is there all alone without a single member of the family to support her."

No one replied.

"Serge was my closest friend," Konstantin said, "and the least I can do is be there now for his wife."

Miechen shuffled uncomfortably, "Zinaida Youssoupova left straight away for Moscow, and Ella's own family will be there soon. Victoria is coming over with Serge's sister and I believe they've contacted Ernie and he should be arriving in a day or two."

Konstantin shook his head, "It seems shameful that they should make that long journey while we, who are already in the country, leave Ella completely on her own."

Mavra reached for his hand, "I heard that Alix wanted to go to her at once."

"That's ridiculous!" Miechen said, "For the Tsarina to go into Moscow now, would be like throwing a match into a powder keg!"

"But she is so distressed by it all and so concerned for Ella. We were supposed to be dining with them at Tsarskoe tonight but, of course, it was cancelled."

"What about Pavel?" Miechen said. "Will he be allowed to return for the funeral?"

Vladimir nodded, "Nicky has granted him that. He'll be heart-broken. He and Serge were always so close and it must be even harder for him to bear, knowing they never had time to settle their differences."

Another uneasy silence ensued until Vladimir, sighing loudly, stood up and clenched his hands into fists, "They caught the assassin. Kalyaev, he's called. Apparently, he didn't even try to escape. He wanted to be caught - another martyr for their cause."

"The way things are going, he won't be the last. But what can we expect when the Tsar is so weak and..."

"No," Konstantin slammed his hand down on the table. "It's not weakness; it's a lack of support from the rest of us. Serge was totally devoted to the Tsar. Everything he did, he did out of love for

Russia and the autocracy. The best way we can honour his memory is to do as he would have done. We should be standing behind the Tsar, not criticising and carping. We should be supporting his decisions and..."

"Decisions? What decisions? One minute he says one thing, the next another!"

"And why is that? Because he hears so many conflicting reports from so many different departments. How can he possibly deal with so much, unaided?"

"Sasha managed it," Miechen said.

"Yes, because Sasha had the full support and respect of the family. Look at us, now! You deliberately defied him by using his box at the theatre. Pavel broke his oath of allegiance and, from what I hear, Kyril is on the point of doing the same."

Miechen, rankled by the mention of her son, shook her head with a smirk of disdain, "What hypocrisy! Alix's brother re-marries and she sends him congratulations while, at the same, insisting that Nicky will never allow the same happiness to his ex-wife. If Ernie can remarry, why shouldn't Ducky?"

"It's not about re-marrying, it's about marrying a cousin. If..."

"Please, please, please!" Vladimir said, putting his hands over his ears. "Arguing among ourselves is the last thing we should be doing tonight."

Konstantin lowered his head in shame, "Forgive me."

Vladimir rested his hand on his shoulder, "We are all deeply shaken and I know you meant no harm. It's only a release from the shock and the tension."

"Our shock and tension," Mavra said quietly, "is nothing compared to what Ella must going through. Kostia, hadn't you better be leaving?"

As he stood up to leave, Miechen leaned across the table, "Give her our sincere condolences."

"Yes," Vladimir said, "and tell her, if it's any comfort at all, we will see that the coward who committed this atrocity is brought to swift justice. I hope they string him up from the Kremlin."

Chapter 36

Almost three days had passed and still the suffocating stench of explosives, blood and mangled flesh clung to Ella's nostrils while the horrific images played and replayed before her eyes. Sometimes numb, sometimes seized by a terrible fear, bewildered and longing to weep, she had somehow continued to function: to breathe, to move, to even think clearly enough to make the funeral arrangements.

"For security, Your Highness," the police had pleaded, "it must be a private ceremony."

"No," her decision was final. "The people must be allowed to pay their respects to the Grand Duke. And I want food made available for all of them on the day of his interment."

His *interment.* It was so final, so hard to believe. Yet harder still to believe was that someone could deliberately perpetrate this evil and intentionally cause such horror and sorrow. She knelt before her icons, "*Why,*" she whispered, "why do they hate us so much that they are driven to such vile destruction?"

Again, she turned the pages of her Bible and read the words of the Gospel: *Father, forgive them, they know not what they do."*

Strangely, there seemed to be nothing to forgive. She bore the killer no malice, had no desire for revenge nor to see him suffer as she suffered now, but she longed to understand. Was this man so filled with hatred that every shred of humanity had been ripped from his heart? And, since he must now face the inevitable consequence of his crime, would he stand before God with that hatred damning his soul?

"If," she prayed, "in some way, we were to blame, if we inspired this hatred by our actions or by our neglect, then our guilt is even greater than his."

She closed her eyes and prayed more fervently for Serge's soul and for the soul of the man who had murdered him. Then, silently, she rose, knowing what she must do. Placing an icon of Christ inside the Bible, she summoned a carriage to take her to the Tanganka prison, where the assassin was being held. For a moment the coachman stared in amazement but, without further explanation, she pulled the black mourning veil over her face and waited to be obeyed.

The flint-like faces of the guards at the prison seemed to blend into the bare bricks of the damp walls. The place stank of unwashed bodies and stale urine, and the dimly lit passageways gave the impression of descending into hell. Too astonished to refuse her request to speak with Kalyaev, one guard turned to the other, who nodded and, nervously jangling his keys, disappeared down to a cellar.

"Your Highness," said the first, "we will take him to our offices and, for your own protection, my colleague and I will stand between you and the killer. If he should insult you in any way or..."

"No. I wish to speak with him alone."

He inhaled as though to reply but she stood intransigent until he acquiesced.

From somewhere along a passage, the jingling of keys came again and the guard directed her towards a stark room in which a gaunt, unshaven man sat on a straight-backed chair. She stepped towards him, closing the door behind her, and her eyes overflowed with tears.

The man looked at her with confusion on his brow.

"I am his wife," she said.

For a moment it seemed he would stand but had no sooner reached the edge of his chair than, as if to make a point, he sat back again. She sat down beside him and, though tears blurred her view of his face, she had the strange sensation that she had seen him somewhere before. She pulled back her veil and her tears seemed to distress him.

"Please, don't cry," he said.

The softness in his tone was so incompatible with the violence he had committed that her bewilderment only increased and the tears flowed more freely.

"Why?" she whispered. "What drove you do such a thing? I only want to understand so that nothing like this need ever happen again."

He laughed exasperatedly but there was no malice in his tone, "*Now* you come and speak to us. It's only when something hurts you that we get your attention. If you had asked that question before it happened, then maybe it wouldn't have been necessary."

If only, she thought, and said aloud, "I wish I had met you before."

"If Grand Duke Serge had listened to us, he could have prevented all of this."

"He tried to listen. He…"

"Like the Tsar listened to the unarmed people who came to petition him in Petersburg? Shooting them down in cold blood! Did the Grand Duke ever listen to our cries or hear us when we tried to tell him how we live? You have no idea! You go from palace to palace, from one ball to the next with your fancy carriages and fine jewels, and all the time, only streets away from those glittering ballrooms, there are babies dying of starvation, children turning to prostitution just to earn enough money to live. Did the Grand Duke care about them when he sent his spies into the city? Did he care about the wives and children left behind when he exiled anyone who spoke up for the poor?"

"He *did* care. He was a good man."

"Good?" He jumped up from the chair and shook his head wildly in frustration, "He was a..." but his eyes alighted upon her and he stopped himself. "I can't discuss this with you. It wasn't my intention to hurt you and I know you are grieving so I will spare your feelings now. My target was the Grand Duke and I succeeded in doing what I set out to do. I have no further grudge against you."

Her head ached and her eyes stung from crying, "In killing him," she said, "you killed me, too."

"There are many widows in Moscow," he said coldly. "The widows of those whom your husband exiled and who froze to death in Siberia. Widows of soldiers who fight your wars, widows of..." He broke off, and sat down again. "Do you hate me?"

"No," she said sincerely.

His eyes softened, "I could have killed you but I risked my life to save you."

She looked at him questioningly.

"The night of the gala performance. I was ready to do it then. I had the bomb; I had the perfect position and everything was planned. A moment later it would all have been over for you but I didn't do it."

"The face at the carriage window," she murmured, remembering now where she had seen him before.

"I was about to do it but, when I ran forwards, it was you I saw, not him, and I couldn't do it."

Suddenly there was hope. This one act of kindness held out an opportunity of redemption and proved that beneath the darkness of his anger, the light of humanity still glimmered in his heart.

"You must have taken a great risk."

He nodded.

"I want you to know that the Grand Duke forgives you," she said but his expression suggested that that was of no consequence to him. "And I want to help you."

"I'm beyond help. They will hang me. But there are thousands of others who are crying out for help and nothing will change for them until the whole autocracy is overthrown."

"No, no," she said, "there *are* ways we can change things without all this violence and anger."

"The people are oppressed and they have no voice to speak. No votes, no elected government. A distant Tsar who has no idea how we live. But there's no point in discussing politics with you. You will never understand how it is for us."

"I didn't come here to discuss politics. I came because I wanted to understand and now I think I *do* understand. And I came because I care about you. I don't know whether or not I am in a position to persuade His Majesty to grant you a pardon…"

"I don't want his pardon. It is he who should be begging our pardon for the ills that we suffer. When they execute me, others will rise to take my place."

She chose not to respond and instead continued, "I care, too, about your soul. For your own sake, not for mine, I beg you to repent of this hatred and anger."

She handed him the Bible and icon and he took them from her.

"I am sorry for your suffering," he said, "but I don't regret what I did. I am proud of it and, if the situation were to arise, I would do exactly the same again. All the same, I am sorry for the grief you are suffering."

She stood up to leave and, as he looked her in the eye, it seemed that on some level a deeper communication was taking place than either of them understood.

"I will pray for you," she promised.

Chapter 37

Zinaida led Konstantin and Pavel to the doorway of the Chudov chapel where Ella knelt in prayer beside the catafalque. Her cheeks were as white as the starched altar cloths and she was still wearing the clothes she had worn the previous evening - evidence that she had kept her lonely vigil all night.

"How is she bearing up?" Pavel whispered.

"Like a saint," Zinaida replied. "She's exhausted, rarely sleeps, has organized everything single-handedly and still her thoughts are only for others."

"Is it true that she visited the assassin?"

Konstantin nodded, "It was supposed to be a private visit but somehow the newspapers got hold of the story and twisted it and made everything worse for her."

"In what way?"

"They reported that he was so touched by her visit that he was filled with remorse and regretted what he'd done. When Kalyaev heard that, he assumed she had given the story to the papers and he wrote her the vilest letter filled with hatred."

"Why *did* she go?"

"To forgive him," Zinaida smiled.

"I wonder," Pavel said dolefully, "if she has also forgiven me."

Zinaida patted his shoulder, "Shall I tell her you've arrived?"

As she tripped slowly towards the catafalque, Pavel turned to Konstantin, "I don't know what to say to her."

"There's so little anyone can say at such a time. Sometimes just being there is enough."

Zinaida whispered to her and Ella turned, unsmiling, and walked towards them.

"Ella, I am *so, so* sorry!" Pavel opened his arms in greeting but she stood some distance from him and, without looking directly at him, said quietly,

"I'm glad Nicky permitted you to come back for the funeral. Serge would have wanted you to be here."

The uncharacteristic coldness in her tone shocked Konstantin and undoubtedly wounded Pavel to the core. His face crumpled and tears filled his eyes, which he wiped away with the back of his hand.

"Many years ago," he said, "Serge gave me a box to be opened after his..." He could not bring himself to say the word. "It contains instructions for his funeral."

"Everything is already arranged," she said but, seeming to think better of it, added, "I will change anything if it is what he requested."

"He particularly stressed that he wished to be placed in his coffin in the uniform of the Preobrazhensky Regiment."

"That won't be possible. He is..." she choked. "His body is too badly mutilated to be removed from the Kiev Regiment coat that he was wearing when the bomb exploded."

Pavel staggered with revulsion and rested against the wall for support. As though by reflex, Ella reached out to him but the moment her hand alighted on his shoulder, she withdrew it as quickly as if the very touch of him had burned her.

"My children," he said, still swaying, "I need to see my children."

She turned away towards the passage connecting the chapel to the palace, and Konstantin, steadying Pavel and uttering something foolish and comforting, led him after her.

The moment Ella opened the door to the reception room, Marie ran to her father and, throwing her arms around him, burst into tears.

"Papa! It's been so awful! I'm so glad you've come!"

"Hush, hush," he soothed, "I'm here now."

"Will you stay?"

He shook his head helplessly "The Tsar won't allow it."

"The Tsar *can't* allow it," Ella corrected in a low voice.

"Will you take me back with you to France?"

"Yes, yes, of course, I will. Of course, I will."

He looked beyond her towards Dmitri, who hung back and, when Pavel's eyes alighted on him, side-stepped closer to Ella.

"Papa," he slid his hand into Ella's, "I can't go back with you. I want to stay with Aunt Ella. Now without Uncle Serge, she needs me more than ever."

Ella ran her hand over his hair and pressed his head to her side, "Your home will always be in Russia," she said.

Pavel, releasing Marie from his embrace, moved closer to Ella and said in a conciliatory tone, "After all that has happened here, my children would be better with me in France."

"With your *other* family?" she said so curtly that Konstantin and Zinaida turned to one another in amazement. "When you abandoned them, the Tsar created Serge their guardian. I intend to continue where he left off. They are true Russians, loyal to the Tsar. If His Majesty allows you to come to visit them more often, I won't object but I cannot extend that courtesy to your wife."

Whether or not the provocation was intentional, it was enough to throw Pavel into a rage, "You've changed beyond recognition, Ella. Such bitterness! I never would have thought it of you. There was a time you would have understood and..."

"There was a time," she interrupted, "when you were loyal to your country and your Tsar."

Before he could reply, she turned and walked from the room.

Later that night when the rest of the household had retired to their rooms, Konstantin, too weary to sleep, paced the corridors with an overwhelming sense that the current maelstrom was but the prologue to a vaster and far wider-reaching storm, perhaps even Armageddon. The silence within the thick walls of the Kremlin belied the chaos that was raging outside. Barricades cluttered the streets; armed gangs held the police and military at bay; and the vast majority of the Imperial Family were too frightened to be seen in public. And now, the family itself, like a microcosm of the whole of Russia, was falling apart with divisions, disputes, disrespect and disagreement. It was as though some kind of seismic shift was taking place; everything was thrown off balance and into such confusion that it was impossible to predict how it would end.

He wandered down the stairs and along the passage leading to the Chudov chapel and, as he stopped at the entrance to stub out his cigarette, the sound of gentle weeping echoed along the walls. Alone by Serge's catafalque, sat Ella, her face buried in her hands and her shoulders rising and falling as she sobbed pitifully. Perhaps it would be better to creep away than to intrude on her grief but, even as that thought crossed his mind, the ineffable longing to ease her pain was so great that he found himself moving towards her as though drawn by a magnet.

Silently, he sat down beside her and, though it was some time before she raised her head from her hands, he had the sense that she knew he was there and appreciated the comfort of his presence.

"You couldn't sleep either," she whispered at last.

"No."

"It's impossible, isn't it, with all that has happened?"

"Pavel said he hasn't slept at all since the news first reached him."

"Pavel," she sighed.

"He *is* heartbroken, too," Konstantin said gently.

She nodded, "You think I am cruel to him?"

"No, of course not, but..." He broke off at the sight of her tear-stained cheeks when she turned to look at him. "It doesn't matter."

"Yes, it *does*," she said. "It matters a lot. It's so wrong, Kostia. It's all so wrong. Serge's whole life was dedicated to serving the Tsar and the honour of the country. Whether or not he made mistakes, his motives were always altruistic and, even when his decisions made him unpopular, he put aside his own desires to do what he thought was best for Russia. He dreamed that one day Holy Rus would be restored and the Kingdom of God established on Russian soil. That was all that mattered to him and he died for his country as surely as if he had been killed on a battlefield."

"Yes," Konstantin stared towards the coffin, "no man could have been more loyal to the Tsar."

"You see, then," she said, with pleading in her eyes, "Serge lived and died to uphold the autocracy while so many others, so many who should be setting a good example and taking seriously the responsibility that comes with our position, are undermining everything he stood for. If Tsardom is destroyed, it won't be the anarchists and revolutionaries who destroy it. It will be the divisions within our own family. Nicky is the Tsar, and Pavel swore before God to obey and support him. By breaking his oath of allegiance, he paves the way for so many other misdemeanours and what might seem as a minor transgression in itself is like another drop in a rising tide that will one day rise up and sweep away everything that we hold dear."

She ran her hands through her hair and sighed deeply, "And then there's the question of example. How can we expect the people to obey His Majesty when they see that even members of his own family go their own way and follow their own selfish desires? Is it any wonder they lose respect for us when all they see are grand dukes and princes, who have been given so many material blessings, absorbed only in indulging themselves regardless of anyone else? Imagine how it looks, Kostia. Imagine living in squalor, toiling away in filthy conditions all day and coming back exhausted in the evening to some overcrowded hovel, while the Imperial Family sinks into decadence and self-indulgence."

He nodded, "There is only so much any of us can do. The problems are so widespread and, as Christ himself said, '*the poor ye always have with you.*'"

"Yes, but whatever little we can do, we *must* do. We are so fortunate and many others are not and one day we will all stand before the throne of God and answer for how we used the gifts he gave us. We have been entrusted with so much and one day we must give an account of it."

She looked again towards the coffin, and the light of the flickering candles glimmered on the tears that hung from her lashes. *Even amid such sorrow and horror,* Konstantin thought, *her beauty is unquenched.*

"Ella," he murmured, "you're exhausted and the funeral tomorrow will be such a strain. Could you not try to sleep, if only for a little while?"

She shook her head, "There is so much on my mind."

In his own weary sleepiness, he thought aloud, "I suppose that the awfulness of what you witnessed must keep recurring like a nightmare."

"It isn't that. It's just that..." she bit her lip then said quietly, "there are so many unanswered questions. Twenty years we were married and yet sometimes I feel I never knew Serge at all." She smiled sadly and shook her head, "If I could never fathom his thoughts and his heart when he was alive, why do I waste time trying to find answers now?"

"He loved you, Ella."

She nodded, "In his way, I know he did."

Konstantin shuffled, wanting to ease her pain, "He told me something once, something that perhaps you would prefer I didn't know."

She glanced at him with renewed horror in her eyes and she swallowed audibly before saying, "Ours was never a...*proper* marriage. He could not love me in that way."

"I know."

She blushed and lowered her eyes, "He told you?"

"Yes, and he told me that that was why he was so angry sometimes. He had all the feelings that other men have, all the desire and emotion but physically was incapable of expressing that to you. He wanted you and knew he could never have you."

Her eyes moved to the coffin, "*Why?* Why didn't he tell me?"

"He was ashamed. He thought he had failed and disappointed you and he couldn't bear that because he loved you so much."

"Oh," she gasped and the tears flooded from her eyes, "poor, poor man. If only I had known. If only he had told me."

Konstantin put his arm around her shoulders and held her till her sobbing eased.

"How he must have suffered," she choked, "and all those rumours and dreadful lies. How they must have hurt him!" She looked up suddenly, "And the worst thing of all, sometimes I half believed them. I wronged him, Kostia. In my thoughts I wronged him. Oh, Serge, I am *so* sorry."

"No, no," he said, his voice becoming louder with emotion, "*you* didn't wrong him. I did." She seemed not to hear but now, as he held her, here in front of Serge's coffin, he had to confess.

"They mistook him for me. The grand duke who frequents the bath-houses, the grand duke and his boys...Ella, it wasn't Serge."

She looked deeply into his eyes, "*You?*"

He nodded and now it was his turn to sob. "I'm so ashamed, so, so ashamed. My poor Mavra and the children!"

"They know?"

"No. It would break their hearts. I love them but sometimes I can't help myself. I'm such a sinner, so vile, so..."

She took his face in her hands, "Kostia, we all have our faults but with God's grace you can overcome anything."

"I've tried and tried."

"And God sees your efforts. You're a good man, Kostia, a true friend, and Serge and I love you."

The catharsis of the previous evening sustained Konstantin through the long and solemn funeral service. His prayers were all for Ella that she, too, might have found some comfort and release through their conversation. Though her face was veiled, the serenity, which he always felt in her presence, brought a greater reassurance than all the long prayers being chanted by the priests. When the service was complete, he and Pavel helped carry the coffin to the crypt where it was sealed in lead. As a memorial, Ella had commissioned the sculptor, Vastnetsov, to design and erect a bronze crucifix, six metres high, on the site of Serge's death. Inscribed around the base were the words:

"FATHER FORGIVE THEM FOR THEY KNOW NOT WHAT THEY DO."

Chapter 38

A veil of snow disguised the familiar scenes of Ilinskoe. Now there were neither cornflowers nor ripe strawberries to gather, only icicles hanging from leafless trees, and frozen ridges of mud lining the forest paths. The boats, no longer bobbing on the waters of the Moskva River, stood locked in sheets of ice, and the cattle had left the fields to huddle in barns against the winter winds.

Draped in black furs, Ella made her way to the village church, recalling the summer twenty years before, when she fell in love with the man whom the villagers had gathered to mourn. This was the image she wanted to keep of Serge. Overlooking the years of misunderstanding, frustration and loneliness, and casting aside the horrific images of his murder, she would think only of the kindness that he had shown her when she first came to Russia and the happiness they had shared in Ilinskoe.

As she left the church, crunching over the icy paths, a fresh wind blew through the claustrophobic gloom of recent weeks. Ella looked up at the wintry-blue sky with a sudden and unexpected sense of liberation, so powerful that she actually longed to skip or run through the snow. Was this the way, she wondered, that widows were supposed to behave? From childhood, she was used to great displays of excessive grief. Her earliest recollections of Grandmama were of the 'Widow of Windsor', dressed habitually in black, obsessed with preserving the memory of her dead husband. For many years after Grandpapa's death, Grandmama refused to appear in public, unable to bear the thought that her subjects would see her 'alone'. For the rest of her life, Grandpapa's shaving water was refreshed every day, his bed linen was frequently changed and the room in which he had died became little less than a shrine.

The rest of the family followed her lead. In Prussia, Aunt Vicky was much criticised for what was seen as extreme mourning when her two-year-old son, Sigismund, died of meningitis. She had gone so far as to have a figurine of the baby placed in his cot. Mama, too, mourned little Frittie to the end of her life and, after Mama's death, Grandmama was gratified to discover that her room in the New Palace in Darmstadt was left untouched.

"Heaven," Ella whispered to herself as she made her way to the house, "if they are in heaven, we should rejoice for them, not grieve forever. And, as our lives can be cut short so unexpectedly, we should live every moment as though it is all we have."

Painful as it had been, she had already sorted through Serge's papers at the Governor General's house and in the Kremlin offices and now here, in the privacy of Ilinskoe, she could begin to plan for the future. Returning to the house, she sat by the open window and made several lists of all that needed to be done. First, there were practical matters to deal with. Serge's will was missing and she needed to know exactly what she owned and what responsibilities he had bequeathed her. Of course, Nicky had offered her all the help she required, with financial advisers and comptrollers, but, after twenty years as a passive wife, she was not content to reap the benefits and leave the running of her estates to others. She would be accountable for her own court, for the tenants of Ilinskoe and the numerous retainers in Moscow; and there were changes she wanted to make.

Unlike the privately owned Beloselsky Belozersky Palace or Ilinskoe, the Kremlin palaces belonged to the Crown so she must write at once to Nicky, requesting permission to make adjustments to her apartments. No longer obliged to entertain on a lavish scale, she had little use for the accoutrements of imperialism. It would be better, she decided, to have much of the antique furniture placed in storage. Before anything was moved, she would make detailed plans so that everything could be returned to its original position when she left the Kremlin. Corridors needed to be constructed so that the rooms might be reached more easily and to provide greater privacy. Her private apartments could so easily be divested of their expensive furnishings and decorated more simply.

Along with the palaces, jewels and wealth, Serge had also bequeathed her many responsibilities and she could not abandon any projects he had begun. Among his papers she had found the details of his chairmanship of the Palestine Society and, judging by so many unanswered letters, it seemed that the pressures of his office had led him to neglect that role. She added to her list the need to work through the backlog and reorganize the accounts. The Elizabethan Society still prospered, and her Red Cross charities continued to demand her attention; then there were the charitable institutions attached to Serge's regiments: funding the education of officers' children and arranging support for their widows.

When the list of all the charities was complete, she sighed at the thought of the most difficult decision of all: Marie and Dmitri. It had been a relief when Pavel eventually returned to France without his children, but the vitriol in his accusations still resounded in her ears. She must make amends to them, she decided, for any coldness she had shown in the past. Taking up her pen again, she wrote the names of their tutors with a view to supervising their curriculum.

At last, when all the lists were complete, she leaned back and inhaled the fresh country air. How recuperative it was being here, after the smog of Moscow. There could be nowhere on earth more conducive to regaining the vitality that had drained from her with the shock of the murder. An idea dawned on her and she reached again for the pen - as the numbers of casualties, pouring into the hospitals from the Japanese war, continued to rise, could there be a more perfect spot for them to recover from their injuries? She sketched a rough ground-plan of the house. What an ideal place to establish hospital wards.

Her thoughts drifted back to Moscow, to the men she had seen in the hospital and to Metropolitan Leontius' and Kalyaev's descriptions of life in the Zamoskvoreche region of the city. Serge's death had done nothing to ease the dissent and sense of imminent revolution. Moscow was virtually under siege. Shootings and disturbances in the streets, barricades and crossfire between soldiers and anarchists but, among them, she thought, there were souls who had never known anything of beauty and perhaps they had never known love.

She folded her lists and stood up. There was no doubt whatsoever in her mind. She must return to the city at once and find a way to bring love and light into the darkness.

"Your Highness, please forgive me," said Djunkovsky, "but I have to speak out. As the Grand

Duke's former aide-de-camp, I feel it's my duty to do all I can to protect his widow."

Ella smiled and continued fastening her coat.

"The streets aren't safe, particularly at this time of night."

"I appreciate your concern, General, but my life is in God's hands and I trust he will protect me."

Djunkovsky shook his head in despair, "At least allow me to arrange a police escort."

She laughed, "What better way to draw attention to myself than a police escort? If I'm to go incognito, the last thing I need is any sign of a police presence."

"But even if you're not recognized, Your Highness, the streets are unsafe for anyone at the moment, and a beautiful woman alone is…"

She patted his arm, "Thank you for your compliment. Rest assured I will come back safe and sound."

Before he could protest any further, she stepped into the carriage and gave instructions, "South of the river. Stop when you reach the Zamoskvoreche area and wait for me there."

Heedless of the coachman's warnings, she alighted on Ordynka Street and, with determined steps, made her way into the heart of the most squalid part of the city. Clouds of noxious fumes from the few factories unaffected by the strikes, hung in the air and smothered the derelict buildings, yards and alleys, echoing with the sound of shattering glass, wailing babies, drunken voices and aggressive oaths. Ragged children sat in gutters that were filled with every imaginable kind of filth: dead creatures, animal bones, live rats, excrement and broken bottles. The stench was overwhelming and the air so rancid that every breath felt like the assault of a virulent contagion in her lungs. From behind the rotten wood of half closed doors, came clashing and clattering and the screams of women undoubtedly enduring unspeakable violence. In squalid doorways, young girls with ancient faces stood waiting to trade their bodies for a few kopeks.

Pulling the veil further over her face, Ella stepped through the open door of a tenement block and found herself in a hallway lit only by a single dim gas lamp. Plaster peeled away from the walls and fell into the foul-smelling pools that stained the floor. A rickety staircase led up to a series of doors, from behind one of which came raised voices.

Ella knocked at the door and from inside an anxious voice responded, "Who is it?"

She pushed it open, "May I come in?"

Her eyes darted around the room; overturned chairs lay beside broken plates scattered across the floor where remnants of half-eaten food were trodden into the ridges between the wooden boards. A nauseous stench emanated from below the closed window where, beneath a heap of sodden blankets on a makeshift bed, a man lay sweating and groaning in his sleep.

A young girl, standing beside him, dropped a filthy rag into a bucket of scummy water and, wiping the back of her hand across her mouth, turned, stared aghast then dropped to her knees in a flurry of embarrassment.

"Is it really…Are you…" she stuttered, "Your Highness?"

Ella offered her hand to raise her to her feet but the girl began kissing her fingers in deference.

"I was in the square, Your Highness. I saw you the day the Grand Duke…"

"Please get up," Ella gently interrupted. "I heard a commotion and wondered if there is anything I can do to help?"

The girl stared at her in utter bewilderment but, when Ella looked towards the bed, the girl followed her eyes.

"It's my father. He took bad this morning. He was raving all day. It was all I could do to restrain him so he didn't hurt himself."

Ella, her shoes sticking to pools of half-dried filth, approached the bed beside which lay an empty bottle. Avoiding the jagged fragments around its shattered neck, she picked it up and inhaled a strong smell of alcohol.

"Is this the cause?"

"No, Your Highness, not this time. He said he wasn't well and he needed a drink but when he reached for the bottle he dropped it before he'd even taken a drop. That's what set him off." Her voice cracked with fraught emotion as her eyes moved wildly over the surrounding chaos. "He started searching everywhere for another bottle, turning things over, throwing things about. It went on all day until he exhausted himself and collapsed on the floor, calling for my mother."

"Where is your mother?"

"Dead, Your Highness. Died of consumption two years ago. I laid him on there and he's been like this ever since."

Ella sat down on the side of the bed and gently laid her hand on the man's brow. His forehead was burning and clammy and, though his eyes opened briefly and moved in her direction, he seemed unaware of her presence. She leaned further over him, "He's very hot. Do you have a little water to cool him?"

The girl, almost falling over herself with fatigue and eagerness to oblige, clattered across the room and, as Ella loosened the man's collar, he raised his hands to his ears with a pained expression and groaned loudly. The stench of his breath in Ella's face turned her stomach but she tried not to wince as the girl placed an enamel bowl on the floor beside her.

"It isn't his fault, Your Highness. He didn't drink at all when my mother was living."

Ella took her handkerchief, dipped it into the water and dabbed his forehead and neck. His shirt was wet with sweat and, as she unfastened the buttons, her eyes were drawn to a rash of flat red spots across his chest.

"This isn't the drink," she whispered. "Your father has typhoid." She glanced up at the girl whose face had turned white with fear, "He needs a doctor."

"We have no doctor, Your Highness. None of them comes here."

"I will send one to you."

She stood up and moved quickly towards the door, "Give him a few sips of water as often as you can. Keep the room dark and try to make as little noise as possible."

The girl, rubbing her eyes as though unsure whether or not she were dreaming, made a slight curtsey as Ella returned to the street.

On a corner stood a girl who, even allowing for the malnourishment that kept them so wasted and small, could not have been more than twelve or thirteen years old. Like the others who hovered in doorways, her purpose in loitering there was quite obvious, the more so when a man approached and held out a fist of coins.

The child nodded and Ella hesitated, longing to intervene yet uncertain how best to respond, when the man turned, put his arm around the child and led her towards an alley. It was then that Ella saw that he was wearing the coat of the Kiev Regiment and, suddenly incensed, she ran towards him, "Stop! Let the child go!"

The child, uttering an expletive, looked at her, "Find your own customers!"

Ella seized the man's arm, "You are wearing the uniform of His Majesty's army. You're a disgrace to your regiment!"

The man looked at her hand on his arm and laughed coarsely, breathing the stench of stale alcohol into her face, "Don't worry, lady, when I've finished with her, I'll take you as well."

Standing her ground, she gripped his sleeve more tightly, "This will be reported to your commanding officer."

"Oh yeah!" he laughed. "And why should he believe a whore?"

She raised the veil from her face, "Oh, he certainly will believe me."

The soldier squinted, moved closer to examine her features, then stepped back, attempted some kind of drunken salute and bowing, staggered quickly into the alley.

As the echo of his footsteps faded into the darkness, Ella was aware that the child was staring at her with an expression of contempt.

"Well thanks a lot," she said. "He would have paid over the odds."

"How old are you?" Ella said.

"Mind your own bloody business!" Her eyes moved along the street, searching for other clients.

"You are only a child," Ella said more to herself than the girl.

"I *was* a child but I'm not anymore. We grow up quickly round here." She laughed ironically and looked up at Ella, "I'm sure you're not from round here."

"Listen," Ella said, "tell me how much you expected to earn tonight and I will pay you double that amount to go home."

"Why?" she frowned. "Who the hell are you, anyway?"

"It doesn't matter who I am. What matters is who you are and why you are living like this."

"Pays well and I have to eat."

"What of your family?"

"I don't have a family. There's just me now."

"No one takes care of you?"

"I take care of myself. I do alright."

"No," Ella shook her head, "not like this. You should be in school, having lessons not…"

"Oh, that's easy to say. What would I live on?"

"Is there no other work you can do?"

"I might as well get paid for it. If I worked in one of the factories, the foreman would force me to do it anyway for nothing."

Ella rubbed her hands together in desperation and the diamond ring on her finger brushed against her skin. She pulled it off and held it out to the child, "Take this. You can sell it. It will provide you with more than enough to keep you. You can go to school, have an education and move away from here."

The girl took the ring and, holding it up to the dim gaslight, stared at it with amazement, "Is this *real*?"

"Yes. Take it. It's probably worth…"

The girl laughed loudly and held it towards Ella, "I can't keep that! If anyone around here knew I had it, they'd kill me for it. And if I tried to sell it, they'd arrest me. They'd want to know where it came from."

"Tell them Her Imperial Highness Grand Duchess Elizabeth gave it to you."

"Yeah, 'course I could!" she laughed. "And why on earth would they believe that a grand duchess would give anything to me?"

"Because, if they come and ask me, I will tell them I did."

The girl stopped laughing, "You mean you..."

Ella nodded.

"My God!" she gasped. "I heard about you. I heard you were..." She handed back the ring, "Thank you, Your Highness, but I can't keep it. I can't."

She backed away and Ella called after her, "Please, let me help you."

"You can't. It's a different world here. It's *different* for you," and she scurried off into the night.

Ella looked at the ring on the palm of her hand. The diamond, flickering in the glow of the gaslight, was the only thing of beauty in the midst of this squalor.

"So small a thing," she thought sadly, "yet it could probably buy all these derelict buildings and change all these derelict lives."

The filth, the foulness, the stench and depravity weighed heavily on her heart as she drifted back towards the carriage, "How can they find beauty in their souls when they are surrounded by nothing but ugliness?"

Chapter 39 - St. Petersburg – Autumn 1905

"Ah, Kostia, at last!" Miechen beamed as he stepped into the Grand Drawing Room of the Vladimir Palace. "We're so glad you could join us. We have musicians, singers, poetry recitals, everything one could wish for in our little celebration."

"Celebration?" he said gloomily, returning her kiss. "Is there anything at all to celebrate?"

"You have heard of a Victory Ball? Well, this is our Defeat Soirée. Considering the reasonable terms the Japanese accepted, all we have lost is our pride."

"And the lives of so many soldiers, for nothing."

She nodded to her other guests and led Konstantin towards a chair.

"We were defeated more by the unrest at home than the superior strength of the Japanese. If we'd had a stronger Tsar, everything would have been different. And now, he's been forced into accepting this ridiculous constitution with the Duma, effectively signing away three hundred years of autocracy."

"It's hardly Nicky's fault," Konstantin dropped into the chair. "What else could he do when all of his ministers and advisers told him that was the only way to prevent a full-scale revolution?"

"I hear Alix is incensed by it," she said with a gleeful glint in her eye. "She's so keen to preserve the autocracy and thinks Nicky was bullied into agreeing to call the Duma."

"Under the circumstances, I think he made the wisest decision. At least there is a semblance of order in the streets again and the factories have re-opened."

"And at what cost to the honour of the Imperial Family?"

"The honour of the family?" Konstantin cynically raised his eyebrows, "How can Nicky hope to preserve the honour of the family, when members of that family act dishonourably in failing to show him the allegiance he deserves."

She laughed superficially, "I take it that that remark is aimed at my son?"

"Is it true that Kyril has married Ducky, despite Nicky's refusal to sanction the wedding?"

"Yes, it is true and it's quite appalling that someone of his calibre, who risked his life and was almost killed fighting for his country, has been forced into exile in France. Alix has made it perfectly clear that he is *persona non grata* with her and, when he went to the Alexander Palace to explain his actions, she had the audacity to refuse him admittance. What gratitude for a war hero!"

"How could she do otherwise? Nicky can't go against the ruling of the Church, nor can he have one rule for one person and a different rule for another. After what happened with Pavel, Kyril knew exactly what to expect if he flouted the Tsar's authority."

"Well," she said, coldly, "it remains to be seen whether Nicky will be such a stickler when the situation is closer to home."

Konstantin shook his head, indicating he had no idea what she meant. She leaned closer, "Nicky's own brother made an attempt to elope with a lady-in-waiting."

"Misha!" Konstantin sat forward in shock.

"Apparently, Minnie heard about it and managed to intervene at the last minute. If she hadn't and Misha had succeeded in his plan, would Nicky have been so quick to banish *him*?"

Konstantin sighed deeply, "What on earth is the matter with everyone? How can we expect the country to remain loyal to the Tsar, when we ourselves are so blatantly going against all the demands of loyalty and service?"

Miechen shrugged, "If he doesn't inspire loyalty, what can he expect?"

Konstantin shook his head, "No, we are all responsible for our own actions. Blaming Nicky for our selfishness only compounds our guilt. Besides, we…"

"Ah, the first performance!" she said, raising her finger to silence him as the quartet bowed to the assembled gathering and began their recitation.

For a while Konstantin relaxed. The music washed over the Renaissance furnishings and artwork, and he was transported back to another era until he caught sight of Sandro, gesticulating to him from a corner of the room.

Inconspicuously, he slipped from his chair and followed him into a hallway where Sandro offered a cigarette and, with an anxious expression, said, "Kostia, have you heard anything of Ella recently?"

"We've been in touch several times since my return from Moscow."

"How is she?"

"Remarkably composed, considering all she has been through."

"Hmm," Sandro frowned thoughtfully and drummed his fingers on the wall. "Do you know what she plans to do now? We assumed she would return to Petersburg and settle in the Beloselsky

Belozersky Palace again but, apart from her visit at Easter, no one has seen her."

"I don't think she intends to return here at all. She plans to stay in Moscow."

"Really? Do you think she will re-marry? She's still only forty and as beautiful as ever. There would be dozens of suitors who would leap at the opportunity of bringing her the happiness that Serge failed to give."

"No," Konstantin said seriously, "I don't think she will ever re-marry. I think she has a very different plan."

Sandro nodded knowingly, "This is quite worrying, isn't it? Is it the shock, do you think? I mean having actually seen what was left of him, and then dealing with everything on her own - it would be enough to shatter the strongest of nerves. Is there anything we can do to help her?"

"I don't know what you're talking about," Konstantin said sincerely.

"The word is that she must be having some kind of mental breakdown."

"I have no idea where that came from but I have seen no evidence of it. On the contrary, she is one of the sanest people I have ever met. If you hear any more rumours like this, you can refute them at once. Didn't she suffer enough from the gossip-mongers' tongues when Serge was alive?"

"This isn't a rumour, Kostia. I heard it from Dmitri himself when he was staying with Nicky, and, if anyone knows the truth, he should since he lives with her."

Konstantin, baffled, shook his head, "What did he say?"

"She has stripped her private apartments of virtually all their furnishings and turned her bedroom into something that bears closer resemblance to a nun's cell than a grand duchess' boudoir."

"Perhaps she prefers simpler styles. And she was always very devout. When Serge was alive, she had to think of his wishes, too. Now she can do as she pleases. There's nothing strange in that."

"That's not all. Serge's will stated that after his and Ella's death, the Beloselsky Belozersky Palace would go to Dmitri. Ella has already signed the necessary papers to hand it over to Dmitri as soon as he comes of age."

"That's perfectly rational, too. If she intends to stay in Moscow, she has no need of it."

"Wait, there's more. She has been giving away so many of her possessions as gifts to various members of the family, but many more of them she has sold. All kinds of things - jewels, dresses, even her wedding presents. They must be worth a fortune; and do you know what she's planning to do with it?"

Konstantin shrugged, "Buy an estate elsewhere?"

"You're on the right lines but you'd never believe the place she's chosen."

"Surprise me!" Konstantin smiled.

"A slum district in the middle of Moscow."

"What?" he laughed in disbelief.

"Apparently, she has an idea that she is going to build a hospital, a chapel, an orphanage - a whole community - in just the very worst part of the city. According to Dmitri, she's been speaking with the best artists and architects in the country because she wants it to be like a palace for the poor. She's going to hire doctors and nurses, and - this is the worst part of all - Dmitri thinks she might actually be planning to go and live there. He thinks she wants to take care of all these people, personally!"

The memory of her beautiful eyes as she prayed beside Serge's coffin, drifted through Konstantin's mind, and the thought of how she had forgiven Kalyaev filled him with awe.

"It's unbelievable!" he said.

"Isn't it? How can we stop her?"

"Stop her?"

"We must! It's madness, utter madness. It's the shock of Serge's death and, once she recovers and realizes what a terrible mistake she has made, it will be too late."

"Sandro," Konstantin said quietly, resting his hand on his arm, "this isn't madness. Don't you see? She *is* a saint. She is doing exactly what Christ commanded: *Sell what you have, give it to the poor and then follow me.* "

"Didn't he also warn about not casting pearls before swine? How long will such a place last? Beautiful art in the middle of a pack of thieves and drunkards! They'll loot and wreck the place even before she's finished building it."

"There's the difference between Ella and us," Konstantin smiled. "We fear the worst of people. She sees the best. And, in my heart of hearts, I honestly believe that they will repay her trust with gratitude and respect."

Sandro shook his head, "Apart from everything else, it's demeaning. Dmitri says she has been reading medical books and studying anatomy and reading about that English Miss Nightingale's work. Don't you see what that means? She must be planning to nurse these people herself!"

"Ella never does anything by halves."

"A grand duchess working as a nurse! We'll be the laughing stock of Europe. Whatever respect the people have for us will collapse in an instant."

"No," Konstantin said, "perhaps, in her humility, they will see that we really do care about them and, apart from the beauty she will bring to those people's lives, she will do more for the reputation of the family than the rest of us put together."

Chapter 40 - Tsarskoe Selo - 1907

A freshening breeze blew through the open windows of the Catherine Palace, filling the corridors with the scents of spring flowers. There was a lightness in Ella's step as she guided Victoria from sumptuous room to sumptuous room, delighting in her sister's company and the prospect of confiding her plans. From the Great Gallery to the Grand Hall, from the Great Bedroom to the Chinese Room, Victoria plied her with questions, wanting to know every detail of the history and furnishings of so magnificent a palace.

Ella held open the door of the Amber Study, and Victoria's awe-struck eyes travelled over the figures of gods and goddesses in Florentine mosaics, the rocaille frames and the tiny pieces of fossil resin covering the wall panels.

"The entire room," Ella said, "was a gift to Tsar Peter from Frederick the Great. It was at the time of..." Startled by the echo of raucous laughter on the corridor outside, she turned abruptly, "Who on earth is that?"

They both stepped from the room to find Dmitri, almost bent double with mirth, beside a tall young woman, holding a fan before her face and equally convulsed with laughter.

"Dmitri! What are you doing here?" Ella held out her arms and he ran to embrace her warmly.

"Nicky told me you'd arrived and I didn't want to waste a minute before seeing my favourite aunt!"

She laughed and, when he had greeted Victoria, turned to the young woman behind him. She made a great, flamboyant curtsey and, though she held the fan in front of her face, there was something vaguely familiar about her eyes.

"Since Dmitri has quite forgotten his manners," the young woman said in a falsetto voice that was almost comical, "I see I am going to have to introduce myself."

Dmitri fell into further paroxysms of laughter, so contagious that Victoria and Ella glanced at one another and laughed, too, without knowing the cause.

The young woman held out her hand as though expecting it to be kissed, "Her Imperial Highness Princess Felicia Youssoupova, at your service."

"Oh good gracious!" Ella laughed, seizing the fan to expose a prettily made-up face with wild, mischievous eyes, "Felix, what on earth are you doing?"

"Can you believe it?" Dmitri laughed. "He has been all round Petersburg dressed like that!"

Felix removed the wig, "And a good many compliments I received from gentlemen."

"Really!" Ella said, "Whose are the clothes?"

"My mother's. She won't mind. She has plenty."

Shaking her head in amusement, Ella turned to Victoria, "You have met my young friend, Felix Youssoupov?"

Victoria smiled, "Felix dined with us several times when he was studying at Oxford."

"I dare say you have never seen him like this before!"

"Ah," said Felix, fluttering his eyelashes, "*you* might not have seen me like this, but your uncle, the King of England, has. He didn't know me, of course, but was so taken by my beauty that I had to make hasty escape to avoid his advances."

Victoria looked at Ella with a bemused smile, "Is that true?"

"Who knows?" she laughed. "Felix is quite mad. I never know what to believe."

"But you love me all the same," he said.

"How could I not love someone who always makes me laugh?" She looked along the corridor, "Come on, we'll go to my apartments before someone sees you and thinks we have all lost our senses."

Because it was Felix, and because he was clearly quite comfortable with his bizarre appearance, there seemed nothing incongruous about taking tea and discussing more sensible matters with a young man dressed in his mother's jewels and gown, his short hair out of place above his heavily-painted features.

As Victoria handed around the cups, Dmitri asked, "Where's Marie? She came with you from Moscow, didn't she?"

"Yes, she did. She was feeling a little under the weather and wanted to rest."

He nodded and Ella explained to Victoria, "Dmitri spends a lot of the time with Nicky and Alix now. I thought, since he is almost sixteen, he needed a father-figure and Nicky so enjoys his company, but it means Marie and I see far less of him."

Dmitri smiled at her, "But there is always plenty of news to catch up on when we meet."

"Yes," she said eagerly, taking the cup from Victoria, "and I suppose Marie has written to tell you her most exciting news?"

His lip twitched, "Concerning the Swedish prince?"

"Yes. We're meeting him for dinner with Nicky and Alix this evening, and she will give him her answer to his proposal."

"Do you know what that answer will be?" Dmitri asked.

"She has assured me that she has thought it through and is happy to accept him."

When Dmitri's brow creased doubtfully, Ella felt obliged to explain, "She was uncertain at first, which is natural, but for over a year she has been telling me she couldn't wait to marry. She likes him, he is quiet and unassuming, and I am sure they will be very happy together."

"She's very young to be marrying," Felix said.

"She's seventeen and will be eighteen by the time of the wedding. That's not too young."

Dmitri, in a manner reminiscent of Serge, fidgeted with the ring on his finger, "The thing is," he said, "I think Marie feels she hardly knows him. She has only met him on a couple of occasions and even then always with a chaperone."

"That's the way of it for people in our position," Ella said and felt Victoria's eyes upon her with an expression of uncertainty.

"And," Dmitri fidgeted more nervously, "Marie feels she can't accept him without our father's permission."

The mention of Pavel provoked the usual jolt in Ella's stomach and her reply came out far more curtly than she intended, "Your father lost all his rights when he abnegated his responsibilities. The Tsar and I are Marie's legal guardians and, since Nicky has granted permission for her to marry, that is all that's necessary."

When Dmitri didn't reply, Ella felt a pang of regret for having spoken so sharply and dampening the lively atmosphere. She glanced towards Felix who seemed to sense what she was thinking and immediately set about raising their spirits again.

"A wedding!" He leaped up and twirled around, "I do hope I shall be invited. Now what shall I wear? My mother's Peregrine pearls - would they match my court dress?"

"No," Dmitri smiled, "we don't want you upstaging the bride!"

Felix laughed and sat down again, "If I could marry anyone, do you know whom I would choose?" He winked at Ella, "Present company excepted, of course."

"One of Nicky's daughters?" Dmitri said.

"Oh no, I wouldn't dream of setting my sights quite so high. Irina."

"Irina?"

"Xenia and Sandro's daughter. She's quite exquisite."

"She's only twelve years old!" Dmitri laughed.

"And I intend to enjoy a few more years of freedom before marrying so, by the time she is old enough, I will be ready to settle down."

"Somehow, Felix," Ella smiled, "I am sure you are far too irrepressible to *ever* quite settle down."

"In that case, when I prove you wrong, I shall have to mark the occasion with the most memorable wedding Russia has ever seen."

"Yes," Dmitri joked, "*you* could wear the wedding gown and veil!"

The idea so amused Felix that he rolled back in the chair and gasped through his laughter, "And my wife would wear a military uniform, all the guests would wear black, and I could have that strange monk fellow to officiate."

"What strange monk?"

"The one you were telling me about. The one who visits the Tsarina."

"Oh, he's not a monk," Dmitri said, suddenly serious. "I don't know what he is exactly - some kind of holy man but definitely not a monk. He has a wife and children somewhere in Siberia."

Holy man... The memory of Alix's description of the prophecy of the charlatan, Philippe, that another guide would follow, caused Ella's heart to sink.

"Who is he?" she whispered.

"Some scruffy peasant," Dmitri said awkwardly, as though torn between loyalty and his true feelings. "He has some kind of healing power so Alix sends for him when the Tsarevich is unwell."

Victoria looked at Ella with consternation.

"He's called Grigory Rasputin. Alix calls him Father Grigory but he isn't a priest and there are all sorts of stories about him. It's hard to know what's true and what isn't."

"What kind of stories?" Victoria said.

"When he's at the palace, he's always polite in a coarse kind of way. He treats Alix and Nicky with deference; and their children, especially Alexei, love him. But he gives me the creeps. There's something about the way he looks at people through very dark eyes that seem to bore through you."

"And what of the stories about him?" Victoria said again.

"Well, they say that his life outside the palace is anything but that of a holy man. He frequents the bath houses and brothels; and women - some from the very best families - are seen going into his rooms at all times of the day and night."

"Does Alix know of these stories?" Victoria asked.

He nodded, "She says calumnies are an occupational hazard for holy men. Christ himself was accused of being a glutton and was criticised for mixing with sinners."

Ella wearily pressed her hand against her forehead with a sense of having been through this before. How intransigent Alix had been in defence of her 'doctor', would she now be the same regarding this Grigory Rasputin?

"Anyway," Dmitri said, shuffling to the edge of his chair, "we don't know if there is any truth in the stories. But there is one odd thing. No matter how ill he has been, Alexei is always better after Rasputin visits." He stood up, "I had better go and see if Marie is feeling better. Would you excuse me?"

"Yes, of course," Ella said, "and would you tell her I will come along shortly to see her?"

"I had better go too," Felix said brightly, "before my mother misses her pearls."

"You're not going back to Petersburg dressed like that?" Ella smiled.

"Why not? It gives me a whole new view of the world!"

When they had gone, Victoria raised her eyebrows to Ella, "Do you think we should speak with Alix about this Rasputin?"

"I don't think it will make any difference if she has made up her mind to trust him."

"We could at least warn her of what is being said."

"And she will give us the same reply as she gave to Dmitri. The more he is criticised, the more holy he will appear to her. Perhaps the best thing is to hope his influence will be as short-lived as Philippe's was."

Victoria's face was grave for a moment then suddenly brightened, "But what of your news? You said you had something to show me?"

"Yes!" Ella took two scrolls from a cupboard and spread them across the table, "The plans for my foundation! I have bought the land, and Nicky has given permission for me to go ahead with it. Shchusev, the architect, has been wonderful and followed my specifications exactly."

Victoria leaned over her shoulder and read from the top of page, "*The House of Martha and Mary.*"

"I thought that name best captured the purpose of it: Martha's practical service and Mary's spirituality. My idea is to establish a religious community of nurses who'll work here in the hospital and visit the sick in their own homes as well. Over here," she pointed to the plan, "the church is the heart of the whole community. I've asked the artist, Nesterov, to paint the ceilings and walls with frescoes. And here, there will be the house for our community, and an orphanage surrounded by gardens and orchards."

Victoria looked at her in amazed admiration, "And this in the middle of a slum district?"

"Their lives are so harsh, Victoria. Is it any wonder there is so much vice and immorality? Surrounded by filth, worn down by disease and exhausted by long hours in sweatshops, how could they raise their hearts to God? That's why everything in my foundation must be beautiful. We'll have white walls and fill the place with flowers so we can bring beauty into their lives."

"And you're going to live there in this community?"

She nodded, "In time I hope the Church will grant us permission to be established as a proper religious order. There is nothing like this in the whole of Russia but, when they see the good we are doing, the bishops will surely grant us convent status. I have spoken with a few of them - Tryphon, Anastassy, Feofan - and they have given me so much support. Some of the others seem less convinced. They think the idea is too Protestant but, once we are established, I am sure they will change their minds."

Victoria sat back, "You really *have* thought it all through, haven't you? I was under the impression from Alix's letters that it was something of whim."

"Oh," she sighed, "so many people, all with good intentions, don't understand at all. They've been telling her that I'm suffering from some kind of breakdown or I'm taking too much on and will regret it, but you know me better than that, Victoria."

She smiled, "Yes, I do and, if she were alive, Mama would understand too."

"We all do what we can. When Serge was alive, I had other duties: receptions, balls, entertaining so many people. Now I have this opportunity to do something else that, with God's blessing, will make such a difference to so many people's lives." A memory flashed through her mind and she felt a need to explain, "I know Serge was anxious that I allow myself to be led astray by my own notions, so I have been especially cautious about that. I haven't done anything without first consulting the elders of the Zosima Hermitage and, more recently, I've found a new spiritual director, Father Mitrophan Serebrinsky. He's a very simple man, a former chaplain to the army, and now has a parish in Orel but I hope that, in time, he will agree to come here and be our chaplain. Only to speak to him for a few minutes, one feels instinctively that he is so modest and pure and he has experience of so many different kinds of people that he would be perfect for our foundation."

"And what about the community? Do you think you will find enough women to want to join you?"

"Six have already approached me and I am sure many more will follow. Obviously, before we can take any patients we will need some kind of training. Several of my Red Cross nurses and doctors have offered their services free of charge."

"I'm amazed, Ella, truly amazed," Victoria smiled, "though I suppose, knowing you as I do, I shouldn't be."

"It's the most wonderful thing for me. At last it's the chance to really live up to Mama's example and use the skills she taught us. For the first time in my life, I feel truly free. Now that Dmitri spends most of his time with Nicky, once Marie is married I will have no other obligations here and can devote myself totally to this and, of course, to my other charities. I don't intend to abandon those."

Victoria looked up pensively, "Marie's wedding," she said.

"What about it?"

She hesitated, "I'm sorry but I have to ask. In all your enthusiasm to see these plans come to fruition, you're not rushing her into it, are you?"

"Not at all. She told me she wants to be married. She told me she was fond of William." She knew how defensive she sounded and, beneath the certainty that she was acting justly, came the niggling fear that perhaps Victoria was correct.

"Alright, she has taken to her bed feigning illness now but it isn't because I have forced her into anything. The choice is hers entirely. The only thing I have insisted upon is that she give him an answer one way or the other."

Victoria's expression suggested she was unconvinced.

"I can't deny that I have never found Marie easy to live with, any more than she has found me easy to live with. Nor can I deny that it wounded me deeply to see Serge showing her and Dmitri the affection he seldom showed me but, after his death, I regretted that fault on my part. I apologised to both of them for any coldness I had shown them in the past. Dmitri and I have been very close ever since. The same, I know, can't be said for Marie but, in spite of all of this, I would never force her into anything against her will. She is often moody and self-absorbed. One minute she wants to marry, the next she doesn't and the poor young Swede is left not knowing where he is. If I have pushed her at all, it is only to make a decision. Now she's reached that decision and, by this time next year, she'll be married."

"And you will be free to commence your new life in The House of Martha and Mary."

Chapter 41 - Moscow - February 1910

Carriages, horse-drawn wagons and motor cars bustled to and fro along Ordynka Street as Konstantin alighted at The House of Martha and Mary. He pushed open the wrought iron gates and the din and clatter of engines and hooves faded like the dying notes of symphony. Behind him, on the street, people jostled and rushed, shouting raucously above the clamour of vehicles, but the few figures he saw before him, moved quietly with such a light serenity in their steps that it seemed he had stepped directly from hell into heaven.

A small woman with a bright smile came towards him, "Your Highness, the Grand Duchess is expecting you, if you would care to follow me."

She led him through a neatly tended garden, past a white-walled church and low buildings from which sacred images gazed serenely across mown lawns and courtyards. Here and there, tranquil figures went about their tasks, sweeping leaves, wheeling patients in chairs, and leading small groups of children whose voices echoed like laughter. Contentment was etched into their faces; they all seemed to be in place and to belong in this haven, the harmony of which was such that Konstantin felt that his own strangeness and inner-discord must stand out like a birthmark across his brow.

"I'm afraid we're a bit disorganised today," his guide said. "A woman was brought in last night covered in burns from an overturned gas-stove. When gangrene set in, the city hospital said there was no hope and they could no longer treat her but the Grand Duchess is convinced we can save her. She has been up all night tending her wounds."

"You receive many patients from other hospitals?" Konstantin said.

"Oh yes. All the ones they consider beyond hope are sent here."

"And they recover?"

She stopped and thought for a moment, "One way or another they find healing. Even if they don't make a physical recovery, they find peace in their souls. The Grand Duchess stays with them through their last hours, helping them to prepare for a happy eternity, and they die in peace."

"In Petersburg they say that the Muscovites call her a saint."

"They do," the woman laughed, "and some go even further, kissing her shadow or the hem of her garments as she passes. The Grand Duchess dislikes flattery and pays no attention to it but she can't help what other people say or do."

She held open a door and guided him into a cosy parlour where Ella, dressed in white, sat at a table covered with letters in orderly piles.

"His Imperial Highness Grand Duke Konstantin Konstantinovich," said the woman.

Ella sprang from the chair, "Kostia, thank you so much for coming!" Her face was radiant with a joy that seemed almost divine. She greeted him with a kiss on both cheeks before turning to his guide. "Thank you, Barbara. If you have a moment would you ask Father Mitrophan to visit our newest patient?"

Barbara nodded, made a slight bow and left.

"Well," said Konstantin, smiling brightly, "once again you exceed my highest expectations! The first time I saw you, I was speechless at the sight of your beauty. Now, twenty-five years on,

I'm speechless in the midst of the beauty you've created."

She laughed dismissively, "We have only just begun. It will be easier in a couple of months when we are officially recognized as a convent."

"Yes, the Tsar told me that the synod had finally seen sense and recognized your foundation as a religious order."

"It's too wonderful for words!" Her eyes shone with delight, "In April we take our vows. Seventeen of us in the first instance but there are others who will follow soon afterwards. It's such an important step for me that I so *wished* Alix and Nicky could come. Unfortunately, they have so many other commitments that it's not possible."

She shook away a momentary frown and, inviting him to sit down, poured tea from an English teapot, "I will show you around later, if you would like."

"I *would* like, if you're not too exhausted. I heard you were up all night with a patient."

"I'm used to getting by on little sleep," she smiled, "and I'd love you to see what we do here. But first," she handed him a cup of tea, "tell me all your news. How is Mavra and your family?"

"Very well," he nodded eagerly. "They are all growing up so quickly! It's hard to believe that Ioann will be twenty-four this year. It seems no time at all since he was just a tiny baby."

"The years fly by, don't they? When we're young, our lives seem to roll out endlessly before us and we think we will continue on the same path forever. One day we wake up and suddenly find everything has changed and we have no idea how it happened or where the time went."

"So many changes," he said, ponderously. "I was sorry to hear of the death of your uncle in England."

"Yes, it is a great sadness. Poor Uncle Bertie had waited so long to be king, only to reign for so short a time."

Konstantin reached into his pocket for a cigarette but thought better of it, "Sandro and his brothers are of the gloomy opinion that, without your uncle to hold the world together, war in Europe is inevitable sooner or later."

"I see no reason why it should be. George, in England, is a great friend of both Nicky and the Kaiser. Cousin Willy might be pompous and bombastic but I am sure he has no more desire for war than we do."

"War would be a disaster for Russia."

"Disaster for the whole of Europe. After the tragedy of the Japanese War, Nicky knows that better than anyone. I'm sure he'll do everything in his power to keep the peace."

Nicky, Konstantin thought and, as he wondered whether to voice his concerns, Ella seemed to read his mind. She smiled at him, "Tell me, what's the latest news from Tsarskoe Selo?"

He frowned, weighing his words before speaking, "I suppose you will have heard what they're saying about this holy man, Rasputin?"

She nodded and sipped her tea, "I saw Zinaida last week and she was concerned about some of the stories that are circulating in Petersburg."

"It seems that the Tsar and Tsarina are very attached to him but no one knows exactly what goes on or why he is allowed such easy access to the palace."

"What have you heard about him, Kostia? Where does he come from and how did he come into contact with Alix?"

"As far as I can make out, he was just a simple peasant, working his father's land and earning a reputation as a foul-mouthed, loose-living ruffian until, he claimed, God called him for greater work."

"He says that?"

"Apparently, shortly after his marriage, he claimed to have had a vision of the Virgin Mary. He was convinced that she was calling him for a higher purpose. He left his wife and family to make a pilgrimage to Jerusalem, via several Russian monasteries and Greece. For two years he travelled, seeking advice from monks, studying the ways of the Staretzy and probably spending time with the Khlysty."

"Khlysty?"

"You've not heard of them? They're a strange sect, condemned by the Church authorities."

"On what grounds?"

"They have very bizarre beliefs and twist theology to suit their own rather depraved ends. They preach that sin is beneficial, since only the sinner can obtain divine forgiveness and draw closer to God. The harder and more often a man sins, the greater will be his humility and hence his sanctity."

Ella shook her head.

"Their services are held in secret but it's said they involve flagellation and frenetic dances culminating in orgies through which they claim their souls are cleansed of pride and sin."

Her frowned deepened, "And this Rasputin is a khlyst?"

"He has never admitted to it but, from what I have heard, he shares many of their beliefs."

"This *is* disturbing."

"What is more disturbing is the number of young women who are taken in by him. I don't know for certain whether or not this is true but the story is that many, many young women of aristocratic families go to his rooms for healing or guidance and he always gives them the same message. They must destroy their pride, which keeps them from God, and he persuades them that the best way to do this is to yield to his sexual advances."

"And they believe him?"

"Apparently, though I must say it is quite unbelievable. He is dirty and unwashed with particles of food caked in his straggly beard, yet many of these women go to him willingly and have become his fervent devotees."

"How does he convince them?" she frowned. "Does he use hypnosis?"

"He denies it but everyone who has met him is struck by the incredible power of his eyes."

"Everyone including Nicky and Alix?"

Konstantin shrugged, "The problem is that at first many leading bishops accepted him. Even the Tsar's spiritual advisor, Archimandrite Theofanes, was so impressed by his spirituality and powers of healing that he had no doubt at all of his sanctity. Others, like Bishop Feofan, esteemed him highly, so it's hardly surprising that the Tsar and Tsarina accepted him when he had the backing of the Church."

"And what of his healing powers?"

"Those who have witnessed them are amazed. Again, I cannot vouch for the truth of this but I was told that the Tsarevich has an illness which is never mentioned." He paused allowing her the opportunity to confirm or deny it, and, though she said nothing, he took her silence as confirmation of the fact. "For this reason, it's said, Rasputin was brought to the Alexander Palace and, though he made no effort to disguise his natural coarseness, the Tsarina was impressed and saw him as the epitome of the true Orthodox Russian, devoted to the Emperor and to God."

Ella smiled ruefully, "Alix has always had great faith in the *real* Russians - the peasants and the simple people - which isn't surprising when you consider the way she has been treated by many of the aristocrats and courtiers."

Konstantin agreed and continued, "Allegedly, at the time Rasputin arrived, the Tsarevich was suffering from a severe episode of his illness and the doctors were quite powerless to ease his pain. Rasputin simply leaned over him, whispered to him and left and, by the following morning, His Highness was healed."

An expression of combined sorrow and consternation settled on Ella's face and for a few minutes she stared into space as if gazing at a memory. Then, as though jolted from sleep, she shook her head, "Rumour and gossip are the most pernicious vices and cause untold harm. Whatever the true reason for this man's visits to the Tsar and Tsarina, is really no one's business but their own."

There was such finality in her tone that Konstantin suspected she was not only hiding some family secret but also confronted by a challenge she had no desire to face. She took his tea cup from him and stood up, "Shall I show you around now?"

Through the tranquil gardens, in and out of hospital wards and schoolrooms, she led him and everywhere the same atmosphere of incense and sanctity pervaded the place. Children kissed her hands as she passed, and patients called from their beds, "Matushka!" and blessed themselves.

Matushka, Konstantin smiled - *little mother!* She, who had so longed for the children that Serge denied her, now had a whole family to care for and to love.

"We usually meet for prayers at seventy-thirty in the morning," she explained as they left the chapel. "After breakfast those not actively involved in nursing or running the house, come back here for other religious services. The rest go about their duties and we meet again at nine in the evening for vespers."

"You didn't have any difficulty recruiting followers?"

"Not at all. Each day more and more young women arrive, eager to dedicate themselves to this way of life. It's wonderful because it means we can expand into so many other areas. The hospital flourishes but not all the sick need hospital treatment; many could be tended in their own homes. Once the convent is officially established, we plan to go out into the community, taking medicines and dressings wherever they are needed."

As they walked past the windows of the orphanage, sadness filled her eyes, "Many of these children have such terrible backgrounds. Some of them I found literally abandoned on the street; others were working as prostitutes."

"*You* go out into the streets to find them? Is that safe?"

"Is it any more dangerous to wander through the streets unguarded than it was for Serge or his father to venture out with a police escort? Our lives are in God's hands and he will protect us for as long as he wishes us to do this work."

Konstantin smiled at her and she laughed as though mildly embarrassed by her own faith, "Truthfully, so far I have met with nothing but respect. Even in some of the worst areas, when people understand our intentions and the hope we are offering their children, they see no need to harm us."

"All these children," he said, looking through the window, "were found on the street?"

"No, not all of them. Some of them came to us through the Elizabethan Society. As far as possible, we like them to remain with their families, so the priests report to us the names of any parishioners who are in dire circumstances and we send money and food to them. Some of our community are preparing to educate the parents in their own homes, too."

"And what will happen to these children when they leave here?"

"Ah," she said, her eyes lighting up with enthusiasm, "I have an idea that I hope to implement as soon as we have made our vows. It's no good sending them back to the mercy of unscrupulous landlords or employers so my thought is that we can set up a series of inexpensive or rent-free hostels for those who wish to study. For those who don't want that, I would like to offer work as messenger boys. There is such a demand for that across the city, and that way we can be sure they are paid fairly and have safe places to return to each evening."

He shook his head in wonder. How little Serge had appreciated so brilliant an imagination and so noble a heart. *No wonder*, he thought, *they hail her as a saint. Even to be in her atmosphere fills my soul with awe. I truly believe I am in the presence of the divine.*

Chapter 42

The pearl grey habit and veil lay across the table. Just a few more weeks, Ella thought, and her old life would be closed forever. Beneath her white dress, the rough hair shirt scratched her skin, and the weights, fastened to her wrists, pulled at the muscles in her arms as she outstretched them in prayer.

"I repent of all the vanities of the past," she murmured. "I repent of my worldly pride. I repent of the urge of the flesh and all unholy desires. I repent…"

The door opened and, startled by the intrusion, she lowered her arms and stood up. A young girl stared at the weights and blushed, "Oh Matushka, I'm so sorry!"

Ella loosed them from her wrists.

"Valentina," she smiled, guiding the girl towards the door, "it is always better to knock before entering a room."

"I am so sorry," Valentina said again, "but there is a young lady here from Petersburg and she wishes to see you urgently."

"Would you show her to the parlour? I will be along in a moment."

She blew out the candles that burned before the icons, and returned the weights to the drawer beside her prayer books, before raising her head and walking from the room.

In the parlour, a well-dressed young woman was nervously pacing to and fro. She curtseyed when Ella entered and, though her face seemed vaguely familiar, Ella couldn't quite place her.

"Your Highness," she said desperately, "please forgive me for coming to you like this. I don't want to cause any trouble."

She was so flustered and anxious that her words ran together, and Ella, taking her hands, led her to a chair, "We have met before?"

"Yes, Your Highness. I was governess to His Majesty's daughters."

"Ah," said Ella, remembering, "Mlle Tyutcheva, I think? I know your parents."

She nodded, "Sophie Ivanovna Tyutcheva."

A frightening thought suddenly struck Ella. "The Tsarevich is well?" she asked urgently.

"Oh yes, yes. At least, he is as well as he…" She fidgeted with her cuffs and her eyes darted anxiously around the room, "Your Highness, this is such a delicate matter and I beg you not to be angry with me. I wouldn't have come but I felt it was my duty. My father said you would be the best person to approach."

"Please," Ella said, "speak freely."

"I am no longer in Their Majesty's employment. I made a terrible mistake and yet I felt I had no option."

"You were dismissed?"

She hung her head in shame, "Yes, Your Highness."

"Why?"

"I am not really sure. I think I offended Her Majesty. I took my responsibilities to the young grand duchesses very seriously so you can, I am sure, imagine my reaction when I saw a rather rough peasant lurking by their rooms as they were preparing for bed. At first I didn't recognize him but then I realized it was Rasputin - the man they call Father Grigory."

Three times, Ella thought, *in one month, I have heard this man's name and each report more disturbing than the last.*

"Of course, I told Her Majesty and she was very angry about it."

"Naturally."

"Oh no, Your Highness, no. She wasn't angry that he had been there. She was angry that I had suggested there was anything untoward about this man of God."

Ella closed her eyes not wanting to imagine the scene.

"I also spoke of it to His Majesty and he said there was nothing for me to worry about, that the man is a holy man and that he prays with the grand duchesses. To avoid any misunderstanding, he said, he would order him to stay away from their rooms but, shortly afterwards, I was dismissed. I came back here to my parents and, when I told them what had happened, they insisted I came to you."

"I'm glad you did."

"Oh, please, Your Highness, don't think I am suggesting any wrongdoing. It is just that this man is giving rise to so many rumours that I fear his presence is damaging to the reputation of the Imperial Family. Her Majesty is devoted to him, and those of us who are aware of the condition of the young Tsarevich can understand why, but there are so many other people who know nothing of that and they jump to all kinds of scandalous conclusions."

"Yes," Ella said, "I understand and I commend your loyalty."

"Besides," she was calmer now, "I know Their Majesties have absolute faith in him. When he is with them, he behaves with decorum but what we hear of his activities in the city made me fearful for the grand duchesses. They are so young and innocent and he is..."

"It's alright," Ella said. "I appreciate what you're saying. I will speak to Their Majesties."

Clearly relieved, Sophie stood up, "Thank you, Your Highness. Obviously, it is not my place to voice these concerns but I thought...my father thought, if perhaps you..."

"Yes, of course," Ella said. "And I trust that I may rely on your discretion?"

Sophie nodded.

"These things have a way of being blown out of all proportion. The sooner any whiff of scandal is extinguished, the better."

The candlelight flickered on the diamonds sewn into Alix' ball gown, so incongruous amid the blood-soaked dressings piled on the floor. Slipping her arm around Alexei's shoulders, she tried to whisper something soothing but his agonized cries drowned her words. The tighter they bound the bandages, the greater his pain and, as the swelling on his knee enlarged, his leg twisted distortedly. The doctor brought brandy and, pouring it onto a teaspoon, Alix held it to his lips. His face was deathly white and clammy, and his weakening cries sounded like the muffled death throes of one being smothered.

"Sip this, my love. It will make you feel better," she whispered. "You will feel better soon, I promise you will."

Alexei choked at the first sip but Alix persisted, waiting patiently for him to regain his breath, holding him securely in her arms and whispering constantly, "It's alright, my darling, everything will be alright."

When the teaspoon was dry she laid him back on the pillow but he had hardly closed his eyes when he lurched forwards again, groaning in agony. Still Alix held him, comforting him with tender whispers.

The doctor backed towards the door, "Shall I ask His Majesty to come?"

She shook her head, "He cannot leave the guests. They will suspect the worst." She looked up suddenly, "Father Grigory has been sent for?"

The doctor's surly expression passed her by unnoticed, "Yes, Your Majesty."

"There now," she whispered to the child, "Our Friend is coming; everything will be alright. Everything will be alright."

The door opened and a goat-like smell filled the room - to Alix the refreshing odour of sanctity and salvation.

"Little Mama!" Even the sound of his voice brought healing and, when he rested his hands on her shoulders, she could feel the power of God within him.

He looked back at the doctor, "Send him away. The doctors distress him with their lies."

She waved dismissively and, though he bristled, the doctor obeyed. When he had gone, Father Grigory moved her from the bed, and lay down beside the Tsarevich.

"Now then, my little one," he pressed his face close to Alexei's. "There is no cause for pain. God is good. He doesn't want his little ones to suffer. This is nothing but a nightmare and you can wake up now. See yourself as you really are. Your spirit dances like sunlight on the Neva. You see it? You are running through fields of summer rain. Your laughter echoes over the river and ripples in joy through your veins."

Softly, soothingly, hypnotically, gently his voice seemed to fill the whole room with an atmosphere of peace. Alexei's breathing deepened. His cries became more infrequent and soon he was sleeping peacefully.

Father Grigory rose from the bed and looked Alix in the eye, "The little one will recover. Don't let the doctors touch him. All they see is illness, evil and disease and they wonder why they cannot cure it. They cannot cure it because they see it. God heals because God sees only perfection."

Again he put his hands on her shoulders and she sank to her knees in gratitude.

"God looks at him through my eyes. Through me God heals him. You understand?"

She didn't understand. She understood only exhaustion, desperation, despair and the blessed relief of his presence. Days and nights and days and nights at Alexei's bedside as he lay there screaming in pain, and the strain of stepping from that scene into the crowded, trivial ballroom with the false smiles and idle chatter, the criticism and the sneers.

"Help me," she murmured.

"Abase yourself," his hands were forceful on her shoulders, pushing her lower as though pressing her into the earth. "You trust yourself and you are nothing so you fail. Trust God alone and trust God in me and you will begin to understand."

She kissed his hands, "Dear friend! My dear, dear friend."

He brushed the tears from her face and pulled her to her feet, "Your guests are waiting."

She looked down at the pale face of the beautiful Tsarevich and longed only to remain by his side, to see him wake, fully restored to health and free of this evil forever. But the diamonds shimmering in her gown spoke only of duty. She called for the maids and gave them orders to remain with her son, then ran along the corridors, trying to restore her calm before stepping back into the mindless cacophony of the ballroom.

"So," Nicky laughed, as he and Ella strode through the early-spring snow of Tsarskoe Selo, "this is the last time I shall see you dressed as a woman of the world?"

She smiled, "Nesterov designed our habits for us. I wanted something simple, obviously, but we owe it to the people we visit and care for, to look respectable."

"Everyone speaks very highly of all the work you're doing."

"From when I first came here, Serge told me that his dream and the dream of Tsardom was to build the Kingdom of God in Russia. We all work towards that goal, each in our own way, so we do what little we can in Moscow."

"I wish you well in it."

"Nicky, I so appreciate your support. Without that, I am sure the synod would never have granted us convent status. Those bishops, like Anastassy and Tryphon, who visited us and have seen our work, were happy to offer us their help but Hermogen and some of the others criticised us without even knowing what we do. It's thanks to you that the synod finally voted in our favour."

He smiled.

"It was even kinder of you to do that for us when you're not totally convinced that I am doing the right thing."

He stopped and frowned.

"I know that Alix thinks this is just a whim," she said.

"She worries about you. We both do. It must be so exhausting for you and we fear for your health."

"Look at me!" she opened her arms. "I am in perfect health. I never felt better!"

He nodded sadly, "So often I wish Alix and I had the freedom to follow our hearts, too, but Providence decides our fate before we are born - one man a peasant, another the Tsar - and we all do the best we can. You know," he smiled dreamily, "if I had a choice, I wouldn't have chosen this. Not at all."

"It *is* a great responsibility but God would never place that burden on someone who wasn't strong enough to carry it."

"It's simply impossible to keep everyone happy. Each day the ministers from so many departments come to me with their proposals for my approval. One comes in, states a very convincing case for spending so much money on education or the railways or the military and I accept what he says. Then the finance minister comes in and states the exact opposite view. If I go back on my word, I am seen a prevaricating and weak. If I keep my word, I am seen as making terrible mistakes. All I want is to do the best for Russia, for my people."

Ella smiled, "So vast a country, so many demands."

"I could accept that," he said, "and I am happy to take criticism but it's vital that the family stand together and support me. Uncle Pavel, Kyril and now Misha..."

"Misha?"

"His mistress is expecting his child so he is pushing me to grant her a divorce from her husband."

"I had no idea," she said sadly. "He isn't expecting you to allow him to marry her?"

"No, not at the moment, but I fear it could become a repeat of what happened with Uncle Pavel."

"That's impossible. Misha is second in line to the throne and if Alexei..." she stopped herself and glanced towards the window where Alix was sitting looking out at them. "Misha is your brother; *he* will never betray you."

He followed her eyes to the window and his face became more serious, "It's so painful for Alix. All this disloyalty and disregard for what is right. Everything she does, she does to support me and to preserve the autocracy for Alexei. When she sees members of my own family chipping away at it for their own selfish reasons, it is so hard for her to bear."

"And Alexei's health must be a constant strain too," Ella said.

"Everything he suffers, she suffers with him. You know how excruciating it is to see someone you love in pain and to feel quite powerless to ease that pain. For Alix that agony is doubled because in some way she feels responsible for it."

Ella looked up at the pale face at the window. How Alix had aged in the past six years since Alexei's birth! The melancholy beauty, which had always graced her features, was replaced now with an indescribable sorrow that surrounded her like a shroud.

"Shall we go to her?" she said.

Nicky nodded and, kicking the snow from their boots, they stepped indoors to the cluttered room with its icons and photographs, its wicker chairs and chintz hangings. Their faces glowing from the snowy wind, they sat by the fire taking tea, and, though the conversation was cordial and made lighter by the arrival of the children, Ella could not help but be aware of the defensiveness in Alix's attitude towards her. Perhaps she already knew what Ella wanted to say. Deliberately steering away from any talk of the Tsarevich and pointedly making no mention of The House of Martha and Mary, she spoke only generally of the weather and seemed relieved each time one of her daughters intervened with a comment about their lessons.

Anastasia, who had been restlessly swinging from a chair, apparently sensed the tension and eventually, no longer able to endure it, swung instead from Nicky's arm.

"Let's go back outside, Papa, and throw snowballs."

"I'm sorry," he began, "I have so much work to do that..."

"Please," she pleaded, "just for a short while. You know the fresh air clears your head and then you can work better."

The temptation was too great and he yielded with a happy smile, "And perhaps Mama and Aunt Ella would like to spend a little time alone."

The expression on Alix's face said the opposite was true and, when the others had left, she yawned as though to preclude conversation.

"I'm so sorry," Ella said, "that you're unable to come to Moscow for our ceremony next month. For me, it's as important as when a young girl takes her vows at her wedding."

"It's quite impossible. You have no idea of all our commitments here."

She smiled affably, "Perhaps you will be able to visit another time. Serge's sister came, and Victoria, of course, and Kostia. They all seemed to enjoy their visits."

"Alexei's health prevents us from travelling as much as we might."

"Of course, I appreciate that and I understand what a terrible strain it places on you."

"I don't think you do," Alix said. "Every single minute of every single day and night, it is like a terrible cloud hanging over him. He wants to play as other children do and, naturally, we must let him but you have no idea how it feels to know that the tiniest knock, the tiniest bump could lead to..." she shook her head. "And when he is ill, like any mother, all I want to do is hold him and care for him but there are always crowds of people expecting me to dance, to smile, to speak with them about *nothing* at all."

"If I were in your position, I am sure I would be so desperate to find relief for him that, if someone were to claim they could help him, I would fall at their feet with gratitude."

"You are not in our position," she said, "so you cannot possibly understand."

Ella moved her chair a little closer, "Alix, I have to tell you what's being said. One after another, people have come to me with stories about this Rasputin and..."

"Lies from people who haven't the faintest idea that the man is a saint."

"A saint!" Ella gasped.

"Oh, forgive me," Alix replied sarcastically, "did you think *you* were the only saint in Russia?"

Ella shook her head, "Don't you see that no matter what he is like, if people perceive him to be something else and don't understand his presence here, it gives rise to so many stories that can only be damaging to you."

"People will always invent stories. I don't intend to risk my son's life - the life of *your* future Emperor - to satisfy the gossips."

"This isn't just the gossips though, is it? Alix, I received a letter from Bishop Feofan…"

"Feofan is a meddling old fool."

"He supported Rasputin. He told me himself, he was so convinced of his holiness that he actually introduced him to many young women of his congregation but, when these same women came back to him to confess to adultery with this so-called holy man, what could he do but denounce him?"

"Adultery!" she huffed. "Of course, what is said in confession cannot be verified so it's an easy accusation to make."

"Feofan is an honest man, why would he lie?"

"For the same reason as the Pharisees and Sanhedrin found it convenient to calumniate Christ. The truth is, Feofan and the others know that Father Grigory is far closer to the true message of the Gospel than they are and that truth frightens them."

"Bath houses, brothels, drunkenness…"

"And they accused Christ of being a glutton and a drunkard."

Ella sat back and sighed, "Alix, I *know* you are desperate to find relief for Alexei but in your position you can't afford to allow your heart to rule your head. You're not only responsible for your own family but for the whole of Russia and…"

"And that is why I do everything I can to preserve the health of Russia's future Tsar. Anyone who can help him is serving their country and anyone who decries that help is guilty of treason."

"Treason?" Ella laughed in exasperation. "Isn't it more treasonous to bring scandal into your home? By giving this moujik free access to your daughters, you are giving rise to all kinds of stories. This man is nothing but a…"

A voice came from behind her, "Man of God."

Ella turned to see Nicky standing in the doorway.

"If I were to tell you," he said quietly, "that with my own eyes I have witnessed his power to heal Alexei when all the doctors had given up hope, you couldn't deny that he is anything other than a saint."

"Alright," Ella conceded, "perhaps he *does* have a gift but not all those who seem sincere, *are* sincere. We can only judge by their lives and their example."

"There is no need to judge at all," Nicky said. *"Judge not lest you be judged."*

Alix leaned forwards, "There are so many mystical things of which you, for all your show of faith, have no idea. Our Friend comes from a simple background with a tradition of ancient truths that have long been forgotten by most of us. Those shamans and staretzy understood all kinds of things that you can't even imagine. Centuries ago, people listened to them and they were peaceful and they

looked after the land, honoured the Holy Mother
and she took care of them. Then in came the bishops
and the priests and you know what they did? They
silenced them, said all their ways were wicked and
nothing more than superstition."

"But some of them *were* wicked, Alix.
Superstition is dangerous and goes against
everything that the Saviour came to teach us."

"He taught love and kindness, forgiveness,
tolerance and healing, just as Our Friend does. He
speaks of a God of love, not a God of suffering and
sacrifice. He heals because he speaks of forgiveness
and mercy, not of a vengeful tyrant who is
described as a loving father one minute and the next
as one who will send us to hell for our sins. As Our
Friend says, God has given us so many gifts and we
must use them, not sacrifice them, not make
ourselves martyrs to satisfy our own sense of self-
righteousness as so many would-be saints and
bishops do."

Ella stood up, "Alix, this is blasphemy! If you
will not listen to me, at least listen to the bishops
and the synod."

"As the people of Israel listened to their
religious leaders and had Christ crucified?"

A pang thudded in Ella's heart and she did not
know whether the discomfort she felt came from
hearing such blasphemy or from a deep suspicion
that Alix was right. She leaned closer and reached
for her hand, "I'm sorry if I've spoken sharply but
you must be careful. It is dangerous to dabble in
things that are beyond our understanding. If we
embark on an unmarked path without the support
and guidance of the Church, there is no telling
where it will end. Many of those who set out with
the purest intentions can become puffed up on their

own power, forgetting that their gifts are from God. Then, instead of using them for good, they use them for their own ends and eventually destroy not only themselves but all those who trust them." She turned to Nicky, "You're the Head of the Orthodox Church. You *have to* set an example to your people. Remember that..."

"No!" Alix interrupted forcefully. "You are speaking to your Emperor, and it behoves *you* to remember your place and respect his judgement."

Chapter 43 - Moscow - Autumn 1912

Felix stood at the entrance to the hospital ward, scarcely daring to venture inside for fear of infection. Ugly faces contorted and spat into pots; chests crackling and gurgling; old people with wrinkled skin; gnarled hands twisted over walking sticks; bent backs; deformed joints; every possible distortion of flesh and bone; the epitome of all that was frightening and repulsive. And yet, in the middle of that horror, stood a beacon of light so radiant that her very presence shone over the disgusting scene and transformed it with a beauty verging on the divine.

She peered into wounds and gave instructions to the younger nuns who floated to and fro at her bidding. She placed her hands on the foreheads of patients and they seized her, smothering her skin with kisses; grotesque lips pressed to those artistic fingers that painted with such grace, and yet in that very touch she raised them from their ugliness into her own radiant atmosphere.

The sight filled Felix with such emotion that he longed to burst into tears but, when she turned and noticed him, he could only play the fool, the dandy - the role he had always played.

He twirled his hand and, with a flamboyant bow, said, "Lady Abbess, Matushka, Imperial Highness! Prince Felix Youssoupov has the honour of presenting himself at your service."

Patients and nurses stared at him, bemused.

"Oh Felix," Ella laughed, "you really are incorrigible!"

"I know. I can't help it."

"Come on," she shook her head in mock-exasperation, "before you disturb all our patients."

She led him from the ward, "I didn't think you would come."

"I promised that I would, and you promised that you would show me the very worst streets in Moscow. You know how I like to be entertained, and the glitz and glamour of Petersburg have become so dull of late."

"If I really believed that was your motive, you know very well I would have given you short shrift."

He laughed.

"But remember, Felix, even though I can see through that veneer, other people don't know you so well so you must be on your best behaviour."

"Upon my honour!"

Calling brief instructions to some of her nuns, she led him through the convent gates and out into the noisy road. Down back streets, through squalor, through stinking hovels and filthy alleyways, into a world so far removed from all he had known before. Never had he encountered such poverty, and the state of many of the people she visited revolted him, yet her kindness and remarkable ability to raise the spirits of even the most abject sufferers convinced him of her sanctity. The roughest, most brutish men, who might well have killed him for his coat had he been alone, tempered their language, stepped back and doffed their caps as she passed. Many blessed themselves or called blessings upon her until Felix felt safer in her gentle company than he would have done with an entire regimental guard at his side.

Quickly, his desire for jokes and histrionics faded. All his playacting suddenly seemed more grotesque than the toothless faces or the twisted limbs of those who hobbled by. In the presence of such goodness, he felt ashamed and worried that he had deceived her. If she knew the truth about him - his dissipated life and his bisexuality - she would not, he thought, have been so willing to receive him.

"I'd like to confess something to you," he said quietly as they made their way back to the convent.

"I am not a priest," she smiled.

"You think you know me but what you know of me is only an act. Have you heard of the British playwright, Oscar Wilde?"

She nodded.

"His story, *The Picture of Dorian Grey*?"

"I don't think so."

"It tells of a man who is physically beautiful but his soul is fouled by debauchery and decadence. He has his portrait painted and, though the man himself remains beautiful to outward appearances, the portrait changes to illustrate the ugliness within."

"A clever idea," she said.

"Ella, these people, all this ugliness, they are only the portrait, aren't they? We are the mask, the outward appearance. The ballrooms, the palaces, the art and culture, all that *we* have is a superficial beauty, but these people, they are the reflection of our soul. It's so wrong. It has to be seen. *Our* ugliness has to be seen for what it is…"

"No," she said, "on the contrary. These people are not ugly. Their situation is ugly but their souls are beautiful. It would be quite wrong of us to sink into ugliness, too. We're here to raise everyone to their true beauty. *That* is the point of all the work in my foundation."

His shame overwhelmed him, "You can see beauty in them because your soul is beautiful. My soul? If you had any idea of the life I have lived!

All of my life is devoted to pleasure, debauchery, self-gratification and..."

"Felix," she rested her hand on his shoulder and smiled, "I know far more about you than you think. Anyone who is capable of devoting himself so wholeheartedly to pleasure, is equally capable of devoting himself wholeheartedly to good."

In a moment of passion he threw back his head and laughed, "Yes! Yes, you are right. I will do exactly what you have done. I am going to give away everything, just as you did. I will build a foundation like yours but mine will be for men and..."

Suddenly he realized that she was laughing, "Oh Felix! I love your enthusiasm but you know this isn't your calling at all."

Immediately deflated and a little relieved, he trudged along beside her into the convent.

"You have a duty to your parents. You stand to inherit huge estates, and many people will be relying on you for work, for fair wages, for a home. Think of all the good you can do. *That* is your calling."

She led him into the cosy parlour and poured tea, "Now," she said, "I think there is something else that you came to ask me?"

He smiled, "You have heard from Dmitri?"

She nodded.

"He told you that we both wanted to marry Sandro's daughter, Irina?"

She nodded again.

"We asked her to choose between us."

"So I heard," she raised her eyebrows, "and I must say, it seemed a rather strange way of going about things. Then again," she smiled, "only what I would expect from you."

He laughed, "I was surprised that she chose me but, unfortunately, her parents are less enthusiastic. They made inquiries into all my activities as a student in England. I think they were shocked by what they discovered."

She silently stirred her tea.

"I wondered if you might put in a good word for me?"

"If you truly love Irina and promise to be a good husband to her, I will speak with Sandro and Xenia on your behalf. At the moment, though," she sighed, "I'm afraid I have little faith in my matchmaking ability. I suppose you have heard that Dmitri's sister is seeking to divorce her Swedish prince? I fear I made a dreadful mistake and rushed her into something that was bound to end in disaster."

"It was her choice in the end."

"But she was so young and I pressurised her."

He couldn't dispute it but wanted to cheer her, "You were successful in bringing the Tsar and Tsarina together!"

She smiled but the sorrowful look in her eye implied she considered that an even greater mistake.

A tap at the door preceded the appearance of a young nun who handed Ella a letter and departed as silently as she had entered.

"It's from Nicky," she said, turning the envelope around in her hand. "Do you mind if I...?"

"No, of course not."

Her face, as she perused the contents became increasingly grave and, as she placed it folded on the table between them, she sighed deeply.

"Bad news?" he said.

"I might as well tell you as you'll hear it soon enough anyway. Misha has married his mistress."

"Without the Tsar's permission?"

"Yes."

"What will happen to him? The Tsar surely won't exile his own brother?"

"He has no choice. He can't make one rule for Pavel and Kyril and another for Misha." She shook her head sadly, "What are they all thinking? Don't they see that Nicky needs them? They don't seem to realize that the Tsar deserves loyalty. He is so thoroughly loyal himself and to repay him like this is too cruel. Who is left to support him now? Vladimir and Serge, dead; Pavel in exile and now Misha..."

"He still has you."

"Yes," she said wearily, "but I see so little of them nowadays. My work here keeps me from Tsarskoe Selo and even when I am there they..." She threw up her hands in despair then recollected herself, "That terrible man does everything to keep us apart."

"Rasputin?"

"*Father Grigory,*" she said with a sigh. "Alix avoids me for fear of what I might say of him, and she makes sure that Nicky and I are never alone so I can't broach the subject with him. On the rare occasions we are together, the spectre of that man hangs over all our conversations so we can never speak freely as we used to."

He hesitated before saying, "I've met him, you know?"

She looked up, interested, "What did you make of him?"

"He's quite unnerving. I have to admit that at first I was fascinated. He has that effect. He looks at you in such a way that you feel he is boring into your soul and reading the deepest recesses of your mind. It's a disconcerting sensation and at the same time attractive, in a strange way."

"Attractive?" she frowned.

"The feeling of being so utterly *known,* and yet, no sooner had I felt that, than I had a powerful sense of the presence of evil. In fact it was quite terrifying."

"Did he speak with you?"

"Yes, for quite some time. He spoke of my mother and of you."

"What did he say?"

The conversation replayed in his mind and he regretted having mentioned it, "I can't really remember," he shrugged.

"Felix, you're as transparent as water. You might as well tell me."

"He said…well, he said the worst sin a woman can commit is celibacy. For a beautiful woman to remain faithful in a loveless marriage is a travesty of the truth. It's only pride that prevents any woman from giving and receiving pleasure and he would have esteemed you more highly had you taken a lover. Even worse, living as a nun, you are wasting the gifts God gave you."

She laughed spontaneously, "And this is the kind of thing he tells Alix?"

"I don't know about that but I know he dislikes my mother, too. She went to the Tsarina to warn her of all the rumours about him. I can only assume that the Tsarina told Rasputin of what she had said. He thinks you both hate him but, in reality, I think he is afraid of you. Being here today and seeing your work, I realized something. Everything you do is totally at odds with his distorted theology. His aim is to drag pious people down to destroy their pride, whereas you raise people up and restore their dignity. Dozens of princesses and wealthy women believe in his power and let him humiliate and humble them, but you? You are far too pure for him to reach."

"The Tsarina has absolute faith in him," she said wearily.

"I know. When my mother approached her about him, she dismissed her at once. "

"It seems the way of it. Anyone who speaks out against him is dismissed. Ministers who criticise him, lose their positions; bishops who condemn him, suddenly find themselves sent off to the remotest parts of the Empire only to be replaced by Rasputin's friends. Poor Bishop Feofan was first removed to the Crimea but, even from there, he continued to rail against him and now he finds himself far away in Astrakhan."

"What of the Tsar? He must realize that what is being said is so damaging?"

"I'm sure he does know and, in his own silent way, he is troubled by it. Did you know the police presented him with a dossier that they compiled after months of round-the-clock surveillance of Rasputin?"

Felix shook his head.

"I heard from Djunkovsky that it contained a lot of sordid information, which, of course, Alix insisted was nothing but lies. All the same, it must have made an impact on Nicky because shortly afterwards Rasputin disappeared home to his wife in Siberia."

Felix frowned, "But he's back now. It's not long since I saw him in Petersburg."

She nodded, "I think that Dmitri has told you of the Tsarevich's illness?"

"Yes," he said with genuine sadness.

"Shortly after Rasputin left Petersburg, the Imperial Family went to the hunting lodge in Spala. While they were there, Alexei fell. The bleeding began at once, his knee swelled and he was in excruciating pain. Doctors were rushed from the capital but it seems it was the worst episode to date."

"Yes," Felix said, "I saw the bulletins in the papers asking for prayers for his recovery. Of course, they didn't describe the nature of his illness but they made it clear that his life was in the balance."

"They had summoned the priests to give him the last rites, and even prepared a proclamation announcing his death."

"Oh Lord! I didn't realize it was so serious."

"I think Nicky had resigned himself to the inevitable but Alix, understandably, wouldn't give up hope. She had a telegram sent to Rasputin. He replied at once, telling her not to be afraid. Almost immediately, Alexei began to recover. To Alix it was a miracle and Rasputin must be a saint."

Felix tried to understand, "It *was* a miracle."

"Perhaps," she said, "and yet I can't help believing it was the prayers of all the people in the country that saved him. Rasputin's part in it was purely coincidental."

"You can understand why the Tsarina is so devoted to him, though, can't you?"

"Oh yes," she nodded, "and my heart goes out to her. What she suffers must be unbearable but her desperation blinds her to the truth. All she is doing, she does with the highest motives but she doesn't see that as long as these rumours persist - and as long as Rasputin is given access to the palace they *will* persist - untold damage is being done to the autocracy. You must have seen the scurrilous cartoons that are being circulated?"

He *had* seen them - a hook-nosed Tsarina sitting on the lascivious peasant's knee while the cuckolded Tsar looked on helplessly.

"If people believe these things, how can they respect the Emperor? He becomes a laughing-stock! And worse, if Rasputin really does have such influence over Alix, and she over Nicky, what kind of man is running the country?"

"What can be done?"

"We can only pray that Alix will see sense and send him back to Siberia for good." She stood up and moved across the room towards a cabinet, "In the meantime, it's important that the Tsar and Tsarina are seen as much as possible, to win the hearts of the people." She opened a drawer and pulled out a letter. "Next year marks the anniversary of three hundred years of Romanov rule. There are many celebrations planned, culminating here in Moscow in May with a big procession to the tomb of the first Romanov tsar. Nicky wrote to me, asking me to take part."

"Naturally," Felix smiled.

A pensive expression settled on her face, "I have stepped down from that position. When I took my vows, I left that glittering world behind, and yet..." she sighed and her eyes moved towards an icon, "more than ever we need a show of solidarity. With so many of the grand dukes disregarding their oath of allegiance, the people need to see that the Tsar still has the support of his family."

"You *must* be part of that," Felix said. "The Muscovites love you and, if you are not seen with the rest of the family, they will jump to their own conclusions."

"Perhaps," she said thoughtfully, "if Nicky allows me to travel in a carriage with his daughters, they would distract attention from me. That might work."

Felix smiled. She had no idea of her own charisma or that the loudest cheers of the crowds would surely belong to her.

Chapter 44

On a beautiful afternoon in the summer of 1913, thousands of Muscovites jostled and strained to catch sight of the glorious procession winding its way through the city. Streets, which eight years before had been filled with barricades and armed revolutionaries, now rang with the echo of church bells as the country united in celebration of three hundred years of the Romanov dynasty. Not since the coronation, had Moscow hosted such a magnificent spectacle of royalty. All along the route from the railway station to the Kremlin, crowds cheered the magnificent parade.

The Tsar and grand dukes, in brilliant uniforms, led the way on horseback, then came carriage after carriage of the rest of the Imperial Family: the Tsarina, grand duchesses and princesses arrayed in jewels, wide-brimmed hats and summer dresses. And somewhat incongruously among them, sharing an open carriage with her nieces, sat the Abbess of The House of Martha and Mary, in a simple pearl grey habit, smiling benignly at the crowd.

For the past few months, Ella had followed, with increasing delight, the newspaper stories describing royal progress in honour of the tercentenary. The Imperial Family had left the seclusion of Tsarskoe Selo at the beginning of the year and moved into the Winter Palace to lead the celebrations in St. Petersburg. From there, they embarked on a pilgrimage to Kostroma, the birthplace of Mikhail, the first Romanov tsar. For the majority of Nicky's hundred and thirty million subjects, this was their chance in a lifetime to catch a glimpse of the Emperor. Everywhere, in the towns and cities, in the open countryside and all along the banks of the Volga, masses of people gathered to demonstrate their fidelity. In the fields and villages, peasants dropped to their knees; from the riverbanks they waded into the water; and in the cities, the police cordons could hardly restrain the throngs eagerly surging forwards to affirm their reverent allegiance.

The cynics might observe that the applause was somewhat half-hearted and criticise the Tsarina for her failure to respond to the show of adulation, but Ella tried to convince herself that the displays of loyalty were genuine and that the Russians loved their Little Father and Little Mother. Even here in Moscow, so often the scene of uprisings and dissent, their subjects had turned out to welcome the Imperial Family. The ministers' warnings of unrest were surely unfounded. The Muscovites were faithful to the Tsar.

Nearing the Spassky Gate of the Kremlin, the procession came to a halt. The Tsar and grand dukes dismounted and led the procession on foot for the culmination of the celebrations - a pilgrimage to the tomb of Mikhail Romanov. They crossed the square and ascended the steps of the Cathedral of the Archangel Michael and there, in the entrance, to Ella's horror, stood Rasputin. Her heart thudded at the sight of the peasant so blatantly displaying his intimacy with the Imperial Family but, for now, she was powerless to intervene.

As prelates offered blessings and choirs sang, the Tsar lit a lamp at the tomb of his ancestor, and prayers were said that the dynasty might last for another three hundred years but, as Ella surveyed the congregation with the memory of Rasputin so fresh in her mind, she couldn't help but feel that beneath the smiles, the pomp and the show of solidarity, irreparable cracks were beginning to show.

Divisions within the family were wider than ever. The old generation had gone; Serge's brothers, Alexei and Vladimir died within three months of each other in the winter of 1908-09. Pavel was in exile and, since the betrayal by Kyril, Alix wanted nothing to do with Miechen and her family. The strained relations between Alix and Ella were common knowledge and, no matter what discretion she showed, she was well aware that everyone suspected it was not simply her commitments in Moscow that kept her away from Tsarskoe Selo for so long. There were so few people left for Alix to rely on. Perhaps, Ella thought, it was small wonder she placed so much faith in 'Our Friend' but that he should be *here,* so visible to the crowds, was more than she could stand. She glanced towards her sister. How tired she looked; how the strain of the celebrations had wearied her!

And when this is over, Ella thought, *she will return to the seclusion of Tsarskoe and close her eyes on the rest of the world.*

The rest of the world...Her mind wandered off at a tangent. It was not only in the family that cracks were beginning to show. Since Uncle Bertie's death, the reports of dissention across all of Europe were becoming regular features of newspaper headlines. Ella tried not to think of it. There was always trouble in the Balkans and, since childhood, belligerent Cousin Willy had loved to strut about in his military uniforms, boasting of German supremacy, but war in Europe was unthinkable. Her first cousins occupied, or were in line to, the thrones of Germany, Britain, Norway, Roumania, Sweden, Greece and Spain. Grandpapa's vision of peace created through family ties seemed to have been realised.

When the celebrations were complete, Ella set out on a series of pilgrimages. From a remote monastery on an island in the White Sea, to the tiny hermitages of recluses and sages, she travelled the length and breadth of Russia, gleaning the wisdom of the ages, before returning, refreshed and inspired with more ideas to expand her Order. Alongside the work in the hospital, the orphanage, the hostels, district nursing and visits to the homes of children at risk, the sisters prepared meals to be distributed free of charge to the poor. The weeks, the seasons passed in the ceaseless round of innovative ideas to bring beauty to the heart of Moscow and beyond. Daily, more volunteers arrived to offer help, and princesses and peasants alike came to ask to be admitted to the Order.

One afternoon in late June, a familiar and much-welcome face appeared at the door of her parlour.

"Kostia!"

"I was in the city," he said, "when I heard you were back from your travels and I couldn't leave without coming to see you. You must have seen the news?"

He thrust a newspaper in front of her face and the glaring headline struck her like a bullet: "ATTEMPTED MURDER OF RASPUTIN!"

"Murder!" she gasped, struggling to contain the mixed emotions of gratitude and horror. "By whom?"

"A madwoman, apparently," Konstantin said, glancing briefly at the story. "He was in Pokrovskoe, his hometown, when a woman he mistook for a beggar approached him. As he reached to hand her a coin, she pulled out a knife and stabbed him."

"May I?" Ella said, taking the paper from him and reading aloud: "...*The woman, a fanatical supporter of Rasputin's former friend, the monk Iliodor, plunged the knife deep into his gut, leaving him writhing on the ground. Bundled onto a sledge, his intestines protruding from the wound, he was taken on an eight-hour journey to a hospital in Tiumen where surgery was carried out without anaesthetic. His miraculous survival may come as a disappointment to many who fear his influence in the highest echelons of power, but they can take comfort in the knowledge that his injuries will keep him away from St. Petersburg for the foreseeable future...*"

Konstantin took back the newspaper, "We must be thankful for small mercies."

She smiled, uncertain whether the small mercy he referred to was the survival of the peasant or his being kept away from the city.

The sunlight shining through the parlour window was too tempting to resist, "Shall we walk in the gardens," she suggested, "and you can tell me all your news?"

They strolled among the roses and the heady scents of summer, resting on the little white benches that dotted the lawns. It was a delight to hear him speak of his children and grandchildren, "...and Ioann didn't become a monk after all. A happily married man now."

"Your family are a credit to you," she enthused, "we only ever hear wonderful reports of them."

"I have been very blessed in my children and in their husbands and wives. You heard Tatiana has just had her second baby?"

"Yes. Congratulations!"

"Her husband is such a fine man," he smiled, contentedly, "Mavra and I couldn't have hoped for a better son-in-law."

"And what of you and Mavra? You're both well?"

"We are, and to make sure we stay that way, we're going to Germany for a few days to visit the health spas."

She smiled.

"What about your family?" he said, "How is your brother and your sisters?"

"All well. As it happens, Victoria is expected here any day. We're planning a pilgrimage to Alapaevsk and she hopes to join us."

"That will be…"

"Matushka, Matushka!" A young nun came running towards them, waving a newspaper, "Have you heard? A terrible murder!"

"Catherine," Ella said gently, "it's not seemly to lose all decorum like this. Calm yourself."

Uttering apologies and half-curtseying to Konstantin, she shook the newspaper, "Forgive me, but the murder…"

Ella took her hand, "*Attempted* murder. Rasputin survived."

"No, no," said Catherine, wafting the paper still more frantically, "the Archduke Franz Ferdinand of Austria and his wife. They have both been murdered in Sarajevo!"

Konstantin reached for the newspaper: "…*The heir to the Austrian throne, Archduke Franz Ferdinand, was carrying out a routine inspection of*

Austrian troops in the Balkans when he made a detour to the Bosnian capital. As his car drove slowly through the streets of Sarajevo, a young Serb named Gavril Princeps stepped out from the crowd and fired a pistol point blank at the illustrious passengers. The Archduke's wife, Sophie, died instantly, her husband a short time later…"

"Franz Ferdinand," Ella murmured. "Serge and I shared a table with him at Grandmama's Diamond Jubilee celebrations. A quiet man and very unassuming."

"How are the Austrians going to react?" Konstantin said anxiously.

An overpowering sense of foreboding shrouded the brightness of the sun.

"Come," Ella said, "we must go to the chapel to pray for him. Catherine, would you assemble as many of the sisters as you can? Kostia, will you join us?"

"Papa," said Alexei, running his finger over the creases on Nicky's brow, "is this serious?"

"Very serious."

"More serious than when they murdered Uncle Serge?"

Nicky leaned back and put his arm around his son, "The murder of any man is serious but in the case of Archduke Franz Ferdinand the consequences could be catastrophic."

"Why?"

"It's complicated," he said, frowning as his eyes scanned the telegrams and documents on the desk before him.

"I'm almost ten. I'm sure I'll understand."

Nicky looked to Alix for reassurance.

She nodded, "Yes, tell him Nicky. The sooner he is introduced to foreign affairs the better."

"Very well," Nicky reached for a map, unfolded it over the desk and, taking Alexei on his knee, ran his finger around the border of the Empire.

"This is Russia and these are the Balkan states: Serbia, Bosnia, Montenegro. They're our friends. Over here, is the Austro-Hungarian Empire, ruled from Vienna by Franz Josef."

"The old man who visited us once?"

"That's right," Nicky smiled. "Franz Josef rules over all of this area but the Serbs want complete independence and a separate South Slav kingdom, free from any interference from Austria."

"And Emperor Franz Josef won't accept that?"

Nicky shook his head, "Franz Josef wants to keep his empire intact and won't enter into discussion with them. Lots of terrorist groups have sprung up and committed many acts of violence to make themselves heard."

"Is that why they shot Franz Ferdinand?"

"Yes. He is Franz Josef's nephew and heir to the Austrian Empire. That's very sad and has made the Austrians very angry. For a long time they have been looking for a way to bring the Serbs into line and this murder has given them the opportunity to crush Serbia once and for all."

"But they can't blame a whole country for what one man did?"

"They're calling it a declaration of war."

"That's madness!" Alexei said.

"It is, but it's the way of things. The Austrians have sent a list of demands to Serbia and, if the Serbs don't accept them, the Austrian army will attack."

Alexei stared at the map, "But Austria is so much bigger. Serbia will easily be defeated."

Nicky nodded gravely, "And that, little fellow, is why it's so serious. Serbia is our friend and we have a duty to support our friends. If someone attacks Serbia, we must help the Serbs."

Alexei leaned back and smiled, "Then Austria would easily be defeated. Look at the size of the Russian Empire compared to the size of Franz Josef's."

"The size of an empire isn't always an advantage. Look how far we would have to transport soldiers, ammunition, supplies before we reached the front line. And besides, Austria has friends, too. Germany is Austria's ally so the Germans would have to come and help Austria."

Alexei's eyes darted towards his mother, "Uncle Willy wouldn't fight us, would he? He's our friend, and Mama is half-German."

"That's why I am writing to him. I don't think he wants war any more than we do. It would be a disaster for everyone. The French are our friends and they despise the Germans so they would join with us and then Germany would have to fight on the east and on the west."

"They would have to go through Belgium first. Whose side are they on?"

"Belgium is neutral and, if cousin Willy were to lead his army onto Belgian soil, Britain would come to the defence of Belgium."

"And then," Alexei shook his head, "nearly the whole of Europe would be fighting."

"Exactly," Nicky said, setting him down from the table, "and that is why the murder of Franz Ferdinand is so serious."

"What are you going to do?"

"I've advised the Serbs to accept virtually all of Austria's demands and they have agreed to do that. There are just one or two tiny things that they couldn't possibly be expected to accept, so I'm writing to Cousin Willy to ask him to reach a compromise."

"Do you think he will?"

"He must," Nicky said. "The alternative would be slaughter on a scale that the world has never seen before."

Chapter 45

"Wasn't it supposed to be a private visit?" Victoria smiled as she and Ella emerged from the church in the little Siberian mining town of Alapaevsk. Crowds cheered, kissing Ella's shadow and touching the hem of her robe, jostling to reach her through the heat of the afternoon sun.

She smiled, "No matter how quietly and unobtrusively we make plans, somehow they always anticipate us."

"They're certainly enthusiastic!"

"It's a demonstration of their allegiance to Nicky," she said, trying to suppress the anxiety that there was something even more frenzied in their applause than the usual displays of affection. Alongside the blessings and cheers, the cries hailing *Holy Mother Russia* echoed like a rising tide of patriotism, welling into a maelstrom.

Victoria obviously felt it, too, and she turned to Ella with a troubled expression, "If they are like this now, what will they be like if…"

"No," Ella cut her short, unwilling to entertain the possibility. "It won't happen. Nicky will find a way to keep the peace. He is doing everything he possibly can."

"But he has mobilised his army."

"He had no alternative. When the Austrians rejected all of the Serbs' offers and declared war on Serbia, what else could he do?"

"You still believe there is hope that this war can be avoided?"

"Yes, I do," she said, clinging to the crucifix around her neck. "All kinds of diplomatic agreements are being worked out behind the scenes."

Victoria was unconvinced, "What of Willy's ultimatum? Unless Nicky stops the mobilisation and withdraws your troops from the Austrian border..."

"Much as Willy loves his uniforms and the trappings of militarism, he has no more stomach for war than we do."

The car passed through the gates of a monastery and the cheering of the crowd faded into the distance. A bearded monk stepped forward to welcome them.

"Seraphim," Ella smiled, "may I introduce my sister, Victoria?"

He bowed and led them from the heat of the sun into the shade of a cloister, where he held out a telegram to Ella, "Your Highness, this came here for you from St. Petersburg."

As she read the contents, she felt the blood rush from her face, "It's from Alix."

Giddiness caused her head to spin and, as the telegram floated to the ground, the arches of the cloister merged and blurred. Shades of darkness clouded the periphery of her vision like the closing of a sliding door. She rocked involuntarily and reached for Victoria's arm to steady herself but the swaying motion increased. Every crease in her skin felt wet, her clothes sticking to her like damp rags, yet she shivered and the darkness closed in until everything was black.

When she opened her eyes, she found herself sitting on a bench, with Seraphim and Victoria peering down at her. Victoria was holding the telegram.

"It's too horrific, isn't it?" Ella whispered.

"There is still *some* hope," Victoria said desperately. "Alix is asking for our prayers. There is still a little time."

Faces flashed before Ella's eyes: the *royal mob* at Grandmama's jubilee celebrations. Ernie, as Grand Duke of Hesse, was committed to the German cause, as was Irène through her marriage to the Kaiser's brother. She, herself, Alix and Victoria would in effect become their enemies. If the situation among siblings looked bleak, the picture was far worse when cousins were taken into account. Relatives, who as children had played and taken holidays together, who had attended the same family weddings and funerals, were suddenly on opposing sides. She closed her eyes and prayed for peace more fervently than she had ever prayed for anything in her life.

There was no question now of continuing the pilgrimage. It was vital to return as soon as possible to the capital. At every station on the long journey back, glaring newspaper headlines proclaimed the latest updates: ultimatum following ultimatum until all hope of peace dwindled away. Europe was in turmoil. Waves of hysteria swept through the cities as masses of people, oblivious of the impending disaster, seized the chance to display their national pride and bayed for war. The wealthy were cutting short their foreign holidays and rushing home before the borders were closed. All transgressions forgiven, the banished grand dukes were permitted to return to Russia with their wives.

By the time they reached St. Petersburg, the inevitable had occurred. The Kaiser, whom Ella might once have married, declared war on the Russia she loved. The next day in the Winter Palace, the Tsar signed the Manifesto of the

Declaration of War and two days later, following the German invasion of neutral Belgium, Britain entered the conflict.

A warm summer rain fell softly as Victoria and Ella wandered dejectedly through the streets of the St. Petersburg. All around them echoed the patriotic songs and excited chatter of crowds. For once, the people were united against a common enemy, and the enemy was Ella's native Germany. In spite of her absolute commitment to Russia, there could be no joy in any victory, knowing that her brother, her sister and numerous cousins would suffer, not to mention the pitiful mass of soldiers who would be decimated in the fray.

Alix, distraught as her sisters, met them in the city and together they returned for dinner at the Winter Palace. It was a solemn affair, no one daring to voice their deepest fears and, when they had finished eating, Victoria hastily packed her bags and prepared to leave for England. She would have to travel overland through the neutral Scandinavian countries and, concerned for the security of her jewels, left them for safekeeping with Alix. Ella watched her go, wondering if she would ever see her again.

Two weeks later, a huge patriotic crowd greeted the Imperial Family when they arrived in Moscow to announce that the country was at war. All discontent forgotten, Russia was ready for action. While the crowds gathered outside, one hundred and twenty five bishops concelebrated Mass, praying for the troops and for Russian success. Now, more than ever, it was imperative that the family should show solidarity and, concealing their differences, Ella and Alix stood side by side in the cathedral. Even Alexei, who had fallen and was suffering from a bleed in his leg, demonstrated his commitment to the country by his presence in spite of having to be carried

After the service, as they emerged from the cathedral to the rousing refrains of the National Anthem, crowds cheered and hailed the Tsar who would lead them to victory.

"You must feel greatly relieved," someone said to Alix, "to see such loyalty and devotion."

But when she turned to Ella, the sorrow in her eyes was unspeakable.

"This isn't about Germany," she said quietly. "The people of Hesse are peace-loving. They want this war no more than we do. This is all down to the despicable Kaiser, dragging the world into this terrible conflict."

Ella reached for her hand and for a moment it seemed all animosity between them was forgotten but, as Alix turned to leave the balcony, she said,

"Father Grigory was insistent that war would be a disaster. If he had been here now, I believe we would have found a way to avoid it."

Ella didn't reply but silently thanked God that, at such a crucial time for the country, the attack on the moujik had kept him far away in Siberia.

All along the route back to the Kremlin, *God Bless the Tsar* rang through the streets.

"We must organize ourselves," Alix said, suddenly animated. "We will have to divide the work of the war charities between us and prepare to receive the wounded."

"Of course," Ella nodded, "I'm at your service."

"I fear that the number of casualties will be far higher than those from the Japanese War." Alix' eyes wandered over the great walls of the Kremlin. "Some of these palaces will need to be converted into hospitals."

"I'll see to it."

"Miechen has already agreed to organize ambulance trains, and Nicky's sisters are setting up hospitals in Petersburg."

"With your permission," Ella said, "I would like to go to the base hospitals at the front line to organize transport back from there."

"Do whatever needs to be done," Alix smiled and, amid all the horror and sorrow, Ella smiled, too. The rift between them had been breached. Perhaps now they could be sisters and friends again.

Only a few months had passed since the crowds cheered the Tsar on the balcony in Moscow but already it felt like a lifetime ago. It had not taken long for the casualties to pour in from the trenches and, in no time, the hospitals were filled to overflowing. Clutching an umbrella, Ella made her way through the quagmire to the stinking base hospital, so close to the Front that the boom of the guns and screeching of shells drowned out the heavy beat of the pouring rain.

So chaotic and hectic was the scene that met her eyes as she entered the makeshift building that, without waiting for introductions, she set to work assisting the doctors and nurses who scurried to and fro in blood-stained uniforms. Everything was filthy, from the mud-splattered sheets to the grimy bandages pressed to open wounds. Screams and groans, unlike anything she had ever heard, sounded with heart-rending ferocity from every corner. Faces, so smashed by shells and shrapnel as to be scarcely recognizable as human, gazed helplessly, more dead than alive. Amputated limbs, stinking of gangrene; frost-bitten fingers; fevered brows; lice-ridden uniforms; trench foot and rat-bitten toes.

She moved from bed to bed, pressing dressings to infected wounds, tightening tourniquets around shattered limbs, holding the hands of grown men who called for their mothers, and whispering words of comfort to those who were dying.

A nurse at the opposite side of a stretcher stared at her, "Your Highness? Forgive me, I didn't recognise you."

Ella shook her head and continued to tend the soldier lying between them.

"You have no idea," said the nurse, "what a difference it makes seeing you here. Our work is so hard but seeing someone like you doing this, too…I heard that even the Tsarina and her elder daughters have trained as nurses now?"

"Yes," Ella said, "we are all in this together."

The soldier turned towards her, "Her Majesty nursed my brother when he lost a leg. She wrote to my mother and said she knew how it felt to watch a son suffer."

Ella ran her hand over his hair, "She does," she whispered, "and she knows how it feels to lose someone you love."

So too, she thought, *does dear Kostia,* and tears filled her eyes at the thought of his sorrow. Young Oleg had always been his favourite son, and now he had not only lost him, but his beloved son-in-law, too.

The soldier took her hand, "Don't cry, princess. It is all worthwhile for the sake of Holy Mother Russia."

She looked along the ward. So many young men! So many wives, sisters, mothers, fathers waiting for news. So much horror, so much death, so much cruelty and destruction.

"For Holy Mother Russia," she whispered and, stepping outside, let her tears fall in the rain.

"Your Highness," a bleary-eyed doctor called over the boom of the guns, "the ambulance train is almost ready to leave."

She wiped away her tears and followed him to the waiting carriage. The train rocked and swayed and every jolt brought more cries from the suffering soldiers. Several died en route and their corpses lay beside the living like an ominous reminder of their own impending fate. Her thoughts returned to Kostia, mourning his young son. Death, not anarchy, not war, was the greatest revolutionary of all. Princes and peasants, grand dukes and artisans: death was no respecter of titles or positions - everyone was equal at its hands.

Eventually, the train drew in to Moscow and, as Ella emerged onto the platform to supervise the unloading of the wounded, a small crowd of onlookers gathered. They doffed their caps to the soldiers, and their faces twisted with fear and horror. When Ella gave instructions to the ambulance drivers, she heard a groan from the crowd.

"They're not taking our heroes to the best hospitals. You know why? Fifteen of them are filled with prisoners of war! The Hun gets all the best treatment and our soldiers get what's left over."

"She speaks German to the prisoners," an old man muttered, "and the other nurses don't know what she's saying."

"She *is* German! Probably passing on secret information."

Ella glanced towards them, "It's true that Moscow has many wounded German prisoners but I have no say in who is sent here."

His lip curled like angry dog, "Hessian witch!" he spat in her face.

Chapter 46 – 1916

"Thank you for coming," Ella said when Djunkovsky stepped into her office in the Nieskcushnoe Palace. She pushed a newspaper across the desk towards him, "I believe you were present at the scene?"

"I was."

"So this is true?"

He nodded.

Ella sat down, resting her head in her hands, "Tell me what happened."

He fumbled in his pocket for a notebook and recited the events of the previous evening as though he were giving evidence in a court of law.

"Following the report of a disturbance, I arrived at the Yar nightclub and found the place crowded with people from all strata of society. Several members of Moscow's leading families were present, including many ladies whose evening had been disturbed by the lewd and intoxicated behaviour of Grigory Rasputin. The management had asked him to leave but he refused to do so. When I arrived, the manager again asked him to go, at which point Rasputin laughed, tugged at his silk shirt and announced that..." Djunkovsky looked up from his notes and cleared his throat nervously.

"Go on," Ella said.

"He announced that 'the old woman' - the Tsarina - had sewn it for him herself."

Ella inhaled sharply and Djunkovsky paused before continuing, "He then began to dance and, opening his trousers, exposed himself, yelling further obscenities to imply that he and the Empress were lovers and he could 'do what he liked with her'."

Ella pressed her hands to her eyes, "And this is reported for all the world to see."

"Yes, Your Highness."

She pushed back her chair and strode towards the window, "I thought he was still in Siberia."

"He returned to Petersburg some months ago and, according to the surveillance reports, he has made several visits to Her Majesty. He arrived in Moscow last week and my officers have been following him. Most of the time he has spent drinking and dancing with his gypsy singers."

"This was bad enough in peacetime but now..." She shook her head desperately. What on earth could Alix be thinking? Didn't she realize that with anti-German feeling running so high, any hint of scandal would only add to the mistrust of the Imperial Family?

"For the good of the country," she said, "and for Their Majesties' safety, this has to stop now."

Djunkovsky stepped back and said quietly, "According to my officers, there is a growing suspicion that Her Majesty uses this peasant to convey Russian military secrets to the enemy. That's how they account for so many Russian losses."

She turned sharply, "You know that is totally untrue!"

"Yes, of course, Your Highness. I am only reporting the general feeling to warn you of the dangers."

She sat down again, "I am well aware of the dangers. The question is, is Her Majesty?"

How is it, she wondered, *that everyone else is aware of the dangers yet Alix refuses to see? What will take to make her see...to make Nicky see?*

Djunkovsky stood before her with his head lowered and his fingers nervously running around the edges of his notebook.

"Will you do something for me?" she said. "Will you compile a new report on all of Rasputin's activities?"

"For the past three months, Your Highness, I have been gathering information about him."

"Good," she nodded. "When the report is complete, you must present it to the Tsar. When His Majesty hears the whole story, he will act swiftly to put an end to this whole sordid business."

"Very good, Your Highness."

When Djunkovsky had gone, Ella summoned a carriage to return to the convent. Along the route, workmen were busily hauling down the shop signs with Germanic names, and boarding up the shop fronts of businesses once owned by Germans. Passers-by paused to watch them, trampling on the signs with such anger that it seemed to Ella that if they could lay their hands on the former owners, they would tear them limb from limb. She pressed her face to the window and suddenly a cry came from the street, "German spy!"

Immediately, ferocious clattering echoed from the roof as those who had once kissed the hem of her robe, pelted the carriage with stones, "German bitch! Hessian traitor!"

"*Dear God,*" she prayed, "*where will it end?*"

Nicky closed Djunkovsky's file, leaned back on his chair and inhaled deeply from his cigarette. The smoke hovered over his desk, scattered with countless notes from Alix: *Our Friend advises this appointment, Our Friend advises that appointment,*

Our Friend says, Our Friend says, Our Friend says...

He had done the right thing. He was certain of it. Rasputin's sway over Alix had gone too far. Of course, he couldn't deny the great service the peasant had performed in easing Alexei's suffering, and it was true that he had been happy to confer with him on matters of religion. Rasputin's views were fascinating and spoken so sincerely that it had been refreshing to hear him speak with such simplicity of spiritual matters. If only it had ended there! Now, he had overstepped the mark. It was irritating, to say the least, to be constantly bombarded with advice on military affairs from a man who made no secret of his opposition to the war. And now this damning report!

There was no way he could allow Rasputin's alleged claims that he and Alix were lovers, to pass unpunished. Even Alix would understand that - surely she would...surely she must. He pushed the file across the desk. Yes, he had done the right thing in sending him back to Siberia. And yet...and yet...and yet...

The conversation replayed in his mind. True, Grigory had appeared suitably repentant, kneeling and pleading that he was a simple man who had been led astray by the wealth and adulation that his devotees showered upon him. True, too, that he vehemently denied having made any reference to the Tsarina. Nicky stared up at the ceiling. Had he been too hasty? Should he have given the healer one more chance? He shook his head decisively. No, in war time when the masses were baying for German blood, it was vital to protect Alix's reputation and that of the whole Imperial Family.

The door burst open and Alix, ashen-faced, stood before him, "Nicky, what have you done!"

"He had to go. I had no choice."

Throwing her hands in the air, she shook her head wildly, "Don't you see what you've done? You have played straight into the hands of his enemies. Traitors and liars, all of them! We're surrounded by intriguers and yet you have sent away our one true friend when, in these terrible times, we have more need of him than ever! Bring him back, Nicky. Show them that you see through their lies and that you're not moved by their disgusting insinuations!"

"Alix," he said quietly, offering her the file, "these aren't lies and rumours. This is an official police report. See for yourself and you'll know why I had no option."

She snatched it from him and hastily flicked through the pages, "Djunkovsky!" she said in exasperation. "I might have known it would come from Moscow. Djunkovsky's sister used to work for Ella - this is all Ella's doing. She's planned this from the start, she and the rest of her bigoted clique."

Nicky moved around the desk and reached to put his arm around her but she stepped back from him, "Djunkovsky's not to be trusted. He needs to be relieved of his office. Let Ella see that *you* are the Tsar and she has no business setting up corrupt policemen to try to undermine you. That Bishop Tryphon, Samarin, Scherbatov, Sophie Tyutcheva, Djunkovsky - *all* of them that speak out against him - they are all Ella's friends. She is behind this, Nicky, and you're letting them win."

"Alix," he sighed, "I'm as grateful as you are for all that Grigory has done for Alexei but sometimes we have to put our own feelings aside for the good of the country. These attacks on him aren't only coming from Moscow. You heard my cousin Nikolai's response when Grigory offered to go to the front line to bless the soldiers?"

She shook her head warily.

"He said, 'Yes, let him come so I can hang him!'"

"Nikolai has been against us from the start. I have *never* trusted him."

"But as the Supreme Commander of the army, he has the full support of the troops. He speaks for the ordinary soldiers and they respect him for it."

"That respect is due to you alone. He has become too puffed up on his own power. He needs to be replaced by someone with more loyalty."

"I would replace him," Nicky conceded, "but there isn't anyone else who is powerful enough to take over that role unless…"

He paused. It wasn't the first time the idea had occurred to him and now, amid the whispers of rising dissent in the city, spy-mania, the irritating spectre of Rasputin, and Alix's wrath, the prospect of taking a more active role in the war, had an even stronger appeal.

"Perhaps *I* should take over Nikolai's position myself."

Startled, she stared at him for a moment, "You would go to the Front and lead the troops yourself?"

"It would mean our being separated for weeks, maybe months at a time but, when so many of our people are enduring that hardship, it would be wrong to refuse the same sacrifice."

Her eyes were sad and her face strained by anxiety.

468

"Yes," she murmured, "and it would boost morale for the soldiers to see you there." She was pensive for a moment, "I will write to Our Friend and ask his advice. If he thinks this decision is for the best, we can ask for his blessing."

With black-edged telegrams bearing bad news every hour of every day to homes across Russia, it seemed almost self-indulgent to Ella, to give way to tears.

"Kostia," she murmured, folding the page as she stepped into the chapel. "Was it all too much for you, dear friend? And now, you're reunited with Oleg and your truest friend, Serge." Even as she prayed for his soul, came the fearful thought that it might only be a matter of time before she, too, joined that happy reunion.

After the funeral, when the mourners had departed, she dined with Mavra and her sons in the glorious surroundings of the Great Palace of Pavlovsk.

"This place," Mavra said sadly, "was the perfect home for him. The parks, the Temple of Friendship, the lakes, the bridges, all of it so suited his poeticism. I think he will be happy to rest here."

"He was such a good father to us all," said Igor. "We couldn't have hoped for a happier or more loving home."

Ioann nodded, "It was because he loved us so much that losing Oleg was too great a sorrow for him to bear. Perhaps his passing is a blessing to spare him still more sorrow. The way things are going, it feels as though we are all spiralling into disaster."

"Let's not be maudlin," Mavra said, "that's the last thing he would want." And she forced herself to say brightly, "Once the Tsar takes over command of the army, our fortunes will surely improve."

"Will they?" young Konstantin said gloomily. "Our soldiers are so short of ammunition that they have to wait for someone else to die in order to get his gun."

"I've heard that the generals aren't happy with the idea," Ioann said. "They feel that His Majesty isn't as experienced as Nikolai Nikolaevich, whom they trust absolutely. I mean he is so huge that his very presence inspires confidence in the men. Will the Tsar inspire the same confidence?"

When he looked to Ella for a response, loyalty compelled her to reply, "The Tsar was always very popular among his comrades when he was a young cadet. He takes all of this very seriously. Did you know that he marched ten miles or more carrying the kit of a foot soldier so that he would know exactly what was being asked of them?"

"Oh, I don't question his commitment at all," Ioann said fervently. "I know His Majesty has always sacrificed his own wishes for the good of his country. But I *do* wonder whether he has the character for a military leader."

"More worrying to me," said Igor, "is what will happen in his absence. Who will take over the running of the country?"

"Alix," Ella said.

"Which, in effect," Igor said quietly, "means Rasputin."

"No, no," Ella insisted, "Rasputin has been sent back to Siberia."

"For how long? Once the Tsar is away at Stavka, who else will Her Majesty rely on? I don't want to be pessimistic but I think His Majesty would be far better remaining in Petersburg.

Without him, I can see the whole country sliding rapidly into chaos."

Chapter 47 - Autumn 1916

Alone at Tsarskoe Selo, Alix worried. Her palpitations were becoming more frequent. Her health felt all but broken by worry and pain. Her fingers ached from writing such long letters to Nicky several times each day, and her mind was plagued with sorrow, longing and ceaseless anxiety. In Nicky's absence, she missed him dreadfully. She longed to hear his voice, to feel the touch of his hand, and to see those beautiful eyes gaze at her with love - so unlike the cold eyes of the ministers and generals who came daily to warn her of impending doom. And she worried about him. She worried because he was too kind to stand up to his enemies. Without her to guide him, she worried that he might even lose faith in Our Friend.

She worried about Alexei who, wanting to participate in the war effort, had joined his father in Mogilev. For the first time in his life, he was far away from her. Supposing a slight knock should start another episode of bleeding? How would he cope without her beside him to soothe his pain?

And she worried about her daughters. Their lives were so insular and sheltered that it was hard to accept that they were no longer children. At twenty-one, Olga might well have been married but no Russian suitor was good enough. Dmitri had been suggested - he was handsome, royal and a competent sportsman - but he spent too much time in the company of unsuitable women, and his health was not good. Hadn't the doctors diagnosed tuberculosis to account for his frequently coughing up blood? Miechen's son, Boris, was also mentioned but he was far, far too rough for her innocent child. In wartime, a foreign marriage was out of the question and, even when the war came to end, the unspoken fear would remain that other Royal Houses might be reluctant to allow the possibility of introducing this tainted blood into their dynasties.

More than ever now, too, she worried about her enemies. Though it seemed that in the midst of her own private war against Moscow, Ella was suing for peace, she could not be trusted. She might write frequently to Nicky, affirming her affection and loyalty, and she might even write to Alix, pitying her loneliness while her husband was away, but her attitude to Our Friend had not softened and, until it did, she would not be welcome in Tsarskoe Selo.

She worried about the war; about her brother and sister in Germany; about the poor wounded soldiers in her hospitals; and the treacherous members of the Imperial Family. With so many anxieties to torture her mind and so few friends to whom she might turn, her sole consolation was Father Grigory. He alone had the power to calm her nerves, to ease her palpitations and reassure her that all would be well. He alone had the power to guide Nicky and bring this hateful war to a swift and victorious conclusion; he alone had the power to save her family.

The November morning was dark and icily cold as Ella made her usual round of the hospital ward. Most of the patients still slept and the dim lamps flickered gloomily as though too weary to give any light. When she was satisfied that everything was in order, Ella wrapped a cloak around her shoulders and stepped outside. Her feet crunched over the ice and her breath froze in the air as, through the hazy dawn, came the outline of Father Mitrophan, trudging slowly from the chapel. As he drew nearer, she could see that his face, usually so serene, was shrouded by an expression of confusion. She hastened towards him, "You look worried, Father. Is something troubling you?"

He nodded, frowning, "Might I speak with you?"

She led him into the parlour and, as she stoked the embers in the grate, he said, "I had a dream, a very disturbing dream. Normally I would pay no attention to dreams but this one was so vivid."

"Sometimes God speaks to us through dreams," she smiled. "Didn't he warn Joseph in a dream to take the Holy Family to Egypt?"

Mitrophan rubbed his hands together in front of the fire, "My dream makes no sense at all to me. Perhaps you will understand it."

She pulled two chairs up to the hearth and Mitrophan's frown deepened as he began, "I saw four images: a beautiful church in flames, a portrait of the Tsarina with a black border, the Archangel Michael holding a flaming sword, and St. Seraphim praying on a rock. Can you make any sense of that?"

She stared into the flames. It was all perfectly clear.

"It's a prophecy," she said. "The flaming church signifies persecution, which is surely coming to us. The Archangel Michael was warning of the horrors that will ravish the country, but eventually, through the prayers of the Holy Virgin and St. Seraphim, the Russian people will find peace and mercy."

"And the black border around the Tsarina's portrait?"

She paused before replying, then stated bluntly, "The Imperial Family will be murdered."

Mitrophan stared at her aghast, "*All* of them?"

"All of us."

"No," he said, "no. This can't be so."

"Look around. It's easy to read the signs of the times. Everywhere, there is a sense of imminent disaster and, as often happens before a major catastrophe, it seems that people have lost their capacity to care. Morale is so low in the army that officers are abandoning their duties. With no hope of victory, they throw themselves instead into a frenzy of desperate pleasure seeking. The government is in such disarray. Ministers are changed at the drop of a hat on the whim of Rasputin, and the whole structure is collapsing. The food supplies, transport, all of it is going to pieces. The country is starving, yet the nightclubs and restaurants are full. The corrupt government is decaying and, helpless to know what to do, people seek escape in the unreality of the music halls and theatres. The world is collapsing around us and people are clutching at any last chance of pleasure before the approaching apocalypse."

A sudden yelling startled them both and they turned in unison towards the window to see a nun running towards the parlour.

Ella dashed outside to meet her, "What's happening, Barbara?"

"Oh Matushka, hide yourself away," she said, bundling her back into the room. "They are coming for you!"

"Who?"

"A mob, a lynch mob by the sound of them."

As the voices grew louder and more threatening, Ella moved towards the door.

"No, please," Barbara pleaded, "it's not safe."

But Ella was already outside. Though her heart was pounding, she raised her head and walked with assumed confidence towards the gates where a hostile gang, armed with sticks and rocks, was screaming obscenities.

Suddenly, she was spotted, "There she is! The German spy! We know what you're doing: passing secrets to the Hun and starving out our own people!"

A shower of stones came flying over the gates, and Mitrophan and Barbara seized her arms and drew her back to the safety of the parlour where the three of them stood at the window.

"They're clambering over the gates!" Barbara said desperately.

"I'll go back to them. It's me they want."

Again, Ella turned to the door but had hardly reached for the handle when Mitrophan called, "Wait! There are soldiers."

Ella continued towards the gates, thanking God for the timely arrival of the passing brigade. The crowd began to disperse but not before Ella had heard them baying for the blood of 'Rasputin's whore.'

She turned and her eyes met Mitrophan's, "She won't listen but I have to try one more time. I must go to Tsarskoe and warn my sister. Pray, please pray, that this time she will listen."

Felix's eyes wandered around the drawing room where the solemn faces and conspiratorial whispers bore closer resemblance to a funeral party than a social gathering. How old and weary everyone appeared! How this war had aged them all! Only his beautiful wife, Irina, retained a youthful vibrancy, and she sat between her parents and their guests like a fresh spring snowdrop among a mass of faded roses. The once-sparkling Dowager Empress Minnie looked jaded and dull; her daughter, Xenia, seemed almost as old as her mother; and Sandro, once the dashing young sailor, looked now like an old sea-dog with wisps of grey in his beard. Pavel's face was lined in wrinkles, and deep crevices marked the sagging skin beneath Miechen's eyes.

"Even Ella can't leave her convent now," Sandro said. "The Muscovites accuse her of harbouring spies. They say that if Alix were to appear in Moscow, they would literally tear her to pieces."

"Alix has brought this on herself," Miechen said, which caused Minnie to gasp in horror. "I don't wish her ill but she will not see reason. How many people have tried to warn her what's happening?"

Sandro nodded gloomily, "My brother, Nikolai, wrote to Nicky at his base in Mogilev, and told him plainly of the damage that Alix's obstinacy is doing to the monarchy. He warned him what the outcome will be unless something is done about it."

"Did Nicky reply?" Minnie asked.

"It seems he sends most of his correspondence back to Tsarskoe, so the letter fell into Alix's hands."

"It would do her good to read the truth," Michen said. "I hope it made an impact on her."

"On the contrary. She accused my brother of treason and asked Nicky to have nothing more to do with him."

"Where is it all going to end?" Xenia said. "Surely even Alix can see that the country is in turmoil. Unless something is done immediately, we could find ourselves in the middle of civil war as well as war in the trenches."

Pavel drew deeply on his cigarette, "The only way to avoid a full scale revolution is for Nicky to grant a constitution."

"Would he even consider it?" Sandro said.

"I spoke of it to Alix but she said it's an impossibility. Nicky is bound by the oath he took at his coronation, to uphold the autocracy."

"Autocracy? What autocracy?" Miechen huffed. "The soldiers are deserting; there's chaos in the streets; transport is virtually at a stand-still. There *is* no leadership or autocracy and this will continue for as long as Nicky is away at Mogilev, leaving everything in Alix's hands."

"She is in a difficult position," Minnie said. "There seem to be no strong ministers left who are capable of taking charge of the situation."

"And why is that? Because anyone who *was* capable has been dismissed on the whim of Rasputin."

Minnie tried to be positive, "According to Nicky, Rasputin's influence isn't nearly as great as people think it is."

"But the public perception," Pavel said, "is that *he* is ruling the country. Whether or not it is true, people believe it and, worse, believe that he and Alix are working for the enemy. It's absolutely vital that he be removed from the scene altogether."

Rasputin...Rasputin...Rasputin, Felix thought. The spectre of the moujik hung over the whole of the country like a great maelstrom of evil.

"When I tried to tell Alix all this," Pavel said, "she cut me off as soon as I mentioned his name. She simply refuses to hear him criticised. '*No prophet is accepted by his own people in his own country,'* she says."

Sandro looked towards Felix, "Didn't your mother meet with a similar response?"

"Worse," Irina said, "the Tsarina told her she was no longer welcome in her company."

A melancholy silence hovered between them in the clouds of cigarette smoke until Miechen spoke again, "The woman is quite mad. Nicky should have her confined in an asylum until the end of the war."

"Oh really!" Minnie shook her head.

"At least pack her off to Livadia where she can do no more harm."

"Nicky would never do that. Besides, it isn't Alix who needs to be removed. It's Rasputin."

"And Alix won't let that happen."

"There is one last chance," Minnie said eventually. "I received a letter from Ella. She is coming to tell Alix of the situation in Moscow and hopefully force her to see sense."

"Ella has tried before and failed."

"Her visit will coincide with Nicky's return from Mogilev so, even if Alix won't listen, perhaps she will be able to explain the situation to him. We can only pray that this time she will be successful."

"And if she isn't?"

No one replied.

Felix turned away. *"If she isn't,"* he thought, *"there is only one drastic alternative."*

Chapter 48 - December 1916

Entering the Alexander Palace, Ella breathed deeply to calm her agitation. The date was auspicious: the anniversary of the death of her mother, on whose prayers she had always relied. Surely, she told herself, *surely* on this occasion, Mama's prayers would be more potent than ever. Everything depended upon this meeting: not only the fate of the Imperial Family, but the future of the whole of Russia. She clasped her hands tightly and, when informed that Her Majesty was ready to receive her, raised her head and walked with determined confidence into the mauve boudoir.

Perhaps, she thought, as she entered the room, Alix sensed what she was about to say for, though she had hardly hoped for a warm welcome, the reception she received was even chillier than she had anticipated. Alix, her face pale and care-worn, neither smiled nor offered any greeting beyond a questioning stare.

Very well, Ella thought, *I will waste no time trying to deliver this gently. The message is too urgent for small talk.*

"Moscow is in chaos."

"The whole world is in chaos."

"Alix, do you have any idea how serious this situation has become? The strength of anti-German feeling is so great that I can't even appear on the street without being spat at, pelted with stones or..."

"You are not the only one who suffers. What you're experiencing is nothing compared to what our soldiers are enduring for the sake of the country."

"I didn't come to speak of my sufferings. I came to warn you for the sake of the country."

Alix threw back her shoulders, "I don't need *you* to tell me what my country needs. You seem to forget that I am your Empress."

"For how much longer? Open your eyes! You've seen the cartoons, the posters, the scurrilous pictures. You know what people are saying of you. It's already gone too far!" Ella stepped closer and, unimpeded by the anger in her sister's eyes, continued more forcefully, "You have only one chance to regain the people's trust and, unless you seize that chance, everything is lost. Get rid of Rasputin, Alix, or the people will get rid of you!"

"You dare to come in here and…"

"Yes, I dare because I have no option! How blind can you be? For Nicky's sake, for the sake of the country, you have to act now and you have to act swiftly. The people are starving and they hold you responsible for it!"

"And what do you expect me to do? Is it *my* fault the trains aren't running? Is it *my* fault that food is in such short supply?"

"Yes, it is. It's your fault for appointing ministers who have no idea what they're doing. For pity's sake, Alix, Marie Antoinette went to the guillotine for less!"

Alix threw up her hands in disgust, "Treason!"

"Treason?" Ella gasped. "I am the one person who genuinely cares about you, about Nicky and about our country."

"Oh yes, of course! *Saint* Elizabeth the self-righteous who presumes to care more for her people than their Empress does."

"For pity's sake, this isn't a competition! There isn't time for these petty arguments. How many more warnings do you need? The country is spiralling into disaster on a scale we can hardly imagine, and still you stand there blind and..."

"You have said what you came to say. You can leave now." She turned away.

"Oh Alix, Alix," Ella sighed desperately, "I didn't come here to argue. On this day of all days, as sisters we should put aside our differences and work together to see what can be done."

"Still," Alix murmured as though speaking to herself, "you try to rule me, thinking you know what is best for me." She looked up and said more firmly, "You have responsibilities in Moscow. I suggest you return there and attend to them, leaving me to attend to my responsibilities here."

Ella shook her head, "I believed in you, Alix. I believed that you would make an excellent Tsarina, true to all we were brought up to believe. I believed you would stand by Nicky and support him, but with your blind superstition and your self-absorption you are dragging him down and the whole of the country is going down with you."

Alix eyes filled with tears of rage, "There's nothing more to say."

"Alix, I..."

"As your Empress, I command you to leave."

Shaking with frustration and anger, Ella turned to the door, "Has Nicky returned from Mogilev?"

"He doesn't arrive until tomorrow."

"I would like see him when he does."

When Alix didn't answer, Ella stormed from the room, out of the palace and back to her apartments in the Catherine Palace where she paced the corridors until her rage subsided into despair. She knelt on the cold, marble floor and prayed through her tears. One final hope: that Nicky might be prepared to listen and to act.

All night she knelt in prayer, fluctuating between faith and desolation and, in the morning before the sun had risen, a messenger arrived bearing a note from the Alexander Palace.

'*The Emperor has returned,*' it was Alix's hand, '*but he is far too busy to receive anyone.*'

Heart-broken and desolate, Ella returned to St. Petersburg and made her way to the Youssoupov Palace where Zinaida and Felix were anxiously waiting for news.

"There's no hope," Ella wept. "Poor Nicky! Poor Russia!"

Felix drummed his thumb against his lips as he paced the pavement on the banks of the Nevka Canal. His breath hung in clouds in the icy December air but the feverish thoughts running through his brain drove away any sense of cold. The memory of Ella's face, so forlorn and distressed, hovered before his eyes, goading him to action and strengthening his resolve. Pavel, Sandro, Nikolai Mikhailovich, the Dowager Empress, Ella, even his own mother - all had tried in vain. What else could he do but take action? The cries of opposition to Rasputin came not only from the family or those who would spring revolution; now the most loyal and staunchest monarchists in the Duma were demanding his removal. Two days after the event, Felix could still hear the tumultuous cheers that greeted the impassioned speech of Vladimir Puriskevich when he called for a halt to the dark forces at work in the country. Even the tempestuous Duma was united in hatred of the peasant.

At length, Dmitri appeared, the collar of his trench coat turned up against the wind, his head lowered as though not wishing to be seen. He strode with determined steps towards Felix and embraced him warmly, "I received your message."

"And you agree?"

"I agree that something has to be done. But murder?"

"Dmitri, men are dying in their millions in the trenches and more will die here on the streets unless we do something. If the Empress won't listen to reason, what's the alternative? Words are meaningless now; it's time for action."

Dmitri exhaled in a long sigh, "You're right, of course, but I wish there were another way."

"So do I, but you know as well as I do that there *is* no other way. As long as he lives, his influence over the Empress will continue. For her sake, for the Emperor's sake and for the sake of Russia, we have to do what many other people are longing to do, but dare not."

Dmitri nodded, "How do you propose to do it?"

Felix put his arm around his shoulder and led him further along the bank, away from prying ears, "I've met him a few times already and think he trusts me. I can build on that, cultivate a friendship with him so he won't suspect anything when I invite him to my apartments."

"You plan to do it in your own home?"

"It's the best place. No one will see or be any the wiser."

"How?"

"Poison. I've spoken with Puriskevich and he knows someone who can provide us with potassium cyanide. All we need to do is ply him with cakes and wine sprinkled with the stuff."

"Poison," Dmitri mumbled. "That's the coward's way. A bullet is so much…"

"Bloodier! We can't take that risk. There must be no evidence."

Dmitri's eyes widened, "Isn't a corpse evidence enough?"

Felix looked over the railings at the frozen waters of the Nevka Canal, "His body won't be discovered until the thaw, by which time we'll have saved the country from disaster."

Dmitri frowned, "Supposing he refuses to come to your apartments?"

"He won't refuse. I have the perfect bait."

Dmitri raised his eyebrows.

"Irina."

"No," Dmitri said, "you can't involve her in this!"

"She won't be involved. She'll be miles away on our estate in the Crimea, but Rasputin won't know that. I'll tell him she's ill and would like him to come and heal her. He can't resist a pretty woman, so he's sure to accept."

Dmitri silently stared into the distance as though imagining the scene in advance.

"Well," Felix said eventually, "are you with me?"

He nodded slowly, "When?"

"A couple of weeks. I need to spend a little more time building our friendship to make sure he suspects nothing."

"Have you told Aunt Ella?"

"No. No one knows except you and Puriskevich."

"I'd like to speak with her first."

Felix was about to protest but Dmitri rested his hand on his shoulder, "We can trust her. I won't tell her the details, just let her know that something is about to happen."

"Alright," Felix yielded, "do whatever you think best."

"Perhaps it would be as well for us to avoid one another as far as possible for now. I'll go to Moscow and, if you let me know when you're ready, I'll be here."

"Good man!" Felix slapped him on the back. "And for now, relax and just think that by New Year it will all be over and we'll have saved the dynasty!"

Candles flickered around the crib in the chapel of The House of Martha and Mary, where Ella knelt before the statue of the infant Jesus. The tenderness on the face of the Holy Virgin gazing serenely at her son, brought to mind the memory of Alix holding the infant Alexei in those few brief weeks before his illness was discovered. Any mother, she thought, would risk everything for the sake of her child, like a tigress defending her young. Even the most docile of creatures could turn and become aggressively protective if the life of her child were in danger. Yes, Alix's desperation to save Alexei was understandable but, when so many other lives were at stake and the country teetered on the brink of disaster, all personal feeling must be put aside.

"*Murder?*" she thought, "*Can murder ever be justified...Thou shalt not kill...*" And yet, when the whole of Europe was engaged in such bloody slaughter, the removal of one dangerous man, one source of evil, seemed so small a thing. Had all this bloodshed and horror hardened her heart, she wondered. Five, ten years ago it would have been unthinkable to even entertain such a notion but now...desperate times, desperate remedies. She flicked through the pages of her Bible to the Gospel of St. John: "*It is better that one man should die for the people, rather than that the whole nation should perish...*"

"Matushka," Mitrophan gently tapped her shoulder, "forgive me, but you look so troubled."

"I *am* troubled, Father, deeply troubled."

He knelt down beside her, "Is there anything I can do?"

"'*It is better that one man should die for the people, rather than that the whole nation should perish.*'" she read aloud. "That's what they said of Christ. Those who killed him believed they were acting for the common good. Do you think that the death of one man could prevent the destruction of a nation?"

"Every nation chooses its own scapegoats. It is easier to lay the responsibility for all our ills at the feet of someone else than to accept that we have brought calamity onto ourselves."

"But if one man were truly destroying the country and..."

"Could one man do that without the tacit consent of all his fellow countrymen? Evil is like a plant - it can't flourish unless it is fed and watered." He gazed towards the infant in the crib, "By our carelessness and selfishness, we all contribute to its growth and then, when we see what a monster we have created, we attempt to destroy it as though it is external to ourselves."

"Something terrible is about to happen," she whispered. "I have neither condemned nor condoned it but in my heart I think it's the only way."

"With or without your agreement, this terrible thing will happen anyway?"

She nodded.

"Then it's out of your hands and all you can do is place it in the hands of God. Pray that if it is his will, this thing might be averted but, if there is no other way, pray for everyone involved."

She stared at the serene expressions of the statues in the crib. How she longed for peace, for an end to all this horror and a return to the beauty that was once her sole preoccupation.

"There was time once," she murmured, "to contemplate everything; to reflect, to *feel*. I was so certain of God's will. Now, with so much to do, so many demands, everything rushes by so quickly and I can hardly discern his voice from my own pride or selfish desires."

He smiled gently, "You have exhausted yourself with all your work here. You seldom sleep, you eat so little and every moment of your day is taken up with other people's needs, not to mention all the cares of your family."

"'*He who sets his hand to the plough...* '" she said.

"Christ himself needed time away from the crowds. *'Come away to a lonely place,'* he said. Why don't you go away for a while, somewhere quiet and free of all this anxiety?"

She was about to reply but he shook his head, "As your confessor, I advise it."

She smiled gratefully, "I would like to make a pilgrimage to Sarov. I was there with the Tsar and Tsarina when St. Seraphim was canonised and we witnessed many miracles. Seraphim has always held a special place in the heart of the Imperial Family." Even as she spoke she remembered a prophecy alleged to have been made by the saint, and she wondered if Mitrophan had heard it, too. The saint had said that he would be canonised during the reign of Tsar Nicholas II, and that his canonisation would be followed by a bloody revolution.

"At this critical time," she whispered, "I still hope for a miracle."

Chapter 49

Felix' hand shook as he poured brandy from the decanter, and Dmitri, chain-smoking, trembled so violently he could hardly take the glass from him.

Rasputin was not proving easy to kill.

"Unbelievable!" Felix whispered. "On the cakes alone, there was enough cyanide to kill a horse, not to mention the other sachets that we added to the wine. And he's still sitting there, rambling on! It hasn't touched him at all."

"The devil incarnate," Dmitri said. "Send him home and let's forget the whole thing before it goes any further."

"It's too late for that. We've come this far, we can't stop here."

From the basement apartment, the voice of the moujik sounded like a tethered bear growing restless and aggressive, "Where is she? Is she not coming?"

Dmitri, in great agitation, pushed Felix towards the door, "Make an excuse. Say she's gone to sleep and tell him to go home. Just get rid of him."

Felix seized his collar and shook him, "Calm down or he'll hear you!" He fumbled over Dmitri's body, "You have a gun?"

"Yes but..."

"Give it to me."

He snatched the revolver and returned to the room where Rasputin sprawled drowsily, gulping the poisoned wine.

"For the honour of the Tsar and Holy Mother Russia!" he raised his arm and fired directly at him.

With a growl like a wounded animal, Rasputin slumped to the floor at the same moment that Dmitri and Puriskevich rushed into the room. For a second, all three stood in stunned silence, half-expecting him to rise up like a phoenix from the ashes, but he was still.

Puriskevich spoke first, "We have to get him out of here. Find something to wrap him in. Come on, it will be light soon!"

They ran up the stairs and, while Puriskevich went to collect the car, Felix found a bearskin, which he and Dmitri dragged towards the basement but, as they neared the door, they gasped in horror to see Rasputin scurrying out of the palace.

"Stop him, for Christ's sake!"

They followed him into the courtyard, juggling the revolver between them and firing shot after shot but only after a fourth bullet had hit him, did he finally collapse in the snow. Even then it was hard to believe he was dead.

"Bind his hands," Felix said and between them they bundled the body into the car, sped to the bank and hurled him into the icy waters of the Nevka Canal.

"Welcome home, Matushka!" Barbara called, hurrying across the convent courtyard. "How was your pilgrimage?"

"Wonderfully refreshing," Ella smiled, "and it's good to be back."

"We've missed you so much! The whole place has such a different feel about it when you're not here."

Ella laughed and Barbara took the packages from beneath her arm.

"I brought some icons from Dveev and Sarov, which I thought would fit beautifully in the hospital. Sarov is filled with the most exquisite icons! I sent some to Her Majesty in the hope that..." She stopped herself and walked on into the parlour, "Have I missed anything, while I was away?"

Barbara put the icons down on the table and, as Ella began to unwrap them, she said, "You've heard the news from Petersburg, I'm sure."

"What news is that?"

"Grigory Rasputin is dead."

Ella dropped the icons and stared at her, "When? How?"

"It's rather mysterious. Not all of the details have been released yet. They found his body in a break in the ice off one of the bridges on the Nevka Canal. They said he'd been missing for two days and it seems he was murdered."

"*Murdered,*" Ella murmured, hardly able to reconcile the vileness of the word with the elation in her heart.

"And that's not all," Barbara continued. "In His Majesty's absence, the Tsarina has issued an order for Grand Duke Dmitri Pavlovich and Prince Felix Youssoupov to be placed under house arrest."

"They've done it!" Ella whispered, trying to imagine what terrible qualms of conscience Felix must have endured in carrying out such an act. Felix, who hated the sight of blood and was so opposed to killing that he would not enlist in the army and offered his services instead to the medical corps. "Only his great love of his country impelled him to do this," she thought aloud. "I need to send telegrams at once."

She sat down and prepared her messages: one to Dmitri and one to Zinaida, assuring them of her prayers and offering thanks for such an act of patriotism.

Alix slumped into a chair and her eyes wandered wearily over the piles of letters and telegrams scattered across the desk. There was no doubt at all who was responsible for so heinous a crime. The night of Our Friend's disappearance, the police said, he had set out to the Youssoupov Palace and witnesses in the vicinity claimed to have heard gun shots. And where was his body found? Not far from the Beloselsky Belozersky Palace.

"Dmitri, Felix…" she pressed her hands to her eyes, recalling Our Friend's terrible warning. "If I die at the hands of peasants," he had said, "you have nothing to fear. If your own relatives are responsible for my death, your entire family will be dead within two years." Felix was married to Nicky's niece; Dmitri was his cousin.

Everything was over but justice must be done.

She swished through the papers: a package from Sarov in Ella's handwriting. She put it to one side to wade through the letters and telegrams that the police had intercepted en route to the suspects: letters from well-wishers and strangers. How could so many people offer support to cold-blooded killers? And two more telegrams:

"No!" she choked, "No!"

"What is it, Mama?" Olga said, and Alix handed over a telegram:

"Your son deserves the thanks of the entire nation for his act of patriotism. Ella"

Olga shook her head, "Aunt Ella was a part of this?"

"There is no one left for us to trust." Alix swept the unopened package from Sarov off the desk, "Have these returned to sender. In supporting this crime, Ella is as guilty as those who carried it out. We have nothing more to say to one another."

When Sandro stepped into the drawing room of the Vladimir Palace, he found Miechen and her sons, Kyril, Boris and Andrei, engrossed in a heated conversation with Pavel. Indignation was etched on their faces, as Pavel recounted his meeting with Nicky, earlier that evening.

"…and I told him," he was saying, "that Dmitri has given me his word that he did not kill the peasant."

"The people think he did," said Miechen. "They are flocking in their hundreds to the cathedrals to light candles in his honour. He's quite a national hero."

"He doesn't want any of that," Pavel said firmly.

"Did Nicky believe you?" Sandro asked.

Pavel shrugged, "He said he can't lift the order of house arrest until the investigation is over."

"The fact is," Miechen said, "Nicky didn't give that order in the first place. Alix did, and she had no right to do it."

"I mentioned that to Nicky but he said it was issued on his authority, which we know isn't true. The order came from Alix and he's just covering for her."

Sandro sat down beside him, "I have to say, I never thought my son-in-law had the strength of nerve to do such a thing. He's gone up in my estimation for his part in this. In his heart of hearts, I'll bet Nicky is as relieved as everyone else that the peasant has finally received his just desserts."

"No," Pavel said, "he doesn't see it that way at all. Murder is murder, he says, and when so many of our soldiers are dying at the hands of the enemy, it's unforgivable that any Russian should be killed by his own people."

"What's he going to do about it?" Miechen asked.

"It's not decided yet."

Sandro smiled, "Felix is quite confident that he won't do anything. He thinks he's protected by some lucky star and, besides, since they have the support of so many people, he believes that no one would dare take any action against them."

Pavel shook his head, "Nicky hinted that Felix will be banished to his estate in Kursk, which is hardly any hardship at all, but he feels that Dmitri, being a member of his own family, has the greater guilt. He mentioned the possibility of posting him to the Persian front."

"How ridiculous!" Miechen said. "Dmitri's health isn't strong enough to withstand that climate."

"I said that to Nicky but he is adamant that justice be done."

"Justice?" Miechen said. "Where's the justice in sending a national hero to his death?"

"Perhaps," Sandro suggested, "if Ella were to speak on Dmitri's behalf, Nicky would listen. After all, he was her ward for years."

Pavel sighed, "Alix is convinced that Ella was behind the whole plot. She stands even less chance of being given a hearing than we do."

"In that case," Kyril said, "you should go back and plead Dmitri's cause. Being such a loving father himself, Nicky is sure to listen to you and, if you remind him that the populace is rejoicing over the death of the peasant, he'll see that he cannot go against the will of the people."

"Good grief! *The will of the people,*" Miechen said. "You sound like a revolutionary. Has it come to this?"

Kyril shrugged and his mother frowned, "Never mind the will of the people. We, the family, must make known our opinion. I suggest we all sign a petition asking for Dmitri's house arrest to be lifted and for no further action to be taken."

"I think you're right," Boris said. "Mavra and her sons will join us in that, and your brothers, too, Sandro?"

"I'm sure of it," he nodded but, when he looked towards Pavel, he saw an anxious frown creasing his brow. "You don't agree?"

"I can't help thinking a petition sounds like a threat. We must remember our oath of allegiance."

"It's a bit late for that!" Miechen laughed. "As I recall you broke that oath a long time ago."

"It's different now. In wartime everything is different."

"Exactly! In wartime the killing of this peasant was the most patriotic action anyone could take."

"Maybe so," Pavel sighed, "but the way things are going, I still fear the worst. We've all prayed for so long for the spectre of Rasputin to be exorcised but his death has achieved none of its desired effects. In the fact the opposite is true. It's only brought further divisions into the family, strengthening Alix' conviction that she's surrounded by enemies. It's even shattered that strong bond of affection between Nicky and Ella. The Tsar's reputation is at such a low ebb that I can't help thinking that this act of patriotism has come too late. "

Chapter 50
February - March 1917

Isolated and despondent in Tsarskoe Selo, Alix surrounded herself with icons and candles as she poured out her sorrow and fears in endless letters to Nicky. Her fingers ached from writing, and her heart ached from the sense of complete betrayal by those who owed allegiance to the Tsar. Now, without Our Friend's guidance, she felt more alone than ever. Nicky was so far away in Mogilev and she suspected that he received her incessant exhortations to be strong, with ambivalence. His responses, she was sure, were an attempt to spare her the details of the disastrous course of the war. With his characteristic reluctance to burden her with the seriousness of his situation, he wrote of the weather, of his religious devotions and of his longing to return to the children and the comfort of her arms.

She picked up Nicky's photo and held it to her breast, "God," she whispered, "speed him home to me." Oh, how she longed to hold him! How she longed to be with him again in Livadia, hearing Alexei's laughter and watching the girls run freely among the flowers. The fresh sea air, she was certain, would restore her health and ease this aching in her heart.

But there was so little time for even this brief reverie. More messages arrived from the ministers and police and, if the news from the Front was depressing, the stories of what was happening in the city were even more alarming. The streets, they said, were rife with revolutionary frenzy. Effigies of herself and Nicky were being burned in public places and further obscene pamphlets were scattered among the crowds. Still, the cowards and traitors within the family came to plead desperately with Nicky to grant a constitution before it was too late. Had they no sense of what it meant to have taken an oath before God to uphold the autocracy? Her only satisfaction came from the knowledge that Nicky was far too honourable to listen to such treachery and blasphemy.

She rubbed her eyes and wearily moved across the room and up the staircase. Her joints were stiff and her muscles ached. She felt so old and so tired. If only she could sleep untroubled by nightmares or the ceaseless fretful thoughts that disturbed her rest. If only for one moment she could hear the soft reassuring voice of Father Gregory, but there was no one left to soothe her anxiety and assure her that all was well. And now, more pressing matters demanded her attention. Each of her children had succumbed to an outbreak of measles.

She forced a smile as she pushed open the door to their room and flitted from bed to bed, recording temperatures, mopping brows and uttering cheery words. How sad it was to see the girls with their shaven heads - their beautiful long hair cut off to speed their recovery. There was something so poignant and quite symbolic about it. She smiled sadly, recalling how proud she had been of her own beautiful hair when she was young. It was so long that, when it was loose, she could sit on it - truly her crowning glory. And now, whitened and thinning with worry, that crowning glory had well and truly faded. She brushed away the thought that, with all the chaos in the streets, her children were truly in danger of ever seeing the crowns that were their right.

"Alix," a voice distracted her and she turned to see a grave-faced Pavel standing in the doorway.

In no mood for further confrontations, she said, "You can see how busy I am. I haven't time for..."

"Please," he said, "I have news from Nicky."

The tone of his voice and the expression in his eyes was disconcerting. There was no malice there, no aggression - more sorrow and sympathy. She trembled inside, fearing the worst.

"From Nicky?"

He nodded and she falteringly led him from the room, closing the door behind her.

"Petersburg is in utter chaos," he said. "Coal shortages have virtually paralysed the railways; supplies can barely get through to the soldiers at the Front, let alone the famished civilians here at home. There's rioting in the streets because of the bread shortages and..."

She raised a hand to silence him, "The army has been called in to deal with it."

"But they haven't dealt with it. When they were ordered to open fire on the crowds, they turned their guns on their officers instead."

"One or two mutineers?" she said, not wanting to hear the reply.

He shook his head, "Whole regiments. They've already seized the Peter and Paul Fortress, several government buildings and even the Winter Palace."

"Nicky is on his way back and will arrive in a day or two. Once the soldiers hear that he is in the city, they will return to their duties and all this anger will die down." She spoke in a firm voice that belied the fear in her heart, and she sought to reassure herself as well as him, "We have lived through this kind of disturbance before and there's no reason to believe that this time is any worse than 1905."

Pavel's voice was gentle, "Please, Alix, sit down."

Fear gripped her heart like a vice, and shooting pains ran through her chest and arms, "Nicky?"

"He's alright, don't worry," he said, though his face inspired anything but reassurance. "His train can't get through. He left Mogilev as planned but, when they reached Malaya-Vishera, the track ahead was blocked by revolutionaries."

"Revolutionaries?"

"As far as I can tell, they're diverting to Pskov. Several members of the Duma have set out to meet him there to discuss what can be done."

"Then I'm sure," she swallowed, "yes, I'm sure they will find a perfect solution."

"But we don't know how long it will be before he is able to return here and, in the meantime, I fear for your safety. Let me arrange for you to go to Livadia - you and the children. You'll be safer there."

Her heart melted at the warmth in his voice. It seemed so long since anyone had spoken with such tender kindness, and her eyes filled with tears.

"Pavel," she said, "I am so touched by your concern but my duty is to stay here and wait for the Tsar. Besides, the children aren't well enough to travel yet. You see how things are?"

"Could you not at least leave the city?" he pleaded.

She reached for his hand, "Please, don't worry about us. Whatever is happening in the rest of the army, our guards are totally loyal and, with Kyril as Commander in Chief, I know they won't desert us. We speak with them regularly, take them warm drinks and try to keep their spirits up. They adore the girls and Alexei."

She moved to the window and looked down to where the soldiers usually stood to attention. No one was there. She moved along to another window and another, "They must be…"

"Kyril ordered them to withdraw."

"What!"

Pavel shook his head in sorrow, "He has pledged his allegiance to the Duma and hoisted the red flag of the revolutionaries over his palace."

"And left his Empress and her children defenceless against any attack!"

"Don't you see that you must leave now before it's too late? The Crimea is still peaceful and…"

"No," she said with determination, "the children are not well enough to be moved and, even if they were, I would not leave. Even if they all abandon us, I will not desert my duty. My place is here, waiting for my husband and my Tsar."

Through the silence of the chapel, the revving of a motor car and raucous voices echoed from the convent gates, "Bring out the German spy! Give us the Grand Duchess Serge!"

Ella looked fervently towards the crucifix in Mitrophan's hand. The crucified Messiah hung from the cross with such meek resignation.

"Now," she prayed, "*now*, it is my turn. Oh Lord, give me courage!"

She rose from her prayers and, as she stepped towards the courtyard, a group of her sisters scurried around her, twittering like frightened birds, trying to persuade her not to go. She hardly dared speak with them for fear that her courage would fail, but she walked on, determined to give the appearance of confidence.

At the gate, stood a posse of soldiers. It was clear from their uniforms that these same men were those who had once stepped out before her in march-pasts, saluting and cheering their Commander in Chief. There had been no question of disloyalty then - these same men who carried the wreck of Serge's body to the monastery; these same men who had pledged their life and allegiance to the Tsar.

Children, she thought, *they are like unruly children suddenly free of parental constraint, but they still have noble Russian hearts.*

Heedless of the warnings, she walked towards them, her head held high, "There is no German spy. I am the Abbess of this convent. What do you want with me?"

"We're taking you for trial at the Nicholas Palace. The people will decide how to deal with foreign traitors."

She inhaled deeply, "I will come with you willingly but will you please have the kindness to let me first return to the chapel for the conclusion of our service?"

Clearly disconcerted by her response, they looked from one to another until one of them called, "Why should we trust you?"

"Come with me," she said.

Some laughed, others stared and others called out expletives until, after muttering among themselves, a group of them jumped from the truck and followed her inside. Praying every step of the way and desperately averting her eyes from the sight of her sisters' tears, she walked to the altar where Father Mitrophan held out the crucifix. She knelt and kissed the feet of Christ, then turned to the soldiers, "Perhaps, gentlemen, you would care to venerate the cross, too?"

Without a word or so much as a glance, they filed forwards one after another and, when all had kissed the crucifix, they walked out silently. Ella followed them to the door, expecting them to arrest her, but instead they climbed into their truck and drove away.

"Well," she said, her heart pounding with relief, "it seems that we are still unworthy of the crown of martyrdom."

Leaving the sisters to their prayers of thanksgiving, she returned to the parlour and telephoned her War Charity Committee at the house of the Governor General.

"Who authorised my arrest?"

There was silence on the line until eventually an unfamiliar voice said, "Your Highness, we had no idea about this and will look into it."

She returned to the hospital but hardly had time to complete the round of the patients when an officer arrived at the door.

Respectfully removing his cap and making a slight bow, he said, "What happened earlier was a disgrace. I have come to offer my apologies. The Muscovites are well aware of all you have done for them and I promise you will suffer no further interference in your work here. From now on, an armed guard will be posted at your gates to prevent any disturbance."

Ella thanked him and smiled, "God obviously wishes us to continue our work here."

In the railways sidings at Pskov, Nicky sat in the smoke-filled carriage, his eyes moving sadly over the unyielding faces of the members of the Duma delegation. All around the seat lay telegrams from his military generals, urging him, for the sake of the army, to accept the Duma's request.

The corpulent form of Rodzianko seemed to fill the whole of the carriage, "Sir, we urge you to abdicate in favour of your son."

A thousand conflicting notions rushed through Nicky's head. The words of his coronation oath still ran so easily from his tongue, and Alix's desperate pleading rang through his ears. *I am the Tsar,* he thought, *I didn't choose this; God called me to it and my duty is to follow his will.*

Rodzianko was still speaking, "The country is in chaos, the army demoralized and the people, whom you swore to protect and lead, are starving. Public anger is so great that the only hope you have of saving the dynasty is to give the people a new tsar. For the good of the country, sir, I beg you to accept our proposal."

"For the good of the country," he murmured.

"The only alternative is to gather the few regiments that remain loyal to you, and lead them into St. Petersburg to confront the mutineers and revolutionaries."

He needed air; he needed to think. He stood up and, squeezing past the delegation, strode onto the platform where, drawing on his cigarette, he paced backwards and forwards, trying to ease the weight of his heavy heart. To accept their demands was absurd! What humiliation this would bring to Alix; what shame to his family, his mother and all his relatives across Europe. And yet...and yet...

He walked on. Civil war was unthinkable. He could never lead his troops against his own people and bring disaster to the country he loved. Nor, he thought, could he abandon his allies when the Germans were gaining ground. Turning his troops on his own people, would mean no one was left to continue the European conflict. Cousin George in England had always been a true friend; it would be dishonourable to desert him now. For the sake of his allies and for the sake of his beloved Russia, he must accept this humiliation and bear it with dignity.

He returned to the carriage, "Gentlemen, you have the abdication manifesto?"

Rodzianko placed it on the table in front of him. Determinedly maintaining his dignity, Nicky took the pen, "For the good of my people," he said, signing his name. Then, he sat back, lit another cigarette and, for the first time in twenty-three years, felt a lightness as though a great burden had been lifted from his shoulders.

"I shall go to Livadia," he said, "I like the flowers there."

In his mind, he was already in the Crimea. He could smell the flowers, feel the warmth of Alix's arms around him, see the girls in their lovely white dresses, floating through summer afternoons, and hear Alexei's...

A sudden panic jolted him from the dream and, as Rodzianko, carrying the signed proclamation, moved towards the door, Nicky said, "One moment, please. As my son is only twelve years old, there will be a regency?"

"Yes, sir."

"And to whom will that responsibility be given?"

"It hasn't been decided yet."

It was clear from the tone of Rodzianko's voice that neither he nor Alix would be permitted to take on that role. Undoubtedly, they would both be banished from Petersburg, and the realization that Alexei would be separated from his mother was more than Nicky could bear.

"Would you wait for a little while before leaving? I should like to consult with my doctor."

Graciously, they acquiesced and, when the doctor was finally found, the Duma men waited outside on the platform. Nicky watched them pacing to and fro, relief on their faces as their eyes perused his signature on the document. Without turning to face the doctor, he asked, "There is no cure for my son's illness?"

The doctor answered plainly, "No, sir."

Nicky turned slowly, "In your medical opinion, with his condition, would it be fair to saddle him with the weight of responsibility for an empire? And more, an empire in turmoil?"

The doctor's eyes were filled sympathy, "His Highness will certainly suffer many more prolonged attacks. You know how unbearable his suffering has already been and there is no reason to hope that this will improve. His life is constantly in the balance and, if he were my son, sir, I should want him to live as carefree a life as possible for as long as possible. For that reason, I would hesitate to saddle him with any responsibility whatsoever."

Nicky, restraining his tears, murmured, "Thank you for your honesty. Would you ask the gentlemen of the Duma to return?"

Again they stood before him, sombre-faced and intransigent. He took the abdication manifesto from their hands, struck out Alexei's name and replaced it with that of Misha.

Once so respectful and now so irreverent, soldiers milled around the Alexander Palace, sprawled with their feet up on antique chairs, lit their cigarettes from the candles that burned before sacred icons, and yelled their oaths and coarse stories along corridors. Alix closed the door to her sitting room, trying to close out the world. At least the children were recovering, and soon Nicky would arrive to restore order. The door opened and, as so many times before, she leaped to her feet, anticipating the sight of his beautiful face. Instead, Pavel stood before her with sorrow in his eyes.

"Alix, may I offer my condolences."

Her heart stopped, "Condolences?"

"On the abdication."

"Abdiqué!" she cried, aghast.

Everything she had struggled so hard to uphold - the autocracy, Nicky's dignity and the future of her son - was gone in a single word.

Pavel stared at her in horror, "You didn't know?"

"No. When?"

"Yesterday."

"And no one thought to tell me?"

"I'm sorry. I thought you knew. I…"

"They forced this on him. Oh my poor Nicky, how it must have broken his heart! If only I had been with him to support him!"

"His actions were honourable. He has done this for the sake of his allies and for his own people."

Her heart pounded with palpitations that spread pain from her neck to her fingertips, and she sank into the chair, "Abdiqué!"

So many, many vile words had been levelled at her - German bitch, Rasputin's whore, Hessian witch - but none was ever so wounding as this.

"Everything we have worked for and struggled to maintain is gone in that one word."

Pavel took her hand and sat down beside her.

"Nicky first abdicated in favour of Alexei but, considering his health and not wanting him to be separated from you, he changed that in favour of Misha."

"So Misha is now Tsar?"

He shook his head, "He said he would not accept it unless he had the support of the country. Clearly, that isn't forthcoming. Today he, too, abdicated."

"In favour of?"

"No one."

The tears that burned her eyes rolled down her cheeks, "In one stroke of the pen, three hundred years of a dynasty is wiped away."

He choked and tears rolled down his cheeks, too, and the sight of his grief wrung compassion from her heart.

"My beloved Nicky," she sobbed. "I must write to him at once. No matter what these traitors have done to him, to me he is still and will always be my Tsar and my Emperor."

"At least," Pavel said, wiping the tears from his eyes, "he will be allowed to return to you now and you will all be together again."

"Yes," she said, "we will go away and live quietly, harming no one and just caring for one another."

"Where will you go?"

"Livadia. We have always been so happy there."

Chapter 51

"The worst seems to be over," Mitrophan smiled as Ella turned the pages of the newspaper laid out on the convent table. "Once Their Majesties are settled in Livadia, I am sure everything will calm down. The Provisional Government is doing everything to restore order, and the new Minister of Justice appears to be a very fair man."

Ella nodded, "Kerensky has the respect of the people and seems intent on preventing more bloodshed. What's more, his treatment of Their Majesties has been exemplary. Without his good sense, I fear the mob would have torn them limb from limb."

"The greatest threat now," Mitrophan pointed to a headline, "is the return of this man, Lenin."

"Lenin?"

"A Bolshevik. He left Russia ten years ago and has been wandering around Europe trying to stir up revolution. He thinks the Provisional Government is too moderate and it sounds as though he is winning support by promising to take the country out of the war."

Ella peered at the article, "It seems he hates the Imperial Family and everything we stood for. He won't rest until he has destroyed every Romanov on Russian soil."

"Well," Mitrophan said optimistically, "he won't gain many supporters in that. After all, this commission that Kerensky set up to investigate the Tsarina's supposed treasonable activities, has proved her innocence and satisfied everyone, hasn't it?"

Ella nodded but was unconvinced, "If Lenin is as extreme as this article suggests, I don't think anything would satisfy him short of the execution of the Tsar. We must pray that Kerensky is strong enough to keep the Bolsheviks at bay or else we could still find ourselves in the middle of a civil war."

Mitrophan frowned and ran his hand over his beard, "Perhaps it would be better if Their Majesties were to leave the country while there is still time. Didn't I read that Kerensky has been in contact with the British Embassy, and King George of England has offered them safe haven?"

Ella sighed dreamily as memories of the peace of Osborne in the carefree days of childhood, floated through her mind. "Alix will be happy there. It will feel like going home."

"And you, Matushka, would you think of leaving, too?"

"My place is here," she smiled.

"But if Lenin *does* gain power and is intent on destroying all trace of your family..."

His words washed over her. Her thoughts were far away in Osborne - the breath of sea air and the sound of children's voices echoing around the Swiss Cottage: the tiny tables and chairs, the little wheelbarrows and garden tools; Grandmama's bathing machine. For one happy second it seemed that if she were to return there now, she would step back in time and, as though waking to the dawn of a glorious day, discover that all that had happened since those far off days, had been nothing more than a nightmare. Grandmama would still be trotting around in her little pony-chaise, shaking her head in sham-disapproval at the shrieks from noisy games; and there, she would see Victoria calling to her across the meadow, "Ella, hurry, hurry! Mama is waiting..."

Mitrophan's voice invaded the reverie, "For your own safety, it might be better if you were to leave Russia, too, at least until everything is finally settled. Perhaps returning to England would feel like going home to you, too?"

Home? A rude awakening shook away the dream. Mama and Grandmama were gone; childhood had vanished into the distant past as though it had never happened. England was not the England she had known. That idyll had gone forever, blasted away in this horrible deluge of bloodshed and destruction. *The home I am returning to is quite different.* Fear gripped her and she turned sharply and said again, "My place is here and there is work to be done."

The hospital wards were calm as ever; the same grateful smiles from the patients; the same comforting whispers from the nurses and nuns. As Ella moved from bed to bed and from room to room, there was comfort in the thought that, no matter what was happening in the world outside, this little haven of serenity continued unchanged. Governments might rise and fall; dynasties might topple and be overthrown, but inner peace was something that no war, no revolution could reach. *Peace,* she thought, smiling serenely at each of the patients whom God had entrusted to her care. *Though the world is tearing itself apart with war and cruelty, we must cling to the inner peace, the inner knowing that all is safe in God's hands.*

And so the days continued in their steady routine. Through the chanted *Te Deums* and whispered prayers, peace reigned within the walls of The House of Martha and Mary, even when the rattle of gunfire began to echo across the city. Soon, beyond the white-walled haven on Ordynka Street,

Moscow was being torn apart by a fierce and bloody civil war. Now, as Ella sat through the long night hours at the bedside of a dying patient, whispering softly, "For your loving Father awaits you in our heavenly homeland..." there came the growing sense that she, too, would soon be making that journey home.

"Matushka," Barbara whispered, "some gentlemen from the Provisional Government have arrived and insist on speaking with you."

She blessed the patient and calmly walked to the parlour where two men stood with serious expressions. Without wasting time on formalities, they delivered their message with urgency.

"We are here on behalf of Minister Kerensky. He wants you to know that your safety is of paramount importance to him and he has done all he can to ensure that the great work that you do here continues uninterrupted."

Ella smiled, "We appreciate all he has done for us. His soldiers have even brought food and blankets for the hospital. Please convey our thanks to Mr. Kerensky." She gesticulated towards the chairs but neither of her guests was inclined to sit down.

"You must be aware," one continued urgently, "that the level of unrest in the city has reached such proportions that, much as he wishes to help, Minister Kerensky no longer feels able to guarantee your protection. The Bolsheviks are gaining greater control every day and it's only a matter of time before the whole city falls into their hands. We're here to advise you to leave while there is still time. Perhaps you could find a place at another convent in the Crimea or..."

"Gentlemen," Ella said, "again, please thank Mr. Kerensky for his thoughtfulness but you must know that I have no intention of abandoning my work here."

The two men looked at each other, shaking their heads, "If you're not prepared to leave Moscow, at least take refuge in the Kremlin. It will be easier for us to protect you there."

"I made a vow before God to dedicate my life to caring for this Order as Abbess. I cannot run away from that now."

"Don't you see," the man pleaded, "your veil won't protect you? The Bolsheviks are brutes. They despise Orthodoxy almost as much as they despise the Tsarist regime. You have surely heard that Lenin himself hauled down the cross you erected on the site of your husband's assassination?"

She winced, taken aback for a moment. Seeing her disconcertion, the man seized his chance to press the point home, "Even now bullets are echoing on the walls of the monastery that houses his tomb. You must realize that by remaining here, you are sealing your own fate. Is that what the Grand Duke would have wanted for his wife?"

"The Grand Duke," she said quietly, "did his duty to the end of his life. I must do mine."

"You cannot be persuaded?"

"No, gentlemen. I cannot."

"I admire your commitment," said the one who, until now, had been silent, "but I dread to think what will become of you."

She led them towards the door, eager to change the subject from such ominous thoughts, "When does the former Emperor set sail for England?"

They stopped and looked at each other once more, and the quieter of the two was the first to speak.

"They cannot go to England."

"But Kerensky promised," she frowned. "It was he who was making the arrangements via the British Embassy. Why has he withdrawn that offer?"

"The Minister *didn't* withdraw the offer. The King of England did."

"What!"

"He sent a message via his government to say that, in view of the former Tsarina's German origins and the strong anti-German feeling in Britain, he feels her presence in England would endanger his own security."

"But that's ridiculous! The former Tsarina is only slightly more German than he is. Good heavens! Even his name is German: Saxe-Coburg Gotha!"

"Not any more. He has dropped all German names from the family. I believe they call themselves Windsor now."

Ella laughed ironically at the ridiculousness of it, "George and Nicky were so close," she thought aloud, "friends and cousins. And, for heaven's sake, Nicky abdicated so that the troops would be able to continue to support his allies. How can George abandon him like this?"

"According to our reports, the English king believes that the British public sees the former Emperor as a bloody tyrant who deserves to be left to his fate."

She turned away in disgust, "What is to happen to him and his family now?"

"They've been taken to Tobolsk in Siberia, out of harm's way, while we seek other options and perhaps some other country will offer them asylum."

A rising sense of anger and despair ran through her veins but, glancing at the icon on the wall, she quickly suppressed it.

"It is all God's will. Whatever the outcome, we must resign ourselves to that. And now, gentlemen, if you will excuse me, I have a hospital to run."

Nicky dropped the axe onto the snow and looked down at the pile of chopped logs with satisfaction. There was nothing like strenuous physical work, he thought, to keep out the icy Siberian chill and keep up one's spirits. If he could ignore the little bands of spectators who came to spy through the fence, and overlook the petty rules imposed by some of the guards, life was not too unpleasant in Tobolsk. The days were falling into a happy routine: Alexei's lessons continued and, between brisk walks through the gardens, the girls and Alix occupied their time in reading, learning and prayer. At last, free of the burden of state, there was time to share his love of history, giving lessons to Alexei, according to the timetables that Alix had devised. It was delightful, too, to hear Alix teaching religion as though she had been born to the task. For the first time since childhood, there were even opportunities to play - the long evenings spent creating short dramas and puppet shows.

He gathered the logs into a pile and strode with long steps through the snow. Were it not for the humiliation of enforced captivity and uncertainty about the future, this was exactly the kind of life that he had always dreamed of. No longer responsible for the country, alone with his family he couldn't deny that he was happy. And when this icy winter had passed, there would surely be a return to the old world order. Perhaps George would change his mind - surely he felt some bond of friendship and wouldn't abandon them in their hour of need? Or perhaps they would be allowed to go on to Livadia and live out their days in peace.

The bracing air was invigorating as he strode back towards the house, determinedly ignoring a whispered summons from beyond the fence. Reports of rescue attempts were becoming more frequent but a niggling suspicion warned him that these were probably Bolshevik ploys to trick him into staging an escape that would lead to his death.

Kicking the snow from his boots, he stepped into the little sitting room where Alix sat staring with disgust at a newspaper. He didn't need to ask; he simply looked at her and she nodded as though the news had been half expected.

"The Bolsheviks have signed a treaty with the Germans to end the war."

He took the paper from her and his disgust grew to revulsion as he read the shameful and humiliating terms.

"And they call me a traitor!" he gasped.

Now, everything for which he had abdicated had come to nothing. Civil war mutilated the country as the Bolshevik 'reds' battled for control with the more moderate Menshevik 'whites'; the country had accepted a shameful peace and deserted her allies, and Nicky's closest ally, George, had deserted him.

"Read on," Alix said, pointing to a paragraph, "see, here."

"*It is rumoured that that the German Kaiser Wilhelm II has included a clause in the treaty, guaranteeing the safety of Nicholas Alexandrovich*

Romanov and his family. The Kaiser, it is said, has offered them asylum in Germany.'"

He looked at Alix, "Would Willy stoop so low as to bargain with revolutionaries?"

"Didn't Lenin's train pass through Germany unimpeded? After what they've done to you, I'd rather die here than be saved by the Germans."

"If only George had..."

"They've all betrayed us, Nicky," she said without a hint of self-pity. "You, my love, are the only one among them who has behaved honourably, and this is how they treat you."

He rested his head on her shoulder and she ran her hands through his hair. "Close your eyes," she said softly, "and just for a moment let's forget all of this. Remember Coburg, all those years ago? It was this time of year, spring just beginning, a gentle rain falling..."

"And you made me so happy; happier than I had ever been in my life."

"That is one thing we still have," she soothed, "one thing that they cannot destroy. Even in all this madness, our love prevails and it always will." She kissed him and pressed her lips to his ear, "God bless you, my love. God bless the Tsar."

The moment passed too soon. The door burst open and, as Nicky pulled away from Alix, a tall, dark stranger, appeared in the entrance.

"Your Majesty," he said making a slight bow, "I am Commissar Yakovlev, acting under orders from the Central Committee of Soviets."

Nicky glanced at Alix, confused and slightly alarmed by the man's respect. It seemed like forever since anyone had addressed him as Majesty, and for a moment he suspected that this was yet another plot to have him play into the hands of traitors.

Yakovlev glanced pointedly towards the samovar steaming on the table, and Alix, taking the hint, offered him tea, which he accepted. As he reached to take the cup from her, Nicky observed the smoothness of his hands and the grace of his manners. Whoever this man was, he appeared to be of a higher station than his ordinary sailor's uniform suggested.

"I have instructions to take you from here," he said, sipping the tea, "and must ask you to be ready to leave first thing tomorrow morning."

Nicky looked from him to Alix and back again, "Taken where?"

"I am not at liberty to disclose that at this time but I can assure you that your life is not in danger."

Alix stood up and, with a calmness bordering on nonchalance, said, "I'm afraid that's impossible. Our son is suffering from a haemorrhage and can't possibly travel at such short notice."

Yakovlev, without flinching, nodded, "So I've been told and therefore have telegraphed to Moscow. It has been agreed that it isn't necessary for you all to come, only His Majesty."

A thousand motives and possibilities raced through Nicky's mind. Did they intend to compel him to add his signature to this shameful treaty, withdrawing Russia from the war? Or was it a show trial, they had planned? Even now, perhaps, his executioners were being readied to carry out the death sentence.

He straightened up and, with determined dignity, stated, "I refuse to leave."

To his further amazement, Yakovlev's face softened. "Please," he said, "I urge you to comply. If you don't, they will send other representatives to take you by force and, believe me, they are far harsher men than I am." He bowed to both Nicky and Alix and, as he turned to the door, repeated, "Please be ready to leave first thing in the morning."

The moment the door had closed behind him, the mask of serenity fell from Alix's face, "Alexei can't be moved."

"No, of course not." Nicky took her in his arms, "Don't worry. You stay here with the children. They are probably taking me to Moscow to endorse this shameful treaty and then they'll bring me back."

She shook her head vehemently, "Nicky, you cannot add your name to that. The disgrace would be too great."

"I won't," he said, resting his finger on her lips. "I'll refuse. I promise you."

"And then they will..." she couldn't bring herself to say it. "I'll come with you. We must call the girls and decide what to do for the best."

"There's no need. They will probably bring me straight back here and..." There was no point in continuing the pretence. She knew him too well.

"Nicky," she whispered, "whatever happens, we must stay together. Come on, we must summon the household and tell the children what's happening."

She led him upstairs to where the girls were sitting around Alexei's bed, keeping him amused as he lay, pale and weak, against the pillows. Nicky looked at his beautiful face, and a great weight hung on his heart. What plans he had made, what fine intentions he had had! Alexei would never be as unprepared as he himself had been to take the throne. From his earliest years, Alexei would be trained to rule, to lead and to serve; and one day he would be remembered as the greatest of Romanov tsars. Nicky sighed inwardly to think it had all come to this. Where was that legacy now? Tsardom had been swept away and with it fell the honour of Russia.

Alix was speaking but, too preoccupied with the imminent move and thoughts of what would become of his family when he was gone, Nicky was barely aware of what was being said. Only when she tapped him gently and asked for his approval, did he start from his thoughts.

"Olga, Tatiana and Anastasia will stay with Alexei until our return. Maria and the others will come with us."

His eyes drifted over the members of the household: the maid, Anna Demidova; his personal physician, Dr. Botkin; the former Marshal of the Court, Prince Dolgoruky; the valet, Chemodurov: and the kitchen boy Sednev. What loyalty shone in their eyes, what true nobility!

"At such times," he said, "we discover our truest friends. I am so grateful to all of you." His eyes moved to his son, patiently bearing his pain. Not one word of condemnation had issued from those lips; not one glance of resentment for what he had done in removing his hereditary right to the throne.

"I am touched to the core," he said, kissing the top of Alexei's head. "No matter what happens and no matter how they treat us, I look at you and know that I am the most blessed of men."

Every mile of the three-day journey had been torture to Alix. Anxious about Alexei, ignorant of her destination, her bones ached, her head throbbed and her heart pounded as the cart hurtled over flooded and icy tracks. Then, bundled onto the train that was taking them further and further from her children, it felt as though this journey would end in oblivion.

"Where are we going?" she had asked several times but only now, after so long a journey, did Yakovlev deign to speak.

"Moscow."

Nicky frowned, "We are heading in the wrong direction. When we left Tiumen, we should have headed..."

Yakovlev cleared his throat, "The members of the Ural soviets despise you. For your own safety, we are avoiding that route and..."

Before he could finish, the wheels screeched, hurling him off balance as the train came to a sudden halt. Alix's eyes shot to the window and caught sight of the sign on a station - Kulomzino. Loud male voices echoed from every direction and armed men sped frantically across the platform. As Yakovlev hurried from the carriage, Alix pressed her face to the window, "What's happening?"

Nicky silently reached for her hand.

Soldiers strutted to and fro, pointing ferociously towards the window, and it seemed that Yakovlev had become embroiled in some heated discussion with them.

"Bolsheviks," Nicky said. "They have blocked the track."

Yakovlev vanished from their view and was gone for what seemed an eternity. During his absence, the cries from the platform grew louder and the hostility on the faces peering into the carriage caused Alix to take Marie's hand in her own, gripping it tightly as she uttered unconvincing reassurances.

At last, the door opened and it came as relief to see the now familiar face of Yakovlev.

"There has been a change of plan," he announced resignedly. "My orders are to take you to Ekaterinburg."

Nicky's face fell and, though he tried to conceal his anxiety, Alix saw by the brief flicker of his eyelid that the news had come as deep blow. She held his hand more tightly. Soon the train was moving again and, within a short time, as it drew into Ekaterinburg, it was patently clear that Nicky's anxiety was justified.

The hostility of the locals was apparent from the moment the prisoners set foot in the town. Angry crowds jeered, mocked and bayed for their blood as they were led from the station. It might have come as a relief to reach the security of their destination but it didn't take long to discover that the worst wasn't over.

The house in which they were placed had been recently requisitioned from a merchant named Ipatiev, and ominously renamed 'The House of Special Purpose.' Unlike the guards in Tobolsk, the Red Guards in Ekaterinburg were deliberately going out of their way to insult and debase them. Laughing as they struggled up the stairs with their bags, the soldiers passed lewd comments and, following Maria to the bathroom, refused to allow her to close the door. Alix held her head high, determinedly paying no attention to the graffiti - crude verses about Nicky and pictures of herself and Rasputin in obscene poses - scrawled on the walls for everyone to see.

"Whatever these cowards do, she whispered, "how ever they attempt to debase us, we still have charge of our own dignity and they cannot deprive us of that."

She reached for Nicky's hand - there was still the consolation of his company and, as she prayed, she held steadfastly to the dream of one day returning to Livadia or finding refuge in England.

Chapter 52

At the entrance to the Church of the Intercession of the Virgin on Ordynka Street, stood a tall blonde-haired man who bowed as Ella approached.

"I am the Abbess," she said, "I was told you wish to see me."

His eyes darted warily around as though searching out eavesdroppers, before saying in a sombre whisper, "I have come from the Swedish Embassy with a message for you from…" again he glanced around, "from His Imperial Majesty, Kaiser Wilhelm of Germany. He is aware of the danger you are in, and wishes to offer you safe haven."

"Willy?" Ella whispered. The hateful image of the pompous Kaiser, which had been paraded and desecrated so often these past four years, vanished into the recollection of the small boy issuing orders in childish games.

"If you will accompany me now to our Embassy, we can arrange for you to be safely smuggled to Sweden where your cousin, the Crown Princess, will be happy to receive you until we can arrange for you to be taken to Germany."

"I truly appreciate your offer," she said sincerely, "but I am Abbess here and cannot leave my sisters."

The Swede blinked, "Your Highness, you *do* understand how perilous this situation has become now that the Bolsheviks have taken control of the city?"

Ella smiled, "Even though I have been forbidden to leave the confines of my convent, I manage to keep abreast of what is happening outside."

"You must realize that Trotsky and Lenin have no intention of allowing any Romanov to remain alive on Russian soil. The former Tsar and Tsarina are already in captivity in Ekaterinburg and, from our intelligence, we have discovered that all of their children have now been reunited with them there. Don't you see that it is only because of your popularity among the Muscovites that Lenin hasn't already arrested you?"

She inhaled sharply, "I am aware of what a thorn I am in Lenin's side. Several times he has sent messages asking me if I would like to join my sister but, since I have committed myself for life to the service of my Order, I have declined his offers and will remain here until..."

"Until what?" the Swede interrupted. "Until he feels he is in a strong enough position to arrest you?"

"If that is God's will."

The man shook his head, "What am I to tell the Embassy? And what message are we to take to the German Kaiser?"

She paused for a moment. So much hatred, so much anger, so much blame had been directed at Willy, and she couldn't deny that she had shared that anger and outrage and yet, in her heart of hearts, lay the memory of the lovelorn expression in his eyes as they followed her around the room, so, so long ago.

"Please, thank him for me and tell him I am touched by his kindness."

She returned to the church and, as clouds of incense wafted up to the ornate ceiling, she devoutly participated in the long Holy Week services. The knowledge that the Imperial Family had been removed from Tobolsk and that Alexei and his sisters had finally been reunited with them in Ekaterinburg, convinced her that the final rounding up of the Romanovs had begun. Contemplating the crucifixion of Christ, she sensed her own martyrdom was not far away. She had done all she could to establish the convent; now it seemed that her work on earth was almost complete.

In the midst of the Easter services, the long-awaited moment finally arrived. A group of soldiers jumped out of an armoured car at the convent gates and, rifles in hand, strode to the chapel. Ella met them at the entrance.

"Your safety," they said curtly, "can no longer be guaranteed and therefore, by order of the soviet, you are to be taken to Perm. There is work for you to do there."

She looked around the beautiful buildings and the desperate faces of her sisters, fearing the worst.

"Please," she said, "will you grant me two hours so that I might say goodbye to my patients and give my sisters instructions as to how to continue here?"

"You have thirty minutes, no more."

"Very well," she said and, as the nuns gathered weeping around her, she restrained her tears. She had been expecting this day for many weeks and now she must meet her fate with equanimity.

"It is time for us to bear the cross," she said to herself as much as to them. "Let us try to be worthy of it."

A soldier shuffled as though disconcerted by her composure.

"Seeing that you have not caused us any trouble," he sniffed, "you can choose two others to go with you. Don't worry, we'll make your journey as comfortable as we can and, when we reach

Siberia, you'll be given work with the Red Cross nurses."

The sisters crowded before her, one after another volunteering and pleading to be allowed to accompany her. How could she choose? And how could she know? Would those she chose face death as surely as she would?

"Barbara," she said eventually, "you have been with me from the start, and…" Face after face gazed at her, "Catherine," she said.

The three hastily packed their few belongings and, as the soldiers led them towards the gates, she glanced back, "May this foundation thrive, when I am gone," she prayed.

Unconvincing as were the soldiers' reassurances that their lives were not in danger, it came as a relief that they gave them a private compartment on the train. At least in the silence, as the train chugged from the station, she could concentrate on writing her final instructions to The House of Martha and Mary, urging the nuns to remain faithful to their promises and to graciously accept God's will, never doubting his goodness. As the minarets of Moscow disappeared onto the horizon, her heart ached at the memory of those beloved faces. Her fears for their future and her own, increased with every mile. She looked out at the melting snow. Spring was coming; Easter, Resurrection and the triumph of good over evil. She tried to pray but could only murmur, 'O Lord, I believe, help thou my unbelief.'

The train eventually drew into a station where the soldiers led them to a convent.

"You are free to go into the town," an officer told them, "but if you attempt to leave Ekaterinburg, you will be arrested."

Ekaterinburg... Ella smiled. Perhaps now, after all that had happened, there would be an opportunity to make peace with Alix.

When the soldiers had gone, nuns with kindly faces and welcoming smiles, led them to a refectory and served them food.

The Abbess sat down beside Ella, "Don't be anxious. You're not the only member of your family, here. There are others, too. They must have brought you here for your safety."

"The Tsar is here with his family?"

"Yes," she smiled, "they're staying in the Ipatiev House."

"Will I be able to see them?"

"I doubt it. They're kept under strict guard and not allowed out but, from time to time, the soldiers allow us to take food for them. If you wish, we could deliver a letter or a message."

"Yes, yes," she said eagerly, "I would like that very much."

The aged Abbess patted her hand, "We will see what we can do and, in the meantime, you might be able to meet with the rest of your family. Several of them are under house arrest at a hotel not far from here. I'm sure you'd be allowed to visit."

"Will you show me the way?"

"Wouldn't you like to rest first after such a long journey?"

"No," she said, feeling suddenly more alive, "I would love to know who is here."

As soon as the meal was over, the Abbess summoned a young nun to lead Ella to the hotel, stopping briefly en route to buy chocolate and coffee to send to Alix. No sooner had she stepped into the lobby, than a familiar face appeared.

"Ioann!" she called and he hurried towards her and embraced her warmly. She might have mistaken him for his father - so similar were his mannerisms and tone of voice to Kostia's.

"You too?" he said. "Quite a family party! Come, we'll take tea in my room."

"Are there many more of us?"

"Oh yes. My wife and my brothers, Igor and Konstantin."

"Not your mother?"

"No. She has managed to leave the country. Sooner or later we will find her, no doubt." He strode quickly along the corridors, "Sandro's brother, Serge, is here too with one his attendants, a chap called Remez, and then there's Pavel's son."

"Dmitri!"

Ioann stopped, "No," he said quietly, "Vladimir, his son by his second marriage. He's a wonderful young man - a poet like my father."

Ella smiled sadly. The irony of the situation was so apparent. She had never accepted the children of Pavel's second marriage as part of the family, yet now his son was a prisoner for being a Romanov.

The atmosphere in the hotel room was more like a social gathering than the confinement of prisoners in fear of their lives. The smiles and embraces that greeted Ella were heart-warming and for a moment she quite forgot the shadow looming large over their heads. Soon they were sitting, taking tea and sharing what news they had gleaned of other family members.

Minnie, Ella was told, was with her daughter, Olga, in Livadia, only a few miles south of Xenia and Sandro in Ai-Tudor - more or less out of harm's way.

"As far as we can make out," said Sandro's brother, Serge, "the Bolsheviks have no hold in that area." He smiled to himself, "Ironic, really, that Felix's banishment to the Crimea has worked out perfectly for him. He and Irina are living there as though nothing has happened. Didn't he always say he was born under a lucky star?"

"What about Kyril?" Ioann said. "I heard he flew a red flag over the palace and all but took up with the revolutionaries."

Igor shook his head, "Much good did it do him! He and Ducky fled to Finland a few months ago."

"Did his mother go with him?" Serge asked.

"No. She went with her younger sons to the Caucasus and, the last we heard, they are quite comfortable there."

As they chattered and shared news, a shy young man sat silently, with a pensive expression. Several times Ella glanced at him. There was something of his father in his features - the gentleness that had once so endeared Pavel to her. A sense of guilt clouded her thoughts and she smiled sadly. Would it have made any difference, she wondered, if the grand dukes had adhered to their oath of allegiance and given the Nicky the support he deserved? But what did it matter now that everything was over? And this shy young man, who was never quite part of the family, was hardly to blame for what his father had done.

She moved closer to him, "Vladimir, isn't it?"

"Yes," he said, his youthful eyes shining with poetic light.

"I am...I suppose I am your aunt, Ella."

"I have heard a lot about you," he said. "My father spoke of you often."

"Did he?" *Did he speak of how I judged him; how I refused him access to his children; how I hurried Marie into a disastrous marriage...*

"He told me of all your work in Moscow and he often spoke of the happy times you shared in Ilinskoe."

She smiled with relief, "Your father was very close to my husband."

"Yes," he said timidly, "he was devastated by what happened to him." His eyes moved around the room from one face to another. "Perhaps a similar fate awaits all of us now."

She took his hand, "Whatever happens, we are all in this together and we will strengthen and support one another."

He smiled sincerely, "Thank you. I appreciate that."

They looked at one another and in that moment the guilt of the past was erased.

"Have you heard from your father?" Ella asked. "Did he manage to get away?"

"He hasn't been well so he stayed in Petersburg with Marie. The last I heard, he was under house arrest." His face was sad then suddenly brightened by a smile, "You know Marie remarried?"

"Yes, I heard."

"She's expecting a baby. Beautiful, isn't it, how life goes on even in the middle of all this chaos? Poppies still bloom and birds still sing over battlefields. Even in the middle of so much destruction, new life blossoms and thrives. "

She nodded, "And what of Dmitri, have you heard from him?"

"By refusing to repeal his sentence, the Tsar might have saved his life. He was well away from

Russia and the last my father heard of him, he was seeking a commission in the British army."

"Let's hope he succeeds."

Ioann leaned towards them, "What do you think will happen to us now? Will they send us all into exile?"

"Where would we go?" asked Konstantin.

"Anywhere we like!"

"Britain wouldn't take us. You heard the king refused to grant asylum to Their Majesties, and I very much doubt we'd be welcome in Germany."

Igor said, "The longer we stay here the better. The Whites are gaining more supporters and sooner or later there will be a counter-revolution and a return to Tsardom."

"You really believe that?" Serge said gloomily.

"I do."

"You're fooling yourself. Even if a counter-revolution were successful, who would be Tsar? They'd never hand it back to Nicky, and Alexei isn't well enough to rule."

"Misha?" Igor said.

"Where *is* Misha?" asked Ioann.

"I heard they took him to Perm but the news isn't clear."

"Don't you see," said Serge, "that any talk of a return to Tsardom will only inflame these bloody Bolsheviks. They'd kill us all in one stroke rather than allow us to become magnets for counter-revolutionaries. That's why they've brought us all together. It's easier for them to kill us in one place than have us here, there and everywhere."

"You're a pessimist, Serge," Konstantin said. "I, for one, choose to believe that all this is temporary and any day now we'll wake up and find this was nothing but a nightmare."

The cheeriness in his voice might have raised their spirits but, as Ella looked around the room, she felt that behind the smiles, their fears were as deep as her own. There could be no way back to the old life. There would be no way back to earthly life at all. All that was left now was to effect a reconciliation with Alix, and prepare herself for eternity.

Chapter 53

No sooner had life settled into a comfortable routine in Ekaterinburg than the inevitable order came from the Bolshevik guards. Once again, with only minutes to prepare, the cousins and companions were rounded up and packed onto a train heading north. Where they were to be taken nobody knew, and nobody dared to ask what would happen when they arrived. As the train left the station, Ella clutched the letter that had been handed to her that morning: a lovely note from the Ipatiev House. Her niece, Maria, assured her that Mama had enjoyed the coffee and chocolate and they all wished her well.

Perhaps, she thought, *it was for this that God allowed us this time in Ekaterinburg.* The reconciliation with Alix and Nicky was complete.

The journey through the summer-blessed Siberian countryside was not unpleasant and it wasn't long before familiar scenes came into view.

"Alapaevsk," Ella said, recognising the church, "I was here with my sister, Victoria, the day we heard of the outbreak of war." And she remembered, too, the shock she had felt in the knowledge that that was the beginning of the end. Now, as the train drew into the station, came the sense that *this* was the start of a new beginning.

The soldiers bundled them from the train into carts that took them to an old school house, long fallen into disuse.

"It's filthy," Serge Mikhailovich moaned, stamping from room to room, "and how are we all supposed to fit in here?"

Ella smiled; it was a far cry from the spacious palaces of the grand dukes: only four large and two smaller rooms connected by a series of corridors.

"Clean it yourselves," growled the guard, "and decide who's going to sleep where."

Ella looked at her two companions, "If no one objects, we will share a room. We would like to continue to observe our rule, as far as possible, and, of course, we'll help clean the rest of the house. We can make ourselves quite comfortable here."

Serge stared at her in astonishment.

"There's a garden," she said. "Perhaps they'll allow us to tidy it and plant vegetable and flowers. My father taught me these things when I was child and have been longing for a chance to put them into practice."

Ioann shrugged, "What can't be cured must be endured. We might as well make the best of it."

It was refreshing to engage in physical work, scrubbing the floors, cleaning the grimy windows, weeding and planting and, between the hours of manual labour and the strict regime of prayer, Ella sketched the gardens and the views from the window. Despite the heat, the cramped conditions and the lack of news from the outside world, there was something cathartic in their isolation; the perfect place to prepare for whatever the future might hold. A camaraderie developed between some of the guards and their prisoners and, though one or two seemed set on asserting their authority by imposing irritating and trivial regulations, most allowed the cousins to speak freely and undisturbed.

"Ella," Ioann whispered as they tended the vegetable plots, "look here!"

He glanced around to ensure no guards were within earshot, and scrambled through the soil around the perimeter fence. He pulled out a package, placed it inside his shirt and nodded towards the back of the building. Ella followed him.

"It's addressed to you," he said.

She unwrapped it to find a note pinned to a piece of fine linen, embroidered with a cross.

"What does it say?" Ioann said.

"They remember me from my pilgrimages. They've sent bread and salt from *'the loyal servants of the Tsar and the Motherland, the peasants of the region.'*"

Ioann smiled, "The simple Russian people, whom you always loved, couldn't fail to love you in return."

Suddenly, shouting and banging echoed from inside the building; clattering and angry voices. Ella and Ioann hurried back indoors to find the guards ransacking their rooms, turning out their pockets and throwing their belongings across the floor.

"What are you looking for?" Ella said.

"We have reason to believe that the enemies of the state are planning to rescue you. Any letters you've received must be handed over at once."

"We've heard no such thing," Serge said angrily, trying to gather his belongings.

The guard turned to Barbara and Catherine, "By order of Citizen Beloborodov, leader of the Ekaterinburg soviet, you're to leave."

"What?" Barbara gasped.

"The soviet has no quarrel with you. You are innocent bystanders and there is no reason for you to stay. A truck will be here within an hour. Collect your things."

Catherine turned with such sorrow in her eyes that a lump formed in Ella's throat and she could barely speak.

"Please," Catherine pleaded, "let us stay here. Whatever you plan for the Abbess we…"

"Get your things ready."

"You know what this means?" Serge said. "They're going to kill us."

Ioann stepped towards the guard, "When the sisters go, will you take my wife with them?"

"No!" Helena said, "I must stay with you. We have…"

"The children need you," he said. "Return to Pavlovsk. They won't harm you."

The guard looked at her doubtfully.

"She's a Serb, not Russian. You have no jurisdiction over her."

"Very well," he said churlishly, "but she'd better be quick about it. The truck will be here soon."

Tears stung Ella's eyes. This parting seemed even more difficult than leaving the convent in Moscow. Now she would be alone in the world, wrenched from her true family - the family she had so lovingly born and nurtured. Tears flowed down her cheeks and she sobbed uncontrollably as Barbara and Catherine threw their arms around her murmuring, "We'll go to the soviet and ask them to allow us to come back. We'll find a way."

Ella shook her head, "No. Go back to Moscow. Keep up the work of the foundation. God knows, the people need it more now than ever."

She embraced them tenderly and, as the soldiers dragged them towards the waiting truck, Barbara called, "I *will* come back to you, Matushka. I won't let you face this alone."

A great cloud of gloom descended over the house as Helena, weeping and fearing she would never see her husband again, climbed into the truck.

As it disappeared through a cloud of smoke, Ella and her cousins returned to the house feebly attempting to comfort one another and convinced they were waiting for death.

In a tatty office in Ekaterinburg, an oafish man sat with his feet on a desk, kicking at his name plate - Beloborodov - and pretending to peruse a paper in a deliberate move to keep the petitioners waiting.

Now and again came a guffaw from his attendants, who whispered behind their hands and made lewd remarks, as they looked the two nuns up and down.

Beloborodov eventually swung his feet from the desk, "Well, what is it?"

"We would like your permission to return to the Napolnaya School, to be with our Abbess."

"Would you, now?"

"We've committed no crime, have no political axe to grind and therefore can see no reason why our request should be refused."

Beloborodov laughed coarsely and looked at his soldiers, "They can see no reason! That's because they have lost their reason." He leaned over the desk with a smirk, "I could understand it if you were young, but look at you! I'd have thought you were old enough to have outgrown this infantile devotion to a woman who is an enemy of the state."

"The Abbess has spent her life serving and caring for the Russian people. We have vowed to follow her and we ask only to be allowed to do that."

"Follow her to torture and death?"

"If necessary."

"But it isn't necessary. You're free. Go on, go back to your families!"

"Our Abbess is our family."

Beloborodov shook his head, "I'll tell you what. If you're so set on this madness, I'll compromise. One of you can go back. The older one."

Barbara almost fell to her knees in gratitude but, before she could reply, he added, "First, though, I want your signature to say that I had no part in this. You voluntarily agreed to endure whatever tortures might be inflicted on you."

"Yes," Barbara said, "I'll sign it not only in ink but, if necessary, in my own blood!"

Alix sighed. In the sweltering heat of July, life in the Ipatiev house was becoming more intolerable. The rooms were stifling but the guards refused to allow her to open or even sit near the whitewashed windows for fear she should send signals to the Mensheviks who, they said, were rapidly advancing towards Ekaterinburg. The commandant, Alexander Avdeev, was usually so drunk that he had little control over the unruly soldiers and they frequently helped themselves to the family's belongings. Poor Alexei, confined to bed after yet another fall, wrote daily in his diary of his boredom, while she and Nicky dutifully continued his lessons and recorded the temperature and the minor irritations of life in captivity.

Everything had sunk into a dull and stagnant routine when suddenly a stranger arrived and introduced himself as Jacob Yurovsky, a member of the Bolshevik secret police.

"We have been informed," he said, "that there has been a series of thefts of your belongings. Consequently, I am here to replace Avdeev and can assure you that from now on there will be no more pilfering. I would like you to draw up an inventory of all your possessions. Once that is done, we will seal them into a casket, which will be left in your possession, and the locks will be inspected daily to make sure nothing is missing."

Alix eyed him cautiously. Though he was clearly more diligent and better organized than the incompetent Avdeev, there was something disturbing in his manner. *Why,* she wondered, *would they take such an interest in our belongings, unless they intend to requisition them?* And now it seemed that the precautions she had already taken had been a necessity.

Before leaving Tobolsk, she had instructed her daughters to stitch their 'medicines' - her code word for precious jewels - into their corsets and undergarments. She herself wore a girdle of priceless diamonds and pearls beneath her dress so that when they were eventually released to Livadia or England they would have sufficient funds to support themselves.

Though Yurovsky was polite and efficient, there was something cold and distant in his manner that made her uneasy and suspicious of his motives.

"He's obsessed with security," Nicky said when they were alone. "He's terrified of a rescue attempt."

"Perhaps that's a good sign," Alix smiled. "Any day now someone will come and all this will be over."

But the days dragged on and, as Yurovsky ordered grilles to be fastened to the outside of the windows, the security measures became increasingly stringent. Even the old guards were replaced by more reliable men from the newly formed 'Commission for Struggle against Counter-Revolution or Sabotage' - the Cheka.

"I don't trust this Yurovsky at all," Nicky said. "There's something about him. Something in the way he looks at us. I don't know what it is but I just can't trust him."

Alix couldn't help but agree, even as she conceded, "One thing I will say for him, he is good with Alexei. They seem to have struck up something a friendship."

They walked into the Tsarevich's room, to find Yurovsky sitting on Alexei's bed, chatting in a friendly manner.

He looked up when they entered, "This young man was telling me that he feels much better now. It was nasty knock he took the other day so you'll be happy to see him up and about again."

"He's not up to walking yet," Alix said protectively, "and he has a cold."

"Oh Mama," Alexei smiled, "it's not so bad. Tomorrow I'm sure I'll be completely better."

Yurovsky patted him on the shoulder, "Good man!" He stood up and turned to leave, "By the way, your kitchen boy, Sednev, has gone."

"Gone?" said Nicky, "Where?"

"His uncle was sick and he wanted to go to him. There's nothing to worry about."

With a courteous nod he walked from the room.

"Nothing to worry about?" Alix said. "I wasn't worried until he said that. I don't trust that man."

"He's alright," Alexei smiled. "Much better than Avdeev and at least he keeps the guards in order."

"We must be grateful for small mercies," Nicky nodded.

Alexei lay back on his pillows with a contented smile, "The most wonderful thing about being ill, is when you begin to feel better."

Alix leaned over and kissed the top of his head, "And the most wonderful thing about being in captivity, is that when we are released we will be so grateful for our freedom."

"*Will* we be released?" Alexei said.

"Of course we will," Nicky said firmly and, leaning closer, whispered, "They wouldn't be going to all this trouble about security unless someone is planning to free us. Any day now the White Army will come into the town."

"And then what?"

"Who knows? Maybe Cousin George will relent and send a ship for us. Or there's always Livadia. So," he took Alexei in his arms, "you had better get a good night's sleep so you're ready for a journey."

Alexei smiled and Alix blessed him and kissed him goodnight. She turned out the light, took Nicky's hand and led him to their bedroom.

"A game of cards before we go to sleep?" he said.

He dealt for bezique and, as they played, she looked into his eyes and smiled. His face, for so long lined with care, looked almost young again this evening and, in spite of all the betrayals, the horror, the disappointment and the humiliation, none of the gentle kindness had gone from those beautiful eyes.

"Nicky," she said, "I love you so."

"And I, you."

"Nothing will ever separate us. No betrayal, no revolution, not even death. We are together forever."

They gazed into each other's eyes and, in the wordless love that flowed between them, she felt so immersed in a radiant and divine light that the earth seemed no longer real. There was nothing in the universe only the pure love that bound them together as one.

"Let's leave the game now. Let's just climb into bed and float away together to somewhere beautiful."

Somewhere between wakefulness and dreams, she lay in his arms, listening to the steady ebb and flow of his breath. The muffled banging that sounded through the floorboards, and the growling of engines outside, barely disturbed the deep sense of peace that encompassed her limbs and her heart.

Jacob Yurovsky climbed the stairs from the basement and paused to listen for any sign of movement in the rooms above. Silence. The family were sleeping soundly and everything would go to plan. In an hour or two, it would all be over and he would claim the greatest accolade as the man who oversaw the ultimate downfall of a tyrant. For a split second he hesitated. It would have been so much easier had he simply arrived that evening without having made the acquaintance of these people. Then the tyrant would have been an inhuman figure - a monster to be destroyed. But these days spent in the company of Nicholas Romanov had revealed another side to the man. He was nothing like the arrogant autocrat of popular belief. Far from 'bloody Nicholas the butcher', he appeared to be a man who loved not only his family but also his country and its people. There was even a gentleness about the despised Tsarina, not to mention the naïve simplicity of those innocent girls.

And then there was the boy. Thirteen years old, an invalid, what threat could he possibly pose to the new regime?

"No," Yurovsky deliberately clicked his heels. Great causes demanded great courage and sacrifices. There was no room now for sentimentality. With the Whites rapidly advancing on Ekaterinburg and the sound of their guns echoing through the town, he had to act quickly before the prize possession was whisked from his grasp. Besides, he was following orders. He was not solely responsible for the outcome. Moscow had sanctioned this execution and, since he had planned it with meticulous precision and the utmost secrecy, he was not going to back out now.

The outside world would know nothing of this. Russia needed allies and a formal recognition of her new government. Regicide without trial would damage the Bolsheviks' reputation, and the former Tsar might still be used as a bargaining tool as long as foreign powers believed he was still alive. For that reason, no one could remain alive - not the maid, not the doctor, not the valet - none of them.

Yurovsky ran through his plans, reassuring himself that everything had been arranged with precision. His firing squad had been carefully selected and the site for execution was ideal. The cellar of the house was invisible from the street outside, and its plaster walls would prevent the ricochet of bullets.

At the sound of a lorry drawing up outside, he glanced at his watch - almost midnight - exactly as he had ordered. Its chugging engine would muffle the sound of gunshot, and the bodies would be piled onto it and driven away under cover of darkness for burial in a remote place in the Koptiaka woods. He trusted that the separate squad, under the command of the Commissar Pyotr Ermakov, would be waiting in the woods to prevent the intrusion of any unwelcome witnesses, "And," he murmured, "by dawn it will all be accomplished."

He pushed open the door to the room where the firing squad were waiting, bottles of vodka in their hands, rifles over their shoulders.

"You know exactly what you're to do," he whispered. "Each of you has his own target. Aim for the head or the heart to achieve maximum effect in the minimum time."

They nodded and glugged at their vodka until bravado overcame their squeamishness. He couldn't deny them the strengthening power of the drink; after all, the prospect of murdering four beautiful girls and a sickly boy in cold-blood, would be daunting for even the most heartless of men. He left them in the cellar and climbed the stairs to Doctor Botkin's room. The man woke at once.

"Wake all the others," Yurovsky said. "There's shooting in the town and you'll be safer in the cellar. Hurry!"

Within half an hour, the family was calmly descending the staircase to the death chamber: Nicholas carrying his son. The maid, Demidova, and some of the girls had brought pillows with them, and their little dog followed them down to the cellar.

"If we are to stay here all night," the former Tsarina said, looking around the empty room, "couldn't we at least have some chairs?"

"Of course." Yurovsky ordered two to be taken into the room. Nicholas placed his son one, and the boy's mother sat down beside him while the others crowded around them.

Perfect, Yurovsky thought, *they're in a perfect position.*

He stepped forwards, "In view of the counter-revolutionary plots and the attempts of your family to stage a rescue attempt, by order of the Central Soviet Commission, you are to be executed."

All the women in the room blessed themselves.

"What? What?" Nicholas said in shock.

"Now!" Yurovsky called and the half-drunken firing squad burst into the room and opened fire. Bullets bounced off the plaster walls, filling the cellar with smoke. The Tsar, his wife and their doctor fell at once with bullets through their heads but, as the smoke cleared, it was clear that the girls would prove harder to kill. The maid Demidova was screaming and covering her face with the pillow, and ironically, Alexei, who had come close to death so many times, was also still alive and moaning on the floor.

Yurovsky's clinical preparations were going horribly awry. Perhaps it was because the soldiers' nerves were on edge or their heavy drinking marred their aim but suddenly there was nothing but savage butchery. Alexei was shot through the head but, when the bullets bounced off his sisters, the soldiers repeatedly stabbed at them with bayonets. Still they would not die! It was as though they were wearing armour beneath their dresses and, in a panic, the soldiers struck them with rifle butts before shooting them through their heads. The massacre seemed complete.

Shocked and dazed as the killers were, Yurovsky insisted on carrying out the rest of his plan. As the bodies were piled unceremoniously onto the lorry, a guard reported hearing a cry from one of the girls. She *still* wasn't dead.

The journey to the burial site was equally gruesome and disastrous. The lorry stuck in the mud, and carts had to be brought hastily to transport the corpses before the light of dawn. Ermakov's men were disappointed to discover that the family was already dead - they had hoped to claim that honour for themselves - and set about thieving from the bodies. Only when Yurovsky threatened execution for any man caught stealing, was some semblance of order restored and the grisly cargo reached the burial site - a place known as the Four Brothers.

In the darkness of the woods, Yurovsky gave orders for further indignities to be inflicted on the family, "Strip the bodies so there's nothing to identify them if they should be discovered."

As the soldiers obeyed, jewels trickled from the girls' underclothing - the armour that had prolonged their death. The soldiers fell on the jewels at once, and Yurovsky, exhausted and sickened, was obliged to threaten them with execution if they stole anything. Then he turned away, as some of the soldiers took out their frustration in other ways.

"Well," a crude voice laughed, "it's not every man who gets to fondle a naked Tsarina!"

The massacre was complete.

Chapter 54 - Alapaevsk

Dawn broke over Alapaevsk. Ella rose and, having woken Barbara, together they recited their prayers. Something was amiss. A strange kind of emptiness filled the air. Throughout the morning, the guards seemed more restless than usual; they whispered in corners and several times she thought she heard someone say, "Ekaterinburg", but by lunchtime a different detachment had arrived to replace them. These new Cheka men were very much on edge, hurrying the prisoners through their dinner and informing them that, since they would be moving soon, they must hand over all their remaining possessions and money. The rest of the day passed uneventfully and, in the evening, since there was no further mention of an imminent move, Ella and Barbara retired to their room. They said their prayers, undressed and fell asleep to the sound of carts drawing up outside.

Suddenly, in the middle of the night, two soldiers appeared in their room.

"Your lives are in danger. Get dressed quickly so we can take you to a safer place."

Still half-asleep and uncertain whether these soldiers were rescuers or gaolers, they meekly and silently obeyed. As soon as they were dressed, the soldiers led them out to one of two waiting carts, which immediately set off along the Sinyachikhenskaya road.

They had barely left when the echo of a gunshot startled them and, looking back, Ella saw Serge Mikhailovich being pushed onto the second cart with the other grand dukes. For over half an hour the cart wound its way out of the town, along country roads and through a remote wooded area littered with disused mines. There, as the sun was beginning to rise, they stopped.

"Get out!" a soldier commanded. Calmly Ella and Barbara obeyed.

"Walk!" he said and they did until they drew near to the edge of the mineshaft.

"Keep going!"

Ella glanced at him and, as she turned, the full force of a rifle butt in her face unbalanced her and she fell for what seemed like an eternity into the waterlogged shaft.

Floundering in the icy water, she caught sight of a ledge running the length of the wall above water level, and, in spite of a terrible pain in her head, sustained either by the rifle blow or the fall, she managed to scramble onto it. Soaking wet, her face and head throbbing, she barely had time to take in her surroundings when Barbara was forced in after her.

"Here," Ella called, "take my hand," and, after a struggle, succeeded in pulling her onto the ledge. One after another, Serge Mikhailovich, his companion, Remez, Konstantin's three sons and Vladimir Pavlovich, were bundled in after them.

"I don't believe it; they're alive!" came a voice from the surface. "Why haven't they drowned?"

Seconds later, the pit flashed with bright light and an ear splitting boom as a grenade exploded, hurling bodies to different levels of the shaft. Half blinded by the explosion, Ella blinked, trying to make out the shapes in the darkness. Someone was seriously injured, perhaps someone was dead but, as she edged her way along the ledge, she found Ioann lying beside her. He moaned for a moment then murmured the words of a hymn. *"Lord save your people...*" Ella sang, too, and their voices resounded on the black walls and rose up like incense to the surface.

A crackling above them and more flashes of light, then the pit was filled with the thick scent of wood smoke.

"No," someone called, "they'll burn us alive!"

Ioann and Ella sang their hymn once more and then, but for occasional groans from different levels of the shaft, there was silence.

She reached for Ioann's hand and, as the morning sun climbed higher into the sky, a thin beam of light illuminated his face. His head was bleeding profusely and he was coughing up blood. Regardless of her own pain, she pulled the veil from her head and, ripping it into strips bound his wounds. Then, clinging to the icon that Serge had given her twenty-seven years before, there was nothing to be done but endure the long, slow and agonising wait for death.

Whether minutes had passed or hours, days, even weeks, she did not know. There was silence now as she lay in the darkness soaking wet, cold and starving and yet all the pain had gone. Dawn was breaking, and the rippling shades of the sky above the opening of the mineshaft, spiralled into multi-coloured beams. Her body seemed no longer to belong to her. The whispered words issuing from her lips, *Father, forgive me...*seemed to be spoken by someone else. She was quite separate, enveloped in the beautiful, healing light of the morning sun.

Figures and images drifted on the light beams as though the fifty-three years of her life were being played in reverse: the faces of angry crowds on the streets melted into kindness, the anger in their eyes turning to love; the fall of a dynasty, Alix, Nicky, Alexei...Glorious jubilee processions through London; glittering ballrooms of St. Petersburg when she had stunned every man in the room; a rowing boat gliding over the calm waters of the Moskva River, and Serge whispering softly with love in his eyes. Back, back down the years: Darmstadt, Windsor...Osborne, one beautiful amber afternoon; she was a child, running through a meadow, blowing dandelion clocks as distant voices called to her, "Ella! Schnell, schnell! Mama is waiting..."

The beams of light blended and merged into one. Her eyes filled with tears of joy and, like a bird breaking free from a cage and soaring through the heavens in ecstasy, her soul seemed to rise from her body towards a radiant and beautiful face, *"Dear Mama..."*

Her heart's steady rhythm fell silent and she was free.

EPILOGUE

Distorted and contradictory stories flooded Europe in the immediate aftermath of the slaughter. Bolshevik propaganda stated that the Tsar had been killed but his family had been taken to a safe place, possibly Perm. There was still, as yet, no news of the Empress and her children but rumours were rife. Alix was in captivity with her daughters in Perm; they were ill; they were well; no one could be sure. For almost a month Victoria, Irène and Ernie remained optimistic until the first blow came before the end of August. Though their bodies had not been found, intelligence reports confirmed that Alix and her children had also been murdered.

King George V was the first to hear of the massacre and immediately ordered the newspapers to refrain from printing the story until Victoria had been informed. He wrote a letter, which Alix's close friend and cousin, Princess Marie Louise of Schleswig-Holstein, volunteered to take to her on the Isle of Wight. The letter that Victoria received from George V, could hardly have brought great consolation, considering his refusal to grant them safe haven. According to Marie Louise, Victoria's devastation was 'too overwhelming for mere words' and her immediate response was to work in the garden 'all day and every day for three weeks.'

But, while news of events in Ekaterinburg trickled in from various sources, Victoria heard nothing definite about Ella. Some reports gave her false hope: Ella was still in Alapaevsk; she had escaped to Czechoslovakia; she was safe and well. In spite of the occasional suggestion that she, too, might be dead, Victoria remained optimistic.

Even in Russia, the stories were inconsistent. The Bolsheviks invented an account of the Romanovs' escape, sometimes adding that they had been taken away in an aeroplane. Though many people disbelieved them, few had the courage to challenge the official line until the end of September when the Whites - temporarily - succeeded in taking Alapaevsk and Ekaterinburg.

Freed from the fear of Red retribution, the local people came forward to voice their suspicions. The White commanders, Semenov and Admiral Kolchak, received statements from several witnesses who had seen the carts, heard explosions in the woods and even the voices of the prisoners in the mine. Disgusted that the peasants lacked the courage even to throw food down to the victims, Semenov immediately ordered a full investigation under the leadership of Malshikov.

Painstakingly comparing the witness statements, Malshikov eventually located the mine but the excavation proved difficult. Stones, rubble and charred brushwood blocked the entrance and it took several days to pump out the water before anyone could descend into the shaft. Even then, it was discovered that the grenades had caused many of the wooden planks supporting the walls to collapse, making an immediate search impossible. Not until the beginning of October, were the investigators able to make their way down. On 8th of the month, the body of Serge Mikhailovich's companion, Feodor Remez, was discovered. For three more days Malshikov's men delved deeper into the mine, retrieving five more bodies until finally, on 11th October, they reached Ella and Ioann. Ella's body lay on the ledge, an unexploded grenade at her side and, on her breast, a cedar-wood crucifix and the icon of Christ.

Throughout the excavations, Ella's friend, the monk Seraphim, had been anxiously waiting for news and, on hearing that she had been found, he was given permission to go down into the shaft. He was amazed by her appearance. Apart from a broken noose and a bruise across her forehead, concealing deeper wounds to the cranium, she appeared as though she were simply sleeping peacefully.

The bodies were brought to the surface, where they were examined by doctors who recorded that all - with the possible exception of Serge Mikhailovich (who had been shot) - had died of haemorrhages, infected wounds and starvation. They were placed in public view so that they might be identified and as evidence of the Red Army's butchery. Outraged by the cruel murder of the gentle Grand Duchess Elizaveta, whom they already revered as a saint, hundreds of people from Alapaevsk and the surrounding regions flocked to the church where an official funeral service was held.

In November 1918, as Britain rejoiced in the Armistice celebrations, the news of the discovery in Alapaevsk reached Victoria in England. Having so recently heard of the fate of Nicky, Alix and their children, the death of her closest sister came as a terrible, if not unexpected, blow. Yet Victoria found comfort in the knowledge that Ella's faith would have sustained her to the end, and perhaps it was a relief that she had not lived to see the destruction of her convent. Lenin saw the Orthodox Church as the instrument of imperialism and, with ruthless determination, set about destroying its authority. Convents were disbanded and leading clerics were arrested or exiled. The Communists closed the church on Ordynka Street and moved into The House of Martha and Mary. The saintly Father Mitrophan was arrested and subsequently exiled.

Many years earlier, following her pilgrimage to the Holy Land, Ella had confided to her sister that she would love to be buried in the Orthodox church on the Mount of Olives, but continued unrest in Russia made it impossible for Victoria to comply with her wish. In 1918, as the civil war raged, Victoria could not travel to Alapaevsk or even obtain information about the whereabouts of her sister's body, which was about to embark on a long voyage.

The Whites' control of the Urals was far from secure. The Reds were still the more dominant force in Russia and constantly threatened to regain the province. The monk, Seraphim, was worried. He had heard stories of Bolsheviks digging up graves and desecrating the Romanov tombs in search of treasure. He had promised Ella that he would bury her 'like a Christian,' and he feared what the Reds might do if they regained Alapaevsk.

In the summer of 1919, he approached Semenov to request permission to remove the bodies to a more secure location. Semenov agreed and, in the height of summer, the monk had the coffins loaded onto a train bound for China. The journey was long and the train was terribly slow. In the cramped and stifling compartments, fluid continuously leaked from the coffins and the stench was unbearable but Seraphim noticed that the fluid from Ella's coffin gave off only a fragrant perfume. Prince Felix Youssoupov also later bore witness to this strange phenomenon, writing that his relics of Grand Duchess Elizabeth often exuded the aroma of flowers.

After three weeks, Seraphim arrived in Harbin to be greeted by the Russian diplomat, Nicholas Kudashev, who had known the Imperial Family well, before the revolution. It was Kudashev's unpleasant duty to identify the bodies and write an official report. The Romanovs had been dead for over a year, had been entombed in Alapaevsk for several months and, for the last three weeks had been 'cooking' in the heat of the train. Unsurprisingly, Kudashev approached the coffins with trepidation. When the lids were removed, a ghastly sight met his eyes - a series of completely decayed corpses. His stomach churning, he moved on to the eighth coffin but, when the lid was removed, he was astounded to see that Ella's body was intact and she appeared no different from the last time he had seen her.

Kudashev ordered new coffins for a ceremonial burial in Peking.

Two years passed and Victoria heard nothing. She had no idea that her sister's body had been taken from Russia until, by chance, one day towards the end of 1920, she came upon an illustrated article in an English magazine. It described the Russian Orthodox cemetery in China to which the grand dukes had been taken. At once, Victoria contacted various authorities who put her in touch with Seraphim. The monk offered to help make arrangements for the transfer of Ella and Barbara's bodies to Jerusalem.

On 15th January 1921, Seraphim oversaw the arrival of the coffins in Palestine. Victoria, her husband Louis, and a huge crowd awaited them in Jerusalem. The following day, Ella was laid to rest on the Mount of Olives in the Russian Orthodox Church of St. Mary Magdalene, which she had first visited with Serge thirty-three years before.

Following her interment, numerous miracles were reported by pilgrims, praying at her tomb. Sixty-three years after her death, the Orthodox Church Abroad, canonised the former Princess of Hesse-Darmstadt. Ten years later, following the collapse of Communism, the Orthodox Church in Russia proclaimed the Grand Duchess 'Holy Imperial Martyr Saint Elizaveta Feodorovna.'

The Order, which Ella founded, has, after years of suppression, been revived and the convent, once occupied by the Communists, has now reopened.

About The Author

Christina Croft studied English and Divinity in
Liverpool, and currently lives in Yorkshire.
Her earlier novels include <u>The Counting House</u> and
<u>The Fields Laid Waste</u>, both of which are now
available.

www.christinacroft.com

CPSIA information can be obtained at www.ICGtesting.com
Printed in the USA
BVOW072144110713

325568BV00001B/223/P

9 780955 985300